Little Bit of Wait

Diana Rock

Published by Diana Rock, 2023.

LITTLE BIT OF WAIT
Copyright © 2023 by Denise M. Long
All Rights reserved.
No part of this book may be used or reproduced in any manner whatsoever including audio recording without written permission of the author and Copyright holder.
This author supports the right to free expression and values copyright protection. The scanning, uploading, and distribution of this book in any manner or medium without permission of the copyright holder is theft of the property. Thank you for supporting this author's creative work with your purchase.
PRINT EDITION
Print IBSN: 9798986757148
Digital IBSN: 9798986757155
Editor: Lynne Pearson, All that Editing
This is a work of fiction. Names, characters, places, and incidents either are the product of the author's imagination or are used fictitiously, and any resemblance to actual persons, living or dead, business establishments, organizations, events, locale, or weather events is entirely coincidental.

Also by Diana Rock

Colby County Series
Bid To Love
Courting Choices

Fulton River Falls
Melt My Heart
Proof of Love
Bloomin' In Love
First Christmas Ornament

MovieStuds
Hollywood Hotshot

Standalone
Little Bit of Wait

Watch for more at DianaRock.com.

To LPC

To LPC: For all friendship, love, and support over the years.
Ladies, you ROCK!

EARLY MAY 2017

Finding Heather in cabin four at Lake Terramungus that August morning sixteen years ago blew her thirteen-year-old mind. Just like it did now.

Chelsea escorted her finished manicure client to the salon's front desk. When she turned to get her next client, she couldn't believe her eyes.

"Heather Boyden?" Chelsea's voice held a tremor of surprise, though she was almost one hundred percent sure it was her. The woman looked up with a big smile of recognition blossoming on her lovely face.

"Chelsea?" She jumped out of her chair. "Oh, my God! You work here? Are you cutting my hair?"

"Don't worry, no!" Chelsea advanced to Heather's side. "I just saw you and couldn't believe my eyes. How've ya' been?"

"Not bad, and you?"

They stood on one side of a coffee table stacked with well-thumbed magazines. Five other people sat around them, gawking like a group therapy session gone awry. Her next client stood up, breaking up the reunion. Chelsea flashed the woman her index finger, grabbed Heather's arm, and pulled her aside.

"Let me give you my number. Call me sometime. I'd like to catch up with you."

Heather nodded and waited until she returned with her business card, her home telephone number added on the front.

Pulling Heather farther aside, she lowered her voice. "I do home manicures. Call me, and we can chat while I do your nails. No charge."

"It's Laulier now." She smiled shyly, taking her seat again along the wall.

"You're married?" Chelsea felt her heartbeat quicken.

"With three kids."

Her eyebrows rose. "I guess we have a lot to catch up on. Call me." Chelsea hustled back to her client, apologizing for keeping her waiting and trying to shake off the excitement in her chest.

That night Heather called Chelsea to arrange a meeting.

Days later, they met again.

The sheer cotton voile curtain billowed with the warming breeze invading the window of the retro 1950s kitchen. Chelsea Whitcom, manicurist, smacked the curtain away from her heart-shaped face and returned her attention to Heather on this sunny early May afternoon. It was funny how they not only lived in the same city but also the same neighborhood of Shadyside.

"Thanks for making a house call while the kids are napping," Heather said over the escalating sounds of rush hour traffic clogging Shadyside's main artery a block from her quiet side street. With her free hand, Heather took a sip of soda from the bottle on the Formica table.

"No problem. This is so much more relaxing than at work. I'm thinking of doing this full-time, home manicures. The salon is okay, but I'd like to make my own hours." She glanced out the window as the breeze held the fragrance of lilacs.

A pause in the conversation made Chelsea squirm in her chair.

Heather broke the silence. "Isn't it funny how we haven't seen each other since high school?" She glanced up. "We've known each other since elementary school though we've never been close friends."

"Not until camp." Chelsea kept her eyes on Heather's hands. Would Heather bring up the last night at camp?

"True. And even after camp, we never hung out together although we saw each other a lot in passing at school."

"To be expected. We were in different grades. It made it hard to hang out together." Chelsea wiped Heather's hands dry and reached for the polish color she had selected.

"Is it busy at the shop?"

Chelsea glanced up into the cocoa-brown eyes of her old friend. "Ugh. It's been so busy with pedicures. Everyone wants one now that it's flip-flop season," she mumbled, her green eyes intent on the manicure.

They both watched in silence as the shell-pink polish was expertly applied to the fingernails on Heather's left hand. Their thoughts spun in the air along with the fumes of the polish that dispersed with the breeze.

"Your wedding ring is beautiful," Chelsea said, shifting Heather's hand slightly to view the carved metal. "No engagement ring?"

Heather curtly shook her head. "No."

It seemed odd to Chelsea. No engagement ring. Perhaps Billy couldn't afford one. "I already know exactly what I want for an engagement ring. A marquise cut diamond."

"Did I tell you my brother is getting married?" Heather blurted out as if trying to change the subject.

Was Heather embarrassed she never received an engagement ring? Best to let the subject change. "No. When's that happening?"

"In about five months." Heather shifted uncomfortably in her seat. "I, um—I'm going to a diet program at St. Elizabeth's church. Just to lose a few pounds." She glanced away. "I've been there before. But I'm going to try this time."

The two women locked eyes. "Good luck. Losing weight isn't easy. I tried once back in high school just before prom and promised myself I'd never do it again."

Heather's face closed, her eyes losing their sparkle. A stillness settled between the two women.

Chelsea picked up the polish bottle. "Tell me about your kids and husband."

A blush rose on Heather's pale cheeks. "Another time." She turned her face away to look out the window. "Beautiful day."

The silence returned. Chelsea might have expected an unhappily married woman to not want to discuss her husband and their relationship. But a mother not wanting to talk about her children? Heather's reluctance left a tremor of unease in Chelsea's stomach. It was unnatural. From the look on Heather's face, she was embarrassed by her statement. Rather than probe further, Chelsea changed the subject. "Are you still friends with Monica from high school? She's your next-door neighbor, right?" She pointed to the duplex building out the window.

Heather's eyes brightened as she nodded. "You two were friends in high school."

"We still are friends." Chelsea bent her head conspiratorially. "Do you know if she and Nate are back together for sure now?" She paused in her work long enough to get a mouthful of soda from her own bottle.

Heather's eyes twinkled. "Ooh, yeah. Didn't you hear? Nate proposed on Sunday night after the Pirates won. He put the ring in her dessert at Church View Brews. It's a wonder she didn't swallow it! It was so funny!" Heather nearly shrieked, thumping her feet excitedly on the kitchen's scuffed and spotted linoleum floor.

Seconds later, Heather's baby cried from the other room. Both women cringed and smiled with clenched teeth, eyebrows raised until the baby fell silent again. Chelsea sat back in her vinyl chair, dropping Heather's left hand with the same suddenness as her smile.

Whispering, Chelsea lamented, "So I'm going to be the only one not engaged or married out of all my girlfriends from high school?" Every other one of her girlfriends had moved on in her relationship while she continued to tread water with Seth.

Fingers extended straight, Heather carefully took both Chelsea's hands in her half-painted set. "Don't worry about it, Seth's sure to do something soon."

Chelsea pulled her hands away and pressed her palms to her eyelids, trying to push back the tears. "He damn well better. It's been twelve years, for God's sake," she sniffled. A sunbeam hit her shoulder-length auburn hair, setting it ablaze with reddish tones while she tried not to cry.

"Well, you always have another option," Heather offered mischief in her eyes. "2020 is a leap year." She giggled, nudging her friend's arms playfully.

"That's three years away!" Her damp eyes blinked before Chelsea burst out laughing, then started to hiccup between sniffles, thinking all the while it wasn't a bad idea.

The baby whimpered again. Heather hushed her, and they froze until the baby stopped.

Heather changed the subject this time. "Isn't it kinda funny how you and me are still in contact? I often wonder where the other two are, what they're doin' now."

She sounded wistful, and Chelsea wondered if she was missing Marla. They were most alike in temperament. Both shy and fairly quiet but with a fun mischievous streak which no doubt led them to hang around with Gemma and Chelsea instead of making friends elsewhere. Heather and Marla were used to intervening between Gemma and Chelsea. It was their primary role back when they first met at summer camp on the shores of Lake Mungus.

Chelsea continued painting Heather's nails, thinking of the four of them way back when at Camp Terramungus. A smile spread across her face so wide her eyes scrunched, impairing her vision. Her polish brush stopped in midair as she sat back and chuckled.

"Remember when we stole the camp director's car and pushed it all the way down the dirt access road to the county highway? God!

That was so much fun. You were steering, weren't you? An' Gemma, Marla, and I were pushing the car, right?" Chelsea laughed.

"Oh God! I forgot all about that! Yes!" Heather giggled. "Gemma." She shook her head. "What a bundle of trouble."

Gemma was well versed in trouble from her three elder brothers. Dealing with all their crap honed her with a hard edge, even at that young an age. She was tempered, like steel. Unflustered, always thinking more than one step ahead. Thankfully, her thorough planning kept their asses out of deep trouble the entire two weeks they were there raising havoc.

Camp counselors tried to circumvent their antics, tried to intercept their pranks. They were always ahead of them, thanks to Gemma. They were never actually caught doing any of the pranks, and they made sure there wasn't any evidence left behind. Despite the gossip and accusations, the counselors could do nothing to stop them. "Gemma shutting off the propane gas tanks in the bathhouse so there wasn't any hot water in the showers! Do you remember that?"

"Ha! Yeah, I remember. That was such a fun summer." The brush resumed its motion, slower, haltingly, her nerves on edge. Every time Heather brought up their time at camp Chelsea wanted to bring up the fire.

Heather's mind wandered back to those two weeks. Chelsea had admitted she had never been in much trouble as a kid, but she was in a bad way at camp. Her Dad had died after the previous Christmas. She was filled with misdirected anger, frustration, and grief. It transformed into malice and evil disdain for every girl that snubbed her nose at the four misfits in cabin four.

Heather's family had moved to the Pittsburgh area less than a year prior. Not knowing anyone had made her shy. Her willingness to open her mouth and actively participate in anything at camp was inversely proportional to the number of other girls in attendance.

Like the other three, she didn't have a sister but was attached to her younger brother like an ant to a peony bud. Gregory sent her a letter almost every day. She'd tried passing him off as a boyfriend and was mortified when it came out that he was her brother. "I wish we could find them." The elation of great summer camp memories slid off Heather's face like rain drops off a freshly waxed car.

• • • •

CHELSEA FROZE TO STARE at her friend and client, meeting her large doe eyes. Straightening up in her seat to full height, towering over her friend, she pointed the polish brush at Heather before continuing. "Maybe we can try the internet. It might work. Do you remember where Gemma and Marla were from?" "They were both from New York. Like upstate, not the city," Heather replied, looking up her. Chelsea's six-foot tall, sturdy frame towered over Heather's five-five.

Marla was from somewhere south of Rochester, New York. How she ended up at Camp Terramungus was a mystery until she received a letter from her Aunt Gertrude asking for information on the Camp. Aunt Gert wanted to know how much it had changed in the twenty-five years since she'd been at camp. It was harder for Marla since she didn't know anybody at camp. At least some of the camp girls knew each other from school or at least recognized faces. It was still sort of comforting to see a familiar face. Some girls planned their camp week to coincide with those of their girlfriends. But cabin four was not a pre-matched-up set.

"Worth a try, right?" Chelsea shrugged, trying hard not to get too optimistic. She lifted Heather's right hand and blew on her fingertips before stowing the polish bottle in her manicure bag. "Can you search, Heather?"

Heather blushed. "I— we don't have a computer."

"I'll do some internet searches." Chelsea stood and collected her bag and purse. I have to get going. I'll let you know if I dig anything up." A week later Heather called Chelsea. "Did you have any luck searching for Gemma or Marla?"

"No. I've been so busy at work doing manis and pedis, I haven't thought about it."

LATE MAY 2017

The door to Marla Devine's small, stark white corporate office burst open. Eileen strode to her desk and stopped. "Doing anything Thursday night?"

Marla raised one eyebrow. "No. You know me. I never have any plans."

Eileen exploded with excitement, her hands fisted and raised above her head in victory. "Excellent! You and I are going to the Stones concert!"

Her usual poker-face dissolved into delight as her insides quivered with the thrill. She was going to see the Stones, after all. Warnings flickered in her mind causing a kick in her gut that turned her joy to despair. She rose from her desk chair. "I can't."

"Come on Marla, it's the concert of the century, for God's sake!" Eileen stared her down from the front of her desk, her face broadcasting the same incredulity as her voice. "I know you love the Stones, why won't you go?"

"I just c-can't," Marla stuttered back and turned away to search through her industrial gray metal file cabinet for the last compliance audit report on the Boston laboratory. The one she needed to find just when Eileen barged in without warning.

She glanced out the window of her fourth-floor office, the multi-layered skyline of Pittsburgh not far off in the distance. A sliver of water shimmered beyond where the Allegheny and Monongahela rivers converged to form the Ohio River at Point State Park.

This was her refuge. Her calm and quiet office, a sacred place for her to hide. Other than her boss and Eileen, nobody came to visit the compliance officer willingly. Shifting her vision to the reflection in the window, she could see Eileen standing before her desk. Silently watching her. *Please just leave.* But Eileen didn't move.

Huge raindrops began to fall from the sky. In seconds their numbers grew into a torrent of water. At street level, people walking along the sidewalks or window-shopping the swanky shops of Pittsburgh's Shadyside neighborhood jumped under awnings or into doorways. Anywhere to get out of the sudden deluge.

"What do you mean you can't? It's the Stones!" Eileen's voice cracked, and both arms spread wide. "I can't believe I won two tickets calling the radio station like a maniac all weekend long! Six months ago, we were bummed when we couldn't buy tickets. One minute ago, you said you had *nothing* going on Thursday night," an edge of suspicion saturated Eileen's voice.

Marla could see Eileen's narrowed eyes in the window reflection. They bore a hole in her back. Eileen hadn't told her she was trying for tickets. Six months ago, Marla was relieved when the possibility of attending the Stones concert died. Even though she would have loved to see them in person for the first time. Sam would have too. He would have done anything to see his favorite rock band in person. Seeing them without him felt anything but right.

"I just can't, Eileen. Please leave it at that, okay?" Her eyelids fluttered away the seeding tears blurring the names on the files. With trembling fingers, she worked her way from file folder to file folder. *Go away, please, just go away* her mind repeated, praying Eileen would telepathically hear her plea. She didn't want to have to explain or see that look in Eileen's eyes yet again.

"Marla Devine, you're holding something out on me. What's going on?" Eileen's knuckles rapped on the desktop as if trying to draw her attention. When Marla didn't turn around, she added, trying a gentler tone this time. "Look, I'm still your best friend from college. You can tell me anything."

In the reflection, Marla saw Eileen approach and stand behind her. Eileen gripped Marla's elbow and turned her for a direct confrontation.

Marla bent her head, the multiple folds of her neck making it impossible for her dimpled chin to meet her chest. Shame throbbed through her, bringing itchy, hot splotches to her neck and cheeks. Eileen's hand brushed aside the cascade of long dirty-blonde hair that hid Marla's face.

"Give it up, girl. What's the *real* reason you won't go to the Stones concert with me this Thursday?" asked Eileen softly, her eyes searching Marla's. When Eileen tried to put an arm around her expansive shoulders, Marla's composure crumbled. The dam, the impenetrable emotional fence she worked so hard to shore up, burst. Erratic tears cascaded unimpeded. As they fell, so did her resolve to remain aloof and strong. The stiffness in her spine wavered then collapsed. Hunched over, Marla slumped on Eileen's shoulder.

"S-same reason I-I can't go to the movies anymore. I-I can't fit in the seat." Marla wailed, her tears a torrent running down her plump cheeks. She rested her forehead on her best friend's shoulder for a moment. Eileen's arms stretched halfway around her torso. The comfort they brought allowed Marla to let all her frustration and pain out.

Eileen's pat on the back jolted her to awareness. Marla stepped away. Her face downcast, she struggled to gain control of her spasmodic breathing and stemmed her tears, wiping the last few away with the back of her hands.

"Aw, Marla. We're going to stand the whole time anyway. Who cares if you can't fit into the damn seat?" Eileen shook Marla's shoulder gently as she tried to reason with her.

Control. I must get control. Like the flip of a toggle switch, Marla's shoulders pushed back as her head rose robotically. Back in control again. She was so good at stoicism. Downright tyrannical about keeping her emotions under control all her life for as long as she could remember. Because showing emotion left her vulnerable. It gave her tormentors, enemies, and anyone else a glimpse of her

Achilles heel. No one was supposed to ever see her lose it. Not even Eileen. Especially if it had to do with her body. Or, more correctly, her weight.

They had had this argument many times before, about the theater, the movies, the ballet, and the symphony. Even about eating out at restaurants. Any establishment with booths or tables anchored to the floor or places having seats with armrests that couldn't be adjusted. Seats meant for someone of a normal size. Seats that made it clear that Marla, with her excessive weight, was not welcome in those places.

Four days later, Marla closed her eyes, trying to squeeze back tears. She tried to harness the hollow ache in her chest as her mind replayed the scene and heard the last echo of the conversation.

That morning, she had tottered to Eileen's laboratory workstation, only to find it staffed by someone else. She must have taken the day off or called in sick after Thursday night's concert. *Lucky stiff probably still can't hear right. If she's up yet.* Marla sighed before turning around to return to her office.

Walking back through the maze of biomedical testing equipment in the vast open floor space of the hematology laboratory, Marla remembered their earlier standoff. Keeping her blurring eyes to the polished tile floor, she disregarded the lab technicians she passed, although she sensed them glancing at her with curiosity.

The whir and clicking noise of the automated blood test processing equipment dominated the space and limited conversation between technologists. Until she came into view, and the sounds of whispering started. No doubt wondering why she was in their work area. The compliance inspector's presence always made them nervous, as if she was hoping to spot a problem and make an issue of it. She frowned as she waddled down the aisles. *It was more likely nobody wanted an obese person around.*

Her weight hadn't always been so restrictive. Sure, she had always been larger than others all through school. Even during the first week of college when she and Eileen first met. Back then, Marla's weight didn't matter to Eileen. It had never been a topic of discussion or disdain.

In the seven years since their college graduation, Marla's weight and girth had increased slowly to the state where the seating issue had become problematic. She kept a list of places, particularly restaurants, that could seat her without difficulty. It was these establishments she tried to steer people to when get-togethers were planned. Sometimes Marla took on the responsibility for making reservations so she could be sure to get an accommodating restaurant and sometimes, specific table reservations to prevent public embarrassment.

Face flushing hot, she remembered when Eileen tried to talk her into doing something about her weight gain three years ago. Fed up by then with the harping, Marla had given an ultimatum: shut up, or their friendship was over. Eileen had been shocked and hurt at Marla's ferocity. Nevertheless, Marla had had enough. To this day, she was thankful her only friend had chosen to keep her mouth shut on the issue.

Arriving back at her stark, white-walled office, she removed her white lab coat with her heart still heavy and her stomach burning. Tears welled up again just thinking of the second-row center seats Eileen had won, practically right under Mick's nose. Marla hung the coat up on the brushed chrome coat rack. Turning back to it, she removed the cell phone from the left-hand pocket.

She stared at her phone while leaning against the black bookshelf holding reference books and binders of the city, state, and federal regulations. It was her job to ensure they were all followed. Not just in the Pittsburgh laboratory. In every one of the numerous Peabody Laboratories scattered around the country.

Her finger hovered an inch from the phone's keypad. She wanted to call Eileen to find out about the concert. She wanted to hear how awesome it was, to try to share in the excitement of the event. But she couldn't do it. Times like this, Marla wished she'd listened to Eileen's advice years ago. Then she could have heard the Stones live in person last night instead of on her CD player, all alone in the silent comfort of her king-size bed.

Shaking her head, she dropped the phone into her shirt pocket and sat in her oversized cushy desk chair. She opened the top left-hand drawer of her expansive office desk despite her mind screaming to leave the sixteen-ounce can of salted peanuts alone. Her willpower dissolved when her stomach growled its approval.

The opening poof of the lid revealed the enticing smell of the roasted, salty treats. Popping a handful in her mouth, she sighed as the peanutty delight of her favorite snack teased her tastebuds. Within five minutes, the only thing left in the container was the powdery white salt stuck in the bottom crevices of the can.

• • • •

HERE WE GO AGAIN. Gemma struggled to breathe.

She pushed aside the silk bed linens to sit up on the edge of her bed without opening her eyes. She didn't bother to turn on the light before reaching for the asthma inhaler. Her fingers knew exactly where it was on the corner of her nightstand. She took one deep inhale, held her breath as she counted to ten, and peeled one eyelid open to check the retro alarm clock: 2:16 a.m. *Great.* The next inhale of medication must be at least five minutes later.

Eyes now open, she turned on the lamp. The warm milk-chocolate brown painted walls pressed in on her. Deep shadows hugged the corners of her room. The large gray cat lying beside her on the bed stretched and yawned before settling back into a ball of fur.

Snagging up the bottle of antacid liquid, she chugged a mouthful. On a scale of one to ten, this attack was a seven. Not too bad tonight. Last night it had been an eight. The night before a nine. They were definitely more severe this week. *So much for the stress theory.*

Dr. Hale thought stress brought on the more severe attacks. If that was the case, her worst episodes should have been last month during the national NACET conference when Gemma ran the entire event minus one staff member. And she should not have had any last week while vacationing in Vermont. It made no sense whatsoever.

Gemma shook her head in exasperation at the problem, and speed dialed the cell phone.

"Helloo?" a sleepy Rose Anne whispered in answer.

"Rose," Gemma said breathlessly, trying to stay calm by petting the cat curled up beside her.

"Not again," Rose Anne groaned. Gemma heard the sheets rustling in the background and a click of Rose's lamp switch.

"Yeah ... another one.... Just a seven ... no ambulance this time." *So far, anyway.*

"You better call Dr. Hale in the morning," Rose Anne croaked out. "He's *got* to convince that insurance company. You *need* that surgery."

"Maybe," Gemma said half-heartedly, brushing her short dark brown hair out of her face.

"You've been to the emergency room by ambulance, what, eight times? It's not getting better."

"Seven times," Gemma corrected.

"Seven, eight, *who cares*—last time you were nearly put on a respirator." Tension spilled from her voice through the phone.

It was true. Last time Gemma thought it *was* over. She still remembered the numbness, watching needles sticking into her arms but not feeling anything. Voices surrounded her, but she could not hear their words. Her peripheral vision disappeared until she could only see down a narrow tunnel before her, watching her chest get stripped bare, watching her pale blue feet at the end of the gurney. Her oxygen-deprived mind trying to focus in a Herculean effort to breathe with leaden lungs. Lungs incapable of inflating or exhaling. The thought had swept through her mind—just quit. But some steel force of determination rose in her gut, and she resisted the urge. A week in the hospital, dozens of tests, and still, no one could explain *why* her stomach spewed acid up her esophagus, activating her asthma attacks and nearly killing her in the process.

"Don't know ... what else ... can get ... them ... to authorize ... surgery." Gemma groaned, an overwhelming sense of frustration bearing down on her shoulders as heavily as the feeling in her chest.

"Don't get upset now, you know it makes your breathing worse. Think calmly," Rose Anne cautioned, sounding more awake and alert. "I'm coming over. Give me a few minutes to get dressed—"

"No.... I think the ... attack is subsiding ... I'll let you get ... back to sleep," Gemma said, feeling bad about waking her best friend and cousin.

"Are you sure? You still don't sound so good. I'm just a few blocks away."

"I'm okay. Stay there.... Just promise me something." Gemma worked hard to control her breathing. She repeated the word "control" over and over in the back of her mind.

"Anything."

"If something happens to me ... before I get this surgery, Rose... sue the fucking pants off ... that insurance company, would you?" She looked down at the quietly purring feline beside her and added, "And take care of Wally for me."

"You can bet your ass I will, on both counts. This is costing me a lot of sleep." Rose Anne snorted. "Night, Gemma. Call again if you need me."

"Sure, night." Somehow, she felt better knowing if she died, Rose Anne, a paralegal, and her firm's lawyers would have fun screwing the insurance company.

The weight on her chest was easing. Her breathing was getting better. She re-measured her peak flow, finding it was still suboptimal. For another half hour, Gemma gave herself the step-by-step treatments her doctor had meticulously worked out for her. By three a.m., she was well enough to snuggle up to Wally, the cat, and get another three hours of sleep before her weekday six a.m. alarm rang.

On her way to work the next morning, she stopped at Starbucks to pick up her usual venti, whole milk salted caramel latte, and crumb cake. Dean saw her walking in and started to put her order together.

The barista smirked. "Mornin' sunshine," Dean chirped from behind the green and black coffee bar as he busily rang up her order.

"Give me a blueberry muffin too, would you, Dean?" Gemma handed him a twenty. The anti-inflammatory medication and the steroids made her hungry as hell all the time.

"Another hot night?" Dean wiggled his eyebrows up and down.

"Oh yeah, up 'til three. You know me, wild and crazy sex every night, leaving me breathless. Can't get enough," She joked back. It was their running joke every morning. Dean knew better since he had tried to get into her panties. Gemma didn't let many guys there at all.

In fact, Gemma didn't date. She didn't have time or the patience to play the games associated with early dating. She had tried to hook up with guys she thought were nice looking only to find out—fortunately rather quickly—there wasn't much between the ears to keep her interested. Most men, including Dean, couldn't hold a conversation about anything that didn't involve a sport. Truth was, they didn't want to talk much at all. What they had in mind didn't involve much exercising of the vocal cords beyond moaning.

Besides, the last thing she wanted was an asthma attack in the middle of sex. The embarrassment alone might kill her.

After paying, Gemma moved to the pickup line, waiting for her order. *I should order on the app before I leave the house. Then it would be ready as soon as I arrived.*

The guy in front of her turned to glare at her, then down at her foot. She was tapping it again, and in three-inch stiletto-heeled knee-high black leather boots, it was making a racket.

"Sorry," Gemma mumbled apologetically as the guy waited for his to-go cup.

Again, she cursed the steroid medication prescribed to help her asthma condition. Fourteen months on them and her weight was up fifteen pounds from an insatiable appetite and water retention. *Now I can add irritability to the side effects.* She had to get off them soon, which meant getting that surgery approved.

Gemma watched the surly guy's tight jeans cup his muscular glutes and felt saliva accumulate in her mouth. She tried to think of the last time she had a date. It had been a while. A long while. Maybe a couple years. Not long after dating barista Dean, Gemma quit dating. Not by choice necessarily.

About that same time, her weight started to escalate compliments of her medication, narrowing the field of interested males from a measly few to zilch. As far as she was concerned, sooner or later, some guy would turn up, or he wouldn't.

Sweet buns snagged his cup and walked out the door. Gemma's gaze stayed riveted to his ass as he crossed the parking lot to an Audi. Her cup and paper bag appeared on the counter behind her, and her name was called. Gemma took her order to a vacant table next to the wall of window panes. Sunshine streamed in, making her blink several times. Taking a bite of muffin, she glanced up to see Mei waving at her from the pickup line. Gemma covered her full mouth with her napkin and waved Mei over with her other hand.

"Good morning. How are you? Mind if I join you?" Mei didn't wait for a reply. She flopped into the empty chair opposite Gemma and dropped her oversized shoulder bag to the floor. Gemma had no idea how she still had the shape of an adolescent boy after having twins not long ago.

Her mouth cleared, Gemma answered, "Please. I'm having a lazy morning."

Mei looked at her intently, head tilted. "Oh no, another bad night?" she asked, her shoulders slumping in sympathy for her boss's health issue.

"Yeah, not too bad. Don't worry about it." Gemma patted Mei's forearm reassuringly. *God, now even the office staff is worried about me.*

They sipped their caffeinated drinks in silence for a few moments. Gemma watched as something, nearly voiced, raced across Mei's face, then saw it pulled back abruptly. Whatever it was, Mei wasn't going to say it just yet.

"So, what's up? How's class going?" Gemma smiled, asking the first thing that came to mind.

Mei's chin nearly dropped into her coffee cup, letting her long straight black hair fall across her face like a curtain. Gemma could tell Mei wished she could dive right into her cup. Gemma waited, sipping her coffee. Patience was a virtue and a secret tool. She'd learned that in management training. Give them dead air, and most would fill it with what you wanted to know.

"I ... I'm not taking any this term," she stammered softly, staring at her drink.

Gemma shook her head, thinking she must have heard wrong. Her ears snapped to attention. "What? I thought you were going for that degree in event planning at UPitt?" She'd written letters of reference and recommendation to help Mei get accepted last fall. Now she wasn't going?

"I've been so busy with the babies, and Kim's residency keeps him away sixty to eighty hours a week. I just can't handle the stress right now. I took a leave of absence." Mei's pained smile rose then fell.

Gemma sipped her coffee, eyeing Mei in silence over the rim of her cup, trying to stop the blood from racing through her veins and thundering through her temples. *Control your face, control your words, control everything that wants to scream in fury at a wasted semester.*

"I understand being a mother and wife is difficult. But you deserve to have this for yourself. I was able to work a full-time job at Atlantica Hotels and go to the University of Syracuse full-time to get my degree. I did that for four years. You can't find the time to take one class a semester? The fees are paid for by NACET! You can study on company time!" Gemma desperately tried to keep the sarcastic tone out of her voice. From the look of Mei's face, she didn't succeed.

Teardrops as big as peas slipped from Mei's eyes and rolled down her cheeks unabated. Mei buried her face in her palms and wept in quiet earnest.

Oh, God. I made her cry. Gemma sighed as her mouth went dry. She craned her neck to see how many people had noticed Mei had burst into tears. Too many, and their faces reflected their concern and displeasure.

Deep down, she empathized with the young woman trapped in a slave-like marriage and bound by two infants while her husband completed a surgical residency. Gemma shuddered with visions of her own mother trapped with four kids after her father's abandonment.

She gently lay a hand on Mei's shoulder. "Mei, I'm sorry. That was rude of me. You're not me, and I have no right to bully you into doing something you don't feel you can do right now. Please stop crying," she begged quietly.

A few seconds went by before Mei lifted her head. Gemma handed her some napkins to wipe her face.

"I'm sorry. I just want you to have all the advantages that education can bring. I want you to become a certified meeting planner just like everyone else in the office. It's a great career move. But maybe now isn't the right time for you. I'm sorry I'm being so pushy about it," Gemma confessed, her heart aching now for a woman who tried so hard to please everyone, including her.

"I know you have my best interests at heart. It's just difficult right now with Kim at the medical center. And the twins are three hands full," Mei explained, sniffling into the napkins.

"Would you do me a favor? Go home. I'm giving you the day off. I can't remember the last time you had a day off." Appeasing her guilty soul was the only option Gemma had available.

"I can't do that—" Mei started to say.

"Yes, you can. Just between you and me. No sick time, no vacation time. I'm authorizing it. Leave the kids at daycare, go home, and get some uninterrupted sleep. I'll see you tomorrow," Gemma said, flicking her chin toward the exit door.

A tired, tentative, sweet smile crept part-way across Mei's face. She nodded, got up wearily, and headed for the door.

Gemma watched her go, exhaling when the door shut behind Mei. *You've got to remember, not everyone is as resilient as you are, Gem dear.*

She resumed nibbling on her muffin. She'd much rather scarf it up at this point, but she was, after all, in public. She couldn't stop thinking about Mei's situation: a medical student husband and twin boys.

Serves her right for getting married. Gemma glanced around, afraid she'd said it aloud. No one was paying attention.

Gemma wasn't keen on the idea of marriage, and Mei's predicament and her own mother's marriage showcased why. She definitely didn't want to have children. Her idea of a secure future was not to let a man saddle her with children, only to ignore his responsibilities.

It was funny how most girls played with dolls and dreamed of getting married, raising kids, cleaning a house. She never had. The girls at school made it sound so sweet and romantic. Gemma knew better. She'd had to deal with it from the age of twelve. It was not going to be part of her future.

Like her friends, she started babysitting for money when she turned fourteen, even though she hated it. As soon as she turned sixteen, she got a real job after school at the local hotel assisting with events. It was the start of her quest for a career as an event planner.

Now, she ran the events department at NACET, the National Association of Certified Engineering Technologists, where she managed a small staff of four, planning and running seven major events each year. Her team worked very well together. They didn't let her down.

Before leaving Starbucks, she picked up a yogurt and a pre-made egg salad sandwich, knowing how ugly her schedule looked today. Thinking better of it, she added a fruit salad and another egg salad sandwich. If she didn't get something here, she was at the mercy of the greasy spoon on the first floor of the office building, where the only vegetable on the menu was French fries.

Her stomach was still hungry. She cursed the steroids.

Gemma drove the last mile to the office building, where she spent more time looking for a parking space in the garage than she did driving there. It might have been easier to take a cab or bus or walk. But she didn't walk much. In fact, she didn't exercise much at all. The exertion could also trigger her asthma exacerbations.

That evening on the other side of town, Heather paused outside the doorway only to have two women excuse themselves and step around her. Steeling her shoulders, she entered the large open room.

The lighting was dim; a few of the fluorescent light bulbs had died and not been replaced. Six pillars supporting the church structure were set at regular intervals around the room. It gave the space a tick-tac-toe look. Folding chairs were set up, two to a box. A few early arrivals already sat waiting for the program to begin. The walls were still an early 1940s shade of green, not quite sage. *Some things don't change.*

The line to the payment table was moving fast to get everyone through to weigh in before the seven p.m. program started. After paying her fees from her stash of leftover grocery money, Heather walked over to the weigh-in stations.

There has to be a better way, Heather thought as she waited her turn. *Did I try the Leek Soup Diet?* She rummaged through her memory like a woman searching her purse for loose change. *Maybe not. That's about the only one I didn't try.* Watermelon, Grapefruit, Atkins, Scarsdale, Hollywood, South Beach, Keto, TOPS, Overeaters Anonymous, even gluten-free—she'd tried them all with the same amount of success. None. Well, none that lasted more than a couple weeks.

She stepped onto the scale, averting her eyes to the old tan vinyl tiled floors while the weigh-in assistant checked and recorded her weight. For a house of God, they sure could use a cleaning.

"One seventy-seven," Paige said in a pleasant, upbeat manner.

Like I'm not heavy enough to be a baby elephant or a newborn whale, Heather's sarcastic mind snapped. She retrieved her weigh-in booklet, snapped it shut, and stuffed it into her jeans back pocket before moving on to the congregation of cold, gray folding chairs and the cluster of other clients.

"Pitiful sight," she muttered under her breath, recognizing a few faces from her last attempt. *They're still here.* She bit her tongue when she glimpsed her reflection in a dusty gingham-framed window.

What do you have to say for yourself? Just another Calorie Counters wimp at St. Elizabeth's Church basement.

Heather began praying. *Please, God, my brother's wedding is three months away. I just want to lose a few pounds, maybe fifteen to twenty, by then.* She pictured herself in Billy's arms, dancing at the reception, sleek and sexy in a slinky new dress she was going to buy just for the occasion. Heather would look like a vision of marital happiness in the emerald-green silk wrap dress that went well with her dark brown chin-length hair, and green eyes. Black three-inch sling-back heels on her feet lifted her to five foot eight, gazing height for Billy's own eyes. Billy wouldn't want to let her sit down. He'd be afraid someone else would ask her to dance when he wasn't looking. Heather daydreamed that she'd flirt lightly but decline the gorgeous hunk's offer. After all, she was a married woman and a mother of three young children.

A light nudge to her left arm brought Heather back to the reality surrounding her.

"Yes, you in the Mickey Mouse sweatshirt, would you like to take a seat?" a pixie-haired, stylishly dressed woman asked from the little platform at the front of the audience.

Heather sat in the closest seat in the back row.

The woman was the same leader from the last time Heather had joined. Everything about her was thin: her face, her torso, her limbs. Heather noted even her fingers were long and thin. Perfect for playing the piano, as her mother would say. *What's her name?* Heather searched her brain for a connection and kept coming back to a ketchup bottle image. Priscilla Hunts? No, Heinz. Yes, that's it, Heinz, here in Pittsburgh, but not related to the ketchup conglomerate people.

While her mind was digging for buried information, Pricilla Heinz had gone on with her program. Which, from the few words

Heather caught, might have had something to do with mindful eating. *Whatever that is*, Heather sulked.

"... so, what you want to do is first ask yourself, am I hungry, or is there some other emotion making me want to eat this food?" Pricilla emphasized her point by tapping a yardstick to an outline on a poster board at the front of the group.

"Second, you want to ask yourself, if it's not real hunger, how will eating this food make me feel better? Is it okay to feel this emotion and not eat? Can you do it until the emotion passes?" The yardstick slapped the poster board at the second point.

"And number three, if you eat it, I want you to sit at the table, take a bite and chew each bite at least twenty times, acknowledging the emotion. Before you take another bite, ask yourself if you need another bite. If you do, repeat the process. You want to be fully aware of each bite of food you take and how it makes you feel." The woman crossed to one side of the platform. "I think you'll find that the food doesn't make you feel good at all. In fact, it makes you feel worse for eating something that undermines your weight loss progress." Pricilla fervently offered the crowd. "So, this week, practice mindful eating, and *I think* you'll find you'll eat less. See you all next week."

Heather remained seated, waiting while the crowd surged for the door. She felt drained, and yet her bones felt so heavy, full of lead. Inertia engulfed her. Her hearing dimmed; her eyes felt clouded and unfocused. There were whole meals she ate without tasting them. Entire plates emptied unnoticed as she stuffed down the food while the kids were quiet or before any crying started.

"Are you all right?" Paige asked her, touching her shoulder. Heather's face turned up mechanically, her eyes glazed. For a few seconds her thoughts remained scattered. A little voice in her brain called out *Focus*. With a shake of her head, she was able to pull everything into focus again. Heather smiled softly and made direct eye contact with Paige.

"I'm okay, I think. I ... I think I'm just tired." Heather's voice was weak and cautious. Maybe she should have eaten something before coming tonight. She wanted to weigh in on an empty stomach, so she hadn't eaten anything. It was an old trick she remembered from her last few Calorie Counters go-rounds. She slung her handbag over her shoulder and headed for home.

The last week of the month, Heather called Chelsea again. She had hoped to hear back from her before now. Their brief discussion of reuniting had touched something deep inside her. She remembered their two weeks at summer camp distinctly. Once they got over their initial shyness, they acted as sisters. Or at least how Heather had always thought sisters should act. A sinking feeling in her gut told her Chelsea hadn't even tried the internet yet.

Maybe Chelsea's words were false. Maybe she didn't want them all to get together again. If she remembered correctly, Chelsea and Gemma had vied for Marla and Heather's attention.

Heather gave some consideration to using the library computer to search. She'd have to take the kids with her. Would they behave long enough for her to do a search?

JUNE 2017

On the first Friday in June, Heather got a call at home from Chelsea.

"How's the program going?" Chelsea asked.

"Not so hot. I'll keep trying." Heather's suspicion was piqued. "You aren't just calling me about my weight loss, are you?"

"Nope. I got a couple of hits on the internet." Chelsea's voice held a swagger.

"Really? What? Where?" Heather sputtered, dropping the laundry basket on the kitchen floor, and pulling up a chair, pleased that Chelsea had followed through.

"There's a Gemma Kimble working as a real estate agent out in Nevada. There are a couple in Wisconsin, in the Madison area. One is a college professor. The other might be some kind of political official. And get this, there's another working here in Pittsburgh for an organization called the National Association of Certified Engineering Technologists."

"Which one do you think she is?" Heather asked as she picked up Michelle from the kitchen floor before she pulled everything out of the laundry basket.

"I'm not sure, but checking on the one here in Pittsburgh is the easiest first step," Chelsea said. "Let's hope she isn't married and dropped her maiden name."

"You goin' ta call?" Heather's voice shuddered as she bobbed the baby on her knee to keep her quiet while her brothers were still napping.

"Yup. Here's my plan..."

Finding Gemma was easier than Chelsea ever thought it would be. The Pittsburgh Gemma was the first name they tried due to its proximity. They were pretty sure she was *the* Gemma they were looking for. Heather thought Chelsea's plan was pretty slick too.

When Chelsea finished work the next day, they met at Heather's house. While the children were napping, they called the phone number on the company's website.

"Hello?" The voice was different than either of them remembered. Heather nodded for Chelsea to continue anyway.

"Hello. I'm looking for Gemma Kimble." Chelsea said, a tentative tone in her voice.

"Speaking. What can I do for you?" Gemma's voice was professional yet rather curt.

"I'm calling because you have won a free manicure at the Shimmers Salon on Ellsworth Avenue."

A wariness seeped into Gemma's voice. "I don't recall ever having applied for one." Her voice hardened. "If this is a hoax or scam you can forget about it. I never tried to win a free manicure."

"I pulled your business card from a jar for a free manicure. You won it." Chelsea put an upbeat, exuberant tone into her voice like it was some big deal to have won.

"I don't put my business cards in jars." Gemma's clipped tone continued. "If you'll excuse me, I have work to do."

Chelsea added. "Please don't hang up. It's totally serious and legit. Perhaps someone you work with put your business card in the jar. A coworker?" This Gemma's belligerence certainly sounded like the real Gemma. Perhaps some things hadn't changed. "Let me assure you it's a free manicure service with no strings attached."

Silence on Gemma's end, so Chelsea continued. "Please, can we make an appointment? You can always decide not to show up."

She relented, making an appointment for later in the week. Heather and Chelsea giggled nervously after ending the call. Both of them crossed their fingers for the next five days, hoping Gemma wouldn't call the salon to cancel her appointment.

• • • •

FIVE DAYS LATER, AND five minutes late, Gemma bustled into the salon for her free manicure. Her face flushed; she practically flew in the door on black patent leather stilettos with the fringed ends of her ultra-soft pink scarf fluttering like feathers. She screeched to a halt when she saw Chelsea. Throwing her hands up with a squeal, like a cartoon character spotting a mouse, Gemma grabbed Chelsea in a crushing hug. They spent the entire one-hour appointment yakking about nearly seventeen years of absence.

Before she left, Chelsea called Heather, and the three women arranged a meetup.

Early the next week, Gemma, Heather, and Chelsea met for the first time over coffee at Pamela's Diner on Walnut Street. Formica tables lined the long narrow shop's walls, with pinkish-coral and teal-green cushioned chrome chairs in a vintage 1950s style. The overhead track lighting spotlighted walls festooned with advertising pictures from the same era.

Heather had told Chelsea of the tragic years between high school graduation and now. Chelsea didn't want Gemma sticking her foot into anything sensitive, so she warned her to steer away from asking Heather too many questions. But that wasn't the only reason for the tension between them. So many years, and the question about what happened on the last night of camp still hung between them like a black hole. It was almost as if each of them held their breath, hoping that particular incident wouldn't come up.

It was inevitable they would talk about their camp days and all the trouble they caused. Gemma was in a prankster stage back then, and how could she not be, with three older brothers at home. She'd previously witnessed or heard her brothers and their friends pull off all the pranks they sprang on the other girls at Camp Terramungus. She was a treasure trove of trouble.

The dead fish they tucked under the pillow of the snobbish girl, Veronica, in cabin eight. All four had nearly busted a gut laughing when they heard her screeching bloody murder. The entire camp ran over to find out what was going on. Everyone except the girls in cabin four. Spreading cellophane over a toilet bowl, hiding the oars to the rowboats, replacing the milk chocolate for s'mores with bitter baking chocolate, putting sand in another mean girl's sleeping bag, and adding hot sauce to the pink lemonade were all Gemma's ideas.

The three of them laughed so hard people at nearby tables gave them dirty looks.

"Whatever happened about the fire?" Gemma asked.

"Those were the best pranks," Heather said, her arms crossed over her chest.

"We should try to find Marla," Chelsea replied.

Gemma handed her credit card to the waitress when she approached with the bill. "I can try while I'm at work. I'll let you both know if I find her."

Heather left to go to the ladies' room.

Chelsea leaned over the table toward Gemma conspiratorially. "Hey, don't say anything to Heather, but a bunch of my friends and I are going on a cruise to Jamaica in a month or so. One couple needs to back out but can't get their money back. Would you want to go in their place?" Chelsea continued with the dates and costs.

"Hmm, I'll have to find a cat sitter." Gemma's eyes sparkled. "That sounds like fun. I already have that week scheduled off from work. Would you mind if I asked my cousin to share the cabin?"

"The more the merrier, as they say."

Gemma inclined her chin toward the back when she saw Heather returning. "Can I let you know tomorrow after I talk with Rose Anne?"

Chelsea nodded. "Sure, that's fine. Please don't discuss the cruise in front of Heather. I know she'd love to join us but can't. They can't afford a cruise. And there's the children."

Gemma nodded her understanding with a sympathetic look in her eyes as Heather arrived back at the table.

• • • •

MARLA FINISHED HER report on the St. Louis laboratory inspection an hour later than she expected. It had been a complicated and exhausting report to put together, mainly because of the number of state and federal violations she had found during her inspection last week.

Staring out the window, she pondered the report as it printed, her gut uneasy. The laboratory was seven years old and had been perfectly fine two years ago when it was last inspected. The regulations had changed considerably since then. What had been acceptable then was not acceptable now.

She picked up the freshly printed sheet, only to leave green, red, and yellow smudges wherever her fingertips touched the page. Marla splayed open her hand, finding her fingertips were stained various hues. "So much for 'melts in your mouth, not in your hand.'" She must have been absentmindedly feeding herself M&Ms from the bag in the top left-hand drawer of her desk. It was that time of the month again, and Marla couldn't get enough chocolate to satisfy the cravings. Six more days of this nonsense, Marla thought while wiping her fingers on a tissue. She hit the print key again for a clean copy.

I should just get a hysterectomy. I'll never have a boyfriend, let alone a family of my own. She had come close once in her twenty-nine years, but surely that had been an anomaly. There hadn't been anyone since. Her heart thudded painfully at other memories. The pitying looks and sneers of her classmates in school and at school dances. The stinging slander, cruel taunting, and practical jokes that left her devastated for days. Her parents had been furious at the shenanigans. So much so they wanted to send her to a private school. Marla knew it would be no better there. She'd resolved to stand courageous and defiant against them.

I need real food. Hollowness weighed heavy in the pit of her stomach: cavernous and empty despite the party-sized bag of candy.

Marla emailed the report to her supervisor. They would meet in the morning to discuss it, but at least Beverly would have time to review the findings beforehand. Could her work withstand the scrutiny it would face? Was she being too hardball? Maybe the company didn't want someone who always played by the book? After all, whether nitpicking or justified, her scrutiny cost Peabody money. Frowning with indecision and anxiety, Marla dialed the number for Enrico's Pizza and placed an order for a pickup.

She cleaned up her desk, left the office building, and found her car in the parking garage. She picked up her order at Enrico's on the way to her refurbished Craftsman-style home in the Shadyside neighborhood. The everything-but-anchovies pizza was good tonight, Marla decided after absentmindedly eating three-quarters of the medium pizza. She ignored the salad, dropping it into the fridge to take to work in the morning. She settled back to finish watching *NCIS* while she ate her tiramisu. Enrico made the best tiramisu with real whipped mascarpone cheese. By nine-thirty that night, she gave up trying to keep her eyelids open to watch *Law & Order SVU* and went to bed.

At seven thirty the next morning, she was eating her second Egg McMuffin at her desk, when her supervisor Beverly Breckenridge, called her to postpone their meeting until lunch.

Marla started to pace in her tiny office. After fidgeting with the window blinds, she sat back down in her chair and twirled. She searched her desk for something to eat yet turned up nothing but the leftover salad from the previous night. Her nose wrinkled at the thought of wilted lettuce and soggy croutons. Not wanting to go down to the cafeteria, she began to sweat and dove into paperwork to distract her mind and fingers. If she could only get on with the meeting and present her report, maybe the fluttering in her stomach would end.

After consulting the inspection schedule for the thirty satellite laboratories making up Peabody, Marla put together a mental plan to inspect laboratories in states that had made significant changes to their health and safety regulations. Next, she devised a schedule of inspections for those laboratories over the following year.

Hours later, Marla walked into her boss's office for their meeting. Her eye fell on the narrow chairs in front of the desk. *Why didn't I suggest we meet in my office?* Marla knew that wouldn't have worked. Underlings went to their superior's office. The dozen plaques on the wall—most of them recognizing Beverly as employee of the year—testified to the esteem she had garnered over her thirty-year career. When Marla first joined Peabody, she thought she might like Beverly's job when the older woman retired. After watching her for a few years, Marla was sure no one could fill Beverly's shoes. Not even herself.

The office space was not much bigger than Marla's own. It was warm with the curtains open, allowing sunlight to stream through the window. While not cozy, it gave off a power vibe with vibrantly colored modern paintings on the walls. Beverly's decorating style matched her strong and direct nature.

"Thanks for rescheduling. What's up with your latest inspections?" Beverly asked, glancing over her half-glasses as Marla winced and squirmed to fit herself in the small chair with narrow armrests. Beverly didn't say anything. Instead, she averted her heavy-lidded dark brown eyes to her computer screen.

"My inspections of the Sioux City, Santa Fe, and Providence labs this year went well, as the reports I sent indicate. The inspections at Birmingham and Kansas City found several minor violations. Many major violations were found in Fort Myers."

"What's going on?" asked Beverly. Her brow creased under her short, tightly curled hair. She closed her mouth and pursed her lips. The look might have been one of concern, but it also could be displeasure. Either way, Marla's knees trembled as she began to explain.

"Several states made significant changes to their regulations since the last time those labs were inspected." Marla pressed her palms down on her knees to help calm the quivering.

"Perhaps your predecessor wasn't quite up to standard?" Beverly's thin graying eyebrows rose.

"I'm not aware of his training background, so I can't judge. What I do know is that these three labs have made violations that could have cost Peabody substantial fines if they were caught in federal or state regulatory inspections." Marla explained as judiciously as she could under Beverly's scrutiny. Sweat beads rolled out from under Marla's breasts and down her abdomen until absorbed by her shirt. *My God, I've got to get out of here and get this suit jacket off.* She desperately tried to remain calm and keep her mind on the conversation.

"Good job then. How many other labs do you think might be questionable?" her supervisor asked while scribbling something on a notepad on her desk.

"Five other laboratories are in states that also made the same changes to their regulations. I'd like to make them my priority cases for the rest of the year."

"Sounds like a good plan." Beverly nodded as she continued scribbling notes, then paused and looked up from her notepad. "I've been thinking for a while that you need an assistant to help and to cover for you during vacations and sick time."

The idea blindsided Marla. The more she thought about it, the more she realized it would relieve a lot of her stress. The company was adding more and more locations around the country. Another pair of hands and eyes would be beneficial.

"You would be lead, of course. I'll work on getting this ball rolling with the upper administration." Beverly scribbled a few more notes and underlined something on the page. Suddenly, she stared at Marla. "What about Seattle?"

She'd forgotten about the lab in Seattle currently under construction. "When is it expected to be up and running?" Marla asked, hedging for time.

"Sometime in the next six to twelve months. Keep it in mind. The contractors are working directly with the regulatory people, so you don't need to get involved yet. But once it's open and running..." Beverly sat back in her chair. "The new medical director has already been selected, a clinical pathologist from University of Washington Medical Center, Dr. Timothy Brighton. He's new to Peabody, currently at the Milwaukee facility for training."

Marla's mouth went dry as a desert river wash in August. *Timothy Brighton? Did she say Timothy Brighton?* Her heart fluttered erratically as she tried to focus while Beverly continued speaking. *Should I mention I've met him?* Just as quickly as she thought it, Marla decided to keep that fact to herself.

"The laboratory manager, Andrea Bekkit, is the current manager of Peabody's Atlanta facility. She keeps a tight ship in Atlanta, no doubt she'll do the same in Seattle. Assuming, of course, the inspections have been diligent." A small smirk danced across Beverly's face.

Sweat trickled alongside her backbone, then down the crack of her butt. She hadn't heard a word Beverly had said. And she didn't care. Marla's mind kept repeating *Oh God, Dr. Brighton,* like a blessing from heaven had been bestowed. Her mind reeled with his name again.

"Great job, Marla. I'm impressed with your initiative. Carry on with the revised inspection plan. Let the labs know in advance of the specific dates." Beverly stood and walked around the desk to shake Marla's hand. "Keep up the good work."

"Thank you. I will," was all Marla could muster besides a tentative smile.

Alone in the elevator, she leaned against the cold stainless-steel wall and let out a huge sigh from the very depths of her toes. She had done a good job handling the issues. Beverly had been pleased with her initiative.

Giddiness surged up her chest to her throat until she giggled nervously. Timothy Brighton. Between the praise and the thoughts of seeing Dr. Brighton again, she floated back to her office. After pulling off her suit jacket, she found her linen shirt and bra soaked with sweat and clinging to her skin. Beneath her pantyhose, Marla could tell her panties were likewise soaked from crotch sweat.

She flopped the manila folder down on her desk, dropped into her chair, and laid her forehead on the cool metal desktop. What in God's name was she going to do about Dr. Brighton?

Reaching for the phone, she sat up and pushed speed dial number seven. "Hello, Fajita Grille? Order to go, please."

She drove down the street to pick up her takeout order. Marla celebrated her success with a couple of beef burritos, an order of nachos with guacamole and salsa, and a couple bottles of Pepsi. Returning to the company parking garage, she ate it all while sitting in her car.

Later, in her office, her belly achingly distended with food, she chastised herself for overeating, for being a pig, and looking like a whale. How was she ever going to face Dr. Brighton at over three hundred pounds?

I have to lose weight. Tomorrow, I'm starting a diet, she thought with the rock-solid determination only a full stomach can provide.

••••

HEATHER CONSIDERED her progress as she drove home from her fourth Calorie Counters session. Her weight loss was pretty dismal, totaling only two and three-quarters pounds. An audible snort of disgust came from her throat. The number of months left before her brother's wedding was dwindling.

The problem was Billy. After working up a hearty appetite all day, Billy couldn't be sated with light dinners. Heather had to keep up the heavy meat-and-potatoes meals for him while trying to stick to her plan. It wasn't easy to look at all that food on the table and deny herself. After following the plan for breakfast and lunch each day, Heather let it slide at dinnertime. It was still better than not behaving well at all, which was why she was still losing a tiny bit of weight. Nevertheless, she was not getting the desired results because she couldn't change Billy's food habits and resist her own temptations at dinner every night.

Her meetings with Gemma and Chelsea didn't help either. Gemma was short like her at five foot six. She also had dark brown hair, but hers was cut in a short, angled bob. Chelsea was much taller, and while heavier than they'd been at camp, she carried her weight better than Heather did. The two voracious eaters consumed everything and anything, and it wasn't long before her resolve caved. No wonder she was pear-shaped, heavy in the abdomen and buttocks but with no boobs after breastfeeding all her children through the first four to six months of infancy.

But she was happy the three of them were finally meeting. Now if they could only find Marla, it would be perfect.

••••

CHELSEA AND GEMMA DECIDED to meet despite Heather not being able to join them. Gemma strode up to the tiny table at Jitters Café on Walnut Street after getting some Dave & Andy's Homemade Ice Cream.

"What'd you get?" Chelsea asked and then licked her blueberry cobbler ice cream cone.

Gemma flopped down across from Chelsea. "Mexican Chipotle Chocolate in a cup." Flinging her handbag on the empty chair, she drove her plastic spoon into the cup, pulling up a heap of ice cream that disappeared between her lipstick-painted lips. "MMMM!"

"Yeah. I can't believe you didn't know about this place."

"Me neither." Gemma nodded as she let the creamy coldness saturate her mouth. "I got a sitter for Wally. So, we're all set? Rose Anne and I?"

"Yup. Monica booked your flights. Thanks for taking Tammy and Joe's cabin. They appreciate your reimbursing them the full price for it." Chelsea paused to lick her cone. "Any luck finding Marla yet?"

"No. The search websites haven't turned up anything on her yet. I'm going to have to try another tactic."

"I wish I could remember exactly where she was from in New York. It might help."

Gemma blurted out, "What's up with Heather?"

"She had to bring Michelle to the doctor for something." Chelsea's eyes narrowed slightly though her face held a pinched look. "It was a last-minute development, but not serious."

"That's not what I meant." Gemma sighed. "There's a lot of pain hiding behind those eyes."

Chelsea lowered her voice. "She's had a rough time of it. She and Billy got married when she got pregnant. Probably not a very smart move but anyway. Then the baby was born premature. She only lived a couple of days."

Gemma's heart leaped in sympathy. "Oh, my God. Poor Heather!"

"Yeah. It hit her pretty hard. And their marriage suffered."

"But she has three children now."

"True. They might be the only thing that gets her out of bed in the morning."

"What about her husband?"

A heavy sigh escaped Chelsea. "Between you and me, he's a spoiled jerk. Expects Heather to do everything at the house besides caring for the children. He doesn't make a lot of money which accounts for their financial circumstances."

"That explains the sorrow I see in her eyes."

"She and I met a few times before she told me about it all. Let me tell you, it took my breath away. Heather needed someone, a sister type. I held her while she cried her heart out."

"Such a tragedy," Gemma whispered, wiping her face with her hand. "I won't say anything." Her mind circled around, coming back to the same issue. Another woman married to an ass who took her for granted and chained her to children and an unhappy marriage. It further reinforced Gemma's desire to remain single.

"Let me know if you find anything about Marla."

JULY 2017

Later in the afternoon, Marla's office phone rang as she got her things together to go home.

"Marla, we have a situation at the Phoenix lab. I need you to get there as soon as possible."

Her heart sank as Beverly explained the issues, but Marla hardly heard. She was so looking forward to a quiet evening. Now she'd have to pack and pre-plan her trip. "I'll make the flight reservations right now."

"Don't bother, I had my assistant do it. Your first flight leaves at six in the morning."

Marla slammed her things down on her desk chair. She didn't like having emergency situations like this. She preferred to be totally prepared at all times. These last-minute problems made her uneasy. As if she needed yet another issue to be uneasy about.

She rifled through her file cabinet, grabbed the Phoenix lab file, and stuffed it into her laptop case. *So much for binge-watching Netflix tonight.*

The following day was the worst of her life. Undeniably. As the corporate compliance manager for Peabody Laboratories, Marla periodically traveled to different cities to inspect other company-owned laboratories for compliance with regulatory issues. It was her job. While she didn't mind flying, in fact, she loved to travel, it was always a struggle to travel comfortably.

She had no idea what to expect, and the churning of her stomach intensified on the way to the airport in the cab. She preferred to make her own flight arrangements. Beverly's assistant had booked her in coach—instead of her usual business class—on an airline Marla didn't have frequent flier points with, so upgrading to first class or business class was out of the question. It was a bad omen.

On the flight to St. Louis first thing in the morning, she struggled lifting her carry-on into the overhead bin. The flight attendants indicated the bins in the back of the plane were already full, so Marla had to use one in the front of the cabin. As lightly as she packed, at five foot one, it felt like bench-pressing a forty-pound sack of dog food.

She had nearly dropped the case on someone's head as it started to slide sideways. Luckily, hands flew up behind her from a very helpful young man in army fatigues who proceeded to flip it into the bin as if it was a marshmallow. Marla gave him a whispered "thank you" after swallowing the huge, dry lump in her throat.

Then it everyone with an aisle seat was already in place, so moving down the narrow aircraft aisle was more difficult with her oversized girth. She must have said, "Excuse me," a hundred times as her belly and buttocks brushed arms and legs on her way to seat 20B. She'd been so flushed and sweaty she wanted to park in her seat, plug in her earbuds, pull a blanket over her head, and close her eyes until landing.

The connecting flight from St. Louis to Phoenix was the last straw. Once again, Marla had to sling her case into the overhead bin. This time, she managed to do it with some grace since the bin was empty, as were the seats in front of it, allowing her to get a little closer and heave it. She found her seat, 26B, and squeezed into the middle seat.

Great. Hippo in the middle. She hated that seat most of all. She would ask for another seat, but she knew the flight was full and oversold. If she wasn't on urgent business, she would have given up the seat for a free ticket. *Never fails. It always happens when I can't accept it.*

A blue-eyed, pony-tailed blonde in skintight jeans stopped at the row and announced she had the window seat. Trying to keep a pleasant attitude, Marla stepped out of the row. The girl, an older teenager on closer look, slid into the row without a word of thanks or a smile. As soon as she sat in the window seat, she began rummaging through her handbag.

Not five seconds after settling herself back in her seat, a bright-eyed, spiked-haired, goateed young male sauntered to a stop. His flamboyant outfit and eye makeup struck conservative Marla as odd. But she knew she was the last person who should throw stones.

"I have 26A, the aisle seat," he snipped.

"Okay," Marla said. She adjusted the seatbelt extension over her lower abdomen. It didn't help. She pulled her arms in and squeezed her legs together, trying to stay in her own seat's space. The uncomfortable feeling in her chest had nothing to do with the man's possible sexual orientation. Rather, it had to do with the sneer on his face as he looked down on her. She had seen that look before, and it did not bode well for a pleasant flight. It was the reason she always sat in business class. Silently she cursed the unknown administrative assistant who had saddled her in the coach section.

He waited, his expression one of tight-lipped impatience as if it was killing him to stand another second. Marla reached over to his seat and pulled his seatbelts aside. Without so much as a nod of thanks, he sat down in his aisle seat, shoved his magazine in the seat-back pocket, and began buckling up.

The ruckus started immediately.

"Excuse me, this is my armrest," the pony-tailed teenager sniffed. Marla's right arm overhung the armrest. She tried to shift over to the other side of her seat but bumped shoulders with the man on her left.

"Sorry," Marla said to him as he shot her a hard glare. Readjusting herself, she tried her best to sit in the center of her own seat. There was no help for it. Her spare-tire love handles overhung both armrests. They also prevented her arms from hanging straight down.

"My leg space is cramped enough, do you mind?" the man on her left sneered under his breath.

Looking down, she saw her legs noticeably encroaching into each of their limited leg space.

The pony-tailed teenager unbuckled her seatbelt and partially stood, reaching for the call button but ended up flagging a passing flight attendant instead.

"I can't possibly sit here. This woman is spread into my seat space!" she whined to the middle-aged, weary-eyed flight attendant. "And the odor!"

Marla was meticulous about showering and using a fragrant powder. She knew sometimes her abundant flesh smelled bad no matter what she did to cover it up. If she could have shrunk herself, she would have turned herself into a grain of sand. Her face flamed, her heart raced so fast it might give out at any second, and her breathing became an erratic panting. She closed her eyes, trying to regain calmness. When she opened her eyes, every passenger in the back half of the plane was engrossed in the unfolding drama. All were trying to get a look at her. Trying to see the fat woman in the middle seat.

"Me also, this is toe-tolly unacceptable. I paid over six hundred dollars for this seat, and it's already half taken by this woman!" the young man hissed.

The attendant's jaw tensed. "We are about to push off from the jetway. I can't do anything about your seats at this moment. I'll see who I can move after we're airborne." The attendant said curtly, giving each of them a hard glare.

The engines' discordant whine added to the hostile atmosphere. Whispered muttering buzzed in the seats around them as the three seatmates in row 26 struggled to get some measure of comfort for takeoff.

Marla's chest heaved with deep breaths as she tried to control her pain. Her anguish erupted into tears after spotting her seatmates exchanging fiendish glances. Suddenly it was elementary school all over again. The taunting, the slander, the sly and snide dastardly remarks. With her hands shielding her swollen, tear-drenched face, Marla prayed for death right there, right then.

The roar of the plane's engines was nothing compared to the roaring in her head. A brutal tearing sensation ripped through her chest like a knife excising her soul. Involuntary tremors shook her body, not from the sobbing but from the breaking of her spirit. As tears fell with abandon, she felt her spirit, her life force, and her courage crumble, seeping from her body, weeping from every one of her cells, leaving her limp and worthless.

It felt like an eternity before the flight attendant returned.

"Miss Devine?"

Marla looked up through tear-matted lashes. What more could she want?

The nametag pinned to the flight attendant's uniform identified her as Paula. "Please come with me, I'm moving you back a few rows," she said.

"Thank *Ghodd*!" the man beside her proclaimed, hastening to get up out of his seat to let Marla out.

Marla sidestepped out of the row. *Don't look at anyone. Don't watch them watch you. They want to see the freak you are, the fat lady on the plane.*

Tears continued down her cheeks, soaking into her Oxford shirt; light blue where dry, a darker blue in large patches across her chest where it was soaked wet with tears. Paula directed her to the rear galley area of the plane.

"We don't say this often, but hereafter, Miss Devine, you will have to purchase two seats on this airline instead of one." As Paula spoke quietly, her eyes were clear blue with a tinge of regret and sympathy. Even so, if there were a way to exit the plane, Marla would have jumped, with or without a parachute.

Paula put a gentle hand on her shoulder and gave her a small packet of tissues. "Your new seat is 30A, in this last row, the aisle seat." A nod of her head to the right indicated two open seats beside an elderly man.

Still beet-faced and crying silently, Marla claimed her new seat and closed her eyes to endure the remainder of the three-hour trip. The entire flight, self-castigations roared through her mind. *How did I let myself get this big? Why can't I take some kind of pill to lose weight? How could I possibly manage any kind of healthy eating schedule and exercise program with this type of unpredictable travel?*

Two hours later, she awoke. She glanced around to see if anyone was watching. No one was. She must have fallen asleep due to sheer exhaustion from the emotional calamity. Calmer and slightly refreshed, she dissected the incident behind closed eyes. As the cabin readied for landing, a steely determination built in her chest. She had the beginnings of a plan.

By the time the wheels touched the tarmac in Phoenix, Marla, a woman trained in medical laboratory science, who could take charge, control, and manage all kinds of situations in laboratories around the country, had come to a substantive decision.

I am taking total control of myself until this weight situation is properly resolved. I will use every tool, spare no expense, and not give up until I can look at myself in the mirror and be happy with everything I see. In the meantime, I'm changing my return flight to first class, no matter the cost.

Chelsea and Gemma arrived thirty minutes early so they could discuss the cruise without hurting Heather's feelings. The restaurant was slow that day, giving them a choice of seating.

"I can't believe we're going to Jamaica in the middle of the summer. Who chose the dates?" Gemma whined.

"Why do you think it was so cheap?" Chelsea bit back. "Did you find someone to cat-sit?"

Her martini glass twirled around and around as Gemma fingered the stem. "Yes. Rose Anne's parents are going to watch Wally and his brother, Leo."

"I didn't know you have two."

Gemma shook her head. "I don't. Leo belongs to Rose Anne."

Chelsea, who was watching the restaurant door, suddenly said, "Heather's here."

"Sorry I'm so late," Heather said, flopping into the chair beside Chelsea.

Chelsea patted her hand. "Don't worry. We were just chatting." She turned toward Heather again. "How are the kids?"

Heather groaned. "Ugh. They're running me ragged. I can't get much of anything done unless they're napping. But they can't nap all day either."

"More's the pity, I'm sure," Gemma smirked.

Chelsea glared at her. "Just because you don't enjoy kids doesn't mean nobody else should."

Gemma huffed at the retort, then sipped her fancy drink.

"Anyway, I do like having them home. Peter should be at an age where he can entertain his brother. But he doesn't want to. So we go for a lot of walks with the dog." Heather glanced between her friends. "What's up with you guys?"

Gemma motioned for Chelsea to take the floor.

"I received a lot of feedback and quite a few appointments from the places I put up advertisements. I could probably cut my hours at the salon in half." She grimaced. "Well, not entirely yet. But I can see it happening soon." Chelsea waved for Gemma's turn.

"Hmm, why don't you give me a bunch of flyers, and I'll distribute them around my condo complex. You could probably pick up a few more home manicure clients."

Heather's eyes brightened. "That's a great idea. You should do that Chel."

"And be beholdin' to this witch? Are you crazy?" Chelsea shook her head and crossed her arms over her chest. "I'd never hear the end of it. Besides, Gem will want free manicures for helping."

"You bet I will," Gemma said.

The three of them giggled.

• • • •

MERMAID OF THE WAVES was underway, leaving the Port of Miami for a seven-day cruise to Key West, Jamaica, and Grand Cayman Island. Chelsea and Seth, Diane and Andy, Monica and Nate, Robin and Wes, and Gemma and her cousin Rose Anne gathered at the stern of the ship. It had taken nearly an act of Congress to get them all together for the cruise. Still, Monica's connections with the travel agency had found them passage for two hundred and nineteen dollars each and eighty-nine dollar round trip airfares from Pittsburgh to Miami, which was more than enough arm twisting for many of them.

After two hours on board, they were already buzzed from the stiff drinks served on the Lido deck. A seven-piece band played classic rock hits mid-ship by the lounge chairs. The area was too crowded to be enjoyable, and they could not access their cabins, so the group had gathered by the adults-only pool, eyeing it wantonly but unable to partake without their swimwear.

"Next time, I'm packing my swimsuit in my carry-on bag. I want to be in that pool, NOW," Robin slurred, holding on to her piña colada with one hand and the ship railing with the other.

"Waiting for our cabins and luggage to be ready sucks. How come they don't mention this in the brochure?" asked Rose Anne.

"Because you'd never sign on, that's why," Wes quipped, setting aside yet another dead soldier.

"At least the bar and buffet tables are well stocked," Chelsea offered. "Speaking of which, I think I need more buffalo wings. Anyone want to come with me?"

"Sure," said Rose Anne and Gemma in unison.

"Hun, bring me another cheeseburger, will ya?" Seth asked, giving Chelsea's plump ass a loving rub and then a double pat to shove her off on her mission.

"Anything else?" Chelsea asked, glancing around at the assembly of friends while she swatted Seth's hand away.

"Um, I'll come with you and check it out," Nate said.

"Nate, we're eating dinner about three hours from now!" Monica reminded him.

Nate patted his stomach. "Yeah, well, that's *three hours* from now. I'm a hungry guy, toots. Don't worry, I won't ruin my appetite." He winked and thrust his pelvis in what was probably meant as a seductive gesture but failed miserably.

Monica rolled her eyes and turned away. The high-rise condos of Miami Beach slid by on their right. Their ship cleared the last seawall and instantly had a more buoyant feeling of sailing on open ocean water.

Seth, Wes, and Andy disappeared for drink refills.

"Look, you guys, the pizzeria window is open," Robin exclaimed. "I'm going for a few slices. Want some?"

"Sure, why don't you bring back a couple extra. Maybe Nate will have one," Monica said.

Five minutes later, the troops reconvened from their hunter-gatherer quests with their bounty: five more Budweisers, two piña coladas, two cosmos, three margaritas, four slices of cheese and four of pepperoni pizza, two dozen buffalo wings, four cheeseburgers, and two cafeteria trays, one with a mountain of French fries and the other an exploding volcano of nacho chips oozing salsa and cheese sauce lava.

"Now this is how to go cruisin'," Andy said, raising his bottle in a toast. "To the *Mermaid*, may she grant us a week of good food, good liquor, and good times."

"Here, here" "Yes, sirree!" "Amen" were shouted in reply as they dug into the feast while the horizon melded into the sea.

Three days into their voyage, the ship crossed a two-day-old path left by a category three hurricane. The captain assured the passengers it was a safe maneuver, but seas would be rough for the twelve hours it would take the ship to transect the hurricane's former path. Twelve hours had turned into eighteen with no end in sight. Few passengers were in sight either, most of them flat out in their cabins with seasickness or heeding the captain's suggestion to remain stationary until the ship reached calmer waters. He didn't reckon on two very hungry, non-seasick women still bent on having a great time.

Chelsea and Gemma traveled hand over hand, clinging onto the railing in the ship's corridor, trying to maintain some semblance of balance despite the heaving vessel. Of their entire entourage, only they were not sprawled on their beds, with basins or trash bins within reach for the gastric upheaval that would not subside no matter the repeated applications of various seasickness patches.

"I came for the endless food," Chelsea said as they met outside her cabin.

Gemma quipped, "No, you didn't. You came for the endless alcohol."

They laughed. The ship pitched hard, and the women lost their balance and careened into the hallway wall, making their laughter hysterical.

"Come on. Let's get to the dining room before they close it," Chelsea said as they righted themselves and hastened along the corridor.

In light of the jostling, the elevators were out of service, forcing the women to take the stairs to the dining hall. There, they found a few wait staff and a half dozen like-minded guests trying to find sustenance during the tempest.

The normal dining menu was suspended, as much of the food choices were too hazardous to cook in a wildly pitching ship. Only three options were offered: filet mignon, grilled lamb chops, or baked stuffed shrimp. Gemma chose the filet mignon. Chelsea ordered all three entrees. They settled on a bottle of wine which was opened and poured, though keeping the wineglasses and bottle upright proved difficult during some ocean swells.

The ladies feasted on the food, giggling and gorging themselves. There was no way they were going to let a hurricane's wake ruin their day at sea.

"So, what are you planning to do in Jamaica tomorrow?" Gemma asked, trying to pour herself another glass of wine but missing as the boat shifted. Wine spilled all over the tablecloth. "Oops," she giggled, her head already feeling light and dizzy from the combination.

"Seth and I are doing the falls climb," Chelsea said. "How about you?"

"Rose and I wanted to ride the rainforest zip line, but I exceed the weight restriction. I'm hoping they'll let me go anyway." Gemma's face flushed.

"Don't count on it," Chelsea taunted. Chelsea started to giggle to herself again. It hadn't been easy getting Gemma to go. She had the financial resources, but she had some breathing problems she was worried would interrupt the trip. So far, though, there hadn't been any problems. In fact, Gemma said the ocean air had helped.

"Well, if it doesn't happen, I won't be too upset. I'm afraid of heights, and I'm not that adventurous," Gemma reasoned.

"U-huh!" Chelsea taunted. "Should I bring some leftovers back for Seth, do you think?" she asked with a straight face. But she couldn't hold it for long. She busted out, snickering.

"Only if you wanna see him throw up again—and again—and again!" roared Gemma, nearly unable to find her mouth with the fork.

They cackled heartily, falling over onto the booth bench with a sudden deep sway of the pitching ship.

"Oh God, he really looks a dark shade of green. I took a picture, but he didn't show up as green. I wonder why?" Chelsea stared into her glass, watching the wine swirl and slosh about without her help. Double vision ensued as her eyes crossed. *Yikes! Time to lay off the wine.*

Their waiter approached hesitantly, a wary expression on his face. Chelsea thought he was afraid they would want another bottle of wine. She was beginning to wonder how they were going to get back to their cabins as it were, regardless of the tossing ship. Getting Seth's help was out of the question.

"Would either of you ladies like to see the dessert menu?" The waiter offered each of them a small dessert menu.

"Absolutely," Chelsea said. "Could you read it to me? I can't quite see too well." She couldn't stop herself from cracking jokes about the state of their intoxication. It was funny how drunk she was on this roller-coaster of a ship. She hoped to remember some of this because it sure felt like a fun time. Chelsea focused harder on the dessert menu.

Gemma was having fun. She was happy she was able to join the cruise party. For once, she was letting her hair down, so to speak. It was hard to let down a short, straight bob.

"Most certainly, madam. We have a Bailey's crème brûlée, a chocolate pâté with strawberry sauce, pecan strudel, apple galette, cold lemon-raspberry soufflé or a fresh fruit tart with sabayon. We also have regular and decaf coffees, regular, herbal, decaf teas, cappuccino, lattes, and espresso." He smiled warily.

Chelsea glanced at Gemma for a few seconds, and they replied in unison, "One of each!" then roared with laughter again, falling over in the banquette in drunken glee.

The waiter rolled his eyes and curtly strode away toward the galley.

"I wish Heather was here with us," Chelsea gulped down the last of her wine. "She could use a break from the kids and that husband of hers."

"Mm. I agree." Gemma belatedly used her napkin to sop up the spilled wine. "You know what I don't get?"

Chelsea sat up straighter as if to focus.

"Why every time we bring up the fire, Heather changes the subject," Gemma said conspiratorially.

"It was a traumatic event for her. She did save us all by waking us up."

"That's what I mean. She's the hero, right? Shouldn't she be proud?"

Chelsea shook her head. "That's just not Heather's way. She's bashful and shy."

Their conversation was interrupted by the waiter returning with the dessert-laden serving tray.

"Ohmagod!" Gemma exclaimed wide-eyed with stunned apprehension as she surveyed the five desserts spread from end to end on the table. "How are we gonna eat all that?"

"One delicious spoonful at a time," Chelsea purred, a mischievous glint in her eyes, her spoon already poised above the crème brûlée, ready to submerge.

• • • •

A WEEK AFTER THE CRUISE, the three women were meeting for lunch at Girasole Restaurant over huge bowls of fresh pasta and homemade sauces.

"How's the weight program going?" Gemma asked, observing Heather playing with her lettuce and eyeing her friends' plates.

It was dark in the back of the small restaurant. The only windows were on the street side. The dark stone walls and terracotta tiled floor didn't reflect much light. Local artwork, hanging on the wall, bathed in tiny spotlights, didn't lend much to lighten the restaurant.

"Not so good. It's so hard with Billy around. He wants 'the works' for dinner. Meat and mashed potatoes. He won't even try the vegetables, which makes the kids refuse them as well."

"Monkeys see, monkeys do." Chelsea shrugged. "I couldn't get Seth to do it either. I wouldn't bother trying."

Gemma mashed her lips together. "Don't give up. You still have several weeks before the wedding. Just five pounds will help you feel more confident."

"Huh." Heather snorted as she fiddled with the radicchio.

"I googled Marla Devine. That's her real name, isn't it?" Gemma glanced back and forth between Heather and Chelsea for confirmation.

Heather stopped pushing salad vegetables around her plate and set down her fork. "Yes. Marla is her name. It's not a nickname for Marlene or Marilyn or anything like that, if that's what you mean."

"Great. I couldn't remember, so I went with Marla."

"Whad ya find?" Chelsea asked as she drove her fork into a glistening orange-pink shrimp on a bed of fennel studded with bits of fresh orange and olives.

"I came up with a few hits for a Marla who was a coauthor on several medical, scientific papers; one listing her at Columbia University Medical Center in New York and five others at Johns Hopkins in Baltimore, Maryland."

The three women looked at each other blankly. Gemma paused her forkful of spinach and ricotta ravioli to shrug. "I called HR at both those places but was told that Marla no longer worked at either."

Chelsea shook her head. "Shit. It figures that as easy as it was for us three to find each other, the last would be three times as difficult to find."

"You eat with that mouth?" Gemma quipped, flinging Chelsea a hard glare before breaking into a sly smile and flashing a wink toward Heather. She was pissed at not finding Marla. Failure was not an option, at anything.

Their efforts to find Marla came to a dead end. They ate in silence for a few minutes, deep in their own thoughts. Each of them searching for any ideas about how to go forward.

"How was your cruise?" Heather asked. "Monica said it was an interesting trip."

Gemma and Chelsea looked at each other as if trying to decide who would deal with the question and how much to tell. At last, Gemma spoke up. "It was good. We had a good time."

"The guys were drunk most of the time. When they weren't puking their guts out." Chelsea started to laugh.

Heather gasped, her palm over her mouth. "Oh my! I forgot about seasickness. Were the seas rough?"

Chelsea and Gemma explained about the hurricane's path.

"But don't worry, we ate our weights and then some. Especially Chelsea." Gemma offered with a wink at Heather.

"Hey now, wait one second. You were right there with me the entire time." Chelsea pouted.

"That's why I can attest to that as fact," Gemma smirked. "Hey, I need to tell you guys something. It might be a while before I can meet up again. I'm having surgery next week." She added, "Nothing serious. Just some corrective stomach surgery to stop my nightly asthma problems."

Chelsea took the bait, as Gemma knew she would. "How the hell does surgery on your stomach stop your breathing problem?"

Both of them stopped eating, watching while Gemma segregated out onions on the edge of her plate.

"The stomach surgery will stop stomach acids from rising up my esophagus, as in gastric reflux, where it triggers my asthma symptoms." She speared a ravioli and eyed it. "No, don't ask me how the esophagus activates the asthma wheezing. I can't explain something I don't understand myself."

"Will you need any help? What about Wally? Do you need a ride to the hospital or something?" Heather asked, still picking at her house salad.

"Rose Anne is taking care of Wally. I'll call a cab to get me to Shadyside Hospital. I'll be fine. I'll be home for about six to eight weeks if you want to visit. Maybe we can have lunch?"

"How about we bring a pizza or something like that?" Chelsea offered.

"Whot ebber," Gemma said with a full mouth hidden behind her napkin. While chewing, she looked over at Heather again. She was staring blankly at her plate. "Earth to Heather."

"Hey, I was just thinking of something. What if we send a note to Marla's old address with the thought that perhaps Marla's parents still lived there. If they do, maybe they could forward it to her?"

Chelsea and Gemma stared at each other. "Do you still have it?" Chelsea asked, her tone holding a hint of incredulity.

Heather nodded. "I do. I hand-wrote copies of everyone's letters." At their quizzical looks, she added, "So I could follow the conversations."

It hardly seemed possible they'd remain friends after their one and only summer camp stay together. Like most cabin mates, they swapped addresses, not expecting to write. For each of them, though, having a sister for the first time was kind of neat. And the anonymity of sheets of paper made it easy to spill their guts about life beyond Camp Terrible Fungus, as they had dubbed it by then.

Their letters became fewer, sometimes taking a couple of months to come full circle. Marla was the first to sign off. She was on the fast track in high school to graduate early and head off to the University of Rochester in upstate New York for a medical technology degree. Gemma followed suit, sending out a student mailbox address for Syracuse University, where she signed into the department of hospitality management. Heather and Chelsea were the only ones who didn't go to college. Well, that's not really true. Chelsea took the bus downtown every weekday for a year to the Pittsburgh Beauty Academy for the aesthetician program. Heather took a few courses at the local branch of Allegheny Community College near Shadyside before getting married to her high school beau, Billy Laulier. "Go for it," Chelsea urged while Gemma offered a simultaneous, "Absolutely."

AUGUST 2017

That mortifying airplane debacle ran through Marla's mind for a long time, usually between two and four in the morning, when it woke her up to taunt her. She didn't know how to go about losing weight. She had never tried before. She considered asking Eileen, but didn't want to tell anyone. Just in case she failed.

Early one morning, when the humiliation rushing through her mind and body was intense, she grabbed her laptop and began searching out weight loss methods. While there were some programs that looked promising and had good ratings, she wanted something exclusive to her. A plan or program that did not involve attending meetings with other people.

One Google hit was an article about hiring a dietician specializing in weight loss. Marla liked the idea, and her insurance plan from work would cover the expense. It was a no-brainer.

She searched online until she found a couple of people in Pittsburgh. Later that morning, she would call each of them to ask questions and assess their method. With the comforting thought of a solution close at hand, Marla snuggled back in her bed and slept until it was time to call out sick from work. Her entire day would be focused on finding the answer to her weight loss problem.

Within a week, she had a food plan, a refrigerator full of fresh foods, including fruits and vegetables, and her cupboards were empty of junk food, sweets, and overly processed foods. The dietician had asked her to use a phone app to log her food consumption and exercise. It didn't take long to see the patterns that contributed to Marla's weight problem.

On the dietician's advice, Marla joined a gym and started walking on a treadmill daily. She preferred the quietest hours when no one was there to watch her struggle. The first two weeks, she struggled to finish a mile. She gradually added an extra quarter mile each week.

• • • •

GEMMA WOKE UP SUDDENLY. In her drowsy state, she thought being born must have been like this. A sudden consciousness with no real sense of time or history. Although in her case, there had been plenty of history.

The pain hit like a tsunami a few seconds into wakefulness. The punched-in-the-gut feeling near her diaphragm curbed her breathing to an unnatural, shallow panting. Something squeezed her calves for a few seconds, then let go. She couldn't see what was beneath the sheets, but her legs felt padded around her calves, and they expanded and then deflated. The action happened again a few minutes later.

It was dark outside. Light spilled out her window into leaves on the other side of the pane. There wasn't another patient in her room. *A single?* Strange indeed, since she'd asked the insurance company for a single room but was told all rooms were doubles.

An annoying, intermittent beeping started to her left. An IV pole complete with plastic bags of fluid, hung there, connected to a box emitting flashing lights. A damp feeling along the center of her back became discernible. *Sweat?*

A blonde woman in scrubs breezed into the room. "You're awake." She stopped at the IV box and adjusted something, halting the sound and light show. "How are you feeling?" she asked, a little too brightly for Gemma's taste.

"Kicked in the gut, thanks for asking," Gemma panted.

"Having trouble breathing?" Her eyes fixed on her and traveled head to toe. It was a stern and assessing look.

"Hurts to breathe normally," Gemma uttered.

The nurse's eyes darkened as her forehead furrowed. "It shouldn't be hurting. Can you lean forward a bit? Let me check your epidural line." She gently pushed Gemma's shoulder forward.

Gemma leaned forward, holding her breath, mashing her lips shut to keep from making inhuman sounds as pain ripped through her upper abdomen.

"Okay, I see we have a small leak in your epidural connection. I'm going to try to fix it myself, then call anesthesia to come check it out," she said, fiddling with something on Gemma's back.

Almost instantly, the overwhelming socked-in-the-gut feeling started to disappear. *Ah, Glenda, the good nurse, or was it the good witch? Whatever.* Gemma leaned back slowly, shut her eyes, and let the darkness sweep in again as the pain dissolved away.

She felt much more awake and alert by the next morning, to her dissatisfaction. It became clearer what craziness was going on with her body. The nurse said her legs were encased in inflating thingies meant to prevent post-surgical blood clots from forming and causing something that could kill her within minutes. A nasogastric tube the size of a garden hose was stuffed up her nose. One end rested in her stomach while the other end deposited any stomach fluid into a container beside the bed. It wasn't much. Only water from the ice chips she was allowed to suck on to ease the dryness of her mouth and lips. It would be several days before she was allowed to eat or drink.

Although it didn't hurt, her bladder was catheterized. It was far better than the alternative, but it was yet another tube where tubes never should be. When it got there, Gemma didn't have a clue. She was glad it had been when she was not conscious.

The epidural was still in place, checked by an anesthesiologist during the night, and deemed patent. *Thank God.* There was no way she was ready to feel the full brunt of Dr. Cullen's surgical skill, no matter how spectacular.

Dr. Cullen had been in early that morning and pronounced her healing well so far. Gemma didn't have the nerve to look at her abdominal incision with its thirty-seven stitches. He had wanted to go down her throat to do the surgery, but the thought made Gemma queasy. Instead, she had talked him into plan B. She'd have a heck of a scar. No more bikinis in her future.

Dr. Hale, her lung doctor, had visited as well to give her a once-over and two thumbs up before he disappeared out the door. As he left, an aide delivered two huge, beautiful flower arrangements. One from her boss and one from her coworkers. The sight made her teary, which gave her nose all the more a stuffed-up feeling.

By day three, Gemma was a sobbing mess. Trying to pee now with the catheter removed, her bloating bladder wouldn't cooperate. The anesthesia was so deep during surgery that her bladder had yet to awaken to proper functioning.

The nasogastric tube now felt the size of a firefighter's hose. Earlier in the day, a mirror had been brought so she could comb her hair. The vision in the mirror had scared her and made her feel that much more uncomfortable in her post-surgical recovery.

She was hungry, thirsty, and ready for the shower the nurses refused to allow until the epidural and nasogastric tube came out. Gemma groaned repeatedly. *Let me out of here, and let me take some narcotics with me.*

Finally, Dr. Cullen arrived to quell her fears. He put one hand on her forehead, said, "Hold still," and yanked out the tube with the other hand. It was an instantaneous and miraculous sense of normalcy to the level of homo sapiens again. Within the hour, her nurse brought a generic, "liquids only" lunch tray. She couldn't eat more than a cup of consommé and a half cup of green Jell-O, but it was oh so refreshing.

Nurse Glenda gave her some Tylenol with codeine about half an hour before anesthesia showed up to remove the epidural. It only took a few minutes to remove, but the pain kicked in immediately.

Later in the afternoon, Chelsea arrived carrying a vase of daisies, zinnias, daylilies, and blue cornflowers. "How'ya feeling?" She settled herself on the bedside chair. "These are from Heather and I." She gestured toward the bouquet.

"They're beautiful. Thank you." Gemma glanced away, her hands resetting the sheets around her waist.

"You're doing well?"

"Better now. It was a miserable morning, but it got better with a little food." Gemma gave a slight shrug. "Even if it was only clear liquids."

"Let us know if you need a ride home."

By the next day, number five, she was sick of consommé, clear juices, and Jell-O. On the brighter side, she was getting dressed to go home. Fortunately, she had realized a muumuu-style dress would be needed as nothing could rest on her lower chest and abdomen. Hunched at the waist at a forty-five-degree angle, arms wrapped around her abdomen as if physically holding her guts in, she was up and walking.

"When will your ride home arrive?" Her nurse helped her get the hospital johnny off and slipped the dress over her head.

"I'm going to take a cab. It's not far."

Nurse Glenda stopped what she was doing. "You can't do that. You either have to take a medical cab, which is very expensive and not covered by insurance, or have someone drive you home."

"That doesn't make any sense. The person driving me home will have little to no medical experience anyway." Gemma continued to put the dress on.

"Sorry. It's hospital policy. There must be someone you can call."

Gemma thought for a few minutes. Rose Anne was stuck in court today, so she wasn't available. Remembering Chelsea's offer, she picked up her cell phone and dialed. Chelsea had a client that afternoon, but Heather would be able to drive her home.

It only took a few minutes to get to Gemma's luxury condo in the Squirrel Hill neighborhood adjacent to Shadyside. Heather helped Gemma change into her cotton jersey nightgown. Gemma gingerly lowered herself onto the living room sofa, one hand protectively over her scar. A pile of magazines, books, and a cooler filled with soda was already positioned beside it. Lined up on the coffee table like pawns were her cell phone, TV, DVD, and CD player remotes. She was well-prepped for time out on the couch.

Gemma's stomach groaned a loud, deep, hollow sound not long after she got comfortable. "Well, shit!"

"Oh my! Can I get you anything?" Heather asked.

"I'm not sure what's here I can eat," Gemma said. She had no idea what was in the house. She had still been on clear liquids at the hospital. Rolling sideways, she got on her hands and knees on the rug, worked her feet beneath her, and ever so slowly stood up with Heather's help. Tiny beads of sweat erupted along her forehead and upper lip. Her arms bent protectively over her torso. A quick visual inventory of her kitchen cabinets proved futile. Except for yogurt weeks over the sell date in her fridge, her house was devoid of any soft foods.

Heather interrupted her explorations. "I can bring you some food after I pick up the kids from daycare."

"Nah. I'll place a grocery order for delivery. In the meantime, the Chinese place around the block will deliver." Crawling back to the sofa, she grabbed the phone and ordered a delivery of wonton soup and Mei-fun noodles from the restaurant down the street.

Heather shifted her feet as she stood watching. "Well, I have to go. Call me if you need help with anything. I'll call later to check in with you."

Gemma nodded at her and waved. When Heather was gone, she placed a rapid grocery delivery order of canned soups, pre-made Jell-O, puddings, juices, applesauce, instant mashed potatoes, and more yogurt.

"So much for being prepared," she muttered to herself. She also made a mental note to chew Dr. Cullen and Dr. Hale new assholes for somehow forgetting to mention that after the surgery she wouldn't be able to eat anything beyond the consistency of mud.

Gemma's doorbell rang at the same time her cell phone did the same. Seeing it was Rose Anne calling, she answered the phone.

"Just me. I brought Wally back."

Gemma smiled. She could use the feline's company and comfort. "Door's open. Come on in."

Rose walked in carrying Wally's carrier. When he smelled home he started meowing. A scuffling sound inside the carrier as she tried to tote it into the living room. "Hold still, critter."

She placed it on the floor beside Gemma's couch and opened it. Wally jumped out of the carrier.

Pausing long enough to establish where Gemma was, he jumped up beside her and nuzzled her face.

"Thanks for taking care of him. How did you know I was home?"

Rose shrugged one shoulder. "I called your hospital room. The nurse said you'd already left. I thought you might like to have your big boy home. I'll set out his water and food. And I'll stop by tomorrow if you need me." At Gemma's nod, Rose started for the kitchen. "I hope he doesn't try to sleep on top of your chest."

"You and me both!"

· · · ·

CHELSEA GATHERED THE papers spread out in from of her on the living room floor. Her plan to start a home manicure business was underway, and she already had clients lined up for each Saturday for the next two months.

It hadn't taken much more than posting her new business cards and flyers on supermarket bulletin boards. Gemma's well-placed flyers had also given her half a dozen clients.

She would still have to continue working her usual four days at the salon until the business was self-sustaining. But for now, her shoulders were firmly set, and her prospects were looking good.

Heather and Chelsea met for coffee the next day. This time they decided to try Arrivida Coffee Bar. The back table in the dimly lit rear of the narrow shop was so tiny it nearly didn't fit both of their drinks. Surrounding them were tables full of college students from the nearby campuses.

"How is she?" Chelsea asked before sipping her latte.

Heather set her latte down. "Okay. Not great. But she put a stiff upper lip on and settled down to rest as soon as she was changed. I don't think her doctor gave her much information about post-surgical eating. She had to get a grocery delivery so she would have food to eat."

"I could have gone shopping for her after work."

"She said she'd get it sorted out. When I called back after dinner, she said everything was fine, her groceries got delivered, and she had settled in for the night."

"Maybe I should bring something over for her?" Chelsea nibbled on her lower lip. "What can she eat?" She couldn't help but think of how pale and in pain Gemma had looked when she delivered her flowers at the hospital.

The two women looked at each other. "Not much. You know how Gemma is. She's determined to take care of herself."

"Nonetheless, we should visit soon. "Chelsea gulped down the last of her latte. Seeing Gemma would help alleviate the feeling in her stomach. After offering to pick her up at the hospital, Chelsea felt embarrassed for having to ask Heather to do it.

"Yes, sure. I wouldn't be able to stay long, but at least we can make sure she's okay."

"It must be terrible pain." Chelsea shivered. "It makes my knees weak just thinking about surgery. Imagine looking down and seeing a large, fresh, and painful scar." She had never had so much as a laceration that needed stitches. The idea of a long red scar on her own abdomen made her queasy.

"It's temporary. The pain, I mean. Not the scar. That's there forever." Heather's free hand moved to her abdomen.

Chelsea noticed the gesture. Heather must have had a cesarean at some point. She mashed her lips together and shivered again. "I can't begin to imagine."

"It takes a while to heal. But Gemma's resilient. She'll get through it. And now the asthma won't be disturbing her sleep." Heather changed the subject. "How's your new business going?"

"Good, actually. I got a new setup at the elderly housing complex over in Millvale. My gram used to live there, and I always did her nails. Over time all her neighbors had me doing theirs too. When she died, I stopped going over there. It was too painful. But her friends are thrilled I'm back, even if it isn't free this time."

"That's exciting."

"Yeah, I need more clients, so I'm hoping that word-of-mouth advertising will help me get into some of the other elderly housing complexes in the area."

"I need to get going," Heather said after glancing at her watch. "I'll give Gemma a call to see if she needs anything."

"I'll try to check up on her over the weekend." Chelsea leaned across the small black table. "I've been meaning to ask you. Are you available the second Saturday night in August? Seth wants to get the bunch of us together at Church Brew Bar and Grille."

"With or without Billy?"

"Perhaps Billy can take care of the kids?"

She let loose a tense chuckle and shook her head. "Not likely. Especially when he hears I'm going to a bar." Heather shrugged. "But I'll try."

SEPTEMBER 2017

Marla called her parents once a week every Sunday evening. So, when her cell phone rang with her mother's ringtone, her heart began racing. Something would have to be terribly wrong for her mother to call. "Mom? What's going on? What's happened?" She said, her words rapid-fire, her voice up an octave.

"Nothing, dear. Don't worry. Nothing is wrong." Her mother tried to reassure her. "I wanted to ask you about a letter we received two days ago."

"Letter? Who from?" Her mind searched for someone who might have contacted them. Hopefully, it wasn't a phishing letter. "What does it say?"

"It's from a girl named Heather you went to summer camp with. She says it was Camp Terramungus. She's looking for your contact information. She wants to have a reunion. Isn't that nice?"

Marla couldn't have been more shocked. She and Heather hadn't communicated since before she went to college. "Can you send me the letter? I'll get in contact with her."

"Well," her mother's voice dipped apologetically. "I can send it to you. But—I already sent her a reply with your address and phone number."

Marla paused in silence as she palmed her forehead. Her mind reeled that a) Heather was looking for her after all these years, and b) her mother had willingly given out her personal information.

"Marla, honey. I'm sorry if you didn't want me to do that. I just wasn't thinking." Her mother's voice fluttered like it always did when she was flustered. "When your father found out, he told me to call you immediately to let you know."

"Yeah. Thanks." She tried not to sound upset or angry though both emotions were battling for prominence in her chest. "I'm sure it will be alright." She scowled. "Tell Daddy thanks, and I'll talk to you both in a couple of days."

She disconnected the call. At least she had notice that Heather was likely to be contacting her. The question was, would she answer.

• • • •

FOUR WEEKS POST-OP, it was routine for Gemma to wake up in the middle of the night, absolutely ravishingly hungry and experiencing excruciating hip pains. The hunger and the hunger headaches she understood entirely. She'd found that she couldn't eat more than half a cup of anything at a time and then felt *full* for only one to two hours. She couldn't eat enough at any one time to sate her hunger for longer. Dr. Cullen had decided that the hip pains were probably related to the subsequent weight loss and less fatty padding over all her bony protuberances, similar to how her knees now hurt from rubbing together when she slept without a pillow between them.

The dark red surgical scar ran from the base of her breastbone to her navel, making the wearing of any clothing that pressed on that area still too painful to wear. That meant pants, skirts, and bras were out. She dressed in nightgowns, nightshirts, and baby dolls when inside the condo. When venturing outside for her daily walks, she had to choose loose dresses, low-riding jeans, or her Syracuse University sweatpants loosely tied and slipped down low on her hip bones.

In the course of her surgery, the surgeon had wrapped a portion of her stomach around the sphincter between her esophagus and the rest of her stomach, thereby preventing the reflux. It was similar to a type of bariatric surgery for weight loss, but with Gemma, the aim was to prevent gastric reflux. Still, Dr. Cullen had effectively reduced the size of her stomach to less than half its original size. Not the reason for her surgery, but a good side effect for someone needing to lose a few pounds anyway.

The worst side effect of the surgery was that Gemma could no longer burp. The nurse at the hospital had warned her not to drink any carbonated liquids. Tightening of the sphincter between her esophagus and stomach would prevent her from vomiting.

As a consequence, her entire diet became mundane. It consisted of yogurt, instant oatmeal, crème of wheat, applesauce, mashed potatoes, and orzo pasta with marinara sauce, sometimes with half a mashed meatball mixed in. Nutritionally, not a great diet. Soup was okay, but she'd had her fill of soup and Jell-O in the hospital.

Looking for alternatives to bring some variety to her menu, she spent a lot of time wandering the grocery store, in particular, the baby food aisle. Gemma examined all the jars carefully. After reading the ingredients, she set them back on the shelf and checked others. There were so many unnecessary extra ingredients like cornstarch. She experimented with some upscale baby food, found most of it tasted good with enough salt added, and her eyes closed. The mashed fruits were palatable, and she stocked up on those jars. She became a fan of fresh, mashed sweet potatoes, mashed carrots, and even mashed peas.

Meat was more difficult to visually tolerate when mashed unless smothered in tomato sauce or gravy. Dr. Cullen didn't expect her to be back to solid foods until six to eight weeks post-op, and even then, still on the soft side of normal fare.

She was losing weight steadily. Starting out as a size sixteen, it was going to be interesting to see where she'd end up by the time solid food was back on the menu.

A few coworkers, Mei and Marilyn, had stopped by to visit after calling first. In each instance, it had taken Gemma the entire morning to shower, wash her hair, and dress respectably for her visitors. The preparations wore her out before her guests arrived, leaving her tired, dull, and listless.

Gemma could tell they were shocked to see her out of her usual high energy, go-tackle-the-world attitude, and without her über professional Ann Taylor/Banana Republic business chic. It was a clear sign of how bad she was feeling that she didn't care how wan she looked or that she nodded off during the visits. Embarrassed, she thought maybe it was better if she didn't allow her coworkers to visit. She didn't want word getting back to her boss.

• • • •

CHELSEA AND HEATHER stopped by a couple of times to take Gemma out. They would hop into Chelsea's car to buy ice cream and then drive over to the Phipps Conservatory and Botanical Gardens in Schenley Park. They'd help Gemma shuffle along the paths to the chrysanthemum display now in full bloom. It was heavenly in the humid tropical air of the Palm Court. The three of them would linger, relaxing on a bench under a banana tree and enjoying the peaceful, warm, and quiet space. All so Gemma didn't have to stare at the same four walls all the time.

During one joint visit to Gemma's, Heather reported she'd received a reply to her note to Marla's old address. Marla's mother, Mary Devine, was delighted to hear they wanted to reconnect with her only child. Heather read her letter, which informed them Marla was living and working in their own fair city. The three were open-mouthed, stunned to hear Marla owned a house in their Shadyside neighborhood. Mrs. Devine had given them Marla's address and cell phone number.

It only took a glance between them before hurriedly piling into the car and heading out to Bayard Street. They gawked at the pretty, light yellow painted, well-kept Craftsman-style home on a tiny, well-manicured, grassy lot surrounded by a picket fence. There was no car in the driveway and no sign of anyone being home.

"Maybe we should knock on the front door?" Chelsea suggested.

"Don't," Heather interjected. "We don't know."

Gemma called from the back seat. "Don't know what?"

Heather huffed. "I don't like surprising someone. It would make her feel ambushed. Especially if she isn't happy to see us."

Chelsea nodded. "I get that." She started the car and pulled away from the curb.

They returned to Gemma's condo discussing what to do next. Gemma argued that in the few years of letter writing between them after camp, Marla should know Chelsea and Heather lived in Pittsburgh. If she had wanted to get in contact, she would have before now.

The discussion quickly disintegrated when Chelsea asked if Gemma hadn't contacted them before they contacted her for that very reason. Gemma admitted she hadn't even thought about them when moving to Pittsburgh; she had totally put away memories of Camp Terramungus somewhere in the back of her mind. "It could be the same thing happened with Marla."

Chelsea reluctantly agreed with the reasoning, although she still thought Marla could as likely be avoiding them.

Heather clenched her teeth as the discussion between Chelsea and Gemma became heated over what to do. The tension gave her a tight feeling in her stomach.

"What are you wrinkling your nose about?" Chelsea asked, her eyes meeting Heather's in the rear-view mirror.

"I—" She wanted to say she understood Marla might be less than happy to see them. And yet she wanted to reconnect with Marla. Especially after reading Mary Devine's letter. It sounded like Marla didn't have many friends in Pittsburgh. "I think I'll try to contact her myself. See how she takes it." If nothing else, she could ferret out Marla's willingness to get back with her old friends from Camp Terramungus.

• • • •

BRIDGE TAVERN IN SOUTH-Side was still rocking with DJ music despite being near the end of the reception. Only about twenty of the nearly one hundred guests remained from the wedding ceremony of Greg and Emily Boyden at St. Elizabeth's Church.

"Billy boy, your wife's still a looker," his buddy Nate appraised, leaning heavily on the darkly stained pine bar. Billy glanced at the dance floor where Heather was dancing with her girlfriends. Her hips swiveled to the music alongside Monica and their friend Colleen McCourt.

"Want her? She's all yours. Gotta take the kids too, though," Billy slurred, still on his feet but swaying like a high-rise in a typhoon despite the sturdy bar beneath his right arm.

Billy always got like this when drunk. Not that Billy needed to be drunk to badmouth his wife. He did it far too freely and much too loudly after putting away a six-pack or more. From what Nate could see, Heather was good to him. If Monica put up with as much shit as Heather did, he'd be a lucky man. Not that he intended to treat her like Billy treated Heather. Far from it. The mother of his children would not only continue to receive his love, but she would also receive his help and respect. Sometimes, like tonight, he struggled to restrain his foot from kicking Billy's ass.

"Come on, man. After all the years you two've been t'gether. Went to prom, right?" Nate mused, one eye closed, the other peering down the bottle, checking the amount of beer left.

"Yeah, that's when it started. Cindy dumped me for some jock. I ended up asking Heather to prom instead. Nearly got her knocked up that very night too." His lopsided grin clearly expressed pride in his former prowess.

"No way, man. Really? Get out!"

"Yup, popped her cherry that night." His empty beer bottle hit the wooden bar top and then flopped over on its side. It skidded across the wood surface, over the side, and onto the floor. The bartender gave him the cutoff gesture.

Nate Groaned. *Shit. Now he'll be pestering me to get his brews for him.*

"She used to be hot. Now look at her." Billy grimaced, then turned away and signaled for another beer. The bartender gave him a dirty look and shook his head. In what was left of his peripheral vision, Nate caught Billy flipping the guy off once the bartender's back was turned.

"She don't look too bad for three kids, man," Nate slurred. "I hope Monica looks as good after three." He looked over at his fiancée, Monica, still dancing with Heather and Colleen.

"Yeah, and once you got them, your sex life's over," sneered Billy.

"Gotta give a little to get some, man."

"Only thing I ever get is another kid." Billy's lip curled grotesquely. "Got enough of those."

Across the room on the dance floor, Heather, Colleen, and Monica twisted and shouted barefoot along with the Beatles. At the end of the string of songs, Monica headed for Nate at the bar. Heather and her former high school friend, Colleen, sat at the nearest banquet table. Dessert plates of half-eaten wedding cake, chicken wing bones, plastic cups with stale drink remains, and empty beer bottles littered the tables.

"Billy's giving you the evil eye again," Colleen advised, her fingers combing through her disheveled light brown hair. Bending, she struggled to slip her shoes back on her feet. Their body heat generated by dancing quickly dissipated thanks to the open side door letting in the cool October night air.

"He's such a jerk. I can't believe he hasn't been anywhere near me all night long," Heather fumed, her cheeks red with more than exertion. Their first night out together in years with their kids in Billy's mother's care. Heather knew she looked good tonight. Well, maybe not good; she looked okay. She hadn't lost any more than six pounds going to the program before she gave up. "He didn't want to come tonight. I had to mention it was an open bar for him to agree to come."

"I know just the thing. You two need a little blackberry brandy." Colleen started to giggle, then picked up her beer bottle and placed it to her lips. The mouthful of warm beer she swigged set her off on a coughing fit.

Heather's stomach fell. She gave Colleen a biting glare before turning away to put on her own shoes. "It'd serve you right ta' have beer come out your nose for saying that."

Beer didn't come out her nose, but it did spray across the table and chairs to her right. When she managed to catch her breath and stop laughing, she continued, not heeding Heather's words or tense body language. "It worked for prom. Softened ya' up—"

The heat rose so quickly in her chest and face that Heather couldn't stand it. "That's enough, Colleen. Scared the shit out of me. You know I spent the next three days running pregnancy tests." Uncontrollable tremors shook her body. "Hell. It was hell." Heather groaned, dropping her head into her hands at the memory.

Prom was her and Billy's first date. They talked very little as they were both tense, and she was feeling unusually shy. Until they left the prom. In ten minutes, they both were loosening up enough to talk. By the time the flask was empty, they had loosened most of their clothes and were necking like longtime lovers. Before Heather made it home that night, she was no longer a virgin.

When she woke the next morning and realized what had happened: unprotected sex, hangover, and all, she was frantic to find out if she was pregnant. A quick trip to the drug store Sunday morning for some "supplies," as she told her mom, a stop at the local fast food restaurant's bathroom, and she breathed a huge sigh when the test was negative. She tested for the next two days to be sure it was still negative. During those two school days, she couldn't even look at Billy, let alone speak with him.

He, however, wouldn't leave her alone. All that next school day, she tried to dodge him. She knew it had everything to do with the sex. At least that's what his best friend told her best friend, Colleen.

Two days later, he stalked her into a dead-ending, locker-lined hallway, leaving her only two choices; exit through the alarmed emergency exit or acknowledge him. Resigning herself to being cornered, Heather turned to face him, arms folded across her chest.

"Hey, I've been trying to talk to you." His gleaming eyes never left her face except for furtive glances at her breasts. "Can we talk a minute?"

"Yeah, I guess so," she mumbled, keeping her eyes on the floor. The look of him in those tight Wranglers and cowboy boots made her belly warm and melty.

"You've been avoidin' me. I'd like to take ya out Friday night, maybe go to a movie?" His words came out almost in a rush.

"Um, I'll have to think about it," Heather said, barely breathing, still not meeting his eyes, still clutching her arms across her chest. Her erect nipples tightened, pressing against the sides of her crossed arms, responding of their own accord to his presence. Warmth pooled at the apex of her thighs.

"Look, I know things got out of hand after the prom. That won't happen again, I promise. I mean, unless you want it ta. Um, I'd like it ta, yeah, again, but it's your call," Billy stuttered, his former bravado slipping.

I can't believe he does this to me! Just talking to me! What am I? Heather looked at him, shivers coursing through her body. Seconds ticked by as he held her gaze while she tried to decide what to say. Billy glanced away, shifting his feet under her scrutiny. Knowing what she should say, knowing what she wanted to say. "Okay, what time?"

"Pick ya' up at 6:30?" Billy's voice was more animated, the tone upbeat and louder.

"See you then," she acquiesced, brushing past him. The sleeves of their shirts grazed in a caress that sent jolts of electricity through her arm, into her chest, and down to her fully awakened parts. She hurried away faster.

On Friday, the date started out tense and formal. By the end of the movie, they were hand in hand, kissing in the parking lot after the movie. This time, Billy had condoms with him.

Heather sighed, looking at the deeply scratched wooden floorboards. She and Billy had danced their first dance as newlyweds on this very floor. An event precipitated by Heather's first pregnancy, despite the condoms and the pill. It had been so long ago.

Billy hadn't been thrilled about it, but he'd married her. Twenty-six weeks into her pregnancy, the premature birth of their baby girl, Victoria Marie, brought them closer together for a time. Billy had snapped out of his indifference at the sight of her frail tiny body. Endless hours in the NICU ended with them collapsing in each other's arms over their baby's grave nine days after her birth. Things were different then. Billy was different then. When they sought comfort in each other's arms. It seemed like a lifetime ago.

"You need another drink. If not brandy, what do you want?" Colleen bounced her arm against Heather's, trying to boost her spirits.

"I don't know." It didn't matter now. Heather wiped the tears spilling down her cheeks with the backs of her hands and sniffed. No sense crying now, she chastised herself. With a deep, inhaled breath and heavy sigh, she turned her thoughts to Michelle, Peter, and Nicholas. Better to focus on those who lived and still needed her. With the memory of loss stinging her thoughts, she wanted nothing more than to be home with her remaining children.

Colleen bumped her arm again. "Sex on the Beach?"

"Sure, why not. Hopefully, it's not the only sex I'll get tonight." Heather tried to smile, but the intent never reached her lips. How things had changed.

• • • •

"CHEERS!" CHELSEA SLURRED before up-ending the neon green Jell-O shot at Church Brew Bar and Grill. She wiped her mouth with the back of her hand then pumped her fist in the air. Her diamond engagement ring sparkled as it caught the light.

"Cheers!" Following her example, Gemma, Rose Anne, and Diane echoed in unison. The shot glasses slammed down on the long wooden bar top with a smack. The bartender looked up with a worried expression hoping none of the glasses had cracked. More of their friends sat at tables in groups of three and four on the other side of the room.

At the end of the room, where the altar used to be in the renovated church, giant stainless steel tanks held different types of beer in various stages of production.

"I can't believe he finally asked you after all these years!" Rose Anne gushed, her left hand holding her heart in a romantic gesture. "It's so sweet!"

"It's so late, is more like it." Diane giggled. "It's been twelve years, for Christ's sake. What the hell was he waiting for?"

"Yeah, you guys have been going together since God created the earth. What took him so long?" Rose Anne asked.

"I think he was afraid to grow up like most guys," Chelsea mused. What the heck else could it have been? They'd known each other since kindergarten, going steady since their freshman year in high school. Four years later, their graduation yearbook had anointed them as the couple most likely to marry after graduation. They'd been living together for eight years now.

She glanced over at him, sitting with all the other guys. Without his perpetual ball cap, the crown of his head showed a thick mat of wavy brown hair. Hair on the sides and back of his head was clipped close like an army buzz cut. He must have felt her watching him because he turned and winked at her before returning to the guys' conversation. Chelsea felt her heart skitter in her chest. He had the most beautiful dark brown eyes and full lips that kissed her deliriously. She shivered thinking of their interludes since the engagement last night. She sighed contentedly. *Nothing like an engagement ring to amp up the sex.*

Last night during dinner in their apartment, Seth had gone down on one knee to pick up a dropped fork. He came up with a beautiful marquise-cut engagement ring instead of the fork. He took her hand in his sweaty palm.

"It's been a long time coming, Chelsea. You've been so patient. I know you love me, and I hope you know how much I love you. Will you marry me?" Seth had asked, a tremor altering his voice.

Chelsea had been speechless at first but had finally blurted, "Yes, yes!" and flung her arms around his neck and hugged him so tight he nearly choked. She couldn't believe he had remembered she had told him ages ago she wanted a marquise-cut diamond. He'd actually remembered. Tears of happiness slipped under her eyelids.

It wasn't one of those over-the-top proposals or something shared on TikTok, YouTube, Facebook or even WhatsApp. Chelsea was ecstatic it had come at last.

She knew she could trust him to come through in his own time. Seth worked as a carpenter with his dad, his dad's two brothers, and his own brothers, Joe and Kevin, since he graduated high school. Pounding nails every day, the six-man crew of Symmonds Brothers was complete. Handling all that lumber and building materials kept his sturdy frame muscular in all the right places.

Chelsea sighed with a smile on her face. All her dreams were coming true. Since finishing beautician school, she had religiously saved five percent of her paycheck. Now, she had a nice nest egg saved for the wedding she had dreamed about since she was a little girl. It was time to put those dreams into action.

When told the good news, mother of the bride, Gloria Whitcom, was exceedingly happy for her daughter. "I've known Seth and his family forever." She had no doubt he cared for her daughter. She also knew he would provide for her well enough to keep her happy. "You can use my wedding dress. I still have it."

"We'll see," Chelsea said. She hadn't even thought about getting an appointment at the local bridal shop yet. First, she and Seth had to discuss some things like the date, location, and the bridal party.

• • • •

DESPITE THE VISITATIONS and trips out with Heather and Chelsea, Gemma's days were boring. Twice each day, she walked the roadways of the condo complex, picking up her mail at the mailbox stand on the afternoon trip. Decked out in her old, baggy, gray sweats, the giant orange SU hoodie was loose enough across the chest to disguise her braless condition. Not that she knew anyone except the immediate neighbor to her end unit.

That changed early one morning. Gemma was lumbering along, hunched over, when she passed a newspaper box surrounded by tall shrubs.

"You're walking much better this week," a crisp, male voice praised from behind her.

Gemma turned her whole body around stiffly like she was wearing a full body cast to see a guy with short-cropped, dark hair walking down the sidewalk toward her. A pair of button-fly Levi's hung tight on his medium frame, making her breath stop for a second and her lower belly warm with interest. A faded Tee-shirt featuring a flash-in-the-pan 80s rock group and some fairly new boat shoes, sans socks, finished his look. He had the air of a hip metrosexual rather than an adult bum scrounging a living.

"Thanks, I'm training for the Chicago Marathon in October," she replied, a tired smile on her face. The stutter of her breath made her feel woozy.

"This year or next?" he playfully joked back, his smile friendly and warm.

It was already September twenty second. The marathon was in seventeen days.

"Maybe next year," Gemma smirked back shyly.

"You doing okay? I mean, anything I can do? Walk your dog, get your mail, run an errand?" he dropped his joking manner to become more serious.

"Nothing right now," Gemma said with a slight shake of her head. "Doc says I need to walk until I can do it normally again, whenever the hell that will be. I'm all stocked up for food, and unfortunately, I don't have a dog. I'll be going back to work next week, so I have to get my exercise in."

"Damn, I can't stand not helping a damsel obviously in distress." He cringed and bowed theatrically to underscore his crushing defeat.

"You could do one thing ..."

"Anything," he stated, his eyes darting side to side, hands on his hips.

"Tell me your name?" Gemma asked hesitantly. "I only know one person in this whole complex despite living here for over three years. I'd like to make that two."

He laughed, head thrown back, breeze catching the short tendrils of his hair in a Medusa-like coif, "Charlie Hanover."

"Nice to meet you, Charlie. I'm Gemma Kimble." She offered her hand. She vaguely remembered seeing him a few times at the mailbox stand over the years she had lived in the complex. Always alone.

He grasped her hand and shook firmly. It was warm and soft. If he worked, it wasn't with his hands.

"Great to meet you, Gemma. I've been watching you make this circuit for a few weeks. You've gotten a lot better." He must have seen the disturbed look on her face because he quickly added, "I work at home, and my desk is in the front window." He paused before adding," I have to say, it was hard to watch you that first week. You looked in so much pain I was cringing with every footfall. I wanted to pick you up and carry you back to your condo, but I figured you were doing as the doctor ordered."

"He did. I was and still am, although this scenery is getting boring. I was thinking I should try a mall or find a park for a change."

"Well then, I'm glad I took this opportunity to say hello and introduce myself. If you're looking for a nice park, you should try Frick Park on Beechwood Boulevard. It's public enough for you to feel safe, and the paths are fairly level. The garden club has planted beds, and it's chrysanthemum time. It should be quite lovely," Charlie offered animatedly.

Gemma's belly warmed even more. A man who appreciated flowers and used the word *lovely*. And she couldn't help but think he might look better naked than clothed. "Hmm, I'll have to try it this week then." She glanced away. "I've got to get going. Time for more meds." She shrugged in apology.

"Sure. Do you need help getting back to your door?"

Gemma shook her head. "No, thanks. I'm alright."

"Well, it was nice to meet you. Let me know what you think of Frick." Charlie headed over to the mailboxes.

As Gemma watched, he opened the box for condo 4E. *Okay, that explains which unit he's living in.* "Will do," Gemma said over her shoulder as she turned away on her way back to her condo.

• • • •

MARLA WAS AMAZED AT how her metabolism had spiked so swiftly, and the weight loss had accelerated with the exercise. Between the drop in her daily caloric intake from over five thousand calories to only twelve hundred, plus all the exercise, she was dropping five to eight pounds a week. She thanked her stars, knowing it wasn't always going to be this easy but enjoying it while it lasted. As it was, the ravenous feelings she had two to three hours after a meal made her question her ability to see this endeavor through to the end.

One day Marla hoped to be able to see her toes and wanted to be ready because she intended to touch them someday as well.

In the meantime, she had dug out a picture from a Christmas party at Columbia. The one with Timothy Brighton in it. As a reminder of her goal, she taped it to the refrigerator door.

OCTOBER 2017

When she was down twenty-five pounds, yoga was her third step.

The first class was agony. It started off easy enough, lying flat on her back. She nearly went to sleep. Then she had to sit up in "lotus" position. It was exactly like "Indian style," as everyone called it at Camp Terramungus years ago. Now that term was not politically correct. The instructor used Sanskrit and common names for poses. Marla found it easier to follow what everyone else in the class did, trying to keep up.

Marla tried her damnedest to do everything they could do, but most things were impossible. She couldn't touch her toes in "forward bend." She liked "mountain." It was simply standing straight with your arms at your sides. She also liked "goddess," but it was difficult to hold; her knees kept giving out, but she got a sense of power with her arms out in L shapes, and her knees bent and wide like a ballerina's plié. She also liked "tree," but she couldn't get her foot off the ground, and she tottered so badly, another attendee mentioned a "brisk wind" blowing through the studio. Marla had blushed and given up on the pose. She promised herself she would practice "tree" several times a day to increase her balance.

The real killer was a pose called "downward dog." The instructor kept saying how it was supposed to be a soothing recovery pose. She was damned wrong there. It was a ridiculous pose. Marla started out on her hands and knees in "table" pose, then had to lift only her butt to the sky to get into "downward dog." It was the most uncomfortable pose and one the class frequently used. How it could ever be considered a restorative pose was beyond Marla. It killed her palms and arms to hold her body up, and between being bent in half *and* upside down, she couldn't breathe.

Class ended with them on their backs in "corpse" pose and Marla did fall asleep. She knew because the instructor shook her awake.

When she limped home after class, she spent an hour soaking in a hot bath to ensure her ability to walk the next day.

After the third class, the instructor took Marla aside for a chat. Marla's eyes teared up, waiting for the boot she knew was coming.

"You're working really hard in class. You clearly have a lot of motivation. What's bringing you to yoga?" Donna, the lithe instructor, asked, genuine interest in her eyes.

Marla spilled her intentions with a few errant tears. She didn't keep anything back: being heavy all her life, the things she missed, and the flight from hell. "I'm sorry I'm not able to keep up with the rest of the class. I was hoping it would get easier over time."

"I'm sorry people are so cruel. And I'm happy you are turning this horrific experience into something good." Donna's voice was like velvet. "Yoga is a discipline developed over five thousand years in Northern India. Some people think its purpose was to allow a body to be free to remain in a meditation position for long periods of time. If you think about it, the monks sit to meditate for long periods."

Nodding understanding, Marla urged her to continue.

"Here in the US, we use it more for exercise or for both exercise and stress management," Donna explained.

"Now, I will tell you the most important thing about yoga. It is not a competition. There is no one to try to beat or match. You should only do what your body is capable of doing. And that can change from day to day. Some days I can connect my fingers behind my back; some days, I can't. Like me, you must learn to accept what your body is and is not capable of doing."

Marla stared at Donna for a minute, trying to fathom the notion. "So, what you're saying is, I shouldn't try to raise my leg as high as everyone else in class? Or twist as much?"

"You must *ignore* what everyone else is doing. You must learn to listen to *your* body. Close your eyes if it will keep you from being distracted," Donna suggested. "Have you seen the *Star Wars* film where Yoda says, 'you must feel the force,' to Luke? That is pretty much what I'm talking about. Feel your own force."

"I remember that part," Marla said, smiling back. A shiver of electricity ran down her spine, remembering those words.

"Slowly, over time, your flexibility and balance will improve. As you lose weight, it will also become easier. Do you understand what I'm saying?"

"Yes. I think I do. So don't try so hard. Listen to my body," Marla said softly, then switching to a deeper voice, she added, "'Feel the force.'"

"Exactly!" Donna laughed.

By the next class, Marla was like a new woman mentally. She closed her eyes often to center her thoughts. She breathed and counted. The breathing exercises, called pranayama, gave her mind clarity and focus. As the poses were introduced, she tried to only do what her body said it could by focusing on that inner voice. Marla felt free. Yoga became a refuge instead of a torture she endured twice a week for health benefits.

Donna praised her openly for her form. Praised *her!* At first, she thought there must be another Marla in the room of students. But no, Donna was smiling at her, and so were the other students.

She was the heaviest in the class, but most of the ladies were nice to her. Some even invited her to join them for tea at Tisane Tea Shoppe after class. Marla didn't want to go out all sweaty, stinky, and gross feeling. Once, she accepted the offer but regretted it as the women ignored her for the hour. She needed friends as much as she needed to lose weight, but she didn't feel comfortable yet about socializing.

• • • •

OH MY GOD, NO! HEATHER'S heart jumped in her chest and began racing. She gasped when she saw the thread as she perused the status updates on her Facebook page. Her hand flew to cover her mouth.

"Everything okay?" the librarian asked, glancing over at her cubicle.

"Ah ... fine. Sorry." Heather tried to spit out the words, any words, still shocked by the banter far down on her list of older posts. There it was. Four of her former high school classmates exchanged comments about a ten-year reunion.

Ten years already? Heather squirmed in the wooden library chair as she read the comments several times. They were starting to plan a reunion for May of the coming year, eight months away.

Heather logged out of the site and the computer. She peeked into the community meeting room where Peter and Nick still quietly listened to the children's storyteller. She wheeled a sleeping Michelle in her stroller onto the front stoop of the library and called Colleen on her old flip phone.

"Colleen, it's Heather. I was just on Facebook and saw some comments about a reunion. Did you see them?" Heather asked, her heart beating faster at the prospect.

"I haven't been on lately. What's the date?" Colleen asked.

"They only said they were shooting for May."

"Great! That's what? Eight, nine months away, right?" Colleen asked again.

"Yeah, maybe enough time to lose some of this residual pregnancy weight." Heather patted her bulging lower abdomen, a plan beginning to germinate in her mind.

"Oh, no. Not again. I've been to Calorie Counters with you three times now. You know I'm through with it. They take me as I am or not at all."

"Come on, I need you there with me," Heather put an edge of desperation into her voice to help convince her friend. Her arm wrapped instinctively around her middle.

"No way. I'm not showing my face at Calorie Counters again," Colleen replied firmly.

Heather fumed. "Alright. If you change your mind, give me a call." She picked up the diaper bag. "Got to go, looks like the storyteller is done for the day." A swarm of kids and a few parents poured out of the meeting room doors.

Heather gathered up Peter and Nick and hurried them and Michelle into the car. After a promised stop at Patty Cake Bakery to buy fresh chocolate chip cookies—their reward for being good at the library—they went home. She put the kids down for their afternoon nap after their cookies and milk, then began searching for all her former Calorie Counters materials.

• • • •

GEMMA SPOTTED HEATHER sitting in the crowded café, her eyes seemingly fixated on the bottom of a coffee cup when she and Chelsea arrived. Gemma immediately knew something was wrong. She grabbed Chelsea's elbow rather than get in line for her order. "Something's wrong."

They sat down. Heather's eyes were red and swollen. "What's happened?" Chelsea took Heather's hand in her own.

"I—" Heather swallowed hard as if she had something preventing her words from leaving her throat. "There's going to be a high school reunion."

Chelsea cocked her head. "I went to mine, it should be fun."

"Perhaps it should be, but I can bet money it's going to be a nightmare." Her face was etched with fear. "Maybe we should move or something."

Gemma, who had remained silent, shook her head. "You don't have to go, you know that, don't you?"

Heather rolled her eyes. "You don't know my husband. When he talks, all he talks about are those carefree days of high school. He'll be going."

"Let him go alone. Say you can't find a sitter," Chelsea offered.

"Yeah, right. His mother is always available." Misery masking her face, she said, "I'll have to go to try to keep him out of trouble."

"How was your first week back to work? Chelsea asked, changing the subject.

"Not too bad. I have to say, I enjoyed sleeping in when I was out on sick leave. I miss my leisurely mornings," Gemma said. "My energy level still crashes about 1 p.m., which had been my nap time when I was out. God, I miss those naps."

• • • •

GEMMA DECIDED THAT the walking paths along Frick Park were everything Charlie Hanover claimed they would be. Level, moderately populated for safety's sake, and the garden beds were filled with Halloween decorations of every color and variety despite the bare trees. She had started to walk there every other day for a change of scenery not long after Charlie mentioned it.

Charlie had met Gemma at the mailbox a few times, where they chatted easily for a few minutes before going their own ways. He was pleased to hear she liked Frick so much and had gone shortly after he mentioned it to check on the planting beds herself.

It was an unseasonably warm day when Gemma found him there wrapped in a navy peacoat, looking at his phone as though reading something.

"Howdy stranger. Got a match?" Gemma wondered if he knew the joke.

"Howdy. I haven't had a match since Superman died." Charlie replied without skipping a beat. They both laughed at the absurdity of the old joke.

Flustered, Gemma offered, "Beautiful day for a walk. I don't think we'll get many more of these." *Crap, can't you find anything more original after that lousy start?*

"Even better for vitamin D." Charlie patted the empty bench beside him.

Gemma sat, angling her body to face him better. "What are you reading?"

"A script. I'm a script reader. I work from my home office most of the time, telecommuting."

"I've never met a script reader before. What kinds of scripts do you specialize in?"

"Mainly rom-com. Romantic comedy, that is. Although I look at things outside my area of expertise if it interests me."

"Amazing. I suppose you must have some significant credentials."

"I have a master's in film studies and screenwriting from UC Berkley." Charlie smiled.

Gemma sized him up again for the thirtieth time. He was an enigma. "I'm impressed."

"Don't be. It allows me a freer lifestyle, some travel, and contact with lots of different people. The pressure to find good scripts, though, is pretty tough."

"I can imagine it's hard to find something that could be commercially viable."

"It is. Everyone thinks their idea is valid and new. Most are rehashes of something already filmed or already discredited. Most don't even do a web search to see if their idea is unique. If every script I read was printed on paper, I could burn them one script at a time in my furnace, day in and day out, I would never have to buy fuel oil again." Charlie chuckled as Gemma did.

Gemma pulled her Angora sweater closer around her shoulders and started to button it up.

"I'm sorry, you're cold," Charlie said, a sliver of regret in his voice. He stood and began shrugging off his coat.

"No, please, it's okay. I'm enjoying our conversation. I miss the daily contact with people. Anyway, I find I'm always colder now after my surgery." Gemma explained. He paused and gave her a thoughtful look before pulling his coat back over his neat frame.

"Would you like to continue this conversation over some coffee or tea? Or hot chocolate?"

"Um, sure. How about that Tisane Tea Shoppe a couple of blocks down on Shady Avenue on the left."

"Great place. I'll meet you there."

Charlie stirred his Earl Grey tea, a contemplative expression on his face. Gemma blew on her cup of Mexican hot cocoa and watched him. Her manager's intuition was alerted again; he had questions he struggled with whether to ask.

"Go ahead," Gemma urged.

"What?" Charlie stopped stirring his tea, locking eyes with her.

"Go ahead and ask." Gemma smiled, trying to make him feel comfortable.

"Oookay," he hesitated before adding, "Do you have a significant other?"

"Ah." Gemma laughed nervously. "Not the question I thought you were going to ask." Her cheeks began feeling warm, the feeling moving up to the tips of her ears.

"I'm sorry, but you asked for it." Charlie smiled sheepishly, his cheeks blushing, mimicking hers, no doubt.

"That I did. The answer is no," Gemma admitted, then took a sip of her cocoa to prevent herself from saying anything further.

"The question you thought I would ask was about your surgery?"

"Yes," Gemma said, peering over the rim of her cup.

"Does it matter?" Charlie asked, and then added, "I know it's having a significant impact on your life right now. In the scheme of things, is it significant?"

"I don't know," Gemma said. "It's supposed to help a significant health problem, and it has. The side effects are a complete surprise. I'm still getting used to them."

"Good or bad side effects?" Charlie asked, his chin in his hand.

"A little of both." Gemma sat back in her chair as if trying to get a full view of the issue. "I still can't eat more than a half cup of food at a time, and it holds me for two to three hours. I don't eat much, but I eat much more often. The doctor said that my stomach would go back to normal size eventually. In the meantime, I'm losing weight, and I vacillate between feeling completely full and absolutely starving. I wake up ravenous twice each night, but I'm too lazy to get up to eat," Gemma confessed. She didn't worry about her weight much. The doctor's charts said her five foot six frame should weigh no more than one hundred and fifty, but she was nearly one hundred and ninety-two at the time of her surgery. Since then, she had dropped down to one hundred and sixty-five.

"I noticed you were losing weight. I guess it's safe to mention."

"Yeah, it's safe. Some other weird things I wasn't told beforehand are bad side effects: I can't drink anything carbonated anymore. I can't burp, ever again. It's excruciatingly painful if I have to because I can't, *ever*. I have handfuls of antacids and anti-gas tablets to keep myself comfortable. You know it's amazing how many restaurants don't serve anything non-carbonated except for tea, coffee, or water."

Charlie was pensive as he sipped his tea. Gemma noted he liked it just as she liked Earl Grey tea, with honey and without milk. She also noted he didn't squeeze the tea bag when he removed it from the mug. A sign of a tea purist.

"Not to be gross, but what if you have to get sick?" Charlie asked as delicately as he could.

"Not possible. My stomach will keep trying, but nothing will exit. I, uh, have some special pills in case that situation arises," Gemma surmised.

"Special pill? How can you swallow a pill if your stomach is trying to expel everything?" Charlie wondered.

"Uh, it's not an, uh, oral kind of pill." Gemma turned beet red and refused to make eye contact, sipping her cocoa and staring at the spoon her fingers were now twirling erratically.

"Ooh," Charlie soothed with a note of light humor.

Gemma glanced up at him under her eyelashes. He caught her glance, and they both burst out laughing at the absurdity of the delicate issue. Gemma grabbed her middle, holding her incision, which still seared with pain when she laughed too heartily.

Catching her breath, she said, "Yeah, I'm not looking forward to that experience. I know it's going to happen sooner or later, but I sure hope it's a lot later."

Charlie and Gemma sipped their beverages, smiling at each other intermittently over the rims of their cups. The ache in her incision dulled now that she wasn't laughing, but it didn't go away. It was long past time for pain medication. Tylenol only at this point, but Gemma was trying to give her liver and kidneys a break after months of pharmaceutical abuse.

"You know I'm a script reader, what do you do?" Charlie inquired.

"I'm a certified event planner working for a large professional organization. They have several huge events during the year. I'm in charge of a small team of planners that put the events together, make sure they get set up correctly, run smoothly, and then we critique our outcomes."

"The production company I work for could sure use someone like you," Charlie said with a little awe. "How big are your biggest events?"

"The week-long national convention is once a year and travels to a different city each year. The attendance runs about thirty-six hundred. We also have six smaller educational events, each lasting four days, spread throughout the year and across the country to cover every region. The attendance at those events runs about five to six hundred."

"You must do a lot of traveling."

"It's not too bad. I'm definitely at the national convention site and three or four smaller events. Other members of my staff handle the smaller events with supervision, but I try to give them their heads, let them do their jobs. They're a good team. They know what they're doing. Much of my time is spent doing advanced planning. We have to book convention sites and hotels sometimes up to five years out. Much of my yearly travel is checking out future sites. I love to travel, see new places, so it's good for me," Gemma explained happily.

"Have you traveled much?" she asked Charlie.

"The usual places: LA, San Francisco, New York, Chicago, Phoenix. I've been to Toronto, Vancouver, London, Cannes, Berlin, and Rome." Charlie shrugged. "I like traveling, but I have never traveled for pleasure, now that I think about it. It's always been for work."

"Why do you love to travel so much? New scenery?" Charlie asked, trying to understand her motivation.

"Everything about a new place. The scenery, the people, the different cultures, the different ways they do things. But the food, I love to explore a region's food," Gemma offered. "The most telling place to visit when you go to a new country is the food stores and markets. A food store tells you so much about the country and the people you are visiting."

Charlie smiled. "I've never thought of that. I bet you're right."

"Speaking of which, I have to get to the grocery store," Gemma said, gathering her sweater. "Thank you so much for my cocoa. I've enjoyed our conversation."

"It's been my pleasure. I hope you'll join me again soon," Charlie added, chivalrously standing up when she did.

"Absolutely. Bye." Gemma headed for the door, feeling strangely elated.

NOVEMBER 2017

Breakfast started out peacefully, as usual for a Sunday morning. Until Seth blew it by bringing up their need to set a date for the wedding. The crisp, sunny day quickly deteriorated into the argument Chelsea had been avoiding for months. Even the sunlight stopped shining through the kitchen window of their apartment.

"Why are you being so pushy about the date?" It was so unlike Seth to press her about anything. Something was upsetting his usual patient and calm demeanor.

He blushed but said nothing.

"What is it?" Chelsea's stomach began to ache. Ache with the uncertainty of his insistence and his silence. Was he really in a hurry? What could be so serious he was tight-lipped and blushing?

He glanced away, his fingers shredding his paper napkin. "It took me six years to save up for your engagement ring. It took longer than I thought it would, what with totaling my pickup at that job site two years ago. I've waited all these years to propose. I'm tired of waiting."

Chelsea's insides melted at his explanation. She knew he loved her, would do anything for her. "You don't want to wait anymore?"

"No. It's taken so long to get you the style of ring you've always wanted. And I wanted it to be as big as I could afford." He shrugged. "It isn't as large as I wanted, but I hope you like it."

Her mouth dropped open. "Like it? Are you serious? It's perfect, and I love it. And I love you for trying so hard to make me happy."

They clung to each other for several minutes. Her head resting on his shoulder, her arms tight around his waist. The warmth between them building until they had to break apart. They settled at the kitchen table, Seth still holding her hand.

"So, you'll consider a date?" He squeezed her hand. "How about six months from now? An April wedding?"

"Seth, I need more time!" Chelsea pleaded. "I need to lose weight. I need another year." She got up from the solid wood table Seth had crafted and began pacing until he met her by the sink.

"I don't understand why you need to lose weight. You're perfect the way you are." Seth explained reassuringly, wrapping his arms around her ample waist, trying to snuggle her close again.

Chelsea squirmed, trying to shimmy out of his grasp. She had to stand her ground, and it was a lot easier if he wasn't close enough to use his hands or his lips to physically manipulate her into changing her mind. "I want to look absolutely gorgeous walking down that aisle on my uncle's arm. I have to lose another forty-five pounds or so."

His face darkened. The rigidity of his jaw clued her in that the ice she was treading was wafer thin. Chelsea began to sweat in earnest and hurriedly continued with her reasoning before Seth could find his voice. He rarely got angry. She knew she was pushing his limit. "I've had this dream about my wedding dress since childhood. I know exactly what it looks like. It is so awesome, but it hugs every curve, and I have way more curves and bumps than I should have. I *really* want to wear that wedding dress."

Following her again, Seth found breath. He tried another persuasive vein. "I'll hug every curve and bump. You haven't bought it yet, have you? Pick something else. Something you don't have to lose weight to fit into."

"I want *that* dress. It's *THE* dress. I need time to find it or something very close." Chelsea said, the hard edge in her voice saying the issue of the dress was closed. She folded her arms across her chest for emphasis. "Please, give me a few more weeks to find it, okay?"

• • • •

AGAIN, ON THE ADVICE of her dietician, Marla hired a personal trainer, but the woman was much too harsh. She thought

Marla should put two hours a day into weight training and cardio classes at the gym. She told her the yoga wasn't doing her any real good as far as her weight loss was concerned. Marla told her that she didn't want a drill sergeant. She wasn't trying to mimic *The Biggest Loser* show. She needed a mentor. There was time for weight training and time for cardio classes later, but first, Marla had to get a little more fit before even *attempting* that level of exercise. She'd stick with walking and yoga for now, happy with the results so far.

Each pound was like another spark of fire. It kept her determination burning, kept her going on the diet, going to the treadmill and yoga classes. It made all the sweat, effort, and strain worth every ounce of it.

• • • •

THE THREE WOMEN SAT around Gemma's kitchen table, mugs of steaming tea warming in their hands. "How's everyone's weight loss going?" she asked.

Heather mumbled, "I guess I'll be going back to Calorie Counters. I need to lose a couple dozen pounds before the reunion."

"I'm down to one-forty," Gemma said with a smug grin. Her hand stroked Wally who was balanced on her thighs.

Chelsea pointed her finger at her. "You don't count. You don't even have to try."

Heather and Chelsea looked at each other shaking their heads.

Chelsea shrugged. "I was hoping to do it on my own, so haven't started anything yet. I should get on the ball cuz if anything, I've probably gained more weight."

They were silent, sipping their tea for a few minutes before Gemma added, "I'm down a lot. Which is nice, but this hip pain, both hips are killing me, especially at night." She glanced at their unsympathetic faces. "Okay, so what else is going on?"

Chelsea had told them about her argument with Seth.

Heather thought it romantic the way he didn't want to wait any longer.

"Is it wise? I mean, you've waited so long for him to propose. And he's waited so long to propose to you. If I were you, I'd have dragged him down the aisle the next morning." Heather blew on her tea to cool it enough for a sip.

"Yeah, why the issue with the dress? I don't get it," Gemma said with suspicion in her voice.

Chelsea stared at her engagement ring, her hand wrapped around the mug. "All my childhood, Diane and I played wedding. We even had those icky-tasting NECCO wafers to use as a communion host during the ceremony. I always dreamed of my dress. What it would look like." Chelsea's voice was firm. "I want to find something as close to it as possible."

"That particular one you dreamed of is necessary?" Gemma asked with unmasked incredulity in her voice.

"It is to me." Chelsea frowned. "All my life growing up, I had to wear secondhand clothes. Everything except socks and underwear. My father didn't make a lot of money, and my mom stayed at home. I never got a chance to choose my own clothes. They would magically appear in my closet or dresser." She frowned before continuing. "I don't begrudge them for that. But I swore when I grew up, I'd buy my own style of clothes. And my wedding dress would be exactly what I wanted. I *will* get whatever it is I want. No substitutions, and no settling on something that doesn't thrill me."

Heather nodded slightly, her lips mashed together. "I get it. It was similar for me as a kid. At least I didn't have to wear my brother's clothes. He was younger than me."

Her comment broke them up into giggles.

"So when are we going wedding dress shopping?" Gemma asked, pulling out her phone. "Let's see the calendar...hmm, next Saturday's good for me."

The others pulled out their phones and began scrolling their calendars. They settled for two Saturdays hence.

"There. Was that so hard? At least you can tell Seth you're working on the wedding plans, and you won't have to push his good nature." Gemma stowed her phone away.

"He's pretty pliable. He has a tell when he's really angry. I haven't seen it rear its head yet."

"Oh, what is it?" Gemma asked, a little too enthusiastic for Chelsea's comfort.

"He wrinkles his nose when he's about to cross the line." Chelsea's demonstration made the others giggle.

"Good thing for a wife to know," Gemma said.

• • • •

MARLA SPRINTED THE last hundred feet to the end of her driveway and the end of her run. Hands on hips, head tilted back, eyes glazed, she panted and walked aimlessly around her tiny backyard, feeling the sweat still pouring from her skin, droplets sluicing down her cleavage and back. When her breathing returned to a more normal state, she treated herself to a shower to wash away the sweat and dust of her five-mile jog.

This was always the best part, the fresh, clean feeling under the blast of hot water while the endorphins still surged. Humph, five miles. That first morning she could barely walk down and back up her driveway. Now she was jogging five miles a day. Marla's grin stretched ear to ear.

Using constructive imagery, Marla envisioned every mile jogged was a pound lost, even though technically it wasn't that much. The more pounds off, the easier it was to jog *and* to breathe while jogging. *Breathing helps.* Marla smirked her sideways smile to herself.

Four months and ninety pounds down. Way to go! She praised herself in the mirror, checking out her new body. Well, still the old body, just a little lighter. She was starting to see curves where they should be, curving the way they should be, not in the opposite direction.

The reflected face frowned; there were still bulges. It was going to take another sixty-plus pounds of weight loss before those bulges were permanently gone. By summer, Marla hoped her reflection would no longer be top-heavy with boobs and be slimmer around her hips and booty. Maybe then she'd return that unexpected telephone call.

Since her return flight from Phoenix and the start of her diet, changes were noticeable almost immediately. By the end of the first week, changes in the boobs were the most noticeable. The dietician had said the difference between her new diet and her old daily eating did it. Her arms weren't filling out her blouse sleeves as snugly. A few weeks later, her hips and belly had already started to shrink. The waistband of her pants became looser, and the butt sagged. Every extra millimeter in her clothing fortified her quest for weight loss.

Even her sleep apnea doctor had noted the weight loss would make her need for a CPAP machine obsolete.

After four months of strict diet compliance, she was at the mall shopping for new clothing. Buying only a few items to display her emerging figure and look good at her job. She didn't want to buy too much because there was more weight loss to come. And there was no doubt about it – after conquering the last six months; Marla was going all the way.

On the scale, Marla felt powerful and in total control. She shut the bathroom door to look at herself in the full-length mirror. Her grin evaporated, as did her mood. She was a phony. As much as she loved the changes her determination had wrought, she still could look in the mirror and see her old self. She was still Fat Marla.

• • • •

WHEN HER FIRST AND second voice messages went unreturned, Heather tried again. She wanted to hear from Marla's own lips she wasn't interested in getting together. Heather sat down at the kitchen table and steeled herself as she dialed the phone number yet again. On the sixth ring, Marla answered.

"Hello?" a dull, irritated voice asked.

"Marla? It's Heather Boyden. Remember me from camp? I left a couple of messages a week or so ago. How are you?" Heather responded, trying to keep her voice upbeat and excited. She crossed her right leg over her left knee and bounced her foot. She couldn't help but fidget. Her breathing was shallow, her chest tense, not knowing what to expect.

"Uh, Hi."

Heather covered her eyes with her hand. "Do you remember the four of us from Camp Terramungus, cabin four?"

"Yes."

Heather's right leg dropped to the floor, and she shook her head. She tried to hide how pissed she was for getting only monosyllable answers. "Hey, Chelsea, Gemma, and I are all living in the same area as you. We get together and have coffee or a drink once or twice a month. We were hoping you'd join us now that we've found you."

"I don't know, it's been a long time. I'm not sure we have much in common anymore."

Heather abruptly stood and began pacing. There it was. *At least she's being upfront about her doubts.* Or was she afraid the incident would be brought up? "We are all quite different, but you know, we have a good time getting together and yakking anyway. We'd like to see you again, Marla. Could you meet up with us for coffee next Saturday?"

The line was silent for thirty seconds, sixty seconds. If Heather couldn't hear Marla's soft breath through her phone, she might have thought the line was dead. The kitchen clock ticked away seconds lost forever. She picked stray Cheerios off Michelle's highchair and rolled them in her fist. She dropped the cereal in the sink and walked over to the window.

Rain was pelting down, raising puddles on the sidewalk. The sound of a child's pattering footsteps drew her attention. A sleepy Peter shuffled into the kitchen and wrapped his arms around Heather's leg. Her nerves couldn't contain her impatience a second longer. "Marla? Are you still there?"

"Yeah. Okay." Marla's sigh sounded as though she knew Heather wouldn't let her go without a struggle.

"Great! I'm so excited!" Heather couldn't contain herself. "We meet up at seven o'clock at Arriviste Coffee Bar on Ellsworth Avenue."

• • • •

THE THREE WOMEN SAT around the coffee table in the space before the front window. It was the coziest, most comfortable seating in the small but busy shop. They would be sure to see her arriving from their vantage point. Chelsea and Gemma sat in the cushioned armchairs while Heather waited on the bright blue couch. All three stared at the empty space on the sofa they had saved for Marla. With every tinkle of the door opening, their eyes jumped up, as did their hopes.

"What do we do now?" Chelsea whined, her coffee cup poised inches from her lips. Waiting for an answer to her question, she took a sip of the robust-tasting dark roast coffee.

"Maybe she got tied up?" Heather always had a reasonable explanation.

"And maybe she's too good for us," Gemma blurted out as she set her cup down on the table.

Heather's eyes widened in shock at the comment. Then she furiously shook her head. "I don't think so. She sounded afraid."

"Afraid of what?" Gemma snipped.

Heather bit her lip before responding. "Maybe it's too overwhelming for her to see all of us at once. For the first time, anyway. Maybe I should try seeing her alone."

"I don't think that'll help. She's being stubborn. Just like at camp," Gemma retorted.

Chelsea jumped into the fray. "I get it might be too much for her to see us all together. She always was kind of shy."

"It was because of her weight," Gemma curtly added.

Heather held up her hand. "Let me try."

Gemma shrugged before sipping her drink. "Whatever."

But they all knew what the others were thinking. Was Marla avoiding them because she set the cabin on fire? Was she worried they intended to accuse her? It was so many years ago the statute of limitations had no doubt been exceeded.

In all their meetings, they had never brought up that night. It was some kind of unspoken truce.

"Well, at least I'm out of the apartment," Chelsea said.

Heather sighed. "I'll call again."

Gemma changed the subject. Looking pointedly at Heather, she asked, "How's your diet going?"

Heather mashed her lips together. "It's not."

LATE NOVEMBER 2017

Heather's new tactic with Marla was having a better response. They made a date for the following afternoon. But Marla bowed out of that meeting and the next they arranged for a week later. It was an improvement; she had at least called Heather both those times to say she wasn't coming. Even if the excuses had been rather lame.

As she had promised, Heather kept Gemma and Chelsea informed. None of them understood Marla's reluctance unless it did have to do with the cabin fire. It wasn't always easy to arrange their schedules for their meetups. But it was worth it. As different as they were, they enjoyed each other's company. Having these other women to bounce off thoughts, ideas, and life situations was more than a treat; it was a necessity. It was like the seventeen years between them had evaporated into thin air like the steam over their coffee cups.

Heather persisted, setting up a third date with Marla. She fought with the idea this would be the last time she would try to meet with Marla. Each time she had to arrange her mother-in-law as a sitter. While Joyce loved taking care of her grandchildren, it was always a pain to coordinate the time. If the woman didn't show tonight, Heather wouldn't pursue her again.

A light dusting of powdery, soft snowflakes highlighted the surfaces of the moonlit night. Outside the coffee bar window, Heather could see the flakes making their lazy trails down from the sky, falling like leaves, blown first this way, then that by a subtle breeze.

A figure loomed in her peripheral vision. Heather looked up to see a short overweight, woman approaching. Her oversized heavy black wool coat made her look like a squat football player with shoulder pads. The dark purple peasant skirt and untucked white linen blouse underneath looked too big for her. Had she lost weight?

"Heather?"

It was several seconds before Heather could find her voice. When she was able to respond, she did so suddenly with jerking, uncoordinated motions. "Marla! Gosh, I'm so glad you came." Standing suddenly, she jostled the table, sloshing coffee out of her mug onto the black Formica surface. She quickly corralled the spill with a napkin. "I'm such a klutz! God, Marla, please, have a seat."

Marla sat across from Heather and looked at her with not unpleasant eyes. She didn't take off her coat or put down her handbag.

The rest of their half-hour meeting was like High Mass on Easter vigil. Marla solemnly and politely responded with as much enthusiasm as if she were watching flowers wilt. Heather expended an enormous amount of energy, first trying to get Marla to converse openly and then trying not to tell her off.

Clearly, Marla had issues; weight and confidence issues which Heather tried to keep in mind every time she felt like throwing up her hands in exasperation. But it wasn't the physical changes in Marla that dissuaded her; it was her manner. She didn't act like the Marla she remembered, the girl from Camp Terramungus who smiled readily and enjoyed mischief. Nor whom she seemed in those few subsequent years of letters. Something must have happened to force Marla to build an armor.

From what little information Marla shared, she had a successful career. Whatever fortified her shell kept her distant, impenetrable to even the fondest childhood memories. It didn't take a psychiatrist for Heather to discern Marla's self-esteem had suffered badly since their camp days.

Hadn't they all, to some extent? Even Gemma and Chelsea were different. Both were still outgoing, sarcastic and forthright, but there was an edge that had been sharpened over the years. She was different too. Getting married, having four children, dealing with the grief of losing Victoria, all of it had taken an emotional toll on her. Even so, she didn't feel all that different from her camp days.

It was a sign of extraordinary effort and success when Marla smiled slightly by the end of their meeting.

"I've really enjoyed chatting with you. So, do you think we could meet again?" Heather asked, her nerves tingling with hope.

Marla gave a shy smile. "Yeah. I think ..." She paused a few seconds before continuing. "Yeah. I'd like that."

They agreed to meet again the following week. Heather returned home feeling triumphant. She called Gemma and Chelsea to report on the meeting and the new date. All the while, Heather mulled over how she could get Marla's comfort and confidence built up enough to meet with Chelsea and Gemma.

• • • •

MEETING WITH HEATHER terrified Marla. When they finally met, she could see the effect of her appearance in her old friend's eyes. Her gut had dropped as her eyes did from Heather's face. She almost turned on her heels and walked out the door. She had almost left the coffee shop after getting her to-go cup, chickening out at the last minute after watching Heather sitting by the window, studying her while Marla waited for her order.

Heather had gained a bit of weight, which eased Marla's heart. Otherwise, she looked much the same as when she was at camp. Same medium brown hair, same long hair hanging past her shoulders. Her brown eyes were still large and perceptive to the smallest details. Seeing her gave Marla's heart an ache to feel the closeness she had felt with Heather so long ago.

Marla had been shipped off to camp without any notice. Her childhood, up to that point, had been lonely and subdued. As an only child living in a child-free neighborhood, she never had anyone to play with outside her Barbie dolls. Her aunt had convinced her parents she needed more socialization with other girls of the same age.

Opening the door to cabin four had taken every ounce of courage Marla had in her chubby body. Heather had been the only one there. The outgoing, sensitive girl instinctively knew she was frightened and quietly welcomed her. She never forgot her kindness. Over the course of the two weeks, they had understood each other without words. They thought the same, ate the same foods, and were into quieter things like reading books. Marla used to think Heather was her long-lost twin. Their insides were made of the same stuffing, their skin of the same ticking. And yet they had drifted apart as college and babies butt into their lives. It had been so many years since she had heard news from Heather. Marla felt sorry for those lost years. That regret had led her feet to the table.

The conversation was halting at first. Marla couldn't think of much to say despite the fact there were so many questions milling about her brain. Just like at camp, Heather's manner put her at ease. By the time Heather had to leave to get back to her kids, Marla's reserve was loosening up. It was working out okay. Heather was older by more than these last seventeen years but, at heart, still the same. Only wiser. Maybe it had something to do with marriage and children. Something Marla would not know. She had nearly gotten the chance to find out for herself, but destiny had other ideas.

Heather said nothing of Marla's weight issue, and Marla didn't tell her about losing more than a hundred pounds. Marla was grateful enough to make another date. Heather had also not said anything about their last night at camp. Why not reacquaint herself with the only person as close to her as a sister might have been?

The next day she mulled over the meeting while shopping for new clothes again. Her old muffin top was dwindling. She was tired of pinning her waistbands and getting jabbed when the safety pin opened unexpectedly. She was tired of carrying a travel-sized container of baby powder in her handbag so she could spread it on her thighs to prevent chafing as they rubbed together in skirts.

In rebellion, Marla tried to avoid the fat woman clothes store where everything was made with prints loud enough to bark and swags of fabric that made a big woman look even larger and was covered with sequins, glitter, or rhinestones. This time she went to Largesse Consignment Shop for her temporary wardrobe.

She stopped at the Salvation Army clothing store on the way. The ladies on duty were happy with the three trash bags full of all her old, jumbo-sized clothes and the other items she'd found during the closet cleaning. Marla was equally happy with the tax-deductible donation.

Marla shuddered head to toe, remembering the event which had pushed her to this point in the first place.

Later that night, after putting her newer, smaller clothes away in her sparsely filled closet, she danced around the bedroom in her new silky nightgown. The lacy edge fluttered as she twirled like a toddler under a water sprinkler. She was doing it! Doing it right, doing it well, and in the end, she would fill this closet with the most beautiful clothes she could afford on her well-deserved salary.

Sitting on the edge of her bed, she pulled out her box of old photo albums. She pulled one out and flipped through it lazily, finding only a few pictures from her childhood in Galiston, New York, as well as high school and college photos. Even as a child, she had been heavier than her classmates. At the end of the album, Marla's hand paused on one photo.

His eyes sparkled at the camera. His arm swung over Marla's shoulders, the sides of their heads touching. Sam's smile matched his attitude: effervescent. There was no other way to express his personality. Marla closed her eyes and shut the album. Tears seeped out from under her eyelids as the all too familiar crush of sorrow filled her chest. If only he hadn't died, her life would be so very much different.

Dropping the album back in the box, she recognized another as being from her first job. Propping the album on her lap, she opened it, and her breath paused.

The photo was taken when she worked at Columbia University Medical Center in New York City. She pulled the picture out to look more closely. A small group of ten people posed in front of the hospital facade. Marla flipped the snapshot over to read the date, September 23, 2011. It was her going away party. Her last day working at Columbia. Her audible gasp filled her ears as she recognized Dr. Timothy Brighton in the middle row. She had forgotten he had joined the party. *Good God, he was so gorgeous.*

Elation disintegrated when she climbed under the bedcovers still clutching the picture Marla felt struck by a sucker punch in the chest, a deep, hollow pain. All sense of weight loss success was crushed as she looked at the emptiness of the king-sized bed surrounding her. She felt like an impostor. Her outside form may be reduced, but inside, she was still Fat Marla. Her face buried in her pillow, Marla cried herself to sleep, trying not to drown in the engulfing silence of her empty bed.

••••

"WAIT, SHH, HERE SHE comes," Heather said as she approached the table. The announcement stunned Gemma and Chelsea into silence. Their eyes were glued to the door of Jitter's café. Marla caught their stare the moment she entered the shop. She froze, fear in her eyes. At first, she looked like she would bolt back out the door. But a small group of students were coming in, blocking the way.

Heather stood and approached her. "It's okay, Marla. Just come and say hello. They're excited to meet you again."

Marla searched Heather's face as if to see if she was telling the truth. At last, nodding, she approached their table.

"Hi, Marla," Chelsea said as brightly as she could muster without sounding fake. "It's good to see you again after all these years."

Gemma blinked and smiled. "Marla, what would you like to drink? I'll get it for you."

As Heather led her to the open seat, Marla replied, "Uh, black coffee."

"Anyone else?" Gemma asked. Chelsea held up her latte mug wordlessly. "Got it," Gemma replied. "Heather?"

"No thanks, I'm good."

Marla slowly shrugged off her oversized heavy coat. "Thanks." She folded it nicely and set it on the back of her chair.

It wasn't cold enough out today to warrant such a garment. Maybe she was trying to hide herself in it. Chelsea asked, "Are you cold?"

Marla silently shook her head.

"It's good to see you, Marla. We've been trying to find you for over six months. Heather ended up contacting your mother."

Marla nodded. "She told me."

Heather couldn't stand Marla's tentativeness. "Well, I told you all about me at our last meeting. Chelsea is a talented manicurist and part-time business owner. She does home manicures."

"I could do yours. Looks like you go for the neat corporate look."

Marla gave Chelsea a smile and nodded. "I'm not much into color."

Heather lightly touched Marla's arm to redirect her. "Gemma here is a corporate event planner."

"If you ever need a party, give me a call!" Gemma said with a wink and a grin. "Heather, you forgot to mention Chelsea is engaged to be married."

Marla nodded. When it was clear they were expecting a verbal response, she said, "Excellent."

"How was everyone's Thanksgiving?" Heather asked. "Did you go see your parents, Marla?"

"Yes. I drove up on Wednesday and came back on Saturday. It was nice to see them."

Gemma cut in, "I spend Thanksgiving with my aunt and uncle, Rose Anne's parents. They have quite a tribe, so it's always entertaining."

"Seth's parents hosted Thanksgiving this year. They had their usual Turducken." Chelsea said.

Heather's eyebrows rose. "Turducken? I've heard of it before but never knew anyone who had one." She set her empty coffee mug aside. "Anyone want a coffee or something? Marla?"

Marla, Gemma, and Chelsea shook their heads.

Abruptly, Chelsea turned to Marla and asked, "Did you ever marry?"

Marla stood up so abruptly that her knees hit the table, sloshing everyone's drink, including her untouched black coffee. "I've got to go." Chelsea and Heather threw their napkins over the spilled mixture on the table.

Gemma grasped her arm. "You just got here. Skip the question if you don't like it." Her soft touch soothed Marla's nerves enough that she sat back down. "Where do you work?"

Marla rubbed the side of her face with her palm. "Peabody Laboratories over on Fifth Avenue. I'm the corporate compliance officer for the company. One of two."

"No wonder you have a corporate manicure," Chelsea said.

Marla stared at her for so long that all of them held their breath, waiting for Marla's response. All of a sudden, Marla burst out laughing. The other three women looked at each other, their faces showing surprise. They had no idea what was so funny, but in seconds they were all laughing. It was a break in the cold shoulder.

• • • •

GEMMA'S DOORBELL RANG Friday evening not long after she got home from work. It was Charlie.

"I'm sorry if I'm disturbing you," Charlie said, looking a little embarrassed. "I've been trying to run into you, find you, find your phone number in the phone book. Would you have lunch with me tomorrow?"

"Ah," Gemma hemmed. "I'm still not eating much for real food yet."

"I see. What do you think is doable?" Charlie inquired with a playful smile.

"Hmm, how about Lo Mein?"

"Chinese it is! I'll come by at noon? We can walk over to Chow Fun. Does that sound okay?"

"Sounds good. Thanks, Charlie, I'll look forward to seeing you then," Gemma said.

The next day she spent more time than she had in forever trying to figure out what to wear. Charlie's admiring smile made it worthwhile.

"How's the Lo Mein?" Charlie asked, a little concerned.

"It tastes so good. No problems. Thanks for suggesting it," Gemma said happily.

"If you remember, you suggested it! I'm glad it's working out for you."

"Me too. I can't wait until I can get back to my whole repertoire of foods. Doing only this soft stuff is getting boring." Gemma took two more bites and put down her plastic fork.

"Done?" Charlie asked, wiping his mouth free of garlic sauce.

"God, I hate this. It tastes so good, I want to eat more," Gemma grumbled.

"It's okay. We can come back in four hours and eat the rest." Charlie laughed.

Gemma shook her head slowly. "Welcome to my world. Please finish yours."

"Later." Charlie started packing up the aborted lunch.

"Would you like to come back to my place to finish your lunch?"

He paused and nodded. "Yeah, that would be nice. Do you mind?"

"No, not at all. As long as you don't mind eating alone. I can't even think about eating more right now."

They walked back to Gemma's condo, Charlie carrying their lunches.

They sat at the kitchen table together. Charlie ate his lunch while they chatted about town events, condo complex affairs, and travel. Gemma watched his open face and warm smile. He ate with polite gusto. Her interest in this guy was definitely piqued. A man who looked awesome and could hold up his end of a serious conversation.

"Well, I'm sorry you didn't get to enjoy more of your lunch, you were wonderful company for mine," Charlie said.

"Thanks for the offer. It's nice to know someone my own age. The lady next door is about eighty-seven. She's very nice, but there's not much we have in common," Gemma explained.

Charlie picked up his trash, dropping it in the bin under the sink cabinet where Gemma pointed. He grabbed the sponge and wiped his place at the table. "Well, Miss Gemma, I must get back to work. It has been my pleasure to dine with you this afternoon. I hope we can do it again soon." He bowed chivalrously.

"Being back to work has been a challenge after all those weeks off," Gemma said with reluctance in her voice.

Charlie's smile fell. "You must be pleased to get back to normal."

Gemma got up and walked him to the door but stopped short of it. "Not really. I miss getting to sleep in. I hadn't had much time off from work since high school. It was nice to play the lady of leisure while it lasted," Gemma joked. "There are days I wish I could work at home like you."

"It's hard to stay disciplined working at home, but I manage to get about ten hours in over the course of a day. I like the flexibility most of all. I pick my own days and hours, with some exceptions. I feel like I have more of a life even though I work more hours when I'm working at home. You ought to try telecommuting."

"Yeah, not a bad idea. I'll definitely give it some thought. Even a couple days a week would be helpful."

When their eyes locked, there was some unspoken transfer of communication, of honesty, respect, kindness. Charlie blinked and reached behind for the doorknob.

"Off I go to hit the digital script pile," Charlie said, at first turning toward the door, then abruptly turning back.

Charlie leaned to Gemma's left, brushing her cheek with his soft, warm lips. He drew back slightly, locking eyes with her.

Still feeling under the spell of his eye lock, Gemma raised her chin a micrometer as her arms lifted to his shoulders. Charlie hesitantly put his arms around her waist and drew her closer to him as if afraid to hurt her. His lips pressed gently against hers with a softness Gemma found pleasurable. It was a very sweet, undemanding kiss.

"Bye, Gemma," Charlie whispered in her ear, letting her go as lightly as he had held her.

"Bye, Charlie," Gemma whispered back, tingles running down her neck and spine, down her legs to her toes. Before she knew it, he was gone, and she was panting and faint as her heart galloped away with his receding silhouette in the opaque glass of the front door. She leaned against the back of the door, feeling like a lovesick teenager.

DECEMBER 2017

After weeks of cancellations and delays, Chelsea was shopping for her wedding dress.

Her three friends, her cousin Diane, along with her mother, Gloria, and Seth's mother, Peggy, had been at the bridal salon for almost two hours.

"I haven't decided on bridesmaids yet because Seth and I still need to discuss the size of the wedding party. But I want your thoughts on dresses." Before starting the wedding dress hunting, Chelsea asked Gemma, Heather, Monica, and Diane to look over the bridesmaids' dresses and colors. That task had taken an entire hour. In the end, all five agreed on one design, a simple but elegant satin empire-style dress in navy. Along the neckline were tiny off-white pearls trailing over the shoulder and back where the pearl strands crossed over the deeper cut bare back. To finish the look, the saleswoman suggested they wear elbow-length off-white gloves with the same pearl edging at the cuff. It was, after all, a night wedding, so elegance was expected.

With that decision made, it was Chelsea's turn. The rest of her entourage's enthusiasm was waning but found a second wind for the bride's dress search.

"What do you think of this one?" Chelsea sauntered to the pedestal on the bridal salon dais. It lifted her a foot off the floor to let the dress and train hang fully out for detailed inspection. The salon assistant smoothed out the train and stepped back to watch the reaction of the entourage. Chelsea's own eyes were searching theirs in the mirrors for feedback on this fourth dress of the afternoon.

She was becoming tired and disheartened about ever finding the right dress. The vision she'd had of her wedding dress throughout her childhood dreams couldn't be found. Cost was no matter. She'd been saving money since her first job at sixteen for this specific day. All her life, she'd had to do without or go secondhand. For once in her life, she would not shortchange her desires.

While the party discussed leaving for the day, her cousin Diane checked the clearance rack. There she spotted a dress that fit the description Chelsea had given the saleswoman. Chelsea's heart raced, and her spirits rose when she saw it.

The saleswoman tried to dissuade her from the dress. "This style is no longer available from the dressmaker, and this is, err, not your size. Besides, it's beyond your price range."

"I want to see what it looks like on me," Chelsea demanded. Her heart thudded in her chest as she looked at the gown. *This could be the one.* The one meant for her. The one she had dreamed of for all these years.

The saleswoman zipped it up the back as far as it would go, then held it with clips. The size ten demo dress was smaller than she could fit, but it didn't matter to Chelsea. She could see the potential, and her excitement grew in anticipation. With one glance in the fitting room mirror, she loved it.

She stared at her reflection in the mirror again. The dress was an off-white satin side-draped silhouette that hugged her figure snuggly. A spaghetti-strapped bodice was beautifully embellished with a delicate floral beading design. The skirt was made of side-slanting tiered layers of organza ruffles with soft scalloped edges. Without a pucker, it clung to her body in a modern manner. The saleswoman set a thin pearl beaded band on her head with its elbow-length one-tiered organza bridal veil. It had pearl beading on the edge and tiny rhinestones that shimmered in the room's soft pink, fluorescent light.

"Oh, my God! It's beautiful on you!" Gemma exclaimed, her hands going to her mouth in shock.

"Perfect, it's perfect," Monica agreed, getting up to walk around Chelsea on the dais, getting the three-hundred-sixty-degree view.

"It's the one!" Heather concurred, "No doubt." Her head kept nodding like a bobblehead in a pickup truck.

"Well," Chelsea turned to her maid of honor, Diane, "You picked it out. What do you think?" Chelsea met Diane's eyes in the salon mirror. They held. Diane wasn't smiling.

"Stop chewing your lip," Gloria chastised Chelsea, who checked her reflection to see she indeed was chewing her lip.

Still waiting for an answer, Chelsea's eyes darted back to Diane's. There she found a big smile this time.

"I think it's sensational," Diane said, able to read the excitement in Chelsea's eyes.

"Mom? What do you think?" Chelsea asked for the most decisive opinion to come yet.

Gloria couldn't speak; she just nodded her head in assent and cried into her hanky while Diane gave her a hug.

"Peggy?"

Her future mother-in-law stared at her through her plastic-framed glasses hanging on a beaded string. She was the image of a stereotypical librarian; short, weighty with pudgy cheeks, gray hair, and dowdy clothing. But she was one of the kindest people Chelsea had ever met, and she already loved her as family.

"It's gorgeous, honey. It suits you well." Peggy smiled, giving Gloria a hug also.

"Yup, it's the one!" Chelsea squealed, jumping up and down on the dais.

All the women squealed and clapped, including Gemma, giving her a sense of real achievement.

Chelsea turned to the saleswoman. "This is it!" She paraded out of the room with the saleswoman in tow. She couldn't believe her luck at finding the dress she had dreamed about since childhood.

"We'll get you in to see our alterations department right away. They'll have to add panels to the sides to make it fit you. If it's even possible," The woman said, offering the efficiency for which the bridal store was well known.

"No!" Chelsea said loudly enough to shock everyone. "Give me a few days. I'll call you back. There's no hurry."

There was no way she would walk down the aisle in anything but this wedding dress. It was time to kick the dieting into high gear. In the meantime, she would try to find a bigger size online or at other bridal shops as a backup plan. All she had to do was snap a picture of the tag while the saleswoman wasn't looking.

"Can you ask Diane to come in here, please?" Chelsea asked with a shy smile.

"Sure, I'll be right back."

As soon as the changing room door clicked shut between them, her mouth went dry, and sweat started beading on her forehead. Phone in hand, she took several pictures of the wedding dress hanging on the wall hook. Then she snapped a few of the labels inside the dress. The phone slid into her jeans pocket as a knock on the door sounded.

"Come in," Chelsea called, quickly stuffing her feet into her shoes.

Diane waltzed in with the saleswoman on her heels. The woman gathered the dress and stepped out of the room. "What did you want?" Diana asked, a quizzical look on her face.

"Nothing. I needed a few minutes alone with the dress." Chelsea leaned over to tie her shoelaces.

Diane's forehead furrowed deeper. "I don't understand."

Dropping her voice to a whisper, Chelsea said, "I'll tell you later."

Diane drove the car on the ride home. Chelsea noticed her mother was quiet. "What's wrong, Mom?"

Her mother tried to smile at her. "It's a lot of money, sweetheart. Are you sure you won't consider wearing my dress? It might require some alterations, but it would otherwise be free."

Chelsea took her mother's hand. "I know. But I've been dreaming and planning this wedding since I was a little girl. I know exactly what I want. All my life, I've had to make do. I don't regret that. But I don't want to just make do for my wedding day. For once, I want to do it my way." Chelsea squeezed her hand. "Can you understand?"

Tears brimmed in Gloria's eyes. She tugged her hand away to search for a tissue in her purse. Wiping her eyes, she tried to smile. "I know. I do understand. We all had to make do when your father died. But you're right. It is your day. And you have to do what makes you happiest."

Later that evening, Chelsea searched for the same dress online. She couldn't find it anywhere. She truly was going to have to lose weight.

• • • •

GEMMA'S WEEK OF MEETINGS coincided with a week of daily snowfalls, each a mere one to two inches but accumulating to a depth of four and a half inches by Wednesday night. Another six inches of snow fell early Thursday morning, exactly as forecasted. She got up early to try to shovel her short walkway and clean off her car, only to find both chores already done. The walk was shoveled clean and salted, her car brushed clear of snow. Charlie's business card was stuck under her windshield wiper with a note on the back: For a good time, call 555-8792. Gemma couldn't help but break into a silly smile and looked over toward Charlie's condo building. She thought she saw the curtain twitch but couldn't be sure from such an obtuse angle.

Charlie stopped by that evening, not long after she got home.

"You didn't call for a good time," he said, a serious expression on his face. "I'm running a survey to find out your level of satisfaction with the snow removal service."

"It was terrific! I'm sorry I didn't get a chance to call you yet."

"Tell me I beat you to it." Charlie winked.

"You did." Gemma laughed wearily. "Come in. Can I get you something?"

Charlie strode in, each step tentative as if not wanting to dirty the floor even though it was covered with a drip mat.

"I don't want to stay, I just want to make a date for Saturday, July seventh." Soft brown eyes silently pleaded with her to accept.

"Sure. Details?" Gemma slumped against the wall, feet bare, sweater wrapped tight against her body. A timer went off in the kitchen area.

Sensing her exhaustion, he demurred. "I'll call tomorrow with details. Is that okay?" And with Gemma's nod, he was gone. She finished her quick dinner of oatmeal and left for the meetup at Chelsea's house.

• • • •

MARLA DRESSED CAREFULLY for the company Christmas party. She'd gone all out, buying new lingerie and a well-fitting dress for the occasion. She wanted people to notice she had lost weight—almost a hundred and ten pounds.

While she was far from reaching her goal, this was her reward: putting on the prettiest, most flattering dress she could find, no matter the cost. The new outfit made her feel better about going alone.

Determined to lift her mood, Marla thought of other things that were different with her weight loss. While meticulously putting on her makeup, she mused how much her dressing rituals had changed. It amazed her how much extra time it now took to get ready each morning. Before the weight loss, she could easily be up at six a.m. and at work by seven a.m. That included a breakfast stop at McDonald's and her commute to the parking garage. These days she was up at five. Not that she regretted the additional amount of time spent on her appearance. A last look in the bathroom mirror confirmed it was worth the trouble.

Marla smoothed out the flared skirt of her plum-colored silk, wraparound dress. She dropped her new black sling-back kitten heels on the floor to wiggle her feet into.

She gasped, freezing as she looked down her torso. Her toes! She was seeing her very own toes for the first time in more years than she could remember. There they were, just visible beyond the deflating swell of her belly.

She straightened her back and assumed yoga's mountain pose. Bending forward at the waist, Marla stretched into her forward bend yoga pose. With some strain, she got the middle finger of her right hand to touch her right big toe. She rolled upward on her vertebra until she stood tall. Inhaling deeply, she broke into a full smile.

Marla clapped her hands to her mouth, and giggles erupted as she wiggled the purple-painted metatarsals up and down. She watched them dance until she couldn't see them anymore because of her tear-filled eyes.

It was going to be a *terrific* night. If she could see and touch her toes, she decided, it was going to be a great Christmas and an awesome new year!

JANUARY 2018

On Saturday afternoon, Charlie picked Gemma up in his car, taking her to Frick Park for a casual walk. The snowflakes sparkled in all shades of the rainbow in the sunlight. It was a perfectly sunny day, though chilly. As they sat on a park bench, a horse-drawn sleigh arrived.

"Come, our magic sleigh has arrived." Charlie smiled, holding out his hand for Gemma.

Gemma's eyes widened, and her mouth fell open. She took his hand and followed him to the sleigh.

"I can't believe this! Where did you find a horse-drawn sleigh?"

"I have my secret source." Charlie winked at her while he tried to keep a straight face. "Besides, I thought you needed something special to lift your spirits."

Charlie helped Gemma up into the sleigh, settled her in front of a stack of pillows, then tucked thick warm blankets over her lap. Soft music played from his cell phone as he opened a gourmet picnic basket. He poured glasses of wine for each of them and then pulled out a plate of soft cheese spread and pâté on soft, crustless bread. Charlie held one out for Gemma to taste. She leaned over, taking the morsel in her mouth. It was spectacular. Soft, and creamy, it complemented the wine. Charlie settled on the seat beside her.

"Lie back and enjoy the pampering. I don't do this every week, you know," Charlie mused. Gemma leaned back, resting her head on the pillows so she could talk with him and still look at him. She was tickled with all the attention and special treatment. No man had ever treated her with such regard and tenderness. Charlie Hanover was pretty amazing.

They chatted about their respective week's events. Charlie had found two promising manuscripts in the ever-growing pile in his home office. He mentioned he had to fly to New York for a few days the following week to handle some work at headquarters.

Gemma talked about all the event arrangements that had gone on during her absence. An educational session was held a week before she returned. One minor problem had arisen with a newer contractor that needed a follow-up. She also needed to travel to Miami to work on arrangements for a national convention there in two years' time.

"My sister lives in Miami Beach. Do you know when you are going?"

"I don't have a set date yet," Gemma said a little sheepishly, wondering what he was getting at.

"Maybe we could fly down together," Charlie suggested. "I could visit my sister while you're in your meetings. Then maybe we could spend some time together soaking up warm sunshine."

"Maybe," Gemma said non-committal. "I may have to fly right back for work the following day. I'll see what I can do."

Charlie took a long look at Gemma as if questioning what she was saying, what she was not saying. She looked back at him.

"Charlie, I—" Gemma started to say.

"Gemma, please ..." He cut her off and then paused as if thinking better of it.

They stopped and nervously chuckled. Both looked at their feet before regaining composure.

"Please, let me just say, I like you a lot. I want to spend more time with you. I can't see you during the day anymore. You're exhausted at night, so I feel guilty disturbing you then. I'm trying to think of any way I can spend some quality time with you, even if it's in an airplane or on a beach." Charlie blinked several times before averting his eyes.

She watched his confession intently. "Charlie, I like you too. I can't believe how exhausted I am at the end of the day. I barely have enough energy to eat what little I can when I get home. I wish I had more time to spend with you too. I like you. In some ways, this feels too fast. In other ways, it feels not fast enough," Gemma confessed shyly.

"Gemma, you hold the cards. I'm here," he said, his fingers brushing across her cheek.

She leaned forward to stretch her arms up toward his neck. He gathered her into his arms, pulled her into his lap, and kissed her as she had hoped he would for the last week.

When their lips parted, he did not let her go and continued to hold her in his lap, close to his heart.

After a few minutes, Gemma reluctantly returned to her pillows, and they regained their banter, snacking on more food and wine.

When their jaunt through the park was finished, Charlie and Gemma alighted and went back to her condominium, hand in hand.

Inside her foyer, their kissing resumed, more intense in want and need. Gemma's lips parted, and her tongue searched for his. They danced together, leaving her moaning at the intensity of desire that flared between them. His hair slipped through her fingers like satiny ribbons. An aroma, whether shampoo, soap, or aftershave, was spicy and tantalizing, making her salivate. It had been so long since she'd had any interest in intimacy. Far too long.

Charlie's hands traveled lower along her back until they squeezed her buttocks, straining to pull her closer to his taller frame.

And his cell phone began ringing.

Gemma could feel the firm muscles of his back stretching as he held her to him. "Aren't you going to get that?"

"I don't answer when I'm thus occupied." He pressed his erection, so full and firm, against her abdomen. The wetness between her legs was unmistakable. The throbbing of her need for him was undeniable, nearly desperate after so many years. She broke their kiss to whisper, "It's been a very long time for me."

"Are you okay?" Charlie asked quietly, concern coloring his words.

"We'll have to take it slow. It's an ugly scar."

"I'll be as gentle as I can. I don't care how your scar looks. You are beautiful," he whispered. "I'll stop any moment you want me to. Just say the word. Any reason, Gemma."

"Don't stop unless I tell you to," she whispered back, pulling his lips back within kissing range.

• • • •

GEMMA PICKED UP THE ringing phone the next day. "Hello?"

"How was your date?" Heather and Chelsea said together over the phone.

"You guys," She replied with a sigh that was almost a purr. "It was great."

"Wow! I never thought I'd hear you say that." Chelsea laughed. "You hate men."

"Me?" Gemma's voice rose an octave. "I don't hate men. I refuse to trust them. The whole lot of them are untrustworthy. But I do enjoy having someone around for sexual gratification."

"So the sex was good?" Chelsea teased.

"Good enough." Gemma purred. "I think I'll keep Charlie around for a little while."

• • • •

"HI. WELCOME TO SLIMLINE. I'm Rebecca Standish," A pencil-thin, pin-neat brunette said with an overly tense smile. "A new year, a new you!"

For God's sake! The woman was so thin she had no curves. Maybe it was her clothes. A wave of unease rolled through Chelsea's gut. How the heck was someone who clearly didn't have a weight problem going to help her? Maybe she shouldn't have waited until after the holidays to start.

Chelsea shook the outstretched hand and looked to pick the best seat. "Here, please sit here," Rebecca said, gesturing to a nicely upholstered chair.

"Thanks. I'm Chelsea Whitcom." Chelsea shrugged out of her coat before sitting down. She watched Rebecca hang her coat on the back of the office door. Chelsea examined the small meeting room as Rebecca returned to her seat. The plain white walls were devoid of any pictures or charts. Two steel and plastic chairs were placed on opposite sides of the rectangular steel table. She shivered at the cold, stark room's sterile vibe. The only color in the room besides the two people was from a black leather appointment book and a yellow manila file folder on the tabletop.

"I'll be your weight loss counselor for your time at Slimline. Did the reservationist tell you about our initial meeting today?" Rebecca asked after settling herself down in the chair beside Chelsea's.

"Yes, a little. I can't remember."

"This is what we'll do today. First, I'd like to get a baseline on you. We'll get your current weight to start." She gestured toward the bathroom-style scale behind her.

They both stood beside the scale. "Are you ready?" Rebecca asked.

Chelsea ignored the lump in her throat and stepped on the scale. She averted her eyes toward the ceiling rather than look at the digital number.

"One hundred ninety-six," Rebecca said as she wrote the starting number on the file folder.

Wordless, they sat back down at the table.

"Now, I'll ask you some questions about your goals and eating habits to get an idea of who you are. Then we'll discuss how to go about the program. Does that sound familiar?"

Chelsea nodded in agreement. Her scrutiny of this counselor was giving her the willies. The woman's makeup was flawless; her hair was perfectly styled. Her clothes were immaculate and expensive. Not a pill on her cashmere sweater.

"Excellent. So, let's get started. Each week you'll come here for a brief meeting with me. It takes only fifteen minutes or less. We discuss issues that creep up during the last week or challenges you are expecting in the coming week. I'll try to suggest strategies to deal with any problems you need help with. At the end of the session, I'll get the meal plan selections for you, and then you're off. We try very hard to make the weekly meetings quick and painless." Rebecca's cherry-red lipstick accentuated her plump lips as they pursed momentarily before arcing into a gentile smile.

"Sounds good. I work at a beauty salon plus own my own business, so having appointments that stay on time will be appreciated," Chelsea said, swiping back a stray lock of hair.

Rebecca picked up a folder sitting on the desktop. "So, tell me about your eating habits while growing up. Tell me about your family."

Chelsea shifted in her seat. What could she say?

"My father died when I was about eight. My mother worked hard, she spoiled my brother, Toby, and me as much as she could, but we weren't rich. We weren't poor either. We had a roof, we always had food." There was no way she was admitting their clothes came from the Goodwill store, and the food was either from the food pantry at church or bought with state assistance money. Miss Fashion Model, in front of her, might be too revolted.

"What kinds of food do you remember eating as you were growing up?" Rebecca asked, pen poised over the paper inside the folder.

"The usual. Spaghetti, hot dogs, hamburgers, mac-n-cheese. We always had those snack cakes in our lunch bags. Mom would get them at the bakery outlet store. We had pies too. On special days, like birthdays, we had pizza and ice cream."

"What about now? What's your typical breakfast, lunch, and dinner like?"

"Breakfast during the week is a bagel with cream cheese or peanut butter. On weekends we splurge on pancakes or omelets." Chelsea rubbed her chin. "Lunches at work are microwavable frozen foods like Hot Pockets or Lean Cuisines. Dinners are homemade but not always." She glanced away from Rebecca's gaze. "We do eat out a couple times a week."

"What kinds of snacking do you do?" Rebecca asked, pen scribbling and ticking away as she spoke.

"Pretzels, chips, crackers, peanuts. You know, the usual." Chelsea felt her armpits starting to perspire. She readjusted her chair. She knew her eating habits were terrible. The embarrassment of discussing them was making her feel defeated and angry with herself. *I should have tried harder.*

"What types of beverages do you drink throughout the day?"

Clearly, Rebecca was into present-day eating habits. "I have a couple cups of coffee in the morning, a couple sodas at lunchtime and dinner. Maybe a beer or two in the evening, a few times a week, especially if we go out with friends."

Rebecca flipped the paper over. "How often would you say you go out to eat?" The pen continued to dance over the paper. Chelsea could see the cap on the end bobbing and weaving.

"Two or three sometimes, four at most. Depends on the week, or birthdays or whatnot."

Rebecca's eyes locked onto Chelsea's like a bulldog, "How many times a day do you eat a fruit or vegetable?"

"Maybe one of each at most." A blush crept up Chelsea's face while a sinking feeling filled her gut. She knew better. And she knew this would be one of those issues Rebecca would be harping about throughout her time on Slimline. It wasn't that she didn't like vegetables. And she liked fruit. They were just ... boring.

Rebecca smiled at Chelsea. "We're almost done, three more questions to go!" She flipped to a new sheet of paper and continued the inquisition. "How many times have you seriously tried to lose weight before?"

Gazing off into space, Chelsea tried to count them. "Maybe a dozen or so?" Her voice lifted with the uncertainty of the number. It was probably a lot more, but she didn't need to own up to every single one. A dozen was bad enough.

The pen paused again. Rebecca folded her hands together on her lap. She eased back in her chair, and her eyes and hands focused on picking at a microscopic piece of lint on her sleeve. "What types of weight loss options have you tried?"

"Everything. Well—this is the first time I'm trying Slimline, but I've done everything else," Chelsea admitted, a tone of exasperation creeping into her voice.

"Final question: Why do you want to lose weight?" Rebecca's eyes bore into Chelsea's over the small space between them. She said it with the deadly serious tone Chelsea used to hear on the game show, *Who Wants To Be A Millionaire?*

Chelsea's eyes locked on Rebecca's. They stared at each other, speechless. Chelsea shrugged and shook her head. She hadn't expected that question. The second hand on a clock somewhere in the room ticked the length of the silence. What could she say? There were a hundred reasons she'd tried to lose weight before today. Everything from an upcoming vacation to her jeans getting too tight to going to a friend's wedding. None of those reasons had been incentive enough to get the weight down where it should be and keep it off.

But this time, the reason was too important to her to NOT work.

"I'm getting married."

Rebecca smiled broadly. "Congratulations."

Chelsea wasn't sure if she was being congratulated for being engaged or for having a wedding as a reason to lose weight.

She went straight from the Slimline appointment to Jitters Café to meet Gemma and Heather.

She got her favorite coffee drink and sat down wordlessly at the table.

Gemma bumped Heather's shoulder. "Oh no. She has a salted caramel macchiato with chocolate swirls. You know what that means."

Chelsea scowled. "Shut up. Not everyone can have surgery and lose lots of weight." Her eyes glinted with a fierce sparkle. "It's going to be awful. I know it."

The chatter at the table died.

"Let me share some advice I got from one of my previous Calorie Counters sessions," Heather said tentatively. "Pricilla says when most of us come to CC, we think of our weight loss as a struggle. A war is declared on our own bodies, but this thinking is self-defeating. By calling it a struggle, it really becomes a struggle. It doesn't have to be a struggle. Every tool we need is available to us. We live in one of the richest countries in the world. If we want to eat blueberries in January, we can buy them at the local grocer. There is no struggle in our weight loss unless we deem it so."

"Thank you, Buddha," Chelsea said, rolling her eyes up to heaven, not even trying to hide her sarcastic tone of voice.

•　•　•　•

BIG CHANGES WERE GOING on in Marla's body. Parts of her were jiggling and bouncing far more than usual. Her skin was flabby, though the fitness trainer and dietician both assured her it would firm back up. She was young enough to have some elasticity left in her skin. Speaking of elasticity, her socks were staying up on her calves instead of sliding down all the time as she walked.

Her biggest concern now was about jogging. Despite the sports bra, she was concerned the bouncing boobs would knock her out or, at the very least, give her a black eye or bloody nose one of these days.

It was frightening to know that her "firm" had dissolved into something jiggling worse than Jell-O. Every movement she made, Marla swore could be registered on some earth-tremor monitoring equipment somewhere in the world. There was just too much flesh quivering of its own accord. The last thing Marla wanted was a thin body draped in yards of loose, dangling skin. Surgical removal would always be an option, but it wouldn't be her first choice if there were other ways.

• • • •

"DID YOU INVITE MARLA?" Chelsea asked Heather. The three women sat around Chelsea's coffee table in the small apartment living room.

"Of course I did. She made some sorry excuse." Heather turned to Chelsea. "You scared her when you asked about marriage."

Chelsea flung up her hands. "Of course, it's all my fault. Could it be she's just too sensitive?"

"Whatever. Don't ask her about that kind of stuff again," Heather said sternly. "I want her to feel safe and welcome with us. Just like before."

Chelsea started to reach for the plate of rice cakes.

"Don't. You'll regret it." Gemma grasped Chelsea's hand to stop her reach.

"I like him. He's not pushy," Gemma murmured out loud.

"Who's that?" Chelsea asked. She reached for a rice cake when Gemma wasn't looking. She eyed it with narrowed lids, took a bite, and started to chew. Once she swallowed, she stuck out her tongue and pointed her finger down her throat.

"She warned you they weren't worth the calories," Heather reminded her.

Chelsea ignored Heather's comment. "Who are you talking about?"

"The guy I met at my condo complex. He's nice. He asked me out on a date for Saturday," Gemma said.

"What?" Chelsea blurted. "You met a guy, and you didn't tell us?"

"I guess it slipped my mind. I met him in September, I think it was. We've had a few meetups over the last few months."

"Do you think it's safe?" Heather asked.

"He's lived there much longer than I have. I don't see why he wouldn't be. He even cleans the snow off my car and shovels the walk."

Heather interjected again. "But what do you know of him?"

"Enough, but I'm hoping to find out more Saturday," Gemma said, a mischievous smile spreading across her face.

• • • •

MARLA THOUGHT ABOUT the coffee get-together with her old friends from camp. She'd blown off the last scheduled meeting though she did tell Heather she couldn't make it. She hadn't explained why. Marla tried not to let the embarrassment of backing out of the meeting bring down her good mood. Truth was, she was still uncomfortable being with anyone, including these women. Sure, she had known them back in 2001. But that didn't mean she was going to be enthusiastic reuniting with them now. Except for Heather.

When and if Heather called again, and Marla knew she would, she'd deal with the situation. Maybe by then, she'd feel confident enough to meet them again. Chelsea's questioning about marriage had shaken her to her core. She couldn't discuss Sam and what happened. She hadn't been married, but still, if they went further with the inquiry, she would have shattered into a thousand pieces.

LATE JANUARY 2018

I know how this food system works! The food sucks so bad, you don't want to eat any of it! Chelsea dropped her fork in the sink and hurled the barely touched Slimline System "dinner entrée" into the trash can. *How do they make any money with this crap? Only those desperate would eat it.* Her gumption confirmed she wasn't that desperate yet.

There were two rules in Slimline. Never eat while standing, and always eat the prescribed food. She routinely broke both rules. She reached for the Granny Smith apple on the table. This was not allowed in her diet yet, but it was probably more nutritious than that high-fiber meatloaf. She couldn't even swallow a mouthful of the stuff.

Back in the living room, she flipped through the news channels for the weather report. A long hot soak in the bathtub was her intent, but the couch was calling her name. Before she knew it, Chelsea was splayed out like a hussy, watching an *American Idol* episode instead of soaking out the sweat and stiffness of her late afternoon Flex-a-Belle workout.

She hated the circuit fitness machines but hoped to lose weight and be more toned for her wedding. It would be nice to have Michelle Obama arms with her sleeveless dress. The machines helped build up her muscles. She felt more toned, but the weight issue wasn't going anywhere.

Chelsea wasn't too keen on the Slimline System. It was hard to say which was worse, the expensive food or the weekly meetings with her counselor, who tsked over Chelsea's abbreviated food diary and "poor food choices" over the week. After her fifteen minutes of verbal knuckle beatings, she was sent off with some cutesy infuriating phrase like "doing your best for a thinner you." Six weeks into Slimline, and she'd only managed to lose three pounds.

"Rebecca says it's my lack of commitment to the system," Chelsea huffed at the last *Girly* meeting, as the three of them now called their get-togethers.

"Well ..." Gemma glanced down at Chelsea's plate of breaded buffalo wings.

"Don't you start, Gemma. Not everyone can have surgery to lose weight instantly." Gemma and Heather winced at the bitter edge of Chelsea's words. "I haven't lost weight because I've gained muscle mass since I started at Flex-a-Belle. Everyone knows muscle weighs more than fat tissue. And it helps burn more calories."

In theory, it sounded good. In practice, Chelsea knew it was her poor food choices. She couldn't eat Slimline food at every meal. First, it was excessively expensive. Supplementing was allowed, of course, although it "slows the results." How buying their brand of corn flakes was better than Kellogg's Corn Flakes, Rebecca couldn't clearly explain beyond saying it was the "vitamin and mineral" content. *More likely, it was half sawdust, like it tasted.*

Second, the food generally tasted all the same. It all sucked. Every entrée had beans, cumin, and chili powder. Every entrée smelled exactly the same. Well, maybe the breakfast things tasted okay, but the lunch and dinner entrées, which were most of what Chelsea purchased, were like eating chili dressed up a dozen different ways.

She generally only took a couple bites and tossed the remainder. She ate the salad or vegetables. She also ate fruit, which was not part of the early phase of the diet system. It made her feel like she was having a complete meal and satisfied her hunger. And the fruit's sugars satisfied her sweet tooth for the time being.

"Maybe. But you have to admit, wings are not on your diet," shot back Gemma with a look of disdain.

"You're just jealous you can't eat real food yet." She waved a hot sauce-slathered wing in front of Gemma's face with one hand while the other gesticulated at Gemma's crock of pea soup.

Intervening, Heather threw up her arms between them across the tabletop. "Enough already. Sheesh, I hear enough whining at home."

Chelsea felt bad thinking of the incident now. Gemma was right. She never should have had buffalo wings yesterday. Especially since they were breaded *and* fried. But there were some things she couldn't give up totally.

Like bread. She loved bread—any shape, size, or form. She'd nearly walked out of the Slimline Office when Rebecca mentioned bread was on the prohibited list. Much as Chelsea tried, she couldn't break the bread habit. She'd managed to reduce her intake from four to five slices a day to only two. It was the best she could do for now.

To make it even harder, her live-in fiancé was a big, hard-working carpenter. A big guy who liked to eat big meals. She knew Heather had the same sort of problem with Billy. They had talked about it a few times at their *Girly* meetings. Fortunately for her, Seth knew enough cooking to fend for himself when he wanted. Unfortunately, Chelsea felt bad for him most of the time.

While she tried to choke down the Slimline meals, she put her heart and soul into making him a fabulous meal most nights: Steak with oven fries, lasagna, chicken and dumplings, veal parmesan, corned beef with all the fixings, ham steak and scalloped potatoes, lamb chops rubbed with Adobo seasoning and simmered with a spicy sofrito sauce over rice and beans. Of course, she had to taste test as she cooked to make sure the seasoning was okay. They were only tiny bites.

Unlike Heather with her husband, she could sit with Seth while he ate, relishing the gusto with which he dove into each meal while she ate one of her Slimline meals or drank a cup of flavored green tea or a bottle of flavored seltzer.

Chelsea knew that Seth knew the score. He had tried several times to wrestle Chelsea away from the food preparation. But she was clinging to it as a matter of duty. After all, that's what a wife would be expected to do, make meals. He let it go after a couple of fights, knowing sooner or later, either she'd quit the ridiculous plan or she'd quit cooking. Chelsea knew he wasn't usually a betting man, but she wasn't sure which side he'd bet on if asked.

• • • •

"HELLO?" HEATHER JUGGLED the phone on her shoulder while sitting on the living room couch, folding a pair of the boys' pants.

"Hi. Is this Heather?" an overly exhilarated feminine voice said.

"Yes. To whom am I speaking?" Heather asked politely, perplexed at the voice of this person who knew her.

"It's Cindy! Cindy Devenshear! Remember me from high school?" she squealed as her vocal cords strained into higher registers of audible sound.

Reflexively, Heather pulled the receiver a half foot away from her ear to protect her eardrums. "Yes, hi Cindy." She remained polite despite wanting to hang up. *What the heck does she want?* She tucked the phone back on her shoulder and resumed folding clothes at a slower pace.

"Did you hear the news? There's going to be a ten-year reunion! In May! I'm so excited. I'm calling everyone I can find in the phone book to let them know," Cindy prattled swiftly.

"That's great, Cindy. How nice of you to notify everyone," Heather said as kindly as she could muster, tugging too hard on a pant leg and toppling several items out of the laundry basket onto the floor.

"I'm so excited to be seeing y'all again so soon. How've ya been?" Cindy asked, chirping faster than an agitated squirrel.

"Fine, and you?" *How can I get off this phone?* She picked up the dropped items, placing them on her lap.

"I can hardly wait!" Cindy paused for a few seconds. "Is Billy there? Can I tell him the news myself?" Cindy asked, her voice getting a little squeaky and flustered.

"He's on the john," Heather said. "Let me get him for you." *Enjoy that pretty image.* She smirked. Covering the earpiece, she yelled for Billy to get the phone.

Billy came out of the bathroom and flopped the Motor Trend magazine on the recliner. Taking the phone from Heather's hand, he mouthed, "Who is it?"

"Your old girlfriend, you know—the one who dumped you after getting on the cheerleading squad, when she had all the football players sniffing after her, licking their chops." Heather turned back to the TV and resumed folding the tangled mess in the laundry basket. She held a handful of the lavender-scented clothes to her nose and inhaled. Lavender worked to calm the children, but it didn't help her blood pressure.

Billy sauntered back to the kitchen with a quizzical look. "Hello?"

Heather watched him through the kitchen arch. His face lit up with delight.

"Well, I'll be damned. Cindy Devenshear. What a surprise!" Billy chuckled. He listened intently for a few minutes, his smile stretching as the seconds ticked.

"Is that so? No shittin'? That'll be great." Heather watched his chest puff out like an inflating helium balloon. He cocked his hip to one side, striking a jaunty pose only Heather could see.

"Well, *you* can bet your ass I'll be there. Don't know about Heather, but I expect she'll come along too." Billy laughed.

"Okay, Cindy, I'll be lookin' out for the invite. Thanks for callin'. Bye," He cooed into the phone before disconnecting.

Billy swaggered into the living room, his hands on his hips, a grin on his face, and a sparkle in his eyes. "Can you believe it? Cindy Devenshear, callin' about a reunion."

"Yup. In May," Heather replied, snapping the wrinkles out of a hand towel so violently Snoopy startled awake under the coffee table.

"I'll be damned," Billy said, heading back to the kitchen again, the magazine back under his arm. Heather heard the refrigerator door open and the cracking sound of a can of beer opening. Billy kicked a chair out to sit in, spread the magazine on the kitchen table, and began reading.

Heather didn't like the spark of intensity still on his face. He was thinking of something, something he shouldn't be thinking. Heather was sure of that by the glint in his eyes, eyes that weren't reading the newsprint.

• • • •

GEMMA AND CHARLIE SAW each other at least four times a week. He was always available. Sometimes he spent the night. Other nights Gemma sent him home after a quick dinner of takeout. Her days at the office were still tiring her out by the end of the day. She needed to talk to her doctor about that issue. Her weight was down to one hundred fifteen pounds. Maybe it was too low?

• • • •

MARLA HAD BEEN KEEPING up with the progress at the Seattle laboratory. She and Andrea Bekkit talked almost weekly about which inspections were scheduled and when. Andrea also forwarded all the inspection notifications.

Much as she wanted, she never asked about Doctor Brighton. Some days she had to physically bite her tongue to keep from uttering any questions about him. The most she had been able to dig up was that he had completed all the required Peabody training sessions.

At least three to four times a day, she looked at his picture hanging on her refrigerator. She had no idea how much he had changed physically. There wasn't much on the internet. His last job had already scrubbed his name from their websites. One small article came up in her search, basically describing his education. It said nothing about any relationships, marriage, or children.

Marla fervently prayed there weren't any

EARLY FEBRUARY 2018

"Thanks for coming. It was great to see you too," Chelsea and Seth said in unison as the last couple left their party.

"Thanks for the guacamole. It was delicious," Chelsea called out to Eva from next door.

Seth locked the apartment door while Chelsea returned to face the disaster of a living room and kitchen. It was essentially one room. Only a kitchen island separated the two spaces from each other. An island covered with empty beer bottles, dirty margarita glasses, and paper plates of food residue. A crockpot and a few empty platters remained to be washed.

"That was good. Thanks," Seth said, engulfing her in his arms from behind. "I'll give you a hand with the cleanup."

Chelsea sank back into his firm chest, enjoying the warmth, comfort, and support he gave so freely. She wanted to stay like that forever, feeling loved and safe with the man who had become indispensable in her life. She hoped he stayed so demonstrative and helpful after they were married.

Thoughts of her father reared up. He had been indispensable once, too. And yet he had left. He hadn't had much choice in the matter, but still, his unexpected death left a huge hole in her heart. A hole Seth had filled with love and tenderness. It could happen to Seth. What if he died too? Chelsea's entire body shivered with the morbid thought. It was like being doused with a bucket of ice water.

"You darn well better help, this Super Bowl party was for you," she teased back and stepped away to begin the task. She grabbed a handful of empty beer bottles by the neck, carting them to the kitchen sink for rinsing.

Thankfully, she listened to Rebecca's advice for a change.

If you have a party, send leftovers home with the person who brought the dish so you won't have temptation left in the house.

It had worked well, not that there was much food left over, but what little there was, was definitely not on her diet: chips, sour cream dip, BBQ wings, and some artichoke dip. Chelsea didn't keep those kinds of items in the house anymore, even for Seth; she sure as hell wasn't going to put up with them under her nose now.

The living room had been tight with guests. Their group of friends all came. The only person who had declined to attend was Marla. And that was no surprise. Heather, Gemma, and Chelsea frequently invited Marla to go places with them. She always declined, using excuses like personal trainer, dietician, or yoga classes. She did attend their coffee meetings.

Some of the guests had brought junk food, appetizers, and snacks. By arrangement, her closest friends Diane, Colleen, and Gemma all brought something on the healthier side: Diane brought sliced turkey and lean roast beef finger sandwiches, Colleen had brought two different kinds of hummus, and Gemma had brought some cooked shrimp and cocktail sauce. Heather declined the invitation because she didn't want to bring Billy and watch him get embarrassingly drunk in front of her friends.

Monica had brought a vegetarian chili that the guys had scoffed at initially. Until Charlie tried it and gave it two thumbs up. In ten minutes, the guys had emptied her crockpot.

Chelsea had supplied more healthy choices: crudités and fresh fruit kebabs, which were a big hit. All evening she had managed to stay with the healthier snacks.

Unfortunately, she hadn't been able to stay away from the beer, although she did switch to a light variety and alternated it with flavored seltzer water. She'd still consumed more calories in the last five hours than she should have for the next two days.

She felt no remorse. It was the Super Bowl party. And while the Pittsburgh Steelers weren't playing, the game between the Eagles and the Patriots was a nail-biter.

• • • •

MARLA HAD MORE IMPORTANT things to focus her attention on. Problems like her armpits. Shaving her armpits was nearly impossible now. The weight loss had resulted in concave armpits, which were impossible to shave normally. It took some advanced yoga poses to stretch the pit area flat enough for a razor head to do its work. Thank God she'd been doing yoga. There would be no other choice but to ask someone to pull the skin flat while she shaved. And there was *no one* close enough in her life to merit that job.

More importantly, it was time she took the next big step. Her dietician advised her to start seeing a psychologist specializing in eating disorders to tackle any unresolved issues that might be lurking behind Marla's old eating habits. She should have done it sooner but wasn't ready to face one. Furthermore, her binge eating habits had not given her much trouble in the seven months since starting her diet. The trauma of the airplane incident had been that powerful to her psyche.

At her first appointment, the psychologist, Dr. Kennedy, was nice, although he gave Marla a few instructions and some homework after listening to a short recitation of her life history. He asked her to keep a daily journal. To start, she would write the answers to four questions. Dr. Kennedy told her to be as truthful in answering them as she could. It was an exercise meant to help her get to the bottom of her eating habits.

She sat down later than evening with her new spiral-bound notebook and glanced at the first question on the list: Why are you here? Marla mashed her lips together. She proceeded to fill ten pages, front and back, with a description of the airplane incident and how she felt during and after it. How she never wanted to feel so humiliated about her weight ever again. She briefly added how she'd been overweight since she was about six years old, always unable to overcome the temptation of food.

Marla moved on to question two: List the things you didn't do because you felt you were physically unable, psychologically unwilling, or emotionally unready to do because of your weight. Whoa. Marla thought. This was getting pretty deep.

She pondered the first part of the question: physically unable to do because she was too fat. A scene of a trip to Disney World swung through her mind. Yes, she'd been unable to go on several rides at Disney World because she was too fat for the seats. She couldn't fit behind the safety bar and thus could not go on the Thunder Mountain ride. Then more memories came tumbling into focus, one after another, too fast for Marla to write down.

She closed her eyes and flushed with the humiliation of each event as they replayed in her mind. When she could not think of any more, she slowed her panting breath, wiped her tears away, and started writing. In an effort to keep the responses short, she kept the anecdotes down to a couple sentences.

In all, she recalled over thirty-seven different events. The seatbelt extensions on planes and in cars, Changing tables in restaurants when sitting at fixed tables would not accommodate her belly. Having to make special seating arrangements in college classrooms when she could no longer fit into the flip top student desk chairs.

Exhausted by the emotional reenactments each brought, Marla crossed her arms on the table, laid her head down, and was silent for almost an hour in meditation.

When she lifted her head, she was ready to resume the work on those things she was psychologically unwilling to do. Again, the scenes were slow to come, but they accelerated as they accumulated in her remembrances. Missing her best friend's birthday party at the water park because she didn't want anyone to see her in a bathing suit. Taking clothes home from the store to try them on because no one should have to look at her fat, ugly ass in a dressing room. Skipping out on her high school prom, the high school dances. Giving up playing the flute because she didn't want to sit on a stage during concerts and be the object of jeers and jokes. The plays and musicals she so much wanted to participate in but didn't because she didn't want to a) make herself an object of ridicule and b) no one was going to give the fat girl a part anyway. Skipping her pinning ceremony in college because the scholar's gown made her look like a hippo.

Again, Marla laid her head down and chanted a mantra for peaceful meditation, metta, and loving kindness. It was hard to face the past. Especially the past hurt she had avoided and how much it had stolen from her life.

Last, she tackled the emotional uneasiness. All the times she turned down things because of her own self-loathing. The award she refused to accept at the senior awards banquet because she didn't feel worthy of the praise. The job offer she refused because she didn't feel she could handle being a laboratory manager—no one would ever respect a fat manager. It was easier to be the inspector everyone would hate anyway.

She looked over the third question. What single biggest event was the hardest of your life?

Marla toyed with the pen, biting her lip. The sting of tears in her eyes forced her to close them. Then she wrote pages. Wrote about Sam and their wedding day. The wedding she never ever thought she would have as a fat girl. She should have known it was too good to be true. Her body flared with an inferno of heat. No, she couldn't blame Sam. He was true to her. He was her best friend. It wasn't his fault he had died in that car accident on the way to the church. Marla wrote about the policemen coming to the church, where she waited for her groom. Of being brought into a room by the priest. Of being told her fiancé was dead. She set down the pen, unable to see the lines on the page for the flood in her eyes. Huge gulping sobs erupted and continued unabated for what felt like forever.

When Marla cried herself out, she got herself a glass of wine. She deserved it after dealing with all that crap from her past. When the glass was empty, she went to bed.

The next morning, recharged in spirit, she delved into the last question: Imagine what the new you will do. List some of the things you have never experienced that you would like to do when you reach a normal weight.

Holy crap! Marla thought. *I've never even given it any thought. How will I live? Will I change? What would I like to do?* Her pulse raced at the prospect of ... of what? *What do I call it?* In the back of her mind, the word came screaming forward louder and louder, echoing with a richness, a resonance so powerful she was glad she was sitting down. The word was "freedom."

The first word Marla wrote was Massage. She wanted a body massage. She could get one now, but she would feel like the woman would be cringing at the rolls of blubber she would have to push through to reach Marla's muscles. Marla closed her eyes and let her mind wander through the forgotten closets, opening locked doors to peek inside at her most secret desires. When she found one, she wrote it down.

An hour later, when she could not find anything else to add to the list, she sat back and reviewed it. They weren't in any particular order. Marla heard herself giggle, feeling heady with the thought of all these wondrous things now almost within her grasp.

Massage
Swimming & diving
Dancing
Wear a leather skirt
Hiking
Motorcycle riding

Boating
Camping
Skiing
Dating

An image of Dr. Brighton's face blazed through Marla's mind. Impulsively, she added one more word to her list.

Sex.

The heat of a blush rose up her neck and face at the thought of sharing her answers with Dr. Kennedy. That's what this is for, she thought. Getting it out in the open.

• • • •

HEATHER REACHED FOR the door handle, paused a second while taking a deep, determined breath, opened the door, and descended into Calorie Counters.

Again. Here she was again. This time the motivation was her high school reunion in May. Six months ago, she had decided she wanted to look good for her baby brother's wedding. Getting rid of the extra baby fat around her middle had been important, for about five weeks anyway. She gave up after losing only six pounds and hadn't returned.

Prior to that time, she had been there about a year and a half ago. Again, only for about four weeks of the program. She had decided to get rid of the baby fat then, too but gave up when she found out she was pregnant with Michelle.

Back in 2012, Heather tried Calorie Counters after baby number two, Nicholas. Colleen had also gone with her on that attempt and had lost five pounds in the first two weeks, as had Heather. Then Colleen had quit, citing "diet limitation difficulties," which in Colleen's world meant she wasn't giving up her Guinness for no one, no how. Heather didn't want to go alone, so she quit.

Heather gave up when Billy's whining about taking care of the baby became high-octane frustration. He had his baseball games, after all. The team was counting on him to be there. He couldn't disappoint the team on Wednesday evenings because Heather had Calorie Counters. Taking the baby to practice and games didn't work. Nicholas had nearly been hit in his car seat by a pop-up foul ball. Besides, he cried constantly whenever he wasn't with Heather. His team members didn't appreciate it either.

How I even have the gall to show my face here again is beyond me. Heather suddenly understood Colleen's reluctance to join her. There were probably several dozen meetings within the Pittsburgh area or a reasonable distance away. While she would rather go anywhere than back here for the fourth time, this time and location were the most convenient. She didn't have that much time to travel, let alone stay for the entire meeting. Some days it was hard enough to get away for the weekly weigh-in. Chelsea wanted her to go to Slimline with her, but it was way more expensive than Heather's budget could handle. Marla's method sounded reasonable, but Heather knew herself well enough after nearly twenty-nine years to know she needed a structured program with accountability.

The basement was as dingy as she recalled from her last visit. The curtains were still the light blue gingham, pale against the darkness of the night. The registration table was staffed by no one she recognized. Maybe she could get away without being noticed as a habitual repeat failure. A prodigal daughter yet again coming in to roost for a few weeks in her futile quest to be as thin as her high school days.

If I could only get back to that size, Billy would treat me as he did then. Be warm and loving, unable to keep his hands off me. She smiled, thinking of necking in the school's hidden corners and closets. A shiver of excitement ran up her spine at memories of those lust-filled days. It was safer now with her tubes tied; sex could return to being fun again, if she ever felt like her body was worth it. And if Billy thought it was worth the effort too.

Four pregnancies and three kids had ravaged her physically and mentally. Her breasts were worse than partially deflated water balloons, her waist was no longer definable, and her hips and ass were one big round tire above two thickened legs and swollen feet. She refused to undress in front of Billy anymore. He hadn't touched her since Michelle was born over a year ago.

In ten short years, Heather felt she had gone from pretty to childbirth hag. She wanted to see her old friends again; she didn't want anyone else to see her. She didn't want Billy to see all the girls he gave up for her, Cindy Devenshear in particular.

Registration was easy enough as no one recognized her from all her previous attempts. She received the new pocket guide. Flipping through it, it looked as though it might help.

Her weigh-in was one hundred seventy-seven pounds on a five-foot-five, small-boned frame that should only hold one hundred forty at the most. Heather was flabbergasted. She gave up weighing herself after Michelle was born in 2016.

• • • •

GEMMA FLUNG THE BRAS on the checkout counter with a huff.

"Did you find everything you needed?" the salesclerk asked absently, pulling the bras off their hangers and folding them as neatly as an octopus could be folded.

"No," Gemma grated through clenched teeth. She dropped her handbag on the counter and dug for her wallet.

"If you'd like, I can get our personal shopper to assist you right now. Would you like that?" the clerk hesitated in her folding to reach for the phone behind her.

"No, I've already tried on nearly every bra in the last two hours. It seems you don't stock my size, so I'll have to get the closest available." Gemma stared her down until the woman let go of the phone and continued ringing up the sale. No one told her that she'd lose her boobs while losing weight.

Her boobs had fallen out of the bottom of her bra. Added to that stunt, the straps were constantly slipping down her shoulders. It started at Chelsea's Super Bowl party. Fortunately, she was wearing a heavy sweatshirt over a Tee-shirt, so it wasn't noticeable, albeit highly uncomfortable. It was now of the highest priority to replace her bras.

She snatched her bag off the counter and stalked out of the department store. The new ill-fitting bras would have to do until she could make a trip to the specialty lingerie shop downtown.

• • • •

A DOZEN WOMEN WERE gathered in the seating area, sitting on the metal folding chairs, not quite brown, not quite gray in color, but always cold. Heather took an empty seat in the back row. She didn't recognize anyone until the actual program began. Out walked pencil thin, Pricilla Heinz, all five foot eleven, dark maroon lipstick, false lashes, dark brown eyeshadow smeared from the edge of her eyelashes to her eyebrows. Her hair was short and gelled into spikes that stood up on the top of her head like a modified Mohawk. It had been an angled bob last time.

"Hi ladies, welcome back! Oh, and a special welcome back to Heather. So glad you could join us again." Pricilla's voice grated on Heather's nerves like fingernails on a blackboard. Heather nodded a shy acknowledgment, mortified to be singled out when she wanted to remain anonymous.

"Tonight, I'd like to review some tips on how to keep the between-meal snacking to a minimum." Pricilla's voice was heavy with innuendo, like a naughty-nighty demonstrator at an exclusive bachelorette party. "I bet you ladies didn't know your weight loss best friend is your toothbrush."

Good God, next time I'm only coming for the weigh-in.

• • • •

"SO YOU'RE GOING TO the reunion?" Gemma asked, working her way through a small Caesar salad.

"There's no way Billy won't want to go after his old girlfriend called." Heather's face crumpled. She was on the verge of tears. "I started back to Calorie Counters last night."

"Don't cry, Heather." Chelsea took her friend's hand in her own and squeezed it. "It will be alright."

Gemma intervened. "It's okay to cry. I'm sure the entire situation looks like a minefield. All you can do is your best."

"Thank you, Dr. Phil." Chelsea rolled her eyes.

Gemma placed her arm around Heather's shoulders. "It will all work out. Now, Chelsea, how's the business going?"

"I've had to cut my hours at the salon to fit everyone in. The housing complex for the elderly alone gives me a full day of appointments. I don't charge them much, but it's enough for now. I also got some speaking engagements at area senior centers on nail and foot care. They don't pay much either, but I really enjoy those seniors. They remind me of my gram."

Heather cut in, "How is your weight loss program going?"

The woman wrinkled her nose. "It's not. Well, it was until the Super Bowl party. I need to get back on the wagon." She sighed. "It's so hard. I love what I normally eat. I don't want to change my food habits. I just—" She stopped a second to wipe her eyes. "I just want a magic pill or something fast to get this weight off for the wedding and then go back to normal."

"'The definition of insanity is doing the same thing over and over again and expecting different results,'" Heather said. "Even if you only want it off for an event, you have to change some things, no matter how temporary you might make it." She eyed her friend. "Can you follow the program long enough until the wedding?"

Chelsea sighed. "I'll try again."

Gemma piped up, "'Do or do not. There is no try.'"

Chelsea swatted the back of Gemma's head. "Thank you, Yoda."

LATE FEBRUARY 2018

The sun blinded Gemma when she walked out of the Miami airport. Shielding her eyes, she scanned the long line of cars crawling and parked along the arrivals pick-up area outside baggage claim. Where was the electric blue Honda she was supposed to find waiting for her?

"Gemma!" She heard her name called far off on the left. She turned to see a man standing outside a car about a football field away.

Cupping his mouth with his hands, Charlie yelled, "Wait there." He ducked back into the car. She watched it inch its way forward until she couldn't stand it anymore. She grabbed her carry-on bag and wheeled it down the ramp.

He hopped out of the vehicle and gave her a quick hug and kiss on the cheek before throwing the suitcase in the trunk. Gemma got into the car's backseat.

"What a mess!" Gemma said, exasperated. "Is it always like this?"

"I think there's an accident ahead that's fouling everything up," A brunette woman with short, cropped hair said from the driver's seat. Her hoop earrings jiggled as she turned to look at Gemma.

"Gemma, this is my sister Meg. Meg, this is Gemma," Charlie said, obviously remembering his manners. Both women gave each other a quick wave and a "hi" or "hello."

"How was your flight?" Charlie asked, trying to make small talk while Meg drove a slalom course through the arrivals loading area traffic.

"Uneventful. It's getting pretty bad though, even business class is getting cramped. I can't even imagine how bad coach was." Gemma was sorry she'd added the last part, not meaning to sound snobbish.

They were suddenly on an elevated freeway, giving her a view of postage stamp-sized residential yards, dry, dusty streets, and tall waving palm trees. The freeway turned into a causeway, the four lanes of traffic perched on stilts. Looking to the left, she could glimpse the blue of the ocean. Or was it the bay? Whatever they called it.

On the right, three huge cruise ships had docked, disgorging thousands of passengers after their trip. Someday, Gemma thought. I'm going to get back on one of you big bad boys. Or were they girls?

The car windows were all up, the air conditioner blasting. *Great.* After freezing to death on the plane, she could now refreeze in a car all the way to Miami Beach. What was the point of living in Florida, especially southern Florida, if you weren't going to enjoy the heat? *It's as nonsensical as buying a houseboat when you know you're prone to seasickness.* Gemma didn't think she would ever understand.

The silence in the car was deafening. She already felt a compelling regret about not calling a cab. It would have been far simpler and far less stressful. What Meg thought of all this, she had no clue. By her lack of conversation, Gemma figured Meg was either uninterested in Gemma or she was watching the traffic darting all around the car.

Charlie had arrived in Miami earlier in the week to visit his sister and her family. Gemma's plans had changed slightly in that she did not arrive until Thursday instead of Wednesday. He'd confessed on the phone that his nerves were strained by his two-year-old and five-year-old nieces. He insisted on picking her up at the airport, never telling her his sister would be the one driving. Did Meg not want to loan him her car? Was that why she was uncommunicative? Was she pissed at her brother? Why didn't he get his own rental while at the airport? Maybe Gemma should have picked up a rental instead, driven herself to the hotel, and had Charlie meet her there.

"The traffic has us running late, do you mind if we pick up the girls at daycare? We'll be driving right by," Meg explained.

What could she say? Gemma mused it should be a whole lot of fun in the backseat with two tots. She looked at the empty child seat on the opposite end of the back seat. A grungy, well-worn mini Beanie Baby horse dangled from the side strap.

"No problem," she replied, trying to suppress her rising ire. Where was the five-year-old going to sit? On her lap?

"We can trade places when we get to the daycare center." Charlie must have read her thoughts. "Then Nicole could sit on my lap, with Jenny in her car seat."

"Sure, if you think that would be preferred." *Better some five-year-old slobber all over him than me.*

Meg parked the car in front of a tiny, pink stucco, one-story building. The red tiled roof seemed to press firmly down on the rooftop, driving the house into the ground, leaving its walls a foot or two shorter than its neighbors.

As Meg walked into the daycare, Charlie said, "I'm sorry for the trouble. They're sweet kids. You'll like them."

"Aren't we going to switch seats?" Gemma reminded him.

"That's right," Charlie said, exasperated. The South Florida heat hit her like a concrete wall when she got out of the car. She could barely inhale the hot, humid air for a few moments.

"Hi beautiful, I'm glad you're here," Charlie whispered, suddenly pouring on the charm. He wrapped his arms around her waist and bent to kiss her. Gemma tried to relax and enjoy the moment of attention, but it didn't work. She was too wound up from the flight and everything to let go.

"I'm sorry if I'm grumpy. I'm tired and cold. I want to get to my hotel and get comfortable."

"Mmmm, I like that idea a lot. Maybe I can help you get comfortable. Maybe a little nap before dinner?" Charlie suggested with a wicked grin.

"A nap sounds wonderful, but I don't think that is what you really have in mind, is it?" Gemma pursed her lips.

"You are absolutely right." Charlie laughed, hugging her closer.

Gemma and Charlie were, well, not quite an item, but fast approaching being an item. They enjoyed each other's company, could hold a conversation about any topic for hours, and not get bored. They'd had a rough start in bed but were learning the ropes. It was one of the most complicated sexual relationships Gemma had ever had. There was an attraction, but it didn't go further than that for her. The last thing she wanted was a man screwing up her life.

Charlie was good in bed. Not the best, but good. Whether it was a lack of experience or a true constraint, Gemma didn't know. After three episodes, she could say with certainty he wasn't interested in doing some things most guys enjoyed, and most women adored. It was a very unusual sexual experience each time they got together.

On Gemma's side, she didn't hold back. Not even on day one. Everything she had ever read or knew would stimulate a man was game in her book. Most men she had dated literally cried with joy at her lack of inhibitions and her ministrations. Charlie did not. He didn't like her using her mouth to bring him pleasure. While he allowed her to do some things to please him, Charlie liked to be in control. His reactions to her wandering lips and tongue were hesitant.

Meg came back with the kids. Taller, Nicole had dark, silky hair flowing to the middle of her back and dark eyes keen on the car. Little Jenny had bright blonde hair, startling crystal blue eyes, and a tiny button of a nose. They ran to the car when they spotted Uncle Charlie.

Fortunately for "Uncle Charlie," Gemma's hotel was only a few blocks away. While she wasn't displeased he joined her, she had been looking forward to an hour or two by herself to unwind from the flight. Considering how the munchkins had pestered Charlie in the few minutes' drive between the daycare and the hotel, it was no wonder he wanted to bail out of the car with her.

She checked in at the desk with Charlie carrying her bags. Bags he promptly passed off to the bellhop. Up in her room, Charlie patted his pockets and announced he didn't have any change. The tight-lipped bellhop headed out into the hallway. He hadn't gone far when Gemma called him back. She tucked the ten-dollar bill in his hand. "Sorry," she said with a wink. "He's new to fancy hotels."

Returning to the room, the thunderous look on her face kept Charlie silent. "Don't ever do that again," Gemma hissed.

"What did I do?" He scowled back at her.

Gemma wagged her finger. "Don't ever ask a hotel employee to do something for you and then not tip them. Especially when you're with me." She had a reputation to uphold as the negotiator between her company and the hotel chain. "Scrimping on tips could make the contract terms more difficult and make your stay unpleasant."

Charlie shrugged and wandered about the hotel room. The bathroom was impressively large. The subtle elegance of the fixtures, from the walk-in shower, dual sink granite counter, and the black terracotta tiled floors, shone with a sparkle from the crystal pendant light fixtures hanging overhead. Along one wall was a soaker tub complete with an array of bath salts and bubble bath liquids in a variety of scents.

Hotel reward cards were good for some things after all, and her card must have indicated her profession. Of course, this hotel was one of several she was checking out for room blocking for their event.

It behooved them to treat her exceptionally well in any way they could. A shallow bowl of assorted fresh fruit adorned the small dining table, a glass vase of champagne roses on the sofa table, and a bottle of Santa Margherita Sauvignon Blanc, and San Pellegrino sparkling water were on ice. Even the mini fridge was well stocked with cheeses, caviar, and alcohol. They did their homework. Too bad the room was too antiseptic looking to feel comfortable.

Charlie dropped kisses on her neck when he returned from his explorations. Gemma batted him away.

"Give me a few minutes to get my stuff set up. Then we can relax for as long as we want." Gemma tried to smile.

"Okay, okay." Charlie held up his hands and chuckled. He grabbed the TV remote, flopped on the white comforter-covered bed, leaned back on the padded headboard and pillows, and started surfing through the channels. The dirty heels of his shoes rested on the cloth across the foot of the bed.

Gemma hung up her clothing in the closet so the wrinkles had time to fall out and plunked her extra pairs of shoes on the closet floor. The remaining clothes remained in the suitcase lying on the luggage rack. Her toiletries were transferred to the bathroom, her nightgown to the hook on the back of the door. The laptop was set up on the desk, as were the charging cords for the cell phone. Her RFPs for the convention center and four surrounding hotels were stacked beside the laptop. Sometime tonight, she'd have to go through the material one last time before tomorrow's eight a.m. meeting.

Gemma turned to give Charlie some attention only to find him asleep on the bed, TV remote still clutched in his right hand. She lay down beside him as gently as she could so as not to wake him, pulled the extra thick velvety blanket over them, and shut her eyes with a contented sigh.

Four hours later, Gemma and Charlie were on their way to Meg's house in a rental car. It had not taken much arm-twisting to convince Charlie it was more reasonable for the short time she would be in Miami. It was an expense she would personally have to cover, but it would be far better than the kid-stuffed Mom-mobile.

They had dinner with Meg, her husband, Mark, and the two girls. The food was good, the girls were bad, and Gemma couldn't wait for an appropriate time to leave. Feigning a need for sleep, she made her departure before eight o'clock.

Charlie was a little disappointed at first but resigned with the knowledge that sex was a distinct possibility now. She put him off for an hour, wanting to review her materials for her meetings the next day. He pouted a bit but got an hour of her undivided attention before they turned out the lights.

The next morning, Gemma left Charlie sleeping to make her first meeting of the day. When she wearily slouched in eight hours later, all she found was a note,

Gone to the hotel pool. Join me?.

She wanted a nap, but on second thought, decided a few laps in the tiny, oddly shaped pool might be more refreshing. The NACET guys wouldn't be spending their time by the pool. But their wives and girlfriends might like a dip after shopping at the Bayside marketplace along the river walk.

"Hey, handsome," Gemma crooned. "Anybody special sitting here with you?"

"Saving it just for you, beautiful," Charlie said, giving her the once over with his eyes.

"Nice swimsuit. Though I have to say, I was hoping for a bikini."

"Not with this scar," she quipped. "Bad enough I have to see it. Nobody else should."

"It's not that bad," Charlie said.

"Give it up, Charlie. I have mirrors." Gemma frowned. "I'm going in. Want to join me?"

He turned back to face the pool. "Sure, why not?"

They swam around the pool, avoiding the shallow section where adolescent kids played with inflated rafts and foam noodles. When the pool cleared out for dinner, Gemma began doing laps. Charlie hung off to the side, watching her with a bored expression. After twenty-five laps, she quit.

"What was that all about?" Charlie asked.

"Exercise. Don't you do anything for exercise?"

"I walk everywhere I can." He patted his abdomen. "Keeps me fit and trim."

"Huh." A sarcastic edge to her reply and Gemma's twisted smile said it all.

"What? Are you telling me something?" His voice stiffened, as did his entire body.

"Looking a little soft about the waist. You could use some laps," Gemma said playfully.

Charlie stormed up the ladder out of the pool and stalked angrily to their deck chairs. Whipping up his towel, he turned back to glare at her and stalked toward the hotel without another word.

"What the hell?" Gemma muttered under her breath. "So much for honesty."

Within an hour, she managed to apologize to Charlie as much as she could and get them downstairs to the hotel restaurant for dinner. Charlie still had an ice chip on his shoulder, but it slowly dissolved. *The closer it gets to bedtime, the warmer he'll get.*

Charlie warmed up enough to nibble on her neck in the elevator on the way back to the room. Once inside the door, he had his hands up her blouse, teasing her nipples to full attention while his tongue penetrated her mouth, delving deep. Gemma played his tongue with her own, feeling how wet she got thinking how that strong tongue would feel penetrating elsewhere. If only he were into that.

"Don't—wear—it out," Gemma whispered between breaks in their kiss.

"I have another toy if it gets tired," Charlie whispered back.

They stumbled over to the bed, Charlie pulling off her blouse. Her navy lace bra highlighted the stark whiteness of her untanned skin. Charlie slipped the lacy cup down, engulfing her red-tipped nipple with his lips, flicking his tongue across the nub while his other hand kneaded the damp junction of her pants, then unzipped them.

Her knees buckled when he slipped his hand down her pants and thrust his fingertip between her wet folds.

Charlie pushed Gemma roughly onto the bed and yanked her pants down, taking shoes and all with one swipe. He stood over her in the dimmed light, skimming off his polo shirt, dress pants, and boxers swiftly. Dropping to his knees, he pulled Gemma closer to the edge of the bed, settled her legs over his shoulders, and drilled his tongue into her wetness.

She gasped loudly. *Is this the same guy?* In seconds, she exploded into a quaking orgasm she didn't even know was so close to detonation. As the contractions subsided, Charlie climbed on the bed over Gemma, offering his member for reciprocal treatment. Despite the surprise in his sudden change in attitude, she took him wholly, running her tongue along the ridge and down the underside of the thick shaft. He groaned loudly and began thrusting into her mouth, trying to hold out as long as possible.

When his breathing became ragged and throaty, he pulled away and sheathed himself swiftly before rubbing Gemma's nerve bud with the tip. Her hips stretched up in yearning, seeking the divining rod.

"Charlie," Gemma moaned, half out of her mind with need.

"Here I come, Gemma," he whispered triumphantly seconds before thrusting into her. She groaned at the stretching and filling sensation of his thickness. Then he began to move. A millimeter at a time, adding a little more with each push and just a little faster until he was piercing her so rapidly Gemma could only wail as she was thrust over the edge of want into shattering collapse. Only then did Charlie burst out and release amid the rippling waves of her velvet core.

Lying awake half an hour later, Gemma wondered what had brought the change in Charlie. He somehow, suddenly, had become a stud in bed. It felt ironic that she'd finally found her greatest lover in a guy just when her interest was beginning to wane.

After their weekend trip to Miami, Gemma was amazed at the change in their sex life. He must have talked with someone. The change was too dramatic to be anything but frank advice. Perhaps he'd watched a double or triple X-rated porn movie in Miami. Maybe that was it. Whatever it was, Gemma was not complaining at all. Charlie went from drab to fab in bed, seemingly overnight.

• • • •

"NO, NICK, PUT THAT back. Now!" Heather bellowed after spotting her son reaching out of the grocery store cart to snag a bag of M&Ms.

Why do I try to shop with him? Heather wondered, snatching the bag from his fingers and putting it back on the shelf. Nicholas began to wail loudly, which set his sister off. Soon everyone in the store was staring. Heather gathered everything on her shopping list. *I should shop at night, and leave the kids home with Billy to look after them. There's no way I can shop like I'm supposed to for Calorie Counters with two kids in tow.*

Heather's shoulders slumped in resignation that today was not the day to read labels, check points and comparison-shop based on nutritional information. Cost would have to factor into the equation, as in best nutritional value for the least cost. All this extra comparison work made Heather's grocery store visits twice as long.

She was going to have to talk to someone at Calorie Counters about this issue. It was taking way more time than she had available. Maybe some of the other mothers at the meeting could give her some ideas about good products.

The pocket guide was helpful, but she didn't have enough hands to manage everything. She had to consult the guide, secure her handbag, hold onto the car seat balanced precariously across the carriage, and manage Nicholas. He either grabbed food off the shelves or tried to climb out. Reading labels was not an option.

With little time to sit down during the day, she didn't have any trouble fitting in exercise. She was always doing something physical: laundry, making beds, picking up toys. On the days when she and the kids went to a playground, she brought a ball so she and the kids could kick it around like they were playing soccer. Walking Michelle in her stroller with or without Peter and Nicholas and the dog in tow was a pleasant break in her day when the weather permitted.

It was the damn grocery shopping, menu planning, and food preparation that took enormous amounts of her time. Time was a commodity she didn't have to spare.

Then, of course, there were the meetings themselves. It wasn't enough to weigh in and leave. It was helpful to stay for the session. Pricilla said studies proved that social support was an important part of a successful weight loss program.

Heather had to admit she got some good information from the sessions. Especially from the other mothers in the group who chatted before and after the meeting. Someone always had a tip or suggestion to help in a situation. Even swapping names of babysitters. In fact, a few single moms got together, left their kids with one sitter, and split the cost, something Heather would never have thought to do. It took another whole hour of meeting, but Heather thought it was worth it and indulged in the opportunity every chance she got.

Billy didn't care most meeting nights because a sports game was on, and he could sit and watch without interruption since the kids were already in bed. He never asked where the money came from, and she never mentioned it. Her secret petty cash fund was for her use only. Bringing it up would entice Billy to raid it.

Then Billy would be in a bad mood and angry when she got home, like it was all her fault the kids woke up in the first place.

In time Heather liked her meetings as much for the comradery as the escape from the house they provided.

MARCH 2018

"Not my size," Marla surmised, then cringed at the scraping sound of the plastic hanger along the store's metal clothes rod.

"Not my size." Scrape. "Not my size." Scrape. "Oh! Wait a minute. Yes, this is my size, but dammit, it's sleeveless," Marla grumbled.

"Can't you find anything?" Eileen asked, impatience in her voice.

"Clothes shopping is always a ridiculous waste of time. It's not much better now that I'm about a size sixteen." Many of the "normal" clothes shops only carried sizes zero through twelve. Even if they did, the designs were all wrong for someone with her odd body dimensions.

"How about this?" Eileen held up a cute little orange top with ruffles on the sweetheart neckline.

"Cute. But my boobs look big enough without ruffles drawing more attention, thanks."

"Picky, picky." Eileen's eyes rolled to full effect.

This year's fashion was sleeveless tops, a disaster for Marla and her still saggy upper arms. The weight training was working on those areas, but it wasn't working fast enough to make a sleeveless shirt something Marla wanted to be seen in.

Spring's fashionable fabrics were riotous large floral prints in oranges, hot pinks, electric blues, and flaming yellows. Marla's morale sank deeper. *I might as well buy a muumuu and hide until the fall fashions come out.*

"We've been shopping for three hours," whined Eileen. "Is it lunchtime yet?"

Marla sighed. She'd ignored the hunger rumble in her stomach for the last hour. "Yeah, let's go. I don't see anything here. I thought shopping would get easier." The two women headed out the shop doors, Marla sighing out her discontent and frustration while Eileen tried to boost her spirits.

All her life, Marla had worn baggy clothes. Clothes designed and worn with the purpose of hiding her figure or lack thereof. Her image consultant was now advising her to buy and wear fitted clothes. Normal, fitted pants, not pants with elastic waistbands. A-line skirts, not voluminous, puffy skirts that hid her waist, hips, thighs, and knees. Tailored shirts with darts in the bodice to accentuate the thinness of her abdomen in relation to her boobs. This was the other thing Marla was trying to get used to. Allowing anyone to see a true outline of her body was new, alien, and scary. It was like being naked. It was going to take a lot of mental adjustment after thirty-two years of hiding behind yards of fabric.

• • • •

CHELSEA WENT TO HER boss at Shimmers Salon. "Mariah, I can't take clients this Saturday. I thought I sent you an email weeks ago about that. And you replied it was okay."

Mariah turned a cold eye to her briefly and looked away. "Maybe you did, maybe I did. Perhaps the front desk forgot to take your hours off the website schedule."

Trying to control the rising tide of anger in her gut, she said sweetly, "They will have to cancel those appointments and reschedule."

"That's not fair to our clients. You must do it yourself if you can't make that schedule work." Mariah's smirk said everything she wasn't saying with words. Perhaps she had heard Chelsea was running her own manicure business.

She stood still, the wave of tension threatening to erupt. This was unfair and the last straw. One of the reasons she had started her own business on the side was that Mariah refused to give her time off when she needed it. "You know what? I don't think so. I quit."

Chelsea stayed long enough to watch Mariah's jaw drop before she strode to her workstation, packed up her personal tools, and left the salon.

• • • •

DESPITE IT BEING SPRING break for most of the universities and colleges in the area, Jitters Café was jumping, as usual.

"Okay, ladies. It's weight loss check-in time." Chelsea set down her mug and turned to Gemma. "You first."

Gemma raised her eyebrows. "Me? Why am I always first?"

"Because I like you so much." Chelsea stuck out her tongue at Gemma, which set everyone giggling.

She muttered, "One ten. I gained a few back," before turning to Heather.

"One fifty-five," Heather revealed and turned to Marla beside her.

Marla grinned sheepishly. "One forty."

"Ugh, I only lost a pound." Chelsea's smile fell.

Gemma sipped her coffee before saying, "I went shopping the other day for new bras. My old ones were so loose my boobs were falling out."

Marla perked up. For once, she had something to add to the conversation. "I had that happen too. Had to buy all new underwear too. They kept sliding down to my knees at the most inopportune times. I hustled off to the bathroom in the nick of time. They slid to my ankles just inside the bathroom door. And I was wearing a skirt."

The four of them giggled at the image Marla provided.

"Ha!" Gemma blurted. "Oh my God, I better get new underwear before that happens to me. You know, I thought clothes shopping would be easier as my size decreased. But it doesn't feel that way."

"I know. I was out shopping with Eileen and I couldn't find anything in my size."

Chelsea set down her latte. "There's a store over in Millvale that has a wide range of sizes. It even carries petite and tall sizes. We should make a road trip."

"Road trip, road trip," Gemma chanted, staring directly at Marla. Heather and Chelsea joined in. Their voices grew louder, drawing the attention of other patrons.

"Okay, okay. We'll go." Marla laughed.

"Shoot! Look at the time!" Gemma exclaimed. "I've got to get going. I'm meeting Charlie for dinner."

"How's it going with him?" Marla asked, gulping down the last of her beverage.

"He's okay. Kind of moody sometimes. I wish I hadn't invited him along to Rhode Island. I kind of would prefer to go alone. He likes to disappear while I'm working. I don't blame him for not staying in the hotel room. That would be pretty boring. But sometimes it feels like he's hiding something." She turned to look at Chelsea, "And now he's not coming over as much. There are times he's not answering my text messages or phone calls."

As Gemma stood up, Chelsea gripped her arm. "Wait. I have an announcement."

Gemma sat back down. "I'll let him wait for a change."

"The salon manager booked me with a day's worth of clients after I had told her I wasn't available to work that day." Chelsea's grin spread across her face. "I quit."

Heather, Gemma, and Marla began clapping, drawing the stares of the other coffee shop customers.

• • • •

MARLA GOT TO THINKING about all the funny and not-so-funny events that had transpired to bring her to this one hundred forty pound, five-foot-one inch life.

Like the fat pants that she'd hung onto for so long. They became so baggy they started to slide down her hips one day when she was walking from her car in the driveway to her back door while carrying grocery bags. With both hands full, she couldn't drop the bags of eggs, glass jars, produce, and meats to grab her pants.

With each step, the pants fell a little further. By the time she reached her back door, her pants were at her ankles, leaving her pasty ass in baggy granny panties hanging out for all the neighbors to see. Fortunately, no one else had been around. What a scene that must have been. Thank God her back door was shielded from the busy street by shrubs in full leaf at the time.

Then there was the time those baggy granny panties had done a similar maneuver at work. Not wanting to buy new underwear each time she changed a size, Marla had tried to wear them for three or four months. However, the elastics were so stretched out that they didn't retract as her waist shrank.

On that particular day, she was returning to her office from the executive floor. At first, Marla didn't know what was going on. It felt like her pants were slipping, but the waistband was still in place. The panties rode down until they bunched at her crotch. They weren't noticeable under her pants but utterly uncomfortable and downright ludicrous. Again, she was fortunate it was after her usual departure time, well into second shift, so the halls were deserted of employees.

• • • •

ICY-COLD WATER HIT Gemma's left cheek, jarring her mind to full attention. "Thanks, I needed that." she muttered to herself, remembering the ancient Aqua Velva commercial her father used to joke about in her childhood. She tucked her hair behind an ear to keep it dry, then cupped another handful of water and splashed it on the right side of her face. It was set-up day before a four-day NACET regional conference in Providence, Rhode Island, and already, Gemma couldn't wait to get home.

Despite tracking numbers that claimed otherwise, two important cartons had not arrived from their Pittsburgh office, forcing Gemma, Jeremy, and Mei to improvise new name badges for attendees on the spot. The RI Convention Center staff insisted the crates had never arrived, regardless of signatory proof provided by the drayage company. The name of the signee was illegible.

Jeremy had to set up the registration booth and materials by himself while Mei was at the nearest Copy Cart store two blocks away, getting materials for the new badges they would print and assemble in a work session back in the hotel later that night. This meant Gemma was handling the exhibit hall alone, dealing with over a hundred sales representatives, executives, and corporate pains-in-the-ass while each tried to weasel a bigger space, a better location, or a sightline away from their competitors.

Gemma blotted her face to remove the water droplets. She checked her face in the mirror. *I should touch up my makeup but screw it. It doesn't look bad.* She closed her eyes so she didn't have to look at the barren gray concrete walls and satiny, cold, stainless steel bathroom partitions. The shiny maroon tiled floor with glaring white grout lines somehow gave her the creeps, a vision of rows of bloodied teeth in a cavernous smile, a macabre Cheshire cat. Shivers crawled down her spine. *Time to get out of here.*

She put her suit jacket back on and squared her shoulders to her reflection in the mirror. Set up closed in four more hours, then she could crawl back to her hotel room, soak in hot, rose-scented bathwater, glass of pinot on the side, and wait for Charlie to come in from the airport. Until it was time to reconvene in Mei's room for emergency badge-making.

"Shoes," Gemma said, feeling her arches begin to cramp again. *Now, I just need that change of shoes, and I'll almost feel like a new woman.*

"Jeremy?" Gemma said into the walkie-talkie.

"Yup," A staticky male voice that vaguely sounded like Jeremy replied.

"I'm going to the central office. Anything you need?" Gemma headed for the office room, where coats, handouts, and additional teaching materials, including Gemma's two additional pairs of shoes, waited.

"Bud Lite would be nice, but I don't think I packed any this time. Nothing I can think of."

Gemma kicked off the three-inch heels, eased into the kitten-heeled Capezios, and let out an involuntary sigh. Nothing like a fresh, cool, dry pair of shoes halfway through the day.

"Gemma?" the walkie-talkie hanging on her hip called.

"Jjjerrremyyy? What's up?" Gemma asked playfully.

"Someone from Drafting Tooled Lines LLC is here at registration, needs to see about booth space," Jeremy reported.

"Heading that way."

"Mei's getting back now."

"Great to hear, thanks," Gemma replied, heading for the door. As she walked the speckled industrial carpets to the main registration area, she thought of her conversation with Charlie on the telephone the day before she left for TF Green Airport. They'd discussed his spending the four days of the conference with her in Providence.

Gemma didn't have a problem with his being there, as long as he realized she would be putting in fourteen-to-sixteen-hour days. Unlike her convention site scouting trips, she would be unavailable for sightseeing, meals, and just about everything else Charlie might want them to do together. She'd hinted about sex also. By the time she reached the end of the evening duties, it was hard to keep her eyes open long enough to undress and climb into bed. Charlie had assured her he didn't mind so long as he could wake up with her in his arms in the morning. When she clarified that he'd be waking up at five each morning, Charlie had backpedaled jokingly to sleeping with her in his arms.

"Whatever," Gemma mumbled, approaching the registration table and another irate company executive disgruntled about his booth.

• • • •

HEATHER WENT OVER THE Calorie Counters pamphlets trying to decide how the meal she was cooking for lunch worked out for points. Hot dogs were not on the list of good meats, but the kids would eat them. Mac and cheese was, but it alone would put her over her allowed point value for the entire day. Frustrated, she flung the pamphlet across the kitchen toward the trash bin. Snoopy skittered over to it for a sniff.

"Come here, Snoopy." Tears filled her eyes again for the fourth time today. "What the heck is wrong with me?" she asked the white and black beagle-crossed puppy, tousling his floppy ears and giving them a quick scratch.

Too much on your damn plate. Three kids all under the age of ten, and a dog. And you're hangry.

"Why does this have to be so hard?" she glumly asked the dog. Snoopy sat to scratch his own ear. *Because you can't eat your kids' leftovers as your own meal anymore. That's why. You have to get your own meal. A real meal.*

It wouldn't be hard if she could afford the frozen entrées. On one salary, that was out of the question. Billy's job as a forklift operator at the lumberyard was stable as it supplied most of the local building contractors with quality lumber products. He only made $23.55 an hour, but he got paid holidays and sick time, and most importantly, he had free health insurance for the whole family. It was unheard of, and they counted their blessings for it every time one of the kids needed a doctor's visit.

Heather got up to scout out the near-empty refrigerator for something she could eat for lunch that wouldn't destroy her point count. Carrot fingers, as Peter and Nicholas called them; two apples, one celery stalk, butter, a few slices of American cheese, one slice of cold pizza (pepperoni), and assorted condiments. In desperation, she grabbed the carrot bag, a celery stalk, an apple, and one slice of cheese. "So this is what I have to work with," she snarled, suddenly feeling the empty pit of her stomach grumbling.

When the kids' lunch was ready, she rounded them up. Michelle sat nicely in the highchair now, although more food hit the floor than her mouth. Snoopy scoffed it all up in seconds. At least she had help keeping the floor clean of debris.

The boys dallied with their food as usual, "accidentally" dropping pieces of their hotdog to feed Snoopy. The puppy scampered around under the table. Heather tried correcting their behavior, then scolding, pleading, threatening, and then, nearly blue in the face, she lost her patience. She screamed at the boys. In seconds all the kids were crying, and Snoopy was howling along in sympathy. Heather collapsed in her chair and dropped her head to the table. She was hangry. Hunger was making her short-tempered.

"God help me, please," she muttered.

Surprisingly the kids became silent. When she lifted her head, they stared at her in wild-eyed panic.

"Are you okay, Mommy?" Peter asked, real fear in his tiny voice.

"Mommy is very hungry. She wants you to eat so she can eat too," Heather explained calmly. She got up from the table and shut Snoopy in the bathroom.

Tentatively, they all resumed eating. Heather started to eat her carrots, celery, and apple. Before she could finish the first bite of carrot, Nicholas demanded a carrot. Peter then wanted one also, as well as a celery stick. Within minutes, the boys were ignoring their own lunch, eating Heather's instead.

"I like this better, Mommy," Peter said, crunching away, carrot fragments falling out of his open mouth as he spoke.

"Me too, Mommy. Apple too please!" Nick pleaded.

"Appo," Michelle chimed.

"Okay, okay, today you all eat carrots, celery, and apples." Heather shrugged, giving the kids her diet meal. Sensing the mutiny, Snoopy whined behind the bathroom door, probably licking his chops in anticipation of the leftovers.

Now what am I going to eat? I'll have to eat the kids' leftovers. Heather scrounged on their plates for bits of hotdog and forkfuls of cold mac and cheese.

As she chewed, she gave some thought to what had transpired. What if—maybe this isn't as hard as I thought, Heather smirked. Maybe a little reverse psychology with the kids could make her life a little bit easier.

Over the next few days, she tried out her theory. Getting the children on board her weight loss diet had worked out better than she had ever hoped. She made it a game for them, involving the boys in planning the meals so they all had a say in what was on their plate.

There were plenty of times when the attitude changed by the time they sat down at the table. At those times, it was easy enough to substitute peanut butter and jelly sandwiches when someone, usually Nicholas, threw a tantrum about the lunch menu.

He wanted to help Mommy. From that point on, he was better when she involved him in the preparations, either setting the table or getting the fruits and vegetables from the refrigerator. She called him "sous chef Nick" when he helped. She made both boys toque-style hats out of newspaper. They loved their chef hats, and she had two real helpers in the kitchen from then on. It did wonders for their moods and self-esteem.

Even getting in her exercise got a little easier when she involved the kids. Once Peter was off to kindergarten, she'd put Michelle in the stroller, hook Snoopy up to the leash, and off they'd all go, with Nicholas "helping" to push his sister around the block. When they got back, the two kids went down for a nap until Peter came home from school, giving her free time to sit with a cup of tea and read.

• • • •

THE LOOKIN' GOOD CLOTHING store in Millvale was larger than Marla had imagined. Chelsea had explained on the drive that they carried casual, business, and event attire for sizes zero and up. The brightly lit store had motorized carts for the mobility-challenged and park benches at both ends of each aisle. They even had plus-size mannequins showing off the latest fashions.

As the four women paused inside the door, a saleswoman approached. "How can I help you look good today?"

Chelsea stepped forward. "I've been here before, but these three may need your help."

The first saleswoman waved her hand in the air, and two other saleswomen descended on the newcomers. Each of them introduced themselves to Heather, Gemma, and Marla. Fern paired up with Gemma, and walked to the right side of the store, heading for the area labeled event attire. Heather and Karen stepped off to the casual section while Marla and Danielle set out for the business attire section.

As they entered the area, Danielle started talking. "The clothing here is specifically chosen to make you look your best, no matter what article it is. We don't stock items with loud, large prints or anything with pockets, bows, ruffles, and embellishments in the wrong places for bigger women's bodies. We also don't stock capri pants that will make you look shorter or three-quarter-sleeved tops that make your arms look short. If the fabric has stripes, they are vertical to add visual length rather than horizontal stripes that make you look wider."

Marla scanned the racks. "Wow! I had no idea how amazing this place is."

"What exactly are you looking for in business attire?"

"I'd love to find some new business suits."

"Skirts or pants?"

"Both."

"Long or short sleeve?"

"Short, please." Marla was stunned at the number of questions.

Danielle led her to the racks and began pulling out suits of different colors that she thought would look good on Marla. In ten minutes, Marla was in the fitting room with ten different suits.

Marla turned left, then right, to get a better view. "Dark purple has always been my favorite color." She frowned. All she saw in every mirror image was Fat Marla. Could she trust this saleswoman to steer her purchases? She decided she could, even if she couldn't appreciate the reflection.

Within another twenty minutes, she had four beautiful new suits waiting for her at the cash register.

She sought out Heather as they were finishing. Heather only found one item to purchase. It was a cute light blue colored blouse with tiny white polka dots.

Gemma and Chelsea were the last to arrive at the cash registers. Chelsea purchased new dress pants. Gemma found a couple of outfits for her workday and a gorgeous red gown for a ball she would attend in a few months.

On the way home, the ladies chatted without their usual sarcasm or quips.

"Thanks for suggesting that store, Chelsea. It was amazing. I can't believe I didn't even know about it," Gemma said, securely clutching her purchases.

"Thanks, Gem. It opened before Christmas. Every time I've been, the place has been busy."

"I love that they know the merchandise so well they can go to the exact rack for the item you want." Marla sighed, her suits tucked in a garment bag and lying across her knees. "It's sad to think I can only wear them for a short time."

"What do you mean?" Heather asked.

Marla shrugged. "I'm not at my final weight yet. I have more to go. Not much, but these new suits likely won't fit by the fall."

APRIL 2018

"I don't think you're putting as much effort into this as you can. What's holding you back, Chelsea?" Rebecca asked point blank.

Chelsea's teeth clenched so tight her jaw began to hurt. She glared at Rebecca, envisioning an axe embedded in Rebecca's forehead, the one she'd personally like to put there this very minute.

Chelsea growled silently. *Why does she always have to put me on the spot? Why do I have to constantly defend myself? So I cheat on my diet. Slimline gets paid, why do they care? It's more money for them if it takes me longer to lose weight.*

"Look, I have a fiancé who has to eat a real meal. He's a carpenter with a high caloric requirement. I cook for him. I have to season his food. I'm a good cook. I'm a good cook because I taste the food before I serve it to make sure the seasoning is correct. I don't intentionally cheat. It's not like I'm stopping at McDonald's for a couple Quarter Pounders with Cheese and large fries daily." Chelsea seethed, the pain in her jaw extending up her temples.

"How about if Ricky taste-tests the food and tells you if it needs more seasoning?" Rebecca asked politely.

"*Seth* wouldn't be able to tell me what spices need to be adjusted, that's why." She put a hand to her forehead and pressed. "Look, I have a terrible headache. Can we get this over with for today? I need the usual food supplies and an appointment for next week."

"Okay, the same day and time is available next week if that's okay with you." Rebecca was also now in clenched teeth mode but let the words come out in a professional manner. "I'll go get your meals."

Chelsea glanced down at her cell phone for the time while waiting for Rebecca to get back. Hearing the clickity-click of her high heels on the hall tile, she set the phone aside on the tabletop.

"Before our next session, I was wondering if you could do a little homework assignment for me?" Rebecca asked, a little calmer than when she left the office.

Chelsea gave a noncommittal half shrug, half nod.

Rebecca continued, "I'd like you to write a list of all the things you expect weight loss will do for you."

She could feel the surprise on her own face. "Yeah, sure. See you next week," Chelsea mumbled over her shoulder, already half out of her chair, hefting the bag of food. Her navy-blue Corolla was tearing out of the parking lot within sixty seconds.

• • • •

CHARLIE WENT WITH GEMMA on most of her site visits and event trips. At first, it was nice having him around, at least for the sex, and Charlie was generally able to get away. She felt a little guilty leaving him to amuse himself all day, but too many responsibilities or meetings were crammed into one day for her to do anything else. He could work anywhere and always brought along twenty to thirty scripts to review while airborne or at the hotel.

But her attitude had changed. He kept asking her where they were going next like he was inviting himself along on every trip. His continued presence was irksome. More and more often, she tried not to talk about upcoming travel so he wouldn't know until it was too late and the plane ticket too expensive for him to join her at the last minute. He sulked if he couldn't go with her. All the while, Gemma was feeling more and more in need of distance between them, except for the sex part.

She was still perplexed at the change that had come over Charlie during the Miami trip. From routine sex maneuvers to sex God. Gemma wasn't complaining; she was enjoying the hell out of it. After so many years of celibacy, it was an invigorating change of pace. Charlie was always ready, condom in hand, whenever she was willing.

In many cities, Charlie spent his days roaming the streets checking out the convention center's surrounding areas. He liked to think he was part of her surveying team. To a large extent, he was. His male perspective was a welcome addition to Gemma's investigation of each site since the overwhelming majority of the NACET organization's membership was male.

Not that Charlie was like most men, he certainly wasn't. He wasn't into any sports at all. Didn't follow any teams or engage in anything remotely considered exercise. His one interest was to check out the nightclubs. Gemma tagged along but kept her time clubbing short after a long day. Charlie was always a little disappointed. He still had a bundle of energy to expend while Gemma's generator was running on borrowed time.

During their trip to Phoenix, they had taken a few extra days to see the Grand Canyon. Gemma wanted to hike down the Bright Angel trail into the canyon, but Charlie wouldn't have it. They saw the different vistas from various viewing spots along the south rim, Charlie getting on her nerves the entire time. The views were spectacular, and new expanses opened with every step she took. Charlie merely sneered, "It's just rocks!"

"It's America's national treasure! How can you call it 'just rocks'?" Gemma replied, her tone laced with ridicule.

Gemma promised herself she would return someday to hike the beautiful canyon—without Charlie.

A whitewater rafting trip down the canyon was also out of Charlie's comfort zone. Gemma gave serious thought to making the rafting trip without him. In the end, she chickened out too. Instead, they opted to drive over to Las Vegas for an overnight sightseeing trip on the strip.

Pulling some of her professional contact strings, Gemma procured a room at the Bellagio at eighty percent off the regular rate. They hit the strip after dumping their suitcases on the marble tiled floor in the expansive, ornate room.

It was a calm, clear, beautiful night for checking out the various sidewalk shows. They enjoyed the pirate ship battle and strolling through Paris before taking a gondola ride at the Venetian resort. At midnight they watched the Bellagio fountain show and then went for a swim in the famous Bellagio pools. It was still crowded at two a.m. Vegas never slept, and the pool temperatures still hovered near eighty degrees.

They retired for some hot sex in a California king-sized bed. Sated, Gemma nestled into the high thread count sheets and dozed off immediately. She woke about six to find a note from Charlie. Couldn't sleep, checking out the casino downstairs.

Gemma rolled over in the silky sheets and went back to sleep.

When she woke again at about eight, Charlie still wasn't back. She pulled on a robe and called his cell.

"Hey, you coming back sometime today?" Gemma asked. "We need to get back to Phoenix for our flight home, remember?"

"I'm on my way upstairs. See you in a few minutes," Charlie said briskly and hung up.

When Charlie arrived half an hour later, he brought fresh coffee and pastries from the Italian bakery stall in the hotel's lobby.

"How sweet of you to think of bringing breakfast. And you brought my favorite pastries, chocolate croissants," Gemma purred, giving him a sultry good morning kiss. "How'd you do at the tables? Hit the jackpot?"

"Yup." Charlie grinned ear to ear, then took a big bite of a chocolate-filled croissant.

"How much?" Gem paused over her coffee cup. *Was he holding out on her?*

"Broke even in the end." His tone teased, but his gaze remained averted.

"That's better than losing it all."

Charlie shrugged, smiled, and turned away, not meeting her eyes.

Gemma shivered. She didn't know why, but Charlie seemed evasive. Had he won more than he was admitting? Did he think she would demand a share? She sipped her hot coffee trying to warm up again, but it wasn't helping. Her feet were like ice.

She stood up from the bed, brushing her hands free of croissant flakes. The fact she was back to eating regular food was satisfying, even if the portions were still small. "I'm going to hit the shower. I'm feeling cold. The last thing I want is to be sick now."

"Good idea. I'm going to catch a quick nap." He flung himself on the bed, drew up the bed linens, and was softly snoring before Gemma could undress.

At home, Gemma briskly walked the condo complex every day. Her steps swift, and her arms swinging to increase her cardio. As she rounded the corner and walked past Charlie's condo, Mrs. Hoskins, his next-door neighbor, was outside looking into the garden beds. Seeing Gemma, she waved and walked to the driveway. "Hello, you're Gemma, right? You've been dating Charlie?" She thumbed toward his condo next door.

"Yes." Gemma marched in place, trying to keep her heart rate up. She didn't want to be rude to Mrs. Hoskins but hoped the elderly woman wasn't looking for a lengthy conversation.

"You two look nice together."

Gemma wanted to move on. "Thank you."

"It's sweet how you and Charlie are getting along. He must have been pretty lonesome since his last girlfriend left."

"He's a nice man. We enjoy our conversations," Gemma said stiffly, refusing to take the bait about his last girlfriend. "I have to keep going, Mrs. Hoskins. Have a good day." She marched on, putting an end to the conversation while her mind considered the woman's mention of "his last girlfriend."

• • • •

"HERE WE ARE, THE MOMENT of the reveal!" The salon owner, swung the beauty salon chair around to face the mirror, giving Marla a view of his work.

"Tada! What do you think, honey?" Mitchell asked, bouncing like a ball of electricity, apprehension and anxiety.

Marla studied the reflection. She touched her cheek lightly; the mirror image did the same maneuver. She was speechless.

"Say something, for God's sake! I can't stand it!" Mitchell cried, flapping his hands like a baby bird stretching its wings.

"I can't believe it's me. Is it really me?" Marla whispered, meeting Mitchell's eyes in the mirror.

"It's one hundred percent you, honey. I always knew there was a bombshell in there! You are one hot babe!" Mitchell jabbered happily.

Wow, just wow. No wonder Mitchell had been hounding her for months for a complete makeover. New figure, new face, he had said. *Good Lord, he wasn't kidding.*

"That was better than plastic surgery." Marla still couldn't feel herself breathing yet. She sucked in a huge gulp of air and coughed on it.

Mitchell beamed. "You look so amazing, I can't believe it." He started to weep. "*I'm* so amazing. Where's my camera for the after picture?" He strutted off in search of his camera, fanning his face to dry his tears before they smeared his mascara.

Marla had left herself in Mitchell's hands, hands she knew were very competent. She never would have guessed he could have performed a miracle. Where long, thin, dull, dirty-blonde hair had been was now a shiny, vibrant, light strawberry-blonde, cut to shoulder length in a soft angle. Her makeup, light enough to look completely natural, gave her fair skin an egg-shell finish, eyes highlighted, lips made full in a rose-colored neutral tone. The cheekbones that had revealed themselves as the weight dropped were ever so slightly tinted for accent. The reflection was absolutely stunning.

The slim fingers of her hand showed off the French manicure on her medium-length natural nails. Marla knew her tiny toenails were a light rosy pink after her earlier pedicure. It had been a morning of primp and polish, but look what Mitchell had created. She still could not believe it.

Mitchell returned to his workstation with an entourage of stylists, staff, and even a few customers. Marla gripped the chair arms for dear life and saw herself blush deep crimson in the mirror.

"Ladies and gentlemen, Marla Devine!" Mitchell regally announced as he aggressively twirled her chair to face his audience.

The applause was spontaneous. The ohs and ahs were heartfelt. Marla and Mitchell found themselves being congratulated as if parents to a newborn babe. So she was.

She was on top of the world and ready to show off her new look. Her makeover from Mitchell was astonishing and boosted her self-assurance even more than her weight loss had. Her weight had plateaued after she'd lost one hundred sixty-seven pounds. She decided not to push the last ten pounds. They would drop in time. She had total faith in her new lifestyle and food plan now. It got her this far, it would take her all the way and keep her there.

Yoga, jogging, and meditation made her fit, firm, calm, and collected in thought and mind. The personal trainer had guided her to exercises that shrunk her loose skin. Her wardrobe was smashing, everything brand new, from lacy lingerie to Italian stilettos.

There was one downside. Her only real friend at work, Eileen, had abandoned her. For some twisted reason Marla couldn't understand, her best friend no longer wanted to have anything to do with her since she had lost so much weight. Her heart squeezed tight with the thought that Eileen might have only been her friend because, as an obese woman, Marla made Eileen look good.

As Eileen had said, she looked and acted like an entirely different person. On more than one occasion, she had arrived at a work site to do an inspection, only to leave the staff speechless from her change. Marla loved to see the expressions on their faces when they realized it was her, less than half the weight she had been when she started.

She sometimes wished she could take a picture of their faces. It fed her resolve to maintain the lifestyle change that supported her new weight. This was her new reality.

Secretly, she thanked those two rude people on the airplane daily. She owed them the motivation even if the work and sweat had been all her own.

• • • •

A HONK FROM THE CAR behind Heather informed her the stoplight had changed to green while she had daydreamed. It wasn't daydreaming. First, it was night, 8:48 at night, to be exact, from the LCD clock on the Ford Focus's dashboard. Second, it wasn't a dream. It was a rehash of the presentation Pricilla had given tonight.

Heather accelerated through the light slowly, not wishing to return home so soon. She rarely got a break from the three kids, except for weigh-in night once a week and the occasional coffee with the girls. As much as she loved her children, it was a bit much to be with them 24/7/365. *Maybe I should stop somewhere for a cup of coffee or tea?* Heather knew something was bothering her but was not sure exactly. A green and white Starbucks sign up ahead drew her notice. She pulled the rusting car into the parking lot and entered the dimly lit shop.

LITTLE BIT OF WAIT

The aroma of coffee, deep and rich smelling, filled the space, causing her stomach to growl. Ignoring the snacks and the bakery case, she questioned the barista about the chai. Liking the description, she ordered it. It was something she had never tried before. The idea of something different, something out of her ordinary routine, intrigued her.

A little sweeter than she would have liked, but her tongue enjoyed the tantalizing spices that danced across it. Cinnamon, nutmeg, maybe pepper? What else had the teenager said, something mum, cardamom or whatever. The only thing Heather was sure about was that it was her first time tasting this cardamom flavor. The drink's exotic fragrance had Heather closing her eyes, imagining an open veranda, a cushy lounge chair, and the horizon filled with aquamarine waves, palm fronds drooping from their bent tree trunks, scattered coconuts in the soft white sand.

"Good?" the barista asked her, wiping the table beside her clean.

"Oh, yes. I think it's the most exotic drink I've ever had," Heather admitted.

"I like it too. I prefer it hot like they serve it in India."

India, Heather mused. How much more exotic can you get than India? Sipping the spiced elixir, her mind wandered. She had always wanted to travel to exotic places: Morocco, Greece, and Madagascar. Those countries had fascinated her as a child flipping through *National Geographic* magazines at the library. She sighed, her heart sinking. She would never see those places. Not as her life had turned out. In a year, she hardly left the city of Pittsburgh even once. There was no help for it. All her childhood dreams of exploring new sights and cultures were just that. Dreams.

The ringing of her cell phone brought her abruptly back to the moment. She ignored it. This was her time. Then her thoughts drifted back to the meeting.

Her weigh-in had been only one pound down, a total disappointment, but she had to admit, it was a blessing considering how little effort she had put into following the program in the past week. And the week before that, and before that, and before that. Disgusted, she realized that after twelve weeks, she had only managed to lose nine pounds. It's sabotage. Pricilla was right.

Tonight's meeting topic had been sabotage. At first, Heather had scoffed at the topic when Pricilla announced it. She'd nearly walked out of the meeting after the weigh-in, but she decided to stay to hear what Pricilla had to say on the topic.

Initially she said that everyone in the room had at least one saboteur, making their weight loss plan difficult. Pricilla described her mother, who refused to understand the Calorie Counters program.

"My mother thinks a heaping plate of food is the only way to say I love you and to return the sentiment, I *must* empty that entire plate of food into my stomach." The audience chuckled, and heads nodded in sympathy.

"And the phrase 'portion control' is not in her Lithuanian vocabulary." Pricilla giggled.

Then she asked each of them to examine their own lives, their family, friends, and coworkers who intentionally or unintentionally made their weight loss efforts more difficult with sabotaging tactics. Such as the lady next door who brought over more cookies when she saw you were looking a little thinner. Or the office parties that only served bad food choices and the bosses who gave out candy as gifts. Then there were the biggest offenders: the spouses who felt threatened by your weight loss. Who might do things like bring home more ice cream, take you out to dinner more often, or bring you a box of chocolates instead of flowers.

Priscilla said, "The best way to combat the saboteurs is to have the strength to say, 'No, this is important to me,' and stick to your guns. Otherwise, they will continue to hound you. If you resist temptation often enough, they will quit the offensive. Your spouse needs reassurance that you'll still love and need them after you lose the weight."

Heather thought of the spousal sabotage idea. Did Billy sabotage her efforts? In a way, he did. He didn't want to modify his eating habits to fit her weight loss program.

It was hard enough for her to cook a meal for him and a modified meal for each of the three kids based on their needs and likes. To even think of adding her own diet needs was adding more hot coals to her path of mealtime insanity.

Was it deliberate of him? Yes, in a way. Did he mean it to be? Was it fair for her to ask him to change his eating lifestyle to suit her needs?

Heather sipped from her cup, only to realize it was empty. She frowned, set the empty cup down, and contemplated another chai but spotted the clock on the wall. It was after nine-thirty, Billy must be having a fit. She was over a half hour late. There'd be hell to pay for it, even if the kids were already asleep. Heather tossed the empty cup with a sense of regret and hurried out to the car for a quick drive home to face the reckoning.

Despite Heather disliking Pricilla Heinz, she kept going to her weekly Calorie Counters meetings. Her weight was ever so slowly coming off. A pound or less a week. All the ladies at the meetings kept telling her that was great, the "safe way to go." Heather was running out of time before the reunion. At the current rate, she'd only be dropping twelve pounds before the party. Psyching the kids into eating well was working most of the time.

Dinner with Billy was still a problem she dealt with daily. Night after night, she cringed thinking of being so good on the program all day long and blowing her hard work and sacrifice on one meal. A litany of thoughts burst through her mind. Damn it! Why can't

I just stay on program for one damn night? Or if not on program, not eat like I've been on a hunger strike for a week. Why do I feel compelled to eat what the kids don't finish? Why can't I be a good role model for the kids? It was going to take more self-examination and self-control than she ever imagined.

• • • •

THE THREE OF THEM WERE sitting outside on the restaurant's back patio, unaware of Marla's entrance. Heather was the first to glance up. She turned back to what Chelsea was saying, then jerked her head around with recognition. "Hoool-lly shit!" was all she said. The other two stopped their conversation mid-sentence and looked up in the direction Heather was staring.

"Sweet Jesus," Chelsea muttered so low it was almost a whisper as she continued to stare.

"Marla? Is that really you?" Gemma was the only one with enough of her wits left to actually speak a sentence.

Marla sauntered across the patio to their table and gracefully eased into the empty chair. The dumbstruck looks on Chelsea and Heather's faces were starting to feel embarrassing.

"Okay, quit it. Yes, it's me. Mitchell over at Mode Mitch Salon gave me a makeover," she said, glancing at the drinks the other women had ordered.

"Makeover? The man's a genius!" Chelsea gushed. "I don't think I've ever seen someone made over so incredibly."

"What do you think of it all?" Gemma asked. She looked at Marla inquisitively as if waiting to hear her response before passing comment.

"I can't believe it. He's been on my case forever about a makeover. I always put him off. The time felt right now."

Gemma still waited for her answer, "Are you glad you did?"

Marla's smile stretched from ear to ear, and she nodded vigorously, "Absolutely."

"I think I need an appointment," Heather whined softly. "Does Mod Mitch cost a lot?"

You know the phrase ... if you have to ask...?"

Heather flopped back in her chair, then took another slug of beer. "Figures. But wow! It sure looks like it'd be worth it before the reunion."

"You look great just as you are, Heather," Marla encouraged, feeling ashamed for pointing out Heather's financial state.

Gemma jumped into the conversation to steer the discussion. "We were discussing Chelsea's wedding plans."

"What plans do you have?" Marla asked Chelsea after giving the waitress her drink order. Her gut wrenched at having to listen to wedding plans. It was a topic and event she preferred not to engage in.

"She hasn't even started to plan anything yet. They don't even have a date yet." Gemma flung both arms out, palms up.

"That's because we're not in a hurry." Chelsea interrupted, tapping her index finger on the tabletop. "He's asked me. I'm happy. It's not a big deal." Despite her words, the frown lines deepened across her forehead. "I did pick out my dress. That's the hardest part, right?"

Gemma leaned into the table to get her words closer to Chelsea's ears. "You've waited thirteen *years* for him to propose. And you say you're in no hurry? Let me tell you something, Chelsea. There's waiting, and then there's waiting. You've done both. It's time to plan, for God's sake. Getting your contracts might be difficult."

Chelsea's eyes blinked rapidly several times. "Wow, Gemma, you're usually so opposed to marriage."

Heather nodded and said, "She's right."

Marla gave her a one-shoulder shrug.

"Okay, I'll start to work on it. In fact, let's work on it right now. You, you, and you." Chelsea pointed at each of them in turn. "I want you all to be bridesmaids. My cousin Diane's going to be my maid of honor. How's that for making decisions?" she said smugly before taking a long pull from her Bud Lite.

Marla blurted, "I can't do it," before she could hold her tongue. Her shoulders slumped as she stared at her fingers on the glass.

The three of them stared at her with reproachful glares.

"And why not?" Gemma demanded.

Marla closed her eyes and sighed heavily. The last thing she wanted to do was dampen Chelsea's fun with her own bad luck story. She thought of standing impatiently at the altar, getting angrier and angrier at Sam. And then the news. She'd been cursing Sam for being late when in fact, he and his best man were dead, their lifeless bodies cooling in the mangled mess of car and truck. She would have waited at that altar all day if only he would eventually show up.

"Marla, are you okay?" Heather asked gently, placing her hand on Marla's forearm.

Marla's tears pelted down her cheeks. "I—I can't do it. I can't be in the wedding party."

All three of them looked at her with concern in their eyes. Chelsea took Marla's hand. "It's okay. Whatever it is, it's okay."

She closed her eyes and let the tears wash over her face. Yet she didn't make a sound. No sobs, wails, or groans. When she opened her eyes again, their faces looked thunderstruck. "I'm sorry." She rubbed her cheeks and sniffled.

Heather whispered, "It's okay. You're safe with us."

A tight smile flashed across her face, then disappeared. "I was left at the altar. My fiancé, Sam, and his best man were driving to the church. They were running late. They rounded a corner too tight." Tears threatened to re-start, but she rubbed them out of her eyes.

"Right into a delivery truck." She closed her eyes again, not wanting to see the looks on their faces.

"Oh, my God! Marla, I'm so sorry," Gemma and Chelsea whispered nearly in unison.

Heather placed her arm around Marla's shoulders and hugged her tight. "I'm so sorry."

Once again, Marla swiped her tears away and tried to put a brave smile on her face. "I'm okay. I—haven't been to anyone's wedding since."

"Ah, Marla." Chelsea squeezed Marla's hand. "I totally understand." Her nose crinkled. "Should I not send you an invitation?"

Her eyes brightened. "Yes, please do. I would like to be there. Might be in the back pew, but I'll be there."

Gemma held her martini glass up in the air above the center of the table. Heather held her beer bottle as Chelsea did the same. The last to join was Marla.

"Now, what about the reception?" Gemma broke in.

EARLY MAY 2018

Seth had been patient. Chelsea knew he'd been very patient. But his patience was running out. She had canceled their previously arranged wedding date.

"Chel, we need a date. I didn't get engaged to wait another six or more years to get married." As he spoke, the bridge of his nose wrinkled.

Seeing it, Chelsea knew she had to proceed cautiously. "I know you've been patient. But I need more time to lose weight. It's a one-of-a-kind dress, no longer available from the dress company. So my only option is to lose weight."

"Can't they alter the dress to fit?"

When she shook her head, he offered, "I'll get you money for another dress."

Chelsea's blood pressure was raging now. She stamped her foot. "No." Her arms folded across her chest, she stood tall and firm in her decision. Why couldn't he understand about her dreams? Of her wish to not have to compromise that dream for her wedding day of all days.

Seth changed tactics. "What if it takes twelve months to get into it? Have you thought of that?" He asked, playing the devil's advocate as he advanced toward her.

Backed against the kitchen counter now, Chelsea caught the frustration in his voice. He wasn't happy about the date. She sighed deeply. "Please, it's important to me. We can set a date for eighteen months from now. How about that?"

"No, a year from today, no longer." Seth pressed her back into the counter. "That's less than five pounds a month, for God's sake. You can do that easily. I'll help you."

Her shoulders slumped as she heaved a heavy sigh. "I guess you're right." She hated to admit it, but he was right. They had waited all this time to get engaged. It was time to move forward.

He stepped back, giving her room to move. "What date do you want?" Seth pulled out his cell phone and flipped to the calendar app.

Chelsea reclaimed her seat at the table, fumbling with her cold toast and trying to stall. "I don't know. How about July second? I can ask around to see what dates are open." *If I can only get him off the subject.*

"Not this year, July second, but next year?" He looked at her expectantly. That's more than a year, Chel."

"I know, but I like the idea of a July wedding." She knew that he knew she was trying to wiggle more time out of him.

"Tell me more," he said, walking back to the table. He dropped a kiss on the top of her head before taking his seat.

"Let me check with the restaurant. Pick two backup dates in case that date is already booked," Chelsea said while typing a note on her own cell phone.

Looking relieved, Seth continued, "The following Saturday, July 9th. And what do you think about a Friday night wedding, say July 8th?"

"Eh, Fridays are hard for people who work during the day," advised Chelsea, not looking up from her cell phone.

"That's why I said Friday night. Like eight p.m. Then we can party the rest of the night," Seth suggested. "I think it beats a Saturday morning wedding. Plus, it'll give you more time to get ready during the day."

"I want a night wedding anyway. I'll check into it. It might be cheaper than a Saturday night."

"I'll be willing to bet ..." Seth nodded, looking like he was warming up to the idea. "Then we can sneak away to a hotel suite next door at the Hilton for our honeymoon night." His eyes glinted, his voice suggestive.

"I like that idea too. You know, we could even go to the hotel for a change of clothes to be more comfortable after the ceremony formalities," Chelsea offered, her spirits rising with the simplicity of the plan.

"And maybe a little something more like a quickie?" Seth's voice turned husky and mischievous as he winked at her across the table.

"It's a deal. Friday night, July eight, if it's open." Chelsea frowned, worry lines strung across her forehead despite her happy tone. They had finalized their wedding date just over a year away. *When I'm a sexy size twelve.*

Gemma flung her cell phone on her desk as her temper exploded. She was so tired of trying to get in contact with Charlie. He didn't answer her calls most of the time. He never replied to her emails or voice messages. It was like the man was no longer interested in their relationship. If that was the way, why didn't he just say something.

She picked up the cell phone and set it in the spot it always sat on her desk. As she straightened out the papers on her desk, the phone rang. Looking at the screen, she hastened to answer it. "Hello, Charlie?"

"Yeah, babe. I only have a minute. Sorry I missed your call a couple minutes ago. I'm out in LA for a meeting. Can I call you later?"

His voice was apologetic and hesitant. Gemma was sorry she had blown up over his distance. He hadn't mentioned he was going to LA beforehand. If she had known, she wouldn't have tried calling until the evening when he would likely be free. Still, that didn't excuse him from all the other times he'd ignored her. "Men." Gemma shook her head and set down the cell phone before returning to her work.

• • • •

MARLA SAT AT THE BAR of Bellatoni's Restaurant, nursing an excellent pinot noir. She'd eaten her Caesar salad with a cup of minestrone soup. The menu was phenomenal, with so many delicious pizzas and entrées to choose from. Her determination had wavered. But she persevered, keeping her meal's calorie count even smaller by squeezing a lemon over her salad instead of using the anchovy-based dressing.

It was early, and she wasn't quite up to staring at the four walls of house just yet. The bar area of the restaurant provided lots of diversional nuances. Inside these four walls, the aroma of tomato sauce, the clink of cutlery on plates, and the low murmur of surrounding patrons added to the pleasant ambiance.

The bartender had mentioned a pianist would be playing in the bar area starting at nine, so Marla had wandered over there after her dinner. A little night music before bed, with a glass of wine, her first in well over a month, would be far better than another chapter in a romance book or surfing the TV for something intelligent to watch.

A tall, thin, red-haired man in a dark blazer approached the piano at a quarter to nine. He sat down, adjusted the mike, repositioned electrical cords, and placed sheet music on the piano top. He approached the bar, meeting and holding Marla's eyes as he drew closer. He gave her a friendly smile.

"Hello. Here for the music?"

"Yes. Thought I'd check out the local talent," Marla said truthfully, then cringed as his eyebrows shot up slightly at the import of her words.

He stopped a passing waitress and asked for a club soda. "Here's hoping I meet your standards." He smiled broadly, saluting her with a wiggle of his eyebrows before returning to the piano to start his first set.

The music was pleasant. A mix of both instrumental and vocal songs. The musician introduced himself as Stan Carney, saying, "This one's for those in the audience checking out the local talent." He smiled at her pointedly, with a twinkle in his eye. He broke into a sultry rendition of "The Way You Look Tonight," eyeing Marla frequently throughout the song.

Marla smiled back shyly, feeling the heat of a blush rising up her neck to her ear tips.

The first set over, Stan approached her with his empty soda glass in hand. Marla had turned sideways to the bar in her chair, resting her left elbow on the polished black granite surface. Stan stepped into the space beside Marla's bar stool and the next, which was occupied. He asked the bartender for a refill as he placed his empty glass on the bar top.

He remained so close to Marla she could feel his breath on her arm. Then his leg rubbed against hers. He watched the bartender spritz his soda as though nothing was happening below the bar top. Soda in hand, he turned toward her, his eyes half-lidded, a knowing smile on his face. "Well," He seared Marla from head to toe with a heated gaze. "How'd I do?"

"Um ... very well. I'm impressed." She smiled back, trying desperately to muster some molecules of flirtation. She couldn't remember how to flirt.

His cologne was nice. Not too strong or fake. Notes of lemongrass and wood, just right for a man. She liked it, but this guy was coming at her like a steam roller to a butterfly.

"Great," he said, then bent toward her, invading her personal space further. "Hang around 'til the end, and we'll see how impressed you can be," he whispered into her ear.

She couldn't meet his eyes. Marla's face flamed, setting her cheeks and ears ablaze. She wouldn't have been surprised to see smoke wafting off her body.

Frozen in place, she watched him walk over to the restaurant manager for a few words before returning to the piano, settling himself down for another half hour of entertainment.

Once he had started his second set, Marla slugged back the remainder of her wine as another full wineglass was set before her. Glaring at the bartender, she said, "I didn't order another."

"Your friend did." He shrugged toward Stan and walked away.

Marla slid off the bar stool, almost crashing to the floor when her legs wobbled on impact, and fled back to her hotel. Stan's voice faltered behind her.

Alone, back in the safety of her home, she stared at herself in the full-length mirror. Blushing bright pink, she couldn't believe he had flirted with her so openly and so ... so ... naughty! A shiver went up Marla's spine thinking about it. She'd read enough romance books to know flirting and what came of it.

She had never flirted with anyone before. Not even Sam though he had tried to flirt with her. No man had ever touched her intimately. She and Sam had agreed to remain celibate until married. Looking at herself in the mirror, her hands slid down along the smooth contours of her waist, her hips, her thighs, knowing that while her body was primed and ready for such an experience, emotionally and psychologically, she was a novice.

"You're going to have to figure this out before something like this happens again," Marla said to her reflection. This new body would attract male attention whether she wanted it or not.

The shiver that coursed down her spine to the conflux of her thighs told her she definitely wanted it.

• • • •

HEATHER WAS NERVOUS on the night of the reunion. Her parents had picked up the kids for the weekend, so they were all set. She had time during the day to give herself a basic manicure and pedicure. Trying to ease her nerves, she took a bubble bath, shaved her legs, and primped up her hair. The dress was over five years old, but this was the first time she'd been able to wear it since Nicholas was born, so it didn't look threadbare.

Her only problem involved trying to use a slip with a waistband that had lost its elasticity. She used a safety pin to cinch it tight around her waist since there was no time to replace it now. Hopefully, it wouldn't open up during the party, either during dinner or on the dance floor.

Not that she expected Billy to ask her to dance. Billy hadn't danced with her since their wedding day, and that was only because his best man had just about put a gun to his head.

"It's tradition, man," David had said. "Dance with her for a few minutes, get it over with." Billy had begrudgingly complied and happily for him, was left in peace most of the remainder of the night. He had barely helped Heather cut the wedding cake. He was too drunk by then to stand up straight, much less hold a knife steady for pictures.

Billy waited until twenty minutes before they had to leave to begin changing into his outfit for the night. He still fit into the same suit he'd worn to his grandmother's funeral eight years ago. Infuriating, Heather thought, considering the huge meals, beer binges, and junk food snacking he did week after week.

When he couldn't find his dress shoes, he ranted and raved about never being able to find anything in "this house." Heather shook her head and lifted the bed's dust ruffle to expose the dusty shoes hanging out with the dust bunnies under the bed. Billy glared at her with venomous eyes, wiped the dust off with a sock, put on his shoes, and headed for the kitchen, where his suit jacket waited.

They were silent on the way to the restaurant in the Dodge Challenger.

"I only have seventy bucks for drinks for the night. That's it, so stretch them out." He also reminded her "beer was less expensive than wine or cocktails."

Heather seethed silently on her side of the car. The car windows were steaming up, probably from the steam coming from her ears. *Why didn't he think to bring more money, assuming he had more?*

By design or not, they were late for cocktails. So late, they only had enough time to grab their name badges and meal tickets, and find available seats. Much to Heather's chagrin, Billy steered her to a table in the very back, where two seats were available. At the table where Billy's old girlfriend, Cindy Devenshear, was sitting with three other women and two other men.

"Look, Billy Laulier's here, with Heather! Wonderful! Now we have a full table."

Heather winced. Cindy had obviously been here for all of cocktail hour.

After introductions, Heather decided she would have preferred any other table to the one Billy had chosen.

The eight-foot round banquet tables were covered in white tablecloths, the napkins in their school colors of navy and gold. Each table had a vase stuffed with a collection of daffodils and tulips. The lights were up enough to see across the hall. The walls were covered with weathered barn-board, solid wood beams stretched across the plaster ceiling.

She turned around to scan for other possible tables, but it was too late. A hand with a salad plate materialized in front of her. It would indeed be entirely too rude to get up and move now. Not that she thought there was any chance in hell Billy would move to another table for the remainder of the evening. Suck it up, she told herself, pasting on a smile and trying to be pleasant to the man on her right. Just because Billy was going to make an ass of himself didn't mean Heather had to justify his behavior with her own.

Throughout the dinner, Billy ignored Heather in favor of the woman to his left, Cindy. Jackie sat to Cindy's left. Heather made polite small talk with another former classmate's husband, Paul, seated on her right. Paul had kind, brown eyes and a receding hairline, hardly the type for Anita Nostrum. He didn't appear to be enjoying this nightmare table any more than she. Fortunately for Heather, his conversational skills kept her from constantly tuning her ear in to hear Billy and Cindy's conversation, which involved a lot more laughter than was necessary.

Billy elbowed her left arm. "What do you want at the bar?" he asked her when she turned his way.

"Coors Light, please. With a glass," replied Heather as nicely as she could muster after being ignored for the last twenty minutes and being poked so hard.

Billy strode off to the bar as the wait staff cleared the salad plates. When he returned, he had two bottles of beer, one with a glass over the top and two glasses of wine. Heather's eyes became as big as the pasta plate in front of her as he handed the wine to Jackie and Cindy, then passed Heather her beer. She said nothing but gave him a glare he never caught.

Dinner continued with more and more boisterous outbursts from Billy and Jackie and Cindy, who were going stag for the night. Billy was egging them on, having slugged down his entire beer during the pasta course. As a plate of prime rib was set down in front of him, he strode off to the bar again, returning with another beer for himself.

Heather ate in silence, feeling the temperature of her blood rise another five degrees with each outburst of laughter. *Focus. Focus on your food.*

Jackie and Cindy were literally fawning all over Billy with compliments and innuendos throughout dinner. Outrageous stunts and other despicable incidents they had conspired during high school were retold in the hopes of titillating their table mates.

Paul tried to make small talk with Heather, but she shut him down. The hard stare from Paul's wife warned her not to get too chummy with him. Paul didn't look too enthralled with their immature behavior either. Heather slugged back the last of her beer in desolation.

Billy noticed her draining the glass, gave her a wink, then leaned over to whisper in her ear. "I only have enough money for another couple beers. Do you want one now, or do you want to wait?"

Surprised Billy had noticed, she said, "I'll wait until after dinner." Beer wasn't on the Calorie Counters list, but there was no way she was getting through this night without at least one more to soothe her frayed nerves.

Something stabbed Heather in the waist on her right side. She jerked to the left, and the pain disappeared, only to return when she settled herself back level into her chair. Then it dawned on her, the safety pin had either opened or let go. Rather than wait it out, Heather left the table for the ladies' room to fix the pin.

As she walked into the bathroom, the slip slid down her hips into a pile around her ankles. Heather groaned, partly mortified and partly relieved it waited until she was in the bathroom. She stepped out of the slip and picked it up to look for the pin. It was nowhere to be found. *Can this night get any worse?* Her heart sank further.

A couple of women she didn't recognize came into the bathroom. Explaining her situation, one woman dug through her purse, coming up with a paperclip. It wasn't ideal, but Heather didn't have much choice. She rigged up the slip again. Dancing was now completely out of the question, not that she thought Billy would suggest it. Not to her anyway. At least her slip would stay where it belonged, and she wouldn't show her crotch to everybody in attendance.

Billy gave her a dirty look when she returned to the table.

"Where have you been?" he asked angrily.

"Ladies' room, I had a wardrobe malfunction," Heather replied, her blood boiling that she had to account for her fifteen minutes away from the table.

A half-hour later, dessert was served with coffee or tea. She was thirsty. The water carafes at the table were already empty. Anita had asked the wait staff twice for more water, but it never materialized. By the time she'd finished the dry cheesecake and hot coffee, Heather was parched for something ice-cold and refreshing.

She turned to Billy to ask for that beer, only to find him gone. She scanned the room, looking for him, finally seeing him approaching the table from the bar: two glasses of wine in hand and one beer.

Heather watched in disbelief as Billy handed off the wine to Jackie and Cindy again. Then instead of handing it to her, he downed half the beer in one gulp.

"Where's mine?" Heather whispered.

"Sorry, I didn't have enough money," Billy whispered in her ear. He chugged back the last half of the bottle, shrugged his shoulders, and set the empty bottle on the table beside her.

Was he trying to make it look like she had drank it? Heather was stunned speechless. She couldn't believe he'd bought wine for Bimbo One and Bimbo Two and left her bereft for the remainder of the evening.

The hair on the back of her neck stood up as someone came close behind her. Paul resumed his seat beside her and set down a beer in front of her. Billy scowled at the offering.

"Thank you, Paul," Heather said softly. "That was very kind of you."

"My pleasure," Paul replied with a tiny wink.

Beyond Paul, she could see Paul's wife scowl at her.

Heather nursed her beer for another hour. Billy refused to leave the table to mingle with other classmates. He, Jackie, and Cindy were becoming so boisterous Heather was afraid the management would end up throwing them out. Knowing Billy, he wouldn't take that too kindly or calmly, not with a couple beers in him and an audience to impress.

After finishing Paul's sympathy beer, she slipped away to the restroom. When she returned, the table was empty. Billy was on the dance floor with both Jackie and Cindy. The remaining couples were also dancing. Heather refused to sit at the table alone. Instead, she saw some classmates she remembered seated across the hall and went to say hello.

She never returned to the table for the rest of the evening. Billy was either acting like an ass or flirting outrageously with Cindy and Jackie. Probably hoping to catch himself a threesome, Heather mused wryly.

When the band quit playing at midnight, Heather retrieved her coat from the coatroom and waited in the restaurant foyer for Billy.

Over the next half hour, nearly everyone left. Then she saw him coming down the hallway, arm slung over Cindy's shoulder like they were still dating. Before getting to the foyer, they stopped and kissed like it was still high school.

Heather's fury exploded. She stood up, arms crossed, glaring at them.

"Billy!" Heather barked. "What do you think you're doing?"

Billy and Cindy broke off their kiss as gawking people scurried around them, getting out of the line of fire.

"Giving my friend a goodbye kiss," Billy slurred back. Cindy giggled like it was the funniest thing she'd heard all night. Heather cringed at the sickening sound of it, like metal scratching against metal.

Billy sauntered over and tried to swing his arm around Heather's shoulder, but she was too quick for him. She stepped aside as he flung his arm and leaned, letting him drop to the floor. She didn't know how he'd gotten more alcohol or maybe found someone with hash. He was drunk or stoned or both. It didn't matter.

Heather dug the keys from his pants pocket in front of the tittering crowd and stalked out to the car.

Someone must have helped Billy up. He stumbled to the car a few minutes later, dropped into the passenger seat, and flopped his head back against the head rest. A shit-ass grin was wedged on his face, his eyes closed. When the car began moving through the parking lot, he grabbed his stomach and threw up on his shoes.

Heather didn't stop. She lowered the windows and drove home with Billy puking all over himself. The stink of alcohol puke made her gag as she drove. His stomach emptied, he passed out, slumped against the door. That's where Heather left him when she got home. That's where he woke up the following day, cold, hungover, and covered in puke, in the passenger seat of his precious Challenger.

The kids came home that afternoon to find Daddy cleaning out his car and Mommy down in the basement doing laundry, sobbing as she folded clean towels. Heather's mother, Macie, who got the whole story from her daughter, wanted to smack Billy upside the head for acting like a drunk idiot. She tried to console her daughter, but Heather wasn't hearing anything.

As far as Heather was concerned, if Billy wanted Cindy, he could get the hell out of the house this minute. She'd even told him so when he stumbled into the house at about eleven in the morning. Billy said he didn't remember doing any such thing; Heather was making it up. Trouble was, Billy had been so drunk he couldn't remember trying to suck Cindy's fillings out of her teeth.

Heather also knew it was more than just that kiss. It was buying Cindy and Jackie all those glasses of wine, especially after telling her not to order any because it was too expensive. So he could buy it for his former girlfriends but not for his wife? How inconsiderate could he get in front of all those people? She'd had to accept a stranger's generous offer to quench her thirst. Overall, it was not the respectful way to treat your wife in any manner, shape, or form. It was too much. Until he apologized, she wasn't talking to him.

Macie left her daughter and the three kids in the silent house with Snoopy. Heather knew her mother was furious at Billy, but there was nothing she could do. It was up to Billy to apologize.

The next week was also silent. Billy went to work each morning without Heather's carefully made lunches this time. He didn't return home right after work. He'd stopped at the bar, so he said. While he did smell of beer, there was a whiff of perfume lingering underneath.

With kids to feed, Heather made dinner at the usual time. If Billy missed it, tough for him. He knew when dinner was served. If he couldn't be bothered to call to say he'd be late, Heather couldn't be bothered to save him any. When she and the kids were finished eating, Snoopy enjoyed the leftovers.

On Friday evening, Billy didn't come home until after midnight. He reeked of alcohol and marijuana, something she hadn't smelled on him since high school. It wasn't a good sign, but she wasn't his keeper. He knew where the bread was baked. Nonetheless, she worried his job might be in jeopardy if he continued to let his behavior slide. A slowly clenching tightness grew in her gut with another week of erratic behavior.

• • • •

SETH AND CHELSEA SAT in her car outside a reception venue. "You can't be serious, Chel," he said, shaking his head sternly. "We can't afford this place. Two hundred dollars a plate? They're crazy."

She crossed her arms over her chest. "I've always dreamed it would be here."

"I think you're taking this childhood dream stuff too seriously. We *cannot* afford this place. I have given you as much as I can, but I'm not some CEO or corporate executive. I'm a carpenter, working for my family's business. You have to compromise."

Chelsea bit her lip, her body tense. "I don't want to."

Seth sighed, sorrow etching his face. "Then you're marrying the wrong guy."

• • • •

HEATHER'S THREE CHILDREN were in tow when the four women met at the Frick Park children's playground. They watched as the two boys played on the slides and swings. Michelle sat in the sandbox, her sun hat flopping over her eyes while her chubby hands pulled up handfuls of sand and flung them back down again.

"How're things going, Heather?" Marla asked as she put her arm around Heather's shoulders.

"All right. It's tense between Billy and me, but I don't think the kids are sensing it yet."

Chelsea interrupted. "You have to make plans, try to put some money aside. Do you have your own bank account?"

"No. It's a savings account with the children's names on it too." Heather blushed. "But I do have some cash stowed away for emergencies."

"Good, you take that to a different bank and open your own account. And don't tell Billy about it."

The tension in Heather's stomach escalated. "You don't think this is going to end well, do you?" She glanced from one friend to the next and the next.

"No," the three friends answered together.

A few moments of silence echoed between them.

Heather sighed. "I lost my wedding ring."

The others glanced at her vacant ring finger.

"Sometime during the day, between cooking and cleaning, I lost my wedding ring. I've noticed it was a little looser with my weight loss. I've been checking it every once in a while to make sure it wouldn't slide off my finger. Two days ago, it couldn't slip past my knuckle. After doing the dishes today, I dried my hands on the dish towel and noticed it was gone. Gone! I don't know if I lost it here at the park or in the house. It wasn't in the sink or anywhere on the floor." She stopped for a moment to sigh. "When I told Billy, he shrugged and went back to watching the baseball game. He wasn't upset about it or anything. And the more I think about it, I'm not missing it either."

"Speaking about weddings and rings," Chelsea started to explain, "Seth and I had a huge fight over the wedding venue. I can't budge him. He's dug in his heels. He even suggested maybe he's the wrong man for me if I want something so expensive."

The three women had their mouths hanging open when Chelsea told them about the location and the cost.

"My God," Heather said, "You can't seriously be thinking of paying that much money. What are you going to do?"

Tears welled up in Chelsea's eyes. "But I've always dreamed—"

Gemma gripped Chelsea's hand tight. "You have a good man who wants to marry you. Do you want to lose him for the rest of your life over something so insignificant as the site for one night's celebration?"

Wiping her face with her hands, Chelsea shook her head.

• • • •

BILLY'S MOTHER CALLED a few days later.

"Sorry, Joyce, Billy's out," Heather said.

"Where to?" Joyce Lynn asked.

"I don't know. If I had to guess, he's out with some woman, maybe at the Tavern bar."

"Since when does 'e do that?" Joyce Lynn bit back.

"Since I found him making out with his old girlfriend at our high school reunion." Heather sighed heavily.

"That stupit boy. What the hells 'e done that fer?" Joyce Lynn bellowed.

"I don't know, Joyce. Since then, he goes to work, comes home, sometimes not until after midnight."

"T'morrow's Saturday. I'll be over to straighten 'im out. Don't you tell 'im I'm comin'," she ordered.

"No ma'am," Heather said, hanging up with a giddy feeling in her chest. She couldn't wait to see his face when his momma showed up. There'd be hell to pay now his mother knew what was up. If anyone could straighten his ass up, Joyce Lynn would do it.

Joyce Lynn Laulier showed up at nine a.m., four hours after Billy managed to drag his ass home. He still lay passed out on the bed, fully clothed, reeking of cigarette smoke, hash, and alcohol when she poked her salt and pepper-haired head into the bedroom to roust him up for a "talkin' to." Having raised him essentially alone, she knew exactly how to handle him, and she had the cracked veneer to prove it. "Granny" to the kids, she looked every day her fifty-seven years plus another dozen for the hard labor she did in the laundry room at the nearby hospital.

By the time she left an hour later, Billy was awake, showered, shaved, and dressed in clean clothes. She'd reamed him a new hole for acting like an ass, not caring for his children, and treating Heather like slave labor.

After Joyce's intervention, things changed a little. Billy came home from work, ate with his children, helped put them to bed, then left the house without a word to Heather. He'd return home shortly after last call at two a.m. Sometimes he'd return after six a.m., change clothes, then get himself off to work for seven a.m. How he worked on so little sleep, Heather didn't know.

Four weeks after Joyce's intervention, a phone call came after midnight. Thinking something bad might have happened to Billy, Heather answered the phone rather than wait to screen the call. A wispy female voice informed her, in complete detail, what her husband was doing at the Tavern Bar.

"Billy's flirting with Cindy Devenshear, Jackie Lagorin, and a few of their other women friends," the unfamiliar voice reported.

A sinking feeling in Heather's gut took over her body. A few seconds passed before she could reply. "What makes you think I don't already know?"

Ignoring Heather's reply, the woman continued, "Times like this, later in the evening, Cindy and Billy hide themselves in a dark corner. They get *real* intimate for such a public place." Pleasure dripped from the voice. Whoever this woman was, she was enjoying telling Heather, or maybe just snitching on Cindy and Billy. Maybe both.

"Why do you think I care?" Heather replied, putting as much strength into her voice as possible. She couldn't let the caller know how much her words hurt.

"I thought you should know what Billy is up to."

"Thanks, but I don't care to know, " replied Heather, hanging up before she lost her temper or her backbone. She couldn't identify the voice. It didn't matter who called. It only mattered that her words confirmed what Heather had thought.

LATE MAY 2018

Gemma gave her presentation to the board of directors. They approved each site suggestion for their organization's national conventions with the accompanying hotel contracts and the regional meeting sites for the next two years. They had been given Gemma's report, including a summary of the request for proposal responses from the various convention centers and meeting sites, the site review checklists, interpretation reports, and hotel contract drafts a week before the meeting for their review. Having successfully concluded her portion of the board meeting, she left for a relaxing lunch at Bangkok Balcony on Forbes Avenue.

Later that afternoon, the organization's president asked to speak with Gemma in his office.

"Those were terrific reports you put together. The board is exceptionally pleased with the quality of your work," Mike Jonkowski said.

"Thank you, sir. It's a pleasure to work for this organization," Gemma affirmed.

"Yes, well. Gemma, after you left, the board had other issues to discuss. One of those issues was the decline in membership and its financial impact on our organization. Gemma, the board is cutting back on staffing here at the office. They would like to downsize your department."

"I know, I know." Mike immediately held up his hands, palms forward to forestall the outburst Gemma was ready to unleash. "Please let me finish. This is hard enough. You have a good team. But the expenses of the entire team are more than the board is comfortable with at this time. We need you to cut two positions from your staff."

She could see Mike's shoulders tense, see the tick of a muscle in his tightened jaw.

"Two! Mike, my God, how, when?" she asked.

"By next month. If you can figure out who by the end of this week, we can pay them through the end of the month and pay them for unused vacation and sick time," Mike said, palms upward in supplication. "It's not much, but it is better than some people are getting these days."

"Who do you want me to let go?" Gemma asked, her mind still reeling from the news. A headache started to bud in her left temple.

"That's up to you. The board made it clear that's your department, your responsibility, and your decision," Mike reported. "We don't have seniority rights here, so any one of them is eligible. Let me know who you select, by Friday if you can, so we can complete the paperwork."

Gemma stood to leave his office, turned toward the door, and then turned back and approached his desk.

"Mike, how far is this going to go? I mean, how stable are the remaining jobs?" She rested her fingers on the edge of the desktop to keep her steady.

"The economy is tanking. Our membership numbers are down fifteen percent. Where it all will end is anyone's guess," replied Mike, his face looking as miserable as Gemma felt. "It's our full intention to keep the remaining staff."

"Thank Mike," Gemma said before heading for her office, where a super-sized bottle of Extra Strength Tylenol was waiting to intercept the monster headache spreading across her skull.

She left the office early that day, heading for Frick Park for some solitary reflection on what she had been asked to do. Lay off two workers from her staff of four. Walking the paved paths, she reviewed her staff, their credentials, and their performance history.

Marilyn had been her first hire, a graduate of the same program Gemma had attended, but she had no previous experience before coming to NACET.

Jeremy graduated from a program in North Carolina and had two years of experience with the North Carolina American Red Cross. He had been hired second.

Mei also had two years of experience, but with a corporate insurance company in San Francisco, before moving to Pittsburgh for her husband's medical residency. On a leave of absence from UPitt, her education was just starting in the field.

Tony had a bachelor's degree in graphic design. He handled all of the conferences' design factors, including layout of the exhibit halls, brochures, and many other design decisions dealing with the meetings. In that regard, he was less a meeting associate than a member of the overall office staff. Gemma hardly thought the board would see it in that manner and spare his position.

All of these members worked without direct supervision, requiring little effort on her part. They were professional, extremely hard-working, giving their all to the job when required. As teams, Marilyn and Tony worked best together, while Jeremy and Mei made another cohesive team. Marilyn and Jeremy got along okay, but had very different ways of achieving the same end. Working together was sometimes a challenge. So if Mei and Tony were to go, Gemma would have to keep Jeremy and Marilyn on separate tasks until they got better at working together. Gemma would have to go back to supervising all event again. It would be a grueling schedule. Unless the conference schedule was also being downsized in consideration of the economy. *I'll have to check with Mike about it.*

As much as she hated to lose such a hard worker, Mei was the least experienced and least educated on the team. Her name would be one of the two given to Mike. Despite the significant design assistance and the hard work, Tony would have to be the other member of her staff to go. While he helped do many jobs during the events and in the event planning processes, he could not handle any of the contractual processes.

With a heavy heart, Gemma went home and crawled into bed. She tried not to think about the looks on Mei and Tony's faces on Friday. The only bright spot was the thought she could give each of them a glowing recommendation.

Gemma knocked on Charlie's door Friday night, despite all the lights being out. His car sat in the driveway, in its usual parking space. Perhaps he was out with the guys, one of them picking him up.

She hadn't talked with him all week. And he wasn't returning her cell phone messages. The post-it notes she left on his condo door were disappearing but went unanswered.

Did I do something to make him angry?

She knew the answer to that question.

His sudden, unexplained disappearance had her suspicious he was dating someone else. Gemma had no idea how to find out. He was exceptionally discreet about their relationship.

Saturday morning, he knocked on her door at eight a.m. with a box of pastries and her favorite coffee drink from Tisane Tea Shoppe. Gemma staggered to the door, looking like someone the rescue squad had pulled out of a train wreck.

"Charlie. I'm sorry. I'm not in the mood for …" Gemma muttered, feeling even more miserable if that was possible.

"Gem, what happened?" Charlie asked, genuine worry in his voice. He brushed past her and sidestepped Wally to drop the goodies on the table and take her in his arms.

She struggled out of them instantly. She had been up until three a.m. when someone in a Volvo dropped him off. Gemma wasn't sure, but she thought it was a woman. Which she found odd.

Not wanting to bring up the subject, she made her work problem the excuse. "It's been the worst week of my working life. I had to lay off two of my staff yesterday." Her already puffy and sore eyes teared up again.

"Oh, Gemma. I'm so sorry. That had to suck," Charlie said with a deep sigh.

"It did. I hated it more than—crap—it was as bad as losing a friend." She wept openly.

Charlie held open his arms. Gemma couldn't resist. She stepped in and rested her head on his shoulder.

He patted her back, kissing her forehead. "It's okay, Gem. I'm sure they knew you didn't want to do it."

"Yeah, they recognized it wasn't me. It didn't make it any easier, not for me." Gemma wept on, her tears already soaking into his T-shirt.

"Okay, pretty lady. Me thinks you need a chocolate raspberry latte and a chocolate filled croissant," Charlie said, leading her to the table and pulling out a chair. "Tell me everything." And despite her suspicion he was seeing someone else, she did.

• • • •

THROUGHOUT THE TURMOIL with Billy, Heather still went to Calorie Counters. Her mother came over to watch the kids when Billy left after dinner for reasons he wouldn't disclose. It wasn't easy, but Heather thought that if she could lose another twenty-five pounds and get to her high school weight, she could at least compete with Cindy Devenshear.

A guest speaker at one of the Calorie Counters meetings had suggested journaling might be helpful to some of the clients. She noted it was particularly helpful to see if there were patterns to their eating or binging problems.

Heather bought a notebook to try journaling. She tried to write in it at least once a week, keeping track of her own thoughts and feelings about her weight loss journey.

May 11th weight: 153

One of the hardest things for me is making a goal. As Pricilla said, it's all about setting a plan, seeing yourself fulfilling that plan. Making that goal weight. I can't do it. I hate that word "goal." Goal setting was a death sentence for my weight loss plan every other time. It has such a negative connotation for me. So, I don't have a "goal" weight. I can only try to follow the system one day at a time and eat healthier. As best I can on my limited means. Don't anyone dare call that my "goal." The act of even setting one means I won't achieve it.

May 18th weight: 151

Pricilla said that what our inner voice says is what holds us back. For example, when I weighed in this week, I was down three pounds. My weigh-in partner, Nancy congratulated me profusely. I said something like "thank God, I worked hard at it this week. No cheating, no extras, and I exercised every single day." Then the Voice said, "don't worry, you'll be back up three pounds next week." So my unconscious core is another of my saboteurs. I have to face the Voice down, conquer it. The deeper issue is this unconscious core. It makes me a quitter. I cannot follow through on any program or project, including this project. Project Me. I can't believe in myself. The Voice tells me so. I can't believe that just losing weight is going to make my marriage better. I think the bigger question is, do I still want it?

May 25th, weight 148

The Shadow Self, Jung called it. Others have called it the Rot. The part of yourself that is the root of your feelings of unworthiness. Pricilla says we hide from it, withdraw from it, fight it back when it rears its ugly head, fight the negative Voice that echoes from it. It keeps us from being whole and healthy because it is the part of us that makes it impossible to love ourselves. Pricilla says we should make friends with it, make peace. Talk with it, not stuff it back into the closet. It has powerful emotions that need to be confronted. Until we confront them, hear them out, correct their misgivings, we will always struggle with the Rot. We confront it to control it. I guess my Rot is my marriage. Am I really happy married to Billy? If not, what am I going to do about it?

• • • •

THE FOUR WERE SEATED at their usual table at Jitters Café.

Marla started the conversation. "Time to fess up. How is the weight loss going, ladies?" She looked at Heather on her right.

Heather blinked. "It's okay. I can't tell you how much because I haven't weighed myself in days. If I had to guess, I'd say I'm not losing much, if anything, but not gaining either." Heather looked at Gemma.

Gemma mashed her lips together and shook her head. "I've gained a few." She stuck her index finger in the air. "Just a few." Gemma turned to Chelsea, who was shrinking back in her seat. "Chel?"

Chelsea's face flushed, her cheeks bright red. "I'm up a few too."

Gemma smirked, "Care to elaborate? How many?"

"No." Chelsea wiped at a single tear. "You guys. You know how I am with food. And that Slimline food sucks."

"What about your dress?" Heather asked.

Chelsea shook her head, and another tear dripped onto her cheek. "I know. I know. My bad eating habits will never get me into that wedding dress."

Marla butt in, "Why not try another program? I can set you up with my dietician. She's wonderful."

"I can't afford a dietician."

"How about going to Calorie Counters with me?" Heather suggested.

Chelsea's face closed. "I'll think about it."

It was clear to everyone Chelsea didn't want to discuss the issue anymore. Rather than push her, Marla decided to change the subject.

"I was thinking the other day how my weight loss has changed two housekeeping tasks."

She got a blank stare from the other three and continued, "The overall weight of my laundry has decreased. As my clothes become smaller in size, the volume of fabric per article decreases too. There are more articles in a load now, so fewer loads."

"I hadn't noticed because I haven't been paying attention to my laundry," Gemma said. "It makes perfect sense. I'll have to give it some review."

Chelsea butt in, "You can't tell because you drop your laundry off at the cleaners, and they do it."

"Jealous?" Gemma stuck out her tongue at Chelsea and crossed her arms over her chest. "I can tell if I look at the receipts. The weight of a week's worth of clothing is on it. I'll compare my pre-surgery to my post-surgery receipts."

Marla continued, "The other thing I've noticed is how I spend more time grocery shopping and less money on takeout food. And of course, what I buy has changed. No more sodas or snack foods. Instead I buy produce. It feels good in an odd sort of way."

"I wouldn't know. All my food comes in expensive tiny microwavable packages." Chelsea muttered through clenched teeth.

Heather ignored Chelsea's comment. "Yes, I've noticed how my grocery shopping has changed. Though it's only a slight change. It helps the bottom line to not buy those sugary, fatty snacks. I used to think fresh fruit was expensive, but compared to the price per ounce of some snack items, they're a bargain."

"And better for you and the children," Marla offered. "Teaching them to reach for an apple or grapes instead of potato chips is good nutritional education."

"True, but now I have to sneak my own junk food, or they call me out for it," Heather giggled before the rest joined in.

JUNE 2018

Heather awoke as usual when she heard Billy come in the door before dawn. He had disappeared on Friday evening. She spent the entire weekend trying to skirt the issue when the children asked where their father was and why he wasn't home with them. After their pestering, she blurted out, "Working." It silenced their questions for a little while. Until the question changed to "When is Daddy coming home from work?"

Billy reeked of perfume. He was not drunk, not high, only quiet and sober, which was out of the new ordinary. Heather sat up in bed. Usually, he made a lot more noise because he stumbled and talked to himself. Tonight, he was extraordinarily quiet. When Heather could feel his presence in the darkened room, she reached out a hand and turned on the lamp on the bedside table.

"What the heck did ya do that for?" Billy grumbled. He was hunched over, his shoes and a white cloth in hand, caught in the act of tiptoeing into the room.

"I thought I heard something, didn't sound like you," Heather lied, trying to figure out what was going on. Something didn't smell right, beyond the woman's perfume.

"Well, it's me. Shut the light off," Billy barked, continuing his skulk to his side of the bed.

"I will when I'm ready." Heather picked up a paperback book she kept on her bedside table. She started to read strings of words that would not form cohesive phrases or sentences. Something was up. *What is it? What's different?* All her senses arced into simultaneous use, trying to figure out what exactly was going on here.

Billy dropped the shoes then retreated to the bathroom, where Heather could hear him brushing his teeth. He didn't do that any other time he came home. Something strange was happening or had happened.

When Billy strode back into the room, he was naked. *He must have put his clothes in the dirty laundry hamper himself for a change.* Heather glared over the top edge of the book. Something was definitely off.

Billy climbed into bed, plumped the pillow, and turned his back to Heather. "Would you shut the light off? I'm trying to sleep," he grumbled again.

"Maybe you should have come home earlier if you wanted to sleep," Heather said, now determined to read until the alarm clock went off at six a.m.

A mixture of scents lingered above the bed. Billy flapped the bed sheets, sending a puff of air across his body. Sweaty, musky, salty, semen and latex smells wafted through Heather's nostrils. The pit of her stomach ached. She pulled her knees up closer to her chest, resting the book on them. The words blurred as tears filled her eyes. Don't cry, she ordered herself. Don't you dare cry! Heather cleared her throat to disguise a sniffle and clamped down on her emotions.

She had some thinking to do.

Bleary-eyed, she finally shut the light off for good about five thirty, snuggled down in the bed, and fell asleep almost immediately; the last word she heard before dozing off was Billy grumbling about not getting much sleep.

Later in the morning, when she was picking up from the night before, she discovered the white cloth he'd been carrying with his shoes. It was his briefs. That explained why he'd undressed in the bathroom. He didn't want her to see he was coming home commando.

She found other signs of infidelity over the next few weeks. One afternoon she was transferring the clean laundry from the washer to the dryer when she came across an empty condom wrapper. After that, Heather checked his shirt and pants pockets before putting them through the wash.

Another week, she found a Victoria's Secret store receipt. He'd spent fifty dollars on a "silky ensemble." Heather didn't know what that entailed, but didn't think he was doing early Christmas shopping.

During the last week of the month he didn't come home at all one night. She found a hotel receipt stuffed in his pants pocket when he did. He'd spent the night at a hotel.

She didn't confront him about these slip-ups. In fact, she wasn't sure they were real slip-ups. It would be Billy's way to leave clues behind, this paper trail, as a means of letting Heather know where things stood. He wasn't man enough to tell her straight.

She tucked them away in a coffee mug hidden on the top shelf of the pantry. Alongside it was the ceramic teapot she never used. A wedding gift long ago, it now served as her money stash, a bit of Grandma Boyden's marriage advice. Since she'd been married, Heather had tried to tuck five to ten dollars a week away as security for herself. She'd upped it to twenty since Billy's shenanigans at the reunion. Every extra nickel left over at the end of the week went in there too. A couple of times each year, Heather took the teapot's contents down to the bank, a different bank than their regular bank, and deposited the funds into the savings account in her and the children's names. She had just under a thousand dollars after nine years of marriage.

Marla was having more wardrobe adjustments with her continued weight loss. She'd lost a shoe size. The first sign, which she didn't recognize, was while traveling. She struggled with them when trying to catch a connecting flight in O'Hare.

At first, she thought she'd tripped on something. She'd almost gone face-first flat out on the concourse carpet, but a pilot heading in the opposite direction saw her stumble and caught her arm. He'd smiled nicely, setting her straight on her feet. Once assured she was okay, he set off toward his gate. Embarrassed, Marla blushed profusely. He was handsome in his uniform!

Later, when she was inspecting a laboratory, she fell. The administrators worried she had slipped on some illicit spill. Marla assured them she was clumsy. She was too embarrassed to tell them what happened. She'd figured it out. The rest of the day, she had to be mindful to keep her shoe on her foot. Unfortunately, it was a two-inch heeled pump, so she couldn't tighten any strap or buckle to secure it.

That evening she took a taxi to a local shoe store to get a new pair. The salesperson measured her feet when she described what she thought was happening. The measurements confirmed Marla's feet were now a size six and a half instead of a seven. Not that she minded in the end; she liked buying shoes. She wasn't Imelda Marcos, even though she did have enough room for twenty-five to thirty pairs in her walk-in closet.

She purchased two new pairs at that store and another two when she got home. Those four pairs should keep her going during her weight loss. She promised herself she would fill her shoe racks when she reached her goal. She had tossed the oversized pairs in the Salvation Army-bound bag growing exponentially in the corner of her closet.

• • • •

CHELSEA FINALLY SWALLOWED her pride and her dreams. After making up with Seth and telling him she understood his objections, they sat down and made a budget for the wedding. Chelsea and Diane looked for more reasonable wedding sites. They had already checked a half dozen with no luck. Finding something they could afford and something available on the selected wedding date was looking impossible.

Heather was the last to arrive at the coffee shop a week later. Gemma, Chelsea, and Marla already had their beverages. Heather sank into the empty chair without getting herself a drink. The others watched her with suspicious eyes.

"Nice of you to join us," Gemma said before noisily sipping her espresso.

Chelsea caught the look on Heather's face. Something terrible had happened. "What is it? What's wrong?"

All three looked at Heather. As they watched, tears seeped out from under her closed eyelids. Marla, who was closest to her, wrapped her arm around Heather's shoulders. They remained quiet as they waited for her to speak.

"Billy is cheating on me. Over the last few weeks, I've found hotel receipts, condom wrappers, receipts for gifts from Victoria's Secret." She sobbed softly, both hands covering her face. "The stress threw me into a binge-eating fiasco. But it wasn't mindless. I knew when I was eating that it was solving nothing and going against my plan."

Chelsea reached across the table and rested her hand on Heather's arm. "You were looking for comfort. It's totally understandable."

"I didn't do it for comfort. I did it despite all that awareness and knowledge. I'm so disappointed in myself."

The other three women glanced at each other.

Gemma said softly, "Don't you think your disappointment is misplaced?"

Chelsea gave Gemma a jab of her elbow. "Ignore her."

Heather took a tissue offered by Marla. "I'm not blaming Billy for my overeating. I take responsibility for every morsel I put in my mouth and every pound that will result because of it." She straightened her shoulders and looked directly at Chelsea. "I can't control Billy, and I can't control my own eating."

They were silent for a few minutes before Chelsea asked, "What are you going to do?"

"Nothing right now. But it's time to start making plans just in case he abandons us all."

JULY 2018

July 1st, weight 145

This week's homework exercise was to determine what emotion we were feeling when we wanted to, or decided to eat. I found there were many reasons for my eating, but most of the time, it had nothing at all to do with hunger. I realized that I am bored a lot of the time. Sometimes there was guilt, fear, and shame associated with dealing with the kids. I didn't feel like I was doing the right things for them or to them. Most of the time I felt like an incompetent mother. Clearly, they were doing fine. Looking back on those episodes, there is no basis for those feelings of anxiety. Then it dawned on me that as much as I love my children, at this time in my life, I feel like I have no real purpose. Being a mother is not filling some kind of need in me that I can't explain. I will try to pick up my journal and pen when I get into that feeling instead of food. Maybe it will help on two fronts.

July 8th, weight 142.5

Pricilla let us in on a big secret. She said, "Trust me, I have to give my reflection in the mirror the self-love talk each morning." Pricilla has always struck me as a supremely self-confident woman. She is the kind of person who conquers the room when she walks in, and no, she's not a phony-baloney, she's the real deal. I admire this about her. As scary as she can be with her wardrobe and makeup and hairstyles, she's the kind of person who appears to have it all together all the time. It was shocking to learn even Pricilla has to cultivate and nurture herself, every day. And she doesn't see it as "keeping her guard up" but as a natural self-loving part of her day. I'm going to try to look in the mirror every day and say, "Here's Heather, a good mom, and a good wife." Maybe it will help me feel like I'm worthy of success.

Chelsea and Diane looked at all the websites, brochures and information notes they had made while visiting the florist. The price quote for the bridal bouquet pictured would cost over three hundred dollars. Chelsea's heart sank while Diane gasped at the cost. Yet again, the cost was going to prevent her from getting the bouquet she had selected years ago.

"Why does everything have to be so expensive?" Chelsea muttered. A fog of depression loomed over her head, making tears come to her eyes.

"Don't cry," Diane said. "So, you cut back on the out-of-season flowers. I'm sure the woman could put together a gorgeous bridal bouquet that won't be so expensive."

A rising fury made Chelsea clench her teeth. "I think this budget is ridiculous."

• • • •

RAIN BEGAN PELTING Marla's taxi before it pulled up at the Grand Hyatt Hotel in Seattle. Her check-in was expeditious, and the bellman led her to her room on the twenty-fourth floor.

The room was spectacular, one of the finest Marla had ever enjoyed. Maple-toned wood panels covered the hallway walls, and dark green and brown patterned squishy carpets invited her toes to slip out of her shoes as soon as the bellman was gone. Botanical-inspired artwork hung on soft beige walls over the fluffy, sage-colored comforter on the king-size bed. Eight pillows spread across the head of the bed tempted an early bedtime. Floor-to-ceiling sheer beige linen curtains muted the slowly amplifying city lights in the rising dusk. The view of Puget Sound and the Space Needle was spectacular despite the overcast skies, rain, and accumulating night.

Marla ordered a couple bottles of San Pellegrino, a carafe of hot water, some Earl Grey tea, a Caesar salad with chicken (a lemon for dressing on the side), and a fruit salad for dinner.

She stayed busy settling into the room while waiting for it to arrive. Her OCD required her to place toiletries in the beige-marbled bathroom and hang all her clothes in the closet before she could relax. She tried not to think of the man she would see again tomorrow. Tried to still the increasing thud of her heart at the mere thought of him.

"He could be ugly as sin and fatter than I was by now," she reminded herself. "So don't get your new panties in a twist yet. He could very well be married by now. Wait and see. If he's still as hunky as he was at Johns Hopkins, then you can swoon in the ladies' room."

After her dinner, she drew a bath for a luxurious soak in the huge, white, soaking tub, tossing in two lavender-scented fizz bath balls(complimentary), turned on Spotify for some soft classical music, and relaxed before a good night's sleep.

She hit the company cafeteria before seven a.m. to get an undercover feel for the morale of the new place. It wasn't part of the inspection, but Beverly had asked her to assess the employees' satisfaction with the new location. The faces around her appeared content. Laughter and animated conversations pervaded the warmly decorated room. It was a good sign.

A secretary ushered her into the medical director's office precisely at eight. Marla's step faltered when she laid eyes on Dr. Timothy Brighton for the first time in seven years. He was still stunningly drop-me-to-my-knees gorgeous. Dark brown wavy hair, dark brown eyes on a tanned and freckled boyish face. His features were neither hard and angular nor pudgy and rounded. Not quite six feet tall, his lean frame was nicely sculpted, like Michelangelo's "David," only more youthful about the eyes. *And if the rest of him is as sculpted*—Marla's eyes wandered to his left hand before she realized he was introducing her to the other three people in the office.

He led her around, radiating an aura of total relaxation and comfort. Better yet, he still didn't act like he knew how stunning he was.

By the time Marla started hearing words again, it was time for her to speak.

"...so pleased you could come see how well we've put together this satellite laboratory for Peabody. We're sure you'll find everything in order and to the company's liking," finished a mid-fifties aged woman, who must be Andrea Bekkit, the manager.

"I'm happy to be here to tour this new facility. I'm sure you've done everything according to state and federal regulations. My visit will be merely perfunctory—a double-check. I wish to become familiar with the management personnel," Marla said. *What am I talking about! Become familiar with management personnel?* There was only one member of management she wanted to become familiar with, and it was definitely on a personal level, not personnel. Moisture began to sprout on her forehead. *Get a grip, girl.*

"I received your pre-inspection letter with the list of areas of interest and have put together an itinerary. Did you have a chance to review it before your arrival?" Dr. Brighton asked, sitting rather casually on the front corner of a beautiful bird's eye maple desk. Marla noted his physique had filled out, become firmer and more muscular. *Now if he would only turn around so I can see his glutes.*

"It looks delicious," Marla flustered, trying to keep the blush she felt flaming her ear tips from spreading over her cheeks.

"Ah, but first, Ms. Devine. Would you like something to drink or eat?" He gestured to a side table set with assorted juices, coffee, and tea service, as well as a beautiful fresh fruit display and a tray of bagels, muffins, and pastries.

Marla sensed everyone waiting for her to decide on the food. If she passed it by, everyone else would as well, whether they wanted to or not. She selected a bottle of orange juice. The pastry tray looked so tempting Marla's mouth watered; those were first-class French and Italian pastries. She pondered a few seconds and then selected a beautiful, large, ripe strawberry. She placed it on her napkin and stepped aside to gaze out Dr. Brighton's office window. She sensed him behind her immediately, like radar through a fog.

"Spectacular view." Dr. Brighton had a million-dollar view of Mt. Rainer with its snow-capped dome bathed in a soft, gray-blue light from the overcast sky.

"I grew up in its shadow. I never tire of seeing it, here at the office or at home." His shirtsleeve lightly brushed Marla's bare forearm. A shiver of lust ran down her neck, her spine, her legs, weakening her knees as it sped all the way to her toes, curling them in their sensible pumps. She could only smile in response. No words came to her brain, no words could form in her mouth, or on her tongue, or pass her dry lips. Dr. Brighton nodded and, regrettably, walked away, back to his desk.

Her mouth watered, and her mind went blank at the sight of his backside. Gorgeous! *God! What an idiot! Couldn't you have thought of something to say? He's a doctor, a professional like you.* She stared unseeing at the horizon, trying to get a grip on herself, trying to think of something she could have said.

Marla went to bite into the tip of the strawberry. From the corner of her eye she caught Dr. Brighton watching her. When she bit, one of his eyebrows shot up a fraction of a centimeter, then he turned away to listen to something said by another doctor whose name Marla didn't catch earlier. Hmm, that was interesting. *Does Dr.*

Brighton have a sensual streak? Heat crept up her face, heading for her ear tips. She turned away to prevent being seen blushing.

She held the orange juice bottle briefly to her cheek to constrict the blood vessels and get the redness out of her cheeks before the team moved on for the grand tour. She pleaded with her body to stay in control. Melting down in lust would not be professional.

The remainder of the morning was a general tour of the laboratory's facility. It was neat, clean, and well-maintained, albeit new in the first place. Marla was pleased to see it had a friendly, almost congenial atmosphere. She couldn't pin down what made it so, but she could feel it.

Lunch was held in the cafeteria so she could get a feel for the food service and employee morale. They didn't know she had already scoped it out. Several department supervisors joined their group to meet Marla. She endured the light shoptalk with a smile.

The afternoon was spent camped in Andrea Bekkit's office, reviewing the laboratory's major policy and procedural manuals. It was tedious work, but Marla was expected to ensure every state and federal regulation was being followed. She wasn't the kind of inspector who accepted someone's word that it was done. She had to see for herself.

By five thirty, Marla could hardly see straight. She was dropping Visine into her eyes when Dr. Brighton walked in.

"Peabody should buy you a case of that stuff," he said cheerfully. He was leaning against the door jamb of the boardroom she was stationed in during her audit. "Have you had enough punishment for one day?"

"I most certainly have." Marla closed the three-inch binder abruptly and smiled.

"Good, several of us would like to take you out. On company voucher of course so we've picked the best place in town. Are you game?" Dr. Brighton asked.

"That would be wonderful." Marla would have said yes to bungee jumping off the Space Needle if he had suggested it. "Can we swing by my hotel for a few minutes? This outfit is hardly dinner worthy. I promise to take less than ten minutes."

"I think the Hyatt is on the way, so you're in luck. I'm afraid you'll have to stick to that time limit. If I know Andrea, she'll be watching the clock."

"I'll be sure to keep it quick, Dr. Brighton." Marla's tone was as light and airy as the feeling in her chest. He enchanted her with every movement, every word, every meeting of their eyes. Sometimes, she had to stop herself from zoning out dreamily to listen to what was being said.

"Timothy. When we leave this place, you must call me Timothy," he insisted with a conspiratorial whisper and a wink.

She gripped the table edge to keep from melting in a puddle at his feet. Her response was quicker this time. "You must call me Marla," she whispered back, cupping her mouth with her hands.

"It's a deal," he whispered, sticking out his hand to seal the deal with a shake.

"Deal," Marla giggled. His hand was warm, firm, and gentle. She flushed deeply again. For the first time in her life, she wanted that hand and its mirror image to explore her body.

Like a bunch of juniors on the way to prom, the six of them piled into a limo. True to Timothy's prediction, Andrea used her cell phone as a stopwatch to time Marla's trip up to her room.

She frantically threw off her suit while kicking off her sensible shoes. She slipped a dark green dress over her head as her toes dove into black stilettos. She quickly glanced in the mirror and headed for the elevator while pulling the clip out of her hair and shaking it free on the descending elevator ride. She was in the limo door again at nine minutes and fifty-seven seconds.

"Impressive. Is this the same woman? You're welcome to join us dear, but we're waiting for someone else." Dr. Wimker chuckled. Everyone laughed at his witty remark as the limo sped away.

The restaurant was waterfront on Elliott Bay. The seafood was, of course, exceptional. Marla decided to forgo her usual special instructions to the chef, choosing to simply order off the regular menu. Fortunately for her, the restaurant served up seafood in a simplified manner, unadulterated with fatty sauces or overpowering ingredients.

"Are you enjoying the dinner?" Timothy asked, seated to her left.

"Yes, of course. My God, this seafood is the freshest I've ever tasted. It's incredible," Marla praised. It was sensational, so fresh, she could still taste the ocean.

"The seafood's one thing we pride ourselves on here."

"You're said you grew up here in Washington. I think I remember that from your file."

"Uh oh, I have a dossier? That's scary." Timothy smiled, reaching for his wineglass and taking a long sip.

"No, no, nothing like that. I was referring to the files to see where the management staff came from, who was part of the Peabody lab family, who came from outside. It helps understand styles of management and practices."

"I see," Timothy said, giving her a long, thoughtful look. "This is a much more thorough inspection than I thought."

"No, no. Please don't worry. It's *my* thing. It has nothing to do with the inspection. Though I will say, happy employees tend to follow rules and procedures. My interest is studying leaders. I like to figure out how they manage others. Especially the successful leaders. Sometimes I can see or predict problems. The inspection is a set of checklists I go through. Nothing about management is on them." Marla tried to soothe. "I'm impressed with what I see. Of the sixty or so inspections I've done of the company's labs, I have never, ever been taken out for dinner by a group of management staff, let alone any who enjoy each other's company. It's refreshing and exceptionally commendable." Marla gestured toward him, then let her eyes skim over his face.

"Me? You think I had anything to do with this?" Timothy looked bewildered.

"Yes, *you* have brought together a group of people who socialize and work well together. You were the one who picked them, and you provided the open environment in a stressful workplace for their amiable interaction to occur. It's most unusual." Marla sipped her wine.

"I think you are making too much of it," Timothy dismissed her analysis.

"And I think not, Dr. Brighton." Marla smiled, raising her wineglass in a salute.

"Touché," Timothy said, raising his glass to clink against hers.

"Whoa—what's going on down there? Making contracts with the devil now, Marla?" Andrea asked with a burst of laughter.

Marla smiled sweetly and sipped her wine, glancing left at Timothy's eyes over the rim of her glass. His darkly glinting eyes were smiling back at her.

She spent the next two days carefully reviewing and inspecting each department. As a first inspection of a new laboratory, she tried to be meticulous in her assessment. Each day at lunch, several members from management joined her at the company's cafeteria.

Each evening she dined with Dr. Brighton and six other staff members. True to prediction, Timothy brought a diverse selection of staff: secretaries, technologists, lab aides, and support staff. All were good company.

Timothy sat at the opposite end of the table, allowing her to speak with the newer staff members. Every time Marla lifted her eyes toward the end of the table, she caught Timothy's pensive dark eyes staring, analyzing her. Though he smiled at her pleasantly each time he caught her gaze, it was unsettling.

After each dinner, Marla went back to her hotel room wondering what it was about Seattle that made these people so friendly and amiable. And what was Timothy thinking each time he stared at her? She had little experience with this sort of thing. Except for that piano-playing guy at the restaurant, who'd scared her into retreating. No, Timothy's attentiveness was different. Chalking it up to boredom and line of sight, as Timothy was directly in front of her field of vision, she let the thoughts go during the day. Each night after the staff dinners, she slept poorly. His dark luminous eyes raked her skin like a hairshirt in her dreams. Each morning the linens lay strewn beyond the bed.

By Thursday morning, Marla was providing a preliminary assessment of her inspection to Timothy, Andrea Bekkit, and the other senior management staff. She wound up her review with only a few suggestions. Overall, the inspection found only one minor problem.

When the meeting broke up, Marla stayed behind to give Timothy a copy of her written report.

"It's been a real pleasure working with you, Dr. Brighton. You have an exceptional operation here and an even more exceptional group of people staffing it. You must be very proud." Marla kept her hands folded together, her interlaced fingers clenched tight as she tried to look placid.

"Don't I know it. They all give one hundred percent," Timothy said stiffly. His tone sounded off, as if something was wrong.

Was he unhappy with her assessment despite his words?

Her fingers clenched tighter. "Your staff adores you. I can see why," Marla blurted, then stumbled on, "They appreciate good leadership."

"Thank you. I'm honored by your kind words." He shyly dropped his eyes and held out his hand.

Marla took it, feeling her hand engulfed in his. They gazed into each other's eyes for a few seconds, their hands still joined.

Her knees felt weak as her heart thundered in her chest. It felt as though there was something unspoken between them. She couldn't imagine what it might be. Gently, she retracted her hand and headed for the door. Each step away from him dampened her mood.

Timothy's voice carried over her shoulders. "If you don't mind me asking, what are your plans now?"

She stopped in the doorframe and turned back to face him. Her heartbeat escalated back to revving. "I'll take the formal report back to Pittsburgh. There won't be anything else."

His voice softened. "No, I mean, now. Tonight. For dinner. Can you tolerate another dinner with me?"

"Oh—I, uh, I had planned to order room service, but your idea sounds wonderful." Marla clutched the door jamb, afraid to let go of the support.

"Can I pick you up about six thirty?" His voice was tense, like a teenager asking for a date.

"That would be fine. I'll be waiting in the lobby," Marla said, her voice so low she was afraid he hadn't heard her.

"Great, see you then." A sparkle flared in Timothy's eyes, and his tone brightened.

Back at the hotel, Marla hit the hotel fitness center for a quick session on the treadmill. With each step, she couldn't believe what had transpired. She even questioned if she had dreamed it. But she had seen his dark eyes, intent and piercing, as he had asked her to dinner.

After a shower, she scooted over to the hotel spa for the appointments she had fortuitously made earlier that day: a mini manicure, pedicure, and facial. At six fifteen, she was feeling polished and refreshed, pacing the hotel room, her knees weak, her thoughts garbled. A knock on her door stopped her cold. She glanced at the clock. She had said she would meet him in the lobby at six thirty. It must be housekeeping, or they were delivering her itemized bill. Except it was routinely slipped under the door. Advancing toward the door, she glanced through the peephole. Breath stilled in her lungs. It was Timothy.

"Ah, hello. I wanted to make it a little more formal. Thought I'd come up to your door." He glanced down at his shoes, his eyes not meeting hers.

"Come in. I'm almost ready," Marla said, shocked and contemplating the possible meaning of his words.

Timothy walked in, checking out the view from her window. "It is a beautiful view from up here, isn't it?"

"Gorgeous," said Marla, searching through her suitcase for the shawl she always packed when traveling. It often came in handy on the plane, but it was pressed into service tonight for better reasons.

"I'll bet it is with the western view."

"Yes," Marla said, pulling on her shawl. "I'm all set."

"Let's go." Timothy smiled, then gestured up and down with his hand. "You look beautiful."

"Thanks," Marla said, heading for the door. "You look pretty incredible yourself." It was entirely true. Timothy had changed into a high-quality navy-blue suit made from a light wool-silk blend. Cut exceptionally well, it framed his shoulders, hips, and thighs sensually, making Marla's mouth water just looking at him.

Their trip down to Pike Place Market in Timothy's Audi was quiet in comparison to the chatty dinner trips with the lab staff. Marla's palms felt damp, and her demure, shy, former self took over her body. Her sense of balance teetered on the edge of a fence, unsure how to interact one-on-one with Dr. Timothy Brighton without the security of Peabody Laboratory topics. She felt bereft of the social skills and mannerisms that were customary between men and women. Even though Marla knew the dinner invitation was solely a hospitality measure, she was, for the first time in her life, alone with a handsome man who wasn't her fiancé. Sam had been different as a friend of her family. He had been always there, and was as comfortable as an old slipper.

She tried to console herself. They had their shared work concerns to discuss, and it was probably the reason for the dinner offer. He was providing one last hospitality function before she left town.

The restaurant was a quiet little bistro. The Pacific Northwest-influenced menu was imaginative, the staff attentive, and the food exquisite. Marla ate lightly, enjoying the cuisine and savoring the flavors that danced in her mouth. She let each bite sit momentarily on her tongue to capture all the enchanting flavors and textures. It was almost too good to swallow.

She tried to mute the alarm bells going off in her brain about the calorie-laden wine and foods. For once, just this once, she wanted to enjoy a delicious meal with this great guy, and the calories be damned.

The wines selected by the sommelier complemented each course perfectly. It was gourmet heaven. Timothy and Marla chatted about the company and its many facilities across the US and their respective medical training and laboratory work experiences. Marla knew they had both been at Columbia at the same time, then worked at Johns Hopkins Medical Center in Baltimore merely a year apart.

Timothy was flabbergasted to learn this fact.

"Wait—explain that again." He put down his wineglass, leaning toward her.

Marla felt her cheeks burn hotter under his scrutiny. She couldn't meet his eyes as she began, afraid he would remember what she had looked like back then. "When you started your pathology residency at Columbia, I worked in the hematology lab. I left Columbia shortly after for a job at Johns Hopkins. It was May of 2011, a year before you went there. Three months later, I left for Peabody's Pittsburgh headquarters after you started your fellowship at Hopkins."

"You mean to say we worked together at Columbia?" Timothy asked incredulously. He sat back in his chair, wineglass cradled in his palms, holding on to it for dear life, or so it appeared to Marla. His eyes examined every curve of her face.

"Yes. Isn't it funny? And here we are seven years later, meeting again for a third time, on the other side of the continent." Marla smiled back demurely, praying behind her calm facade he would not remember her from back then. Back when she was Fat Marla.

"Why don't I *remember* you?" Timothy pounded his forehead with the heel of his hand. He was silent a few moments then sat forward to whisper, "Do you believe in destiny?"

"As a matter of fact, I do," Marla replied, a serious expression taking over her face. "Some amazing things have happened to me I thought were serendipitous, but I've come to believe it's all connected in some sort of cosmic, destiny-paved pathway. Not that I don't think we still have choices to make. But I think paths cross, incidents occur, for reasons we might not be able to explain or appreciate, but they profoundly affect our lives."

Timothy's eyes were glued to Marla's as she spoke. When she finished, his stare softened, and he sat back in his chair, absentmindedly swirling his wineglass. He watched the liquid swirl then returned to meet Marla's stare.

"To destiny," he saluted, his glass raised shoulder high across the table toward Marla.

"To destiny." Marla saluted back, smiling. They broke eye contact and sipped in silence for a few minutes.

Abruptly Timothy ended the silence. "When is your flight back?" he asked, slowly swirling his pinot noir again.

"Sunday evening."

"Really? You're not heading back tomorrow? Staying the weekend?" Timothy asked, a perk to his voice.

"I came all this way. It's only Thursday. I've always wanted to see Seattle but never stayed long enough to do it, until now."

"That's great. What are you interested in seeing? Perhaps I can act as tour guide." Timothy blinked several times in a shy manner.

"Oh, please, you've done more than enough for me these last four days. Your family must have forgotten what you look like by now." Marla shook her head slowly. "I don't need to tie you up for another three days." *Though I'd love to, quite literally,* she added in the back of her mind. *My God, how raunchy I've gotten. He probably doesn't even think of me in that manner.* He also probably had a wife or a girlfriend, kids, the whole shebang. *Quite possibly, he could even have a boyfriend.* He was too good-looking to be single, one way or another.

"I don't have any obligations. I'd like to show you around town. The only plans I have involve hiking on Sunday in ONP."

"ONP? What's that?" Marla's knees started trembling. She could not believe what was happening. Could she be setting up a weekend-long series of dates with this gorgeous hunk of man flesh? Intelligent, polite, and salivatingly sweet to look at, Timothy Brighton?

"Olympic National Park, most of the Olympic Peninsula—that huge body of land on the other side of Puget Sound—is one large state and federal park. The hiking is phenomenal. Do you hike?" Timothy's voice held an excited hitch.

"Not since I was thirteen and at summer camp. It sounds like fun." Marla's words came out rapidly and filled with excitement.

"There's no place like it in the US. I try to go hiking at least one day each weekend. I have a small cabin out near Forks. I need it to keep my head clear and sane, keep life in perspective." He rested his chin in the palm of his hand, his elbow on the table.

"Ah, that's your secret. Communing with nature." Marla smiled and sipped her wine again. She leaned back in her chair to observe his dreamy, contented look. If she could only take one picture of him, it would definitely have to be this view of total contentment.

"It is, I confess. The outdoors is my counselor, my psychiatrist, my companion." He mashed his lips together. "Pretty sad, huh."

"Why's that? It sounds like a natural anti-depressant, no pun intended of course."

"In this entire city of active people, I usually end up spending my time alone in the woods. I've always enjoyed it in a way. It's how I grew up as a single child. Playing and doing things by myself. I'm my own best company. But always being alone isn't so good. I mean, beyond being dangerous out in the wild with bears, elk, and cougars. There's no one to turn to and say, 'Isn't that the most beautiful vista?'" His voice ended with a melancholy note. He beseeched her with sad, dark brown puppy eyes. "Come hiking with me,"

Marla couldn't help but melt at his words. She knew exactly how it felt to grow up alone. "If you promise to have me to the airport by six p.m. Sunday night, I would love to join you for a hike. Provided it's on an easy trail. All I have are walking sneakers. I didn't come to town prepared to hike up Mt. Rainer." Marla laughed.

"Hmmm, easy trail, you've got it. I know where we can go ... No wait, I just thought of another place ... Okay, which do you prefer, mountains or beaches?" Timothy's words came rapid fire as if he was nearly unable to contain his enthusiasm. His index finger tapped his cheek. "Maybe we'll have time to stop at the Hoh Rain Forest."

"Rainforest? Here?" Marla felt skeptical now. "If it's my choice, then beaches, most definitely. There aren't any out in Pittsburgh," Marla laughed again. "Then again, there aren't any rainforests either."

The next three days were a whirlwind she'd never anticipated. Marla and Timothy were together for most of Friday. They met up to browse the Pike Place Market for lunch, then headed to Seattle Aquarium in the early afternoon. Timothy came up with tickets to the theater, so they dined together for the fifth night in a row before seeing an outstanding performance of "Pericles." Before midnight, their trip to the top of the Space Needle gave them an owl's eye view of the city, the Sound, and the western islands in the distance.

Their banter dropped its work overtones long ago, becoming light and carefree. They talked about college, high school, and growing up in their respective communities. Marla never let on about her lifelong weight problem or her recent transformation. She found out Timothy also exercised daily, although he preferred running outdoors, of course, rain or shine. He also skied, kayaked, played tennis, and enjoyed camping.

Marla told him about her interest in yoga and meditation. Being a city girl for much of her life, she never had the opportunity or the physical ability to try any of the sports Timothy enjoyed. Mountains were far enough off to make skiing an impractical sport. Camping and tennis were not things an overweight adolescent or teenager would enjoy. With the exception of that one summer at Camp Terramungus, Marla had preferred to isolate herself rather than spend summers at camp or partake in girl scouting. Opening herself to bullying and ridicule was difficult enough during school hours; she was not going to extend them into her after-school hours.

After a brief discussion, Timothy and Marla went hiking in ONP on Saturday instead of Sunday. Tim drove them along the Pacific Coast to Rialto Beach, near the confluence of the ocean and the Quillayute River. The driftwood tree trunks were massive, some four times as wide as she was tall. They littered the beaches for miles. Large smooth round stones covered the beach at the water's edge, rolling with each wave, producing a clacking sound like castanets.

They walked the beach, exploring the tide pools during low tide, the Hole-in-the-Wall trail, and up along the coast for hours. Then they traipsed back before the incoming tide stranded them in an untraversable place.

Back at the beachhead, Timothy brought out a picnic basket and cooler he had hidden in the back of his other car, an Acura MDX. They dined on fresh fruit, cheese, shrimp cocktail, and a duck pâté on thick slices of French bread. He even managed to transport two glass champagne flutes and two chilled bottles of Prosecco.

Sitting on the blanket, they were deep in discussion on East Coast versus West Coast living when Marla thought she spotted something unusual in the water a couple of yards off the beach. She stood up to get a better look.

"Timothy, what is that, just off the beach, about eleven o'clock from our position? There's a black nose or something like it, that pops up. There! Just twenty feet over, more to the left. See it?" Marla asked, a little excited.

He stood up beside her, "I think it's a seal. They frequent this area of the coast this time of year. Sometimes I find them basking on the beach if it's quiet enough for them."

They both watched in surprise as a large seal came on shore. Marla was speechless. She grabbed his arm in silent exhilaration. The seal lumbered up onto the deserted beach area, surveyed them a few moments, and, sensing no threat, collapsed into a comfortable spot to rest. They watched him quietly. Marla looked as if she had seen Santa Claus.

"If we leave it alone, it'll sleep there a while," Tim said, placing his free hand over hers, still resting on his arm. He put down his wineglass, then took her glass and did the same. She looked on in puzzlement, thinking maybe he was going to take her for another walk along the beach. Instead, his free hand cupped her shoulder.

She looked at his hand, then looked into his eyes quizzically. Quivers shook inside her body.

Timothy's facial expression showed amusement for a few seconds and then sobered. Maintaining her gaze, he slid his hand down to hers. Holding both hands now, he looked at them, then up into her eyes.

"Would you think it highly inappropriate if I kissed you?"

The wind tousled his dark brown hair about, making the entire scene all the more moviesque. She could not believe what she was hearing, what she was seeing. This couldn't be happening. These things didn't happen to three hundred seven pound Marla. But she wasn't three hundred and seven pounds anymore. She bore no resemblance to the Marla she had been on that plane twelve months ago, one hundred and eighty-seven pounds ago. She was one hundred and twenty pound Marla now. And Timothy wanted to kiss her.

"Marla?" he asked again, a little concerned about the glistening look in her eyes.

"Yes?" Marla responded to her name. "Uh, no, I mean, no, I wouldn't mind." A tremor filled her voice.

It had never occurred to him until that second when she looked at his hand on her shoulder. She didn't have a clue. She couldn't read the clues and body language he'd used all afternoon. That one quizzical look at his hand on her shoulder explained it all. Now he understood the depth of her naivety.

Timothy pulled her to him as he bent to meet her lips. He kissed her ever so gently, immediately sensing her inexperience. He wanted to lean in more to kiss her harder, but he didn't dare. Her lips tasted so sweet, of strawberries and sparkling wine. Her timidity piqued his interest. Her reaction was not phony, of that he was sure. He would wager a year's salary she was still a virgin. Not that it mattered to him.

He preferred his women well-versed in the pleasures of the bedroom. But Marla's naivety and sensitivity heightened his protective instinct.

It also was enflaming his passion based on the increasing tightness of his jeans. How could someone so beautiful, so incredible, have gone this long without—this? How in this world would he be able to curb his desire to make her first time great for both of them?

Oh. My. God! I can't believe Tim is kissing me. Beautiful, smart, funny, exciting Timothy Brighton was kissing Marla.

She reached for him, one hand spread on his chest, the other's fingers sinking deep into his soft dark hair.

She tried to follow what he was doing, tried to kiss him as he was doing to her. This spurred him on to deepen the kiss. He pulled them even closer together until she was pressed fully against him. His lips parted, the tip of his tongue brushing across her lips. Marla could not control the moan that filled her throat. She explored his back, one hand splayed against the muscles of his lower back, the other's fingers still tangled in the curls of his hair. Her tongue tentatively brushed across his lips in return. This time he groaned and hugged her closer. His lips closed for one final, chaste kiss.

"Marla, I've never met anyone like you," Timothy whispered in her ear as she leaned against him. She could hear his heart thudding rapidly beneath her chest, nearly as fast as her own was racing.

She didn't know what to say. She peered over his shoulder at the napping seal, at the waves, felt the warmth of their bodies pressed together. Timothy Brighton was ... amazing. So gentle, so sweet. What to do about it, she did not know, other than tell him the truth.

"I've never, ever felt anything like this in my life. I—" and she stopped, the fire of her blush igniting her cheeks. A part of her wanted to tell him about Sam. But she couldn't. She didn't want to spoil the moment with talk of another man. A former fiancé who had never ignited the feelings Timothy had by just kissing her.

Timothy pushed her back to view her face. "I know," he said, trying to stem her fears, stroking her hands again with his thumbs.

Marla's eyes felt as downcast as her voice. "Is it that obvious?"

"Yes ... and no. You *do* seem to be a fast learner." Timothy's lips curled up at the corners.

They stood silently for a few minutes, looking out to sea, watching the waves crash ashore, her hands still held in his.

"I would like to take you home with me. Make gentle, passionate love to you," he explained softly, searching her eyes for some understanding of his sincerity, expressing his honest understanding of her predicament. "I've watched you all week. I'm enchanted by your mind, your honesty, your freshness."

Eyes as big as the sand dollars they had collected earlier, her throat tensed as she tried to swallow. Worry lines etched across her forehead.

Timothy rubbed her cheek gently, then cupped the side of her face. "I understand if you wish to decline."

Turning her head, she kissed the palm of his hand. She caught the flash of heat in his eyes after she did.

"I can't promise you anything, but I'd like to try," Marla softly replied. *I can't believe this is happening to me! I hope I don't end up making a fool of myself. Oh, God, do I really look okay naked?* She was so scared she couldn't stop trembling.

Wordlessly, they carried everything back to the car, stowed it away, and slid onto the heated leather seats. Tim held her trembling hand throughout the short trip to his cabin. The single-story cabin was rustic appearing, its exterior so worn and saggy it would look abandoned, but for the porch furniture and the well-worn tire tracks in the dirt drive. The inside was completely the opposite.

A fieldstone fireplace dominated the small but open living space. Scattered rag rugs protected the high gloss, wide plank hardwood floors. Along the back corner to the left, a simple kitchen was made up of a wall of counters and cabinets, a sink, and a small gas stove. In front of this was a planked hardwood table with rush-caned chairs that served as the cabin's only dining area. To the right of the door was the living room area with the central stone fireplace, overstuffed chairs, and a sofa made more for comfort than decorator looks. The windows were topped with valances in Stewart tartan, a simple but elegant weave of royal blue with stripes of yellow, red, and white.

Three-foot-tall bookshelves along the outer walls held books and colorful eccentricities. Marla wandered the length of the shelves marveling at the variety of the natural wonders they held: numerous sand dollars, beautiful shells, unusual rocks, a bird's nest, a paper wasp hive, and a whale's tooth. Clearly, they were treasures collected during Timothy's many hiking escapades around the peninsula's beaches. Treasures from his world travels were also scattered about; colorful Mexican pottery, Indian trinkets, Russian nesting dolls, Japanese rice paper cuts, German wood crafts, and Scandinavian tole art. Timothy started a blaze in the fireplace while she explored. He stepped out onto a back porch, pulled up the mud rug on the deck, and opened a secret hatch to grab a couple bottles of wine.

Seeing her inquisitive expression, he explained, "When I first bought the place and fixed it up, it was broken into a number of times. The only thing stolen was the alcohol. So I decided to make a secret storage place for it. They kept breaking in for a time but didn't find anything, so they eventually stopped."

Marla smiled in appreciation of his cleverness and took the bottles from him so he could secure the storage place again. She brought them to the kitchen area and checked a few drawers, finally finding a corkscrew.

"Which would you like me to open?" she called over her shoulder, then startled to find Timothy standing inches behind her. His hands slipped around her waist, hugging her to him until she rested comfortably against his chest. He nuzzled her neck, letting his lips taste the salt clinging to her skin below her earlobe. Butterflies swarmed in her stomach as his breath caressed her neck.

"Open whichever you prefer," Timothy said softly, his voice deep and sensual, like crushed velvet.

Uncontrollably, Marla trembled with each touch of his lips on her neck, feeling her knees weaken perceptibly with each flick of his tongue. Her head lolled back to rest on his chest, giving him better access. Timothy took the invitation, teasing and tasting before groaning and gently pushing her away.

"As much as I would love to ravish you immediately, I want to savor every inch of you over the next few hours." He turned her to face him, locking her eyes, tilting her chin up with his hand. "You are too exquisite to rush."

Marla felt the heat of her blush creeping up her face again, and she cast her eyes down to the floor.

"No. Look at me," he commanded. "Don't be embarrassed. You are a beautiful woman. As beautiful outside as you are inside. I don't know why you waited so long, but I'm glad you waited for me."

He wrapped her in his arms again, holding her softly a minute, then let her go. "So what'll it be? Riesling or pinot grigio?"

"Riesling." Marla straightened her blouse and made for the sofa.

Within minutes Timothy was beside her, wineglasses in hand. Marla took hers and Tim sat down beside her, pulling some pillows in to support his back. He raised his glass in a toast or salute but said nothing, just watching her eyes. She clinked her glass against his, making a silent wish.

Timothy's arm guided Marla backward until she was leaning against his chest. They watched the flames dance in the fireplace, enjoying the heat, the warmth from each other, the knowledge that their silence was mutual and yet said so much about both of them, separately and together.

Marla kicked off her shoes and tucked her feet underneath her on the sofa. His long, strong fingers made lazy circles on her arm. Between the wine and the fire, the day of fresh air on the beach, and the mesmerizing touch of Timothy's fingers, she was more relaxed than she could ever remember being, happier than she could ever remember being in her whole life. Her eyelids became heavy.

Fearing falling asleep, she set her glass down, then took his. She turned to face him, finding herself, rather unexpectedly, but fortuitously, lying across his lap.

A tentative smile showed on his face, his beautiful eyes warm and inviting. Yet he made no move to kiss her, no move at all to embrace her.

She was perplexed for a moment, then understood. She had to initiate the contact now. He had told her of his desire, his wants, but she had not responded verbally or even shown him any initiative.

She reached up with her right hand, nestled her fingers into the curling hair at the nape of his neck, and drew his head down to hers. When his lips were close enough, Marla touched hers to his, tentatively at first, then more aggressively. Her tongue slipped between them, brushing across his closed lips once, twice, and on the third time, Timothy responded. His arms encircled her, pulling her as close to his chest as he could.

He kissed her as he had on the beach. Marla, still timid but wanting this to happen with him more than anything in the world, matched his level of passion and urged him on, meeting him action for action.

Timothy knew the first time was supposedly the worst for a woman. He was determined to make it good for Marla, whatever the cost. While her responses urged him on, leaving him roaring with passion, he reined himself in, trying to slow the pace.

When it became clear clothes were coming off soon, they moved to the bedroom on the other side of the fireplace. It was dusk now, only a single candle illuminated the chamber. There wasn't much light, and he wanted to see her beautiful, naked body, but she refused to let him light any more candles or turn on any lights. He granted her wishes, understanding her modesty on this inaugural event.

Marla's senses swirled as Timothy's kisses and hands roamed over her body, igniting fires and fanning the flames. She had tasted the swell of passion before with Sam during heavy petting sessions, but they never went any further. She hadn't wanted Sam to see her naked. Her insecurity with her own body and her inexperience curtailed their explorations.

But now? Now, she felt thin and beautiful. This was her dream come true. One night stand or not, she wouldn't let anything ruin this time with Timothy.

They continued their play until, over an hour later, Marla panted and vehemently begged him, "Please."

His naked body rested between her firm, satiny thighs. Gazing up at her full breasts, tan-pink nipples erect and glistening with wetness from his lips, he teased her, "Please, what?"

The "what" she knew but did not know fully. By her wetness, by her body arching and reaching for him, she knew there was something desperately missing. When he relented, ending the sweet torture of his fingertips, his lips, and his tongue, they spent the next hour completing her sexual initiation.

• • • •

GEMMA SLUMPED BACK in her desk chair. She could feel the pounding of her heart and the rise of her blood pressure as she fumed about failing yet again. She had been trying to reach Charlie about a change in their flights to Milwaukee. She wondered if he was going off her. He'd blown her off for a Saturday dinner date last weekend. He hadn't called her all week, and now she couldn't get a reply to her text messages or her emails. She went as far as to call him, but it went directly to voicemail.

Shaking her head, she thought perhaps her efforts were starting to look like stalking. She decided to wait to hear back from him in his own good time.

Dropping her cell phone on the desktop, she went back to searching for good restaurants in Milwaukee.

• • • •

CHELSEA, GEMMA, AND Heather crowded around the laptop screen so Marla could see all their faces during their Zoom meeting.

"What's going on, Marla? Are you okay? Why did you want an emergency Zoom meeting?" Chelsea asked before she noticed her face. "Uh, no. You look like you're ready to burst."

"You guys, oh my God, you'll never guess." Marla sputtered with excitement.

"Your face is glowing. I'd guess you met a man and got laid," Gemma said in a rather matter-of-fact tone.

"Ah, look at the blush! If you get any redder, Marla, someone might think you're having a stroke." Chelsea laughed.

"Congratulations, Marla." Heather gave her two Zoom mates a hard glare. "I'm happy for you. I hope he's worth it."

"Don't be Debbie-downer. Tell us all about it!" Chelsea raised her eyebrows twice suggestively.

"When I get back. In the meantime, I'll be home in a few more days."

AUGUST 2018

Over the months, Marla used a vacation day every Friday for extended weekends in Seattle. Extensive airline miles accumulated as she took off from Pittsburgh airport Thursday evenings to fly out to Seattle non-stop. Timothy picked her up at the airport after he left the office. If the lab was running smoothly, he took Friday off as well to spend all three days with her.

When they got there, he gave her an unhurried tour of his condo on Bainbridge Island, showing her the different views of Puget Sound and downtown Seattle from the various levels of the Redwood deck.

His home office was sparsely furnished but warm in colors and textures. A wall of bookshelves was filled with books and unusual objects, probably from his many adventure vacations. He took a moment to check the house phone for messages.

"My sister's supposed to call," he informed her. "No messages yet."

He did not rush. He popped a fresh bottle of chardonnay, poured them wine, even brought out more cheese and crackers. They sat on the deck admiring the view of the ferry boats crossing the Sound. After Marla had relaxed again and they both had time to refresh, he took her in his arms, held her for a long time while her heart raced, then slowed to a steady rhythm.

Marla would never have imagined this possibility in her own life—this level of physical activity. She and Timothy were always hiking, kayaking, or horseback riding. True to his word, he was an extremely active man. On days they didn't feel like expending much energy, they went to vineyards in the area for wine tasting.

One weekend, Timothy booked a spa retreat on Vancouver Island across the Strait of Juan de Fuca into Canada. Marla knew something was up when he asked her to bring her passport. It had been a relaxing and sensual weekend in the most beautiful rustic lodge Marla had ever seen. They made love a number of times each day, unable to get their fill of each other. She was enchanted by the way he could turn her inside out every time they made love.

He was mesmerized by her enjoyment of their escapades. His eyes never left her face as he watched her reach fulfillment. When she questioned him about it, he said seeing her expression change from sensuality to overwhelming ecstasy was enough to make him lose control. It drove him insane with an insatiable passion for her.

Marla explored a sexual freedom she had not dreamed possible. Many times she thought if she had known how incredible an experience it was, she would have lost all that weight so much earlier.

Equally astounding was her ability to keep up with all the physical activities. Beneath his tailored suits, Timothy was all stamina and muscle. Adventure was his middle name.

Unlike during the week, he never sat still for much more than a few hours, and that was only when eating or cuddling with her. Otherwise, they were on their feet, actively engaged in living and life, absorbing the energy of the outdoors surrounding them. She marveled at the new experiences.

Being overweight all those years had given her an excuse to avoid physical challenges. To avoid trying new things and stretching her comfort zone. Now, she felt so strong, physically able and ready to take on any challenge. Her boundaries disappeared.

There was some unease in that at first. Still, Timothy was always there, always ready to assist her, coax her on to accomplish the task at hand, whether it was an eighteen-mile hike up Mt. Olympus to Blue Glacier or a sea kayaking journey along the Straits. She redefined her physical limits on the fly while feeling the safety and security of knowing he was there to rescue her if trouble arose.

She always knew thin people led active lifestyles. Now, she was one of them for the first time in her life. The only thing that sang a sad note to her joyful exploration was the knowledge of how long she had waited, how many years of fun were lost. All the opportunities she had declined over her short, fat lifetime because she wasn't physically able to participate: the high school trip to Greece involving hiking along the islands of Crete and Mythos, the tennis club, her college outing to a whitewater rafting trip. They were all lost opportunities she could never retrieve. Marla tried not to dwell on them much, instead focusing intently on enjoying every moment now—feeling in the moment every time. Making each moment her own, owning it thoroughly.

• • • •

HEATHER TRIED HARD to keep it all together. The children were doing fine, eating better than they ever had in their short lives. Though once in a while, Peter would demand potato chips or French fries with his hamburger instead of salad. It ended with him crying hysterically while Nick and Michelle looked on in amusement.

Their father, on the other hand, was rarely home. She wouldn't see him if he didn't come home every couple of days for clothes.

She didn't know what to do. The embarrassment of the entire situation stilled her lips from telling anyone how bad the situation had become. As the weeks went by, she had no clue how the mess would end. Little did she know it was coming soon.

LATE SEPTEMBER 2018

It was the last day in September when Billy came home from work just after lunchtime. Heather had put Michelle down for her nap while Peter and Nicholas were at school. Billy found her washing the lunch and breakfast dishes in the kitchen.

He slammed the back door shut when he walked into the kitchen, fury on his face, his fists balled up, muscles tensed.

"Shhh, the baby is sleeping!" Heather reprimanded in a whisper, halting her washing mid-swipe.

"I hope you're happy now," Billy seethed through clenched teeth, pacing across the worn linoleum flooring.

"What? What's happened?" Heather asked, drying her hands and turning to face him, not trusting her back to him in his rage.

"What happened?" Billy sneered. "I got fired! That's what happened!" He continued to wear a tread in the flooring, his pace picking up along with his fury. "Thanks to you!"

"What did I do to cause it?" Heather whispered in shock. "How in God's name could I have caused this? Why would I?"

"Oh, you hate my guts, don't you. You're so happy to see me fail, aren't ya, bitch?" Billy seethed, his eyes spewing as much hatred as his words.

She shot back, "Why would I want that? How are we going to feed the children if you fail? Did you ever think that maybe they're my first priority? You can sleep your way around this whole town Billy, but as long as you keep your hands off me and provide for your children, I'll put up with your stupidity."

"Well, game's over. I got fired in the first round. They said my performance has been poor for the last few months," Billy whined, jabbing an accusatory finger in her direction.

"You can't operate on only a few hours of sleep a night. Who do you think you are, Superman?" Heather seethed now. It was his stupidity and selfishness that put his children's comfort in jeopardy. "What are you going to do about it now, Superman?"

"Don't you get smart with me! At least I can provide for this family. You haven't brought a cent into this household since the day we got married. You're nothing but a lazy bitch. Sending the brats off to daycare. Staying at home watching TV all day long." Billy ranted, his face turning bright red in indignation at her sarcastic remark.

"Is that so? Peter and Nicholas have school. Michelle stays home with me most days. And who do you think is doing all the cooking, the shopping, the laundry? Who's making the beds, washing the floors? Who dusts, vacuums, runs the errands? Who takes the kids to the doctor, buys their clothes? And who is walking the dog you brought home? Who, Billy? Who?" Heather spat at him rapid fire. "Most days that TV doesn't get turned on until you get home from work, which isn't very often anymore."

"That's cuz I can't stand you." He paced stiffly back and forth, a few agitated steps in each direction.

She could feel his anger percolating faster and coming to a head. He swung around and she flinched. Ducking in expectation that a fist was coming her way. He was that angry.

He raged through clenched teeth, "You know what? I'm leaving. You can have one less mouth to feed and one less set of clothes to wash. I know where I'm appreciated and where I'm not."

Billy flung the last words over his shoulder as he marched off for the bedroom. Heather could hear dresser drawers flung open and went to the doorway to watch him pull out handfuls of clothing until he juggled a load. Then he stomped out the door to his car, where he threw the clothes into the back seat. Billy marched back in for another load.

It only took a second load, helped with a trash bag she handed him on his way through the kitchen. She returned to washing the dishes, letting him take what he wanted before leaving. As far as

Heather knew, he was only taking his clothing, leaving everything else behind.

He didn't look back, didn't say goodbye to her, nor did he take a peek at his napping daughter before he left.

• • • •

TIMOTHY FLEW OUT TO stay with Marla a couple times. This was more difficult and perilous, since some of her bosses now knew what Dr. Brighton looked like. They weren't ashamed of their relationship. They wanted to keep it between the two of them. It was an unspoken understanding. There was no need for anyone else to know unless things got more serious.

When he was in town, they saw plays and ballets, attended the symphony, or went dancing in swanky clubs where they could nuzzle each other like love birds between sets. Some days, they walked in museums. At the Frick Art Museum, Marla discovered their mutual love of Van Gogh. Timothy's favorite painting was of the almond tree in bloom in Arles. Marla's favorite was the single white iris in a field of yellow and purple irises.

Some days, they'd spend hours in a café over multiple cups of latte or espresso while Timothy told Marla all about the countries he'd visited and the places he'd traveled for adventures.

Having never felt at home in her own skin, let alone her own country, she had no experience traveling abroad. His stories enchanted her with sights, sounds, and even smells. Also intriguing were the different foods he had tried over his travels, from haggis in Scotland to fried ants in Thailand.

Occasionally, he took Marla out to dinner for a new cuisine he knew she had never tried before. He was always a little reluctant to do so because of her finicky nature with food. She admitted to often going days without eating meat, something he found difficult to imagine. He'd noticed her preferred choices were vegetables and fruits, and she always asked for substitutions for fried foods. When he inquired about it, she said she made it a rule to decline fried foods. He wasn't much into fried foods either, but he didn't have a "rule" about it. He wasn't sure what her food issues stemmed from or how they became ingrained. They weren't terribly outrageous, and yet, they were interesting. Someday he wanted to know the story behind them when she was more than willing to let him in on the subject. For some reason, the look on Marla's face changed from open and friendly to closed and terrified when he mentioned her food rules. Whatever was guiding her rulebook, she wasn't ready to divulge.

Marla tried to be extra vigilant with food around Timothy. Not that she hid her interest. Some of her choices piqued his curiosity, but she wasn't ready to explain the reasons behind her food issues. She wasn't sure she would ever be ready. And she had worked too hard for too long to let anything slide now. Moreover, she had too much to lose if her weight did start to creep back.

Timothy Brighton was the most incredible thing that had ever happened to her, and there was no way on this earth she would give him a reason to stop seeing her. If he left for another reason, then so be it. Nevertheless, Marla swore to herself she would never again miss the better things in life over a few moments of pleasurable eating. She finally understood the complete meaning of "nothing tastes as good as thin feels."

• • • •

GEMMA WAS CHECKING out the feasibility of the Milwaukee convention center after lunch at Mader's with a contingent from the hotel and tourism bureau. They were walking along a city street close by the convention center, half a block from Gemma's hotel. Her high heel shoe had cracked its protective heel tip making walking cumbersome. Besides, she'd had them on since early morning; a change of shoes would feel wonderful. Gemma told them to go on.

She'd catch up with them after getting another pair of shoes up in her room.

The schedule for the day had been extended by the staff. Gemma tried to contact Charlie, but he wasn't answering the phone or her text messages. *Probably off on some brewery tour or such.*

She hurried to the elevator, taking it to her twenty-second-floor room. Approaching the door of her room, she saw the "Do Not Disturb" sign hanging on the lever. Thinking Charlie might be napping, Gemma swiped her card and entered as quietly as she could. She stopped at the closet just inside the door to get another pair of shoes, when she saw a pair of candy-apple red high heels lying on the floor.

Shoes that didn't belong to her.

A surreal feeling of numbness overtook her senses. In slow motion, her hand over her mouth and nose so she didn't make a noise, she padded down the short hallway to peer at the bed. Charlie lay sleeping, curled up beside a brunette. Her clothes were puddled in front of the bed like Gemma's ended up when Charlie pulled them off her in pre-coital haste.

Neither of them woke as she stood staring. Gemma was surprised they didn't wake from the thundering of her heart, first with shock, then with rage. She kept her hand over her mouth to keep from screaming while her mind tumbled with a thousand ideas to break up the sweet scene displayed in front of her, on *her* bed.

An idea came to her.

Stepping backward, she retreated silently to the bathroom, closed the door, and used her cell phone to call the room. The room phone rang several times before Charlie answered.

"Hello?"

"Hey," Gemma said softly, hand cupping the cell phone receiver to blunt the ambient sound. "I got out of my meetings earlier than expected. What do you say we catch a quickie as soon as I get back to the room?"

"What? Now? You're heading back now?" Charlie's voice cracked with panic.

"Oooh yeah." She cooed, "See you soon," before disconnecting the call. She opened the bathroom door and silently slid out into the hall to watch the havoc unfold.

Charlie slammed the receiver down, jumped out of bed, and began shaking the woman frantically.

"Miranda! I have to go! You have to go! Urgent call! Come on honey, get your clothes on. It's an emergency!" Charlie pleaded, his movements and voice becoming more agitated the longer she ignored him.

"Oh, Charlie, why can't I stay?" Miranda moaned sleepily.

"Because it's my room," Gemma said loudly and sternly, stepping forward from the hallway.

The bedfellows froze and looked up with terror on their faces.

"Get out, both of you," said Gemma as coolly and calmly as possible.

"Gemma, it's not what you think." Charlie began. "I was—"

"Get. Out. NOW!" Gemma roared, her teeth clenched to keep from shouting louder. "Sixty seconds, then I'm calling security." She checked her watch.

"Gemma, I can explain—"

Her eyes trained on the watch, she said, "Fifty-seven."

As if sensing a bad scene about to get worse, Miranda grabbed a bathrobe on the foot of the bed and slipped it on. She picked up her clothes, slinked by Gemma, grabbed her shoes, and fled the room.

Charlie, pale and naked, tried yet again. "Gemma, please listen—"

"Forty seconds, Charlie," she said calmly, ignoring his pleas.

Charlie wrestled on his pants. He grabbed his remaining clothing. "Can I pack up my things?"

"I'll have them packed and left at the front desk by six o'clock tonight. I'm canceling your flight too. I don't want you to sit next to me on my trip home," Gemma said coldly, stepping aside to let him pass.

Not meeting her eyes, Charlie walked out the door with his head hung low.

Gemma allowed her stiff posture to deflate when the door latch clicked shut. She inhaled, suddenly realizing she had been holding her breath, waiting for Charlie to leave. She slumped against the wall. Her heart rate began to settle as she kept her eyes closed and willed her nerves to calm. A few minutes later, she opened her eyes, dropped her purse on the desk, and picked up the phone.

Gemma called the front desk and asked for the key to her door to be changed. She'd be down in two minutes to pick up the new card, and no, no other cards would be given out to anyone.

Setting down the phone, Gemma glanced around at the rumpled bed, the pillows cast about. The scent of Charlie's sweat, fear, and sexual encounter mixed with another woman's perfume.

She'd ask for a new room.

• • • •

"I'M CALLING THIS EMERGENCY meeting to order," Chelsea said, holding Heather's hand on one side while Marla held her hand on the other. "Heather, do you want to say anything?"

"He's gone. I don't know where though I have my guesses. The kids and I haven't seen him for a week."

"Not to make light of your situation, Heather, but Charlie's gone too. Except I threw that bastard out."

Marla, Heather, and Chelsea gasped. "What happened?"

"Found him in my hotel bed with another woman while I was working in Milwaukee. Threw them both out. That's what I get for trusting a man." Gemma shook her head and went quiet.

Chelsea's heartbeat rose in sudden appreciation for Seth. *He'd never do anything like either Billy or Charlie.* "Well, both of you are strong. You can get through this. And we're all in this together with you. All for one and one for all."

"Oh, please." Gemma rolled her eyes, shaking her head.

"I mean it. We're there for each other. I count that as a blessing," Chelsea said defiantly.

OCTOBER 2018

Heather held her children's lives together as best she could. Billy never came back for any of his possessions. Slowly, she removed them and placed them in the storage area in the basement of their duplex. Only Peter asked about the missing items and his missing father. Heather lied, telling him his daddy was working elsewhere now, so far away he couldn't come home often. Peter then asked if he was a pirate at sea. She had reassured him his daddy was not a pirate, but he was afloat somewhere.

••••

THE THREE WOMEN SIMULTANEOUSLY knocked on Marla's door before barging through it.

"Hey, Marla!" Chelsea called out from the kitchen.

Marla strode into her kitchen. "Hey, ladies. Thanks for moving our coffee meeting to my house."

Gemma's tone was sarcastic and playful. "Nice of you to invite us for *the first time*." She hunted the countertops looking for the coffeemaker. "Where's the coffee, girlfriend?" Spotting it, she whistled. "Oh, aren't we special? A home espresso machine." She fingered the dials and levers. "How do you work it?"

Marla laughed. "Get out of the way. I'll make it. Who wants a latte, or a cappuccino, or espresso?" She walked over to the counter. "Heather, can you get the soy milk out of the fridge?" She pushed the coffee bean grinder button, and the whirr of the machine chomped away at the whole espresso beans filled the kitchen.

"Where would I find a vase?" Chelsea asked as she hunted in one cabinet after another.

"Pantry, around the corner."

Gemma set down the small box of Italian cookies and wandered off. "Mind if I explore?"

"Go ahead. Find the living room."

"Wait for me," Heather and Chelsea both called.

The three of them explored Marla's house. Checking out the space in the living room with its fireplace and window seat nestled between walls of bookcases on either side.

"You play?" Gemma asked as she ran her finger up the keyboard of Marla's baby grand piano.

"Yup," Marla yelled from the kitchen, where she was putting the final touches on the three lattes, placing them on two small trays along with the cookie box. "Can someone help me?"

"Be right there," Heather responded while the other two continued looking around, their comments on the powder room off the kitchen echoing.

They reconvened in the living room. Marla set the tray down, and Gemma and Chelsea pounced on the treats. Marla sat on a tapestry-covered divan. Heather brought her a coffee mug with one cookie on the saucer, then settled on the end. The other two sat on the sofa.

Heather asked, "How are the wedding plans?"

Chelsea rolled her eyes. "We got a location. Other than that, I don't want to talk about it."

"Ooookay, moving on," Gemma said.

"How's it going with you, Marla?" Heather asked, her tone concerned.

"Good. My weight is stable. I still have yoga and the gym a couple times a week."

"Okay, show off. That's enough." Chelsea groaned as she bit into her third cookie.

Gemma gazed up at the medallioned ceiling millwork around the antique hanging lamp. "Love the details. What's upstairs?"

"Second floor is my bedroom, a walk-in closet, two full baths, and my office. The third floor has two small rooms and one more full bath." She sipped at her latte, ignoring the cookie. "There's a finished basement too."

"Heather, your kids could each have their own room," Gemma teased.

Heather blushed. "It might come to that." Before anyone could ask, she changed the subject. "Time for weight check-in. Marla, you can go first."

"I'm holding at one thirty, you're next Chelsea." She picked the cookie off her saucer and tossed it at Chelsea.

Fumbling, Chelsea caught the cookie and set it on her own saucer. "Ugh, I'm not gaining, not losing. Still the same at one seventy-five."

Gemma piped in, "My turn. I've gained some weight back. It got too low. I literally had to eat like a bird to stay a size two. It's not worth it. I like to eat." She bit into her cookie and chewed.

"Amen to that. You looked too thin at size two," Heather said before sighing. "Guess it's my turn. I've been okay. The kids and I are hanging in there. No gain, no loss." She picked another cookie from the box. "I wanted to tell you about my episode at the program this week. It was kind of inspirational."

"Last night's session was about instead of making our weight loss a battle of willpower, we should create a food rule to live by. For example, instead of fighting the urge to eat potato chips or popcorn while watching a movie, you create a rule that you will not eat anything *except* fresh fruit while watching TV. That solves the problem for anything unhealthy you might want to eat. It sounds like a great plan for me, with three kids around. They respond much better to 'it's a rule' than to 'because I said so.'" At least for now. Maybe I can learn to follow the rules too."

"I have several food rules: no eating after eight p.m. and nothing fried." Marla batted her eyelashes with a smirk on her face.

"That's an interesting concept," Gemma said before popping the last of her cookie in her mouth. "I made one about eating out. Especially at work functions, after what happened two weeks ago."

"What happened?" Chelsea asked, eating Marla's cookie.

"My doctor warned me about eating too much at one time, but I did it anyway. I wasn't thinking clearly after my martinis," Gemma shook her head, remembering.

"Alcohol contains a lot of calories," Heather blurted.

Ignoring Heather's statement, Marla asked, "What happened?" She wanted to hear the story.

"It was at an awards dinner Rose Anne and I attended together. Six courses were served: soup, salad, pasta, vegetable, meat, then dessert and coffee. I thought I was pacing myself well.

"A couple bites per course was the plan. Except the soup was great, the best minestrone I've ever had, so I had a couple too many spoonsful. The salad I set aside. It was a plain old salad. Not worth eating. The pasta sauce was obviously made with fire-roasted tomatoes and maybe even fried pancetta. It was phenomenal, so I ate about four forkfuls before I realized it.

"The roasted vegetables with olive oil, parmesan cheese, and pine nuts were delicious; I only tried one each of the five vegetables." She paused before sighing. "Then the meat entrée arrived. The beef filet was so tender, so succulent. I couldn't resist four or five pieces. By then, it was too late. I went from uncomfortable to ill. I could actually feel the food backed up in my esophagus, waiting for room to enter my tiny stomach."

"Eww." Heather's hand covered her own mouth after grimacing.

"The heartburn didn't have the usual acidic feel. It was like a heavy weight on my chest. I was sweating and gasping for breath. I had to excuse myself and hang over the toilet in the ladies' room, hoping some of the food would reverse course. It didn't because it couldn't. Rose Anne brought a cup of tea to help wash the food down. It didn't help much. I simply had to wait it out. It was an hour, maybe more, before I felt well enough to return to my seat at the table."

"Did they have dessert?" Chelsea asked.

Marla and Heather shook their heads in disbelief. Chelsea loved her desserts. Leave it to her to want to know what the dessert course consisted of.

"Chocolate raspberry mousse cake. I shoved the plate to Rose Anne. And I swore I would never, ever, overeat again."

All four women were silent.

"Wow. I can't even imagine," Marla murmured.

Gemma shrugged. "The surgeon warned me it was possible to stretch out the stomach if it was overfilled like that repeatedly. Gastric band or stomach reduction patients encounter the same problem. If they fail to attain and keep new eating habits, including proper portion sizes, their stomachs will stretch, allowing them to eat more than they should, and end up gaining the weight back. If that happens, there is no going back again."

Marla didn't like those types of dinners for that reason. Little control over the menu. Dining out with Timothy was hard enough. "I guess if that situation arises for any of us, we should pre-plan. One bite from each plate or skip a couple of courses."

Gemma cocked her head and screwed up her mouth. "Let me tell you, if the food is great, it's impossible to stick to a plan."

"I'd skip everything except the dessert." Chelsea stood up. "Anyone want another coffee?"

"So, where's everyone going for Thanksgiving?" Marla asked.

"The kids and I are going to my parents' house," Heather reported. "We're going to be moving in with them after the holiday."

The stares surrounding her propelled her to add, "Billy isn't paying the rent. We can't stay at the apartment much longer."

"That's a good plan. I think the kids will love camping out at Granny and Grampy's," Chelsea said. "Seth and I and my mother are all going to Seth's parents' house for Thanksgiving. I'm bringing a homemade pumpkin pie."

"Ooo, fancy that, Chelsea can bake a pie. Is it a Sara Lee frozen pie?" Gemma's sarcastic tone bit all of them sharply.

Heather wondered why she had to bait Chelsea like that and snapped, "Enough, Gemma."

"How about you, Marla? Going to see Timothy?" Heather asked, ignoring the thirty-somethings acting like the age of her boys.

"No. He's going to his sister's. I'll be going to my parents' house as well," Marla said quietly. "A few days after, we're going skiing in the Cascades."

"I didn't know you skied." Heather gave her a hug.

Marla blinked wildly. "I don't. I'll be taking some lessons while we're there. It's going to be great to see him again. It's been a few weeks since we've been together."

"Think of the spectacular lost time makeup sex you're going to have!" Gemma laughed.

"By the way," she added. "Rose Anne and I are going to Jamaica over the holiday weekend."

Heather asked, "Who's watching Wally?"

"Got it covered. Rose Anne's mom is taking him and his brother, who belongs to Rose, in for the week."

Chelsea's eyes narrowed. "A cruise?"

"No, we got a good deal for Ocho Rios. Six days of sun, sand, and relaxation."

"Watch out for the food buffets!"

• • • •

"OKAY," CHELSEA SAID to Seth as they sat at the kitchen table. "I've found a venue and a DJ within our budget."

Seth nestled her hand in his and stared into her eyes. "Thank you." He kissed her, leaving her breathless. "I know this has been hard on you. But let's focus on what's important. We're getting married after all these years. We're going to grow old and arthritic together. Maybe me faster than you."

She smiled and nodded. "Don't worry. I'll take care of you."

He raised one eyebrow, with a saucy smirk on his face Chelsea could not miss. "Promise?"

LATE NOVEMBER 2018

Jamaica was still beautiful this time of year, though a little on the cooler side of hot. Temperatures at the beach-front hotel resort were in the low seventies. Still far better than the mid-forties and early snow flurries hitting the Pittsburgh area while Gemma and Rose Anne were enjoying the tropical sunshine. After the Charlie fiasco, Gemma decided it was time for a real vacation. Heather's friend, Monica, found them a cheap package deal in Ocho Rios. It wasn't another cruise, which was what Gemma really wanted, but there was far more sand on the resort than on the cruise ship.

They hadn't done much while on the tropical isle. Some shopping, but it became a hassle as they were constantly harassed by the merchants and natives trying to peddle their wares. After that fruitless adventure, they stuck to the resort beach and nightclub and two side trips: the Dunn's River Falls and the zipline Gemma had tried to ride the last time they were in Jamaica.

It sounded and looked like great fun. Gemma was thrilled she wasn't being turned away again because of her weight. Now, she was having second thoughts. Hundreds of them.

She couldn't stop shaking. Dangling a hundred feet above the rainforest, she was harnessed into the zipline system and it was her turn to fly. It sounds so innocuous in the brochure, "Rainforest Zipline On The Island Of Jamaica," she thought. Somehow one hundred feet seemed like a mile from the top, the zipline no more than a wire clothesline, her harness not much more than a belt with leg loops. Gemma tried to swallow the huge knot in her throat, but her throat was too dry. Nothing would go down.

Despite the shouts of encouragement behind her, she could not let go of the deck railing beside her. White-knuckled, she clung to the wood, unable to surrender to the moment.

"Gemma, let go. There's a long line of people waiting," Rose Anne pleaded.

"I can't. Just let me climb down."

"Not possible," Rose Anne said from behind her. Then she shoved Gemma hard, sending her careening down the line, eyes closed, stomach knotted, screeching like a monkey.

After ten seconds, she opened her eyes to see where she was, still flying through the lower canopy of the forest. She flew past a colorful parrot within arm's reach, startling it from its perch. She slowly became less tense and started enjoying the ride. She wasn't ready to relinquish the zipline at the end of the run. Although she wanted to see it again, there was no way in hell she was going up on that platform again.

Her thinner, lighter body may have made it possible for her to participate in activities she would never have been able to before. The problem now was her limited comfort zone. It was difficult for her to push beyond the boundaries that had long defined her sense of safety. They were deeply ingrained. Some of those boundaries were once defined by her weight. Mustering courage and tamping down fears were far more difficult than she thought they would be.

• • • •

MARLA'S FIRST SENSATION was hearing her name being called by several voices. Voices she did not recognize. One voice she did, Timothy's. The terror in his voice, when he called her name, stunned her. What could make him so upset?

Her next sense was of biting cold. Her nose was cold, her face and her hands. Pain promptly followed, starting as a dull throb that escalated into an excruciating, unrelenting stabbing in her left thigh. She tried to open her eyes, but they were covered by a cloth of some sort. Sunlight showed through with shadows bending over her and retreating. She tried to lift her head but couldn't do it. It wouldn't move.

"Stay still, Marla," Timothy's voice quivered. "The ski patrol is here. You're going to be alright." Something squeezed her hand.

"Tim?" She tried to say, but it felt more like a mumble or a whisper; the word was so indistinct.

"I'm here, Marla," Timothy said beside her right ear. "Just relax, let the EMTs do their job. You've had a bad fall."

A dozen voices and streams of words scattered around her ears. Marla could not keep up or concentrate on any of them long enough to translate their meaning. "Where am I?" she slurred.

"Glacial Springs Ski Resort, on the black diamond trail. Do you remember?" another male voice said.

Ski resort? Marla's mind tried to sift through images. Hiking, kayaking, sailing around the San Juan islands. Whitewater rafting, biking, jogging. Skiing?

Then Marla remembered she had taken a short course in skiing at Glacial Springs Ski Resort, where Timothy had a season pass. She had followed him on the black diamond chairlift and skied past him at the top.

"We're moving you to the litter and taking you down the mountain to the first aid station. This is going to hurt."

Marla's consciousness drifted off only to be jarred back when she was bodily lifted onto the litter. She cried out, wailing and sobbing, as the pain seared through her left leg. It was the most extreme pain she had ever felt.

An engine broke the quiet calm around her, and she felt her body jostle on the litter, heading downward on the slope. Timothy called to her, some ways off to the side now. Every bump was torture, yet with each, the engine roaring faded in and out, as did the voices and sea of light shining through her covered eyelids. Morphine? Endorphins? In a moment of scientific clarity, she knew nothing would save her from this immediate pain. Another jarring tossed Marla around on the oversized litter, leaving her screaming.

At last, she was carried in the cold, steel litter to the first aid station, where a team of paramedics waited.

Positioned under intense bright, fluorescent lights, Marla squinted to see faces above her. Her heart raced frantically while her eyes searched for that gorgeous, freckled face. She sighed audibly when she saw him peering over the shoulders of a uniformed man. Marla tried to answer their questions, but everything was hazy in her mind. After an IV was started and some injections were given, the pain eased ever so slightly, and she became drowsy.

Timothy stayed with her the entire time. As a medical doctor, the paramedics gave him the professional courtesy of staying by her side. Marla was only partially aware of being transported by ambulance to the emergency department at the University of Washington Medical Center in Seattle, where Timothy met her, having driven in his SUV.

By the end of the day, Marla was admitted with a broken femur. Though a closed fracture, surgery to pin the thighbone back together was scheduled for the next morning. Because of her loss of consciousness, she was presumed to have suffered a concussion and would stay as an inpatient for several days until medically cleared to go home.

Timothy stayed with her throughout the entire ordeal in the ER and waited while she was transferred to her room. He signed for a private room, not wanting Marla to deal with nosy roommates.

"Should I call anyone for you?" Timothy gestured to her cell phone on the bedside stand. "You should contact Beverly."

Marla's eyes blinked several times as the gears turned in her brain. "I know. But I can't let her know I'm with you. Corporate HR might cause a problem." She laid her head back on the pillow, pain and exhaustion clouding her thoughts. "Can you get my parents on the phone?"

Timothy did as he was asked, handing the phone to Marla once her mother answered.

"Hey, Mom. I kinda fell while skiing and broke my leg." She listened as her mother reacted and then must have turned to tell her father what happened.

"Where are you? Do you need us to pick you up?" Her father asked. Her mother must have put her on speaker.

"I'm in Washington State, in the Cascade Range. I'm okay, and I have a friend here with me. But I need you to do something. I'm sorry, but it involves telling a lie."

It took some convincing, but her father agreed to call Beverly to report Marla had a broken leg and wouldn't be returning to work for the foreseeable future.

That issue settled, Timothy called his secretary to tell her he would be out of work for a few more days but gave no reason.

When Marla glared, he shrugged. "I intend to stay with you until you're released and settled, wherever that may be. Either with me on the island or back in Pittsburgh." He held her hand, his thumb stroking the back of it. "I doubt your doctors would want you taking a long flight anywhere, even if it is home. Not yet anyway."

She knew exactly what he was referring to. The risk of blood clots and fat emboli forming after a long bone fracture could be fatal.

Several days later, Marla was discharged into the care of her own attentive doctor, who had her transported by ambulance to his home on Bainbridge Island.

Timothy set Marla up with a temporary health aide to help her bathe, get dressed, and make her lunch. His usual maid would do the laundry and clean as normal. It was not the best of circumstances. He would have rather stayed home with her, but his work schedule didn't permit him to take any additional time off that week until possibly Friday.

Marla tried to resist the Oxycodone the orthopedic doctor had prescribed. She relied on Tylenol and Naproxen during the daytime. Nights were a different story. Intense pain repeatedly wracked her leg in the middle of the night. Only oxy could ease the pain and allow her to sleep when that happened.

She called Beverly, trying to get some paperwork. Her laptop was with her wherever she traveled, but no one would cooperate. Beverly told her to take it easy for a few weeks. Her assistant would handle the minor things and cancel her next couple of inspections. Marla could reschedule everything when she was fully back to work.

She was rapidly going out of her mind with boredom until Timothy came home on Tuesday with a stack of DVDs, CDs, and books he had seen in the Barnes & Noble down the street from the laboratory. So equipped, Marla kept occupied, if not busy, until Friday afternoon when Timothy arrived home early to make her a proper supper of lasagna and salad.

The inability to exercise and all the food shoved in her direction made her peevish. She feared her weight would increase again, so she ate little despite the hunger that came in waves.

The weekend was spent trying to get Marla more mobile. She had instructions and a referral for an orthopedic doctor back in Pittsburgh whom she would pursue once back home. Her going home became a topic of heated disagreement.

"Take a family leave. Stay here. I'll take care of you," Timothy argued. "You can start physical therapy here and keep seeing the same orthopedist in Seattle."

Shaking her head, Marla said, "I know you're taking good care of me. But I want to get back to my own house, my own things, my own bed." And back to work where she wouldn't feel like her brain was going numb, but she didn't tell Timothy that. By Tuesday morning, Marla had won out from sheer force of will.

After riding out another few days of delirious boredom, Timothy took Marla to SeaTac Airport for her flight home. Anger and disappointment etched lines in his face, stealing his boyish charm, but he said no more. Marla kept silent as well. What more could be said that they hadn't argued about already? A heavy foreboding settled over her as her wheelchair was rolled past the TSA checkpoint. She couldn't shake the feeling that somehow a chapter was closing on this wonderful experience in her life and this wonderful man's part in it.

• • • •

REBECCA HELD THE DOOR to her office open, her face expressionless, her eyes not meeting Chelsea's.

To Chelsea, the open door looked like the yawning jaws of a whale ready to swallow her whole. She hated this part of the diet system more than anything else, this confession of dietary sins and excesses every week to Rebecca. Chelsea's teeth clenched in anticipation of the verbal whipping.

It wasn't so bad, but she hated facing Rebecca. Hated it with a passion that nearly had her canceling every appointment, every week. It took Seth's urging to keep her going.

"You know she's on your side," he'd reminded her over breakfast.

"Well, it doesn't feel like it. She keeps telling me what I'm doing wrong and what I should be doing. I know what I should be doing. I just ... I just can't get it all together and keep doing it," Chelsea sputtered in frustration, her head slumped into her hands already this fine brisk day.

"You mean you don't like to hear you screwed up again." The determined look on his face revealed he knew he was treading on cracking ice.

"YES! I screw up daily. I admit it. Alright?" Chelsea cried, feeling her blood beginning to boil. "Besides, it was Thanksgiving. My favorite holiday."

"Chelsea? Are you okay?" Rebecca asked, breaking into her silent remembrance of this morning's argument.

"Yeah, I'm okay. It's been a hard week."

"Let's see your daily food diary." Rebecca held out her manicured hand for the sheets.

Chelsea's shoulders slumped even lower, then she dug into her bag for the papers and handed them over to Rebecca.

"Hmm. All these blank areas, are they missed meals or entries you didn't record?" Rebecca asked after sitting back in her ergonomic office chair. "Did you have Thanksgiving?"

"Yes," Chelsea replied distantly. "I didn't record anything."

"Chelsea, we've been through this so many times. I can't possibly help you if you don't help yourself by filling in this form," Rebecca said with gentle but insistent exasperation.

"I know, I know. Sometimes, I've gone off the program, and I can't bring myself to write down what I've eaten," Chelsea murmured, chin down and tears starting to trickle down her cheeks.

"Okay, look. Here's what I want you to do. Take one day at a time. If you complete a whole day's food diary, I want you to reward yourself with a treat. Write everything down. I can't see if you have food craving issues or mood/food connections if you don't record the information," Rebecca explained. "Can you do this for me? Write and set up a reward system for completing a daily entry?"

"What kind of reward? Like a candy bar or something?" Chelsea asked with interest.

"No, any kind of treat but food. You have to find replacements for every food reward you give yourself. There are better rewards available than food. A hot bath, a manicure, a facial, a foot massage, a new book. Can you figure something out? It could even be a phone call to a friend, a drive in the country, or a walk in the park. A movie, a new CD. You choose the rewards, but *no food rewards*," Rebecca said. "Can you do it?"

Chelsea perked up, thinking of all the things she enjoyed that she could use as rewards. Some she would need Seth's help with, but she didn't think she'd have too much trouble talking him into a few of them. "Yeah, I think I can do this."

"Good. I hope to see a full food diary next week." Rebecca smiled.

"So long as you don't ask me what rewards I took." Chelsea gave her a shy, almost smile.

Rebecca broke her professional countenance and laughed out loud for the first time.

EARLY DECEMBER 2018

Over the next weeks, Marla struggled to get around with a full leg cast. During the first week back in Pittsburgh, she checked in with her new orthopedist and arranged for physical therapy at home. She worked from home as much as Beverly would let her, which wasn't much.

By the end of her second week home, she was more agile on crutches but also more wan. With clearance from her doctor, she trekked to work after three weeks, taking a cab each day since driving was no longer possible. On Friday, Marla hadn't been home for more than twenty minutes when someone knocked on the back door. She thought it might be Heather.

Marla looked through the peephole, but all she could see were irises. Yellow and purple irises. She flung open the door to find a huge bouquet of dozens yellow and purple irises, with one white iris in the center. Just like her favorite Van Gogh painting.

"I hear there's a beautiful woman here who desperately needs to be swept off her feet." Timothy peered around the bouquet, a contrite smile on his face.

"I think you've been misinformed, sir. There's no one here who *needs* to be swept off her feet."

Timothy handed her the bouquet. "Maybe she *wants* to be?" His eyes twinkled with mischief, sending her heartbeat racing.

He carefully swooped her up in his arms and carried her to the living room, where he gently deposited her on the sofa. Marla scooted over, giving him room to sit beside her. She dropped the bouquet on the end table.

He cradled her in his arms as tenderly as he could, kissing her with a hunger that would not be quenched so easily. Marla put all the loneliness and longing she'd felt in the last weeks into her lips, letting him know how much he was missed.

"So, beautiful lady, I'm starving. Damn airline didn't even serve a tiny bag of pretzels. What do you suggest?"

"Hmm, I could cook here, although I wasn't expecting dinner for two tonight. But I'm sure there's something we can heat up," Marla teased him, pulling at his top shirt button. One by one, the buttons of his dress shirt came loose under her nimble fingers.

Timothy's fingers worked at the buttons of her shirt, exposing her lacy pink bra. "We could order in ... ah ... something hot, spicy, succulent ..." His teeth sank lightly into her earlobe. He cupped her breasts, his thumbs stroking her nipples to full attention. Marla's fingers skipped across the contours of his naked chest.

"We could," she whispered, pulling his lips back in range for a tongue-lashing kiss.

Dinner, Thai by consensus, was delivered two and a half hours later.

After breakfast the next morning, they left the house in Marla's car. A long leisurely drive along the road that skirted the Deer River, then headed up into the foothills. They stopped for a late lunch at a small inn before heading back to town.

It was a relaxing day. Marla gazed in silence at the passing scenery on the way home. It wasn't unpleasant for her. She enjoyed being able to physically do something besides keep a couch warm. Never in a million years did she ever think she would hike Mt. Olympus, see a glacier, and then hike back down all in one day. Although her body protested the rough climb and the elevation change, she'd been exhilarated at the accomplishment. It gave her a new appreciation for her weight loss.

Timothy was an avid outdoorsman. The outdoors refreshed his soul. Marla could understand why and had begun to feel the same. She now had a body capable of hiking, kayaking, going on extended bike rides, and even skiing. The skiing was something he said he deeply regretted now. Marla didn't. She loved swooshing down the slopes, feeling like a bird in flight.

She was a little in awe of herself for being so adventurous. It wasn't a character trait that she felt totally comfortable with yet. She'd spent thirty-two years inside her protective shell, trying to avoid mean looks, hurtful comments, and as much physical exertion as possible. Not being afraid of any of those things was exhilarating and opened a very new life.

The change in weight had been slow in coming, but the emotional and psychological change was still settling in. Marla wasn't always sure who she was without her comforting and protective shell of fat. An incredible array of amazing things had happened since the weight loss: an amazing boyfriend, sex, and more physical activity in one day than she had previously fit into a year. It was too much to fathom at times.

Beeping sounds erupted in the car, waking Marla from a doze.

Timothy steered the car to the side of the road and stopped. "What the—?" He reached for his beeper. A beeper was more likely to have a connection anywhere a cell phone might not, so he always carried one when not in Seattle. "It must be an emergency, a real emergency, if they're contacting me." He checked the display and dialed his cell phone.

"Dr. Brighton speaking, what is it?"

Marla watched as his face paled. He collapsed back in his seat, one hand on his forehead.

"My God! Any injuries? Okay, Good. Were any specimens lost? Right, right ... Can you put him on? Thanks, I'll wait."

"Fire in the histology lab," Timothy said, covering the phone to give her a quick update.

Her stomach dropped as shock spread through Marla's gut. It was incredible to think such a thing could happen. Everything appeared fine when she inspected the lab. Glancing over at Timothy to ask a question, she saw distress etching his face. He cared deeply for all his employees, that some of them had been in danger must be excruciating. She placed her hand on his thigh to comfort him.

"Yes, Chief Holgram. What needs to be done? Closing it down? The whole laboratory ...We have patient specimens that will need to be moved to another testing facility ... Yes, I can appreciate your situation. You have to understand some of these specimens are irreplaceable." He listened intently before adding, "Dr. Wimker is the assistant director, he'll control the evacuation in my absence. I'm on the East Coast, I'll be there by eleven p.m. tonight. Thank you." He disconnected the call and rested his head on the steering wheel.

It was agony waiting for Timothy to share the news with her. She rubbed his right shoulder.

"There's been a flammable liquid fire in the histology lab. The sprinklers knocked it down somewhat, but some of the flammable liquids floated on top of the water, burning. Thank God, no one was seriously hurt. The fire chief wants the entire lab closed immediately. No chance to move patient samples out until the fire marshal and building inspector say the building is safe and secure." He looked at Marla with huge sad eyes. "I have to get back tonight," Timothy groaned.

"My God, of course, Tim," she said.

"I was so looking forward to spending the weekend with you," Timothy whispered, taking her hand in his and softly rubbing his thumb across her knuckles.

"We'll have more weekends. Don't think about me right now. I'll be here. The cast will be off in a few weeks and I can fly out there," Marla said as cheerfully as she could. "And I expect I'll be sent over to the lab to re-inspect once it's up and running again, so you had better get things in proper order." She smiled broadly, trying to tease a smile out of him. It didn't work. He shifted the car in gear, and they drove on toward Pittsburgh, concern etching his handsome face.

Timothy Brighton was already three thousand miles away.

• • • •

"THANKS, DADDY," HEATHER said quietly, tears rolling down her face. Her heart swelled with the love her parents gave her. Their love had sustained her and the kids through Thanksgiving.

"Don't worry, Heather. Everything will turn out all right," her father said reassuringly. "Do you remember the time I got laid off from the paper plant in Maine? You were pretty little back then, you might not remember." He started up the truck, pulling away from the place Heather, Billy, and the children had called home for over five years.

"I'm not sure. I remember we went to Grandma's house for vacation," Heather said, watching the duplex diminish in size in the side mirror before Harold Boyden turned the corner.

"Yup, that's the time. We moved because your Momma and I couldn't afford the house in Maine after I lost the job. We went to stay with Grandma for about six months. It was getting to be spring in Georgia at the time, so you probably thought it was summer." Harold smiled at her. "It took a little while to get back on our feet, but we did. You'll get there too."

Heather didn't have any response to his words of encouragement. While Billy had found another job quickly enough with his forklift operator skills, it still looked bleak. She couldn't see how she and the children were going to survive this abandonment.

Her parents' house in Morningside was big enough for all of them. The two boys stayed together in one guest room while Heather and Michelle had the other. The house was close to Highland Park and the Pittsburgh Zoo and Aquarium. A huge bonus as far as the kids were concerned.

Being left by your husband for another woman was bad enough, but to be evicted from their home because Billy wouldn't pay the required child support was miserable. Payments he knew kept the roof over their heads. There was no hope for much cooperation anytime soon either. And Heather knew her parents were in no position to help them with that much money.

While the state tried to garnish his wages, Heather had nothing to pay rent, electricity, gas, water, or keep a car running. Not to mention feeding three growing children and herself. She had to file for welfare and WIC benefits for the children's sake. How this temporary move-in with her parents was going to affect those benefits, she didn't know. She was too numb from all the issues to even consider the possible ramifications.

The first business was to get the children safe and secure with her parents, then move the contents of the house. Next was getting the kids enrolled in school and after-school daycare. Her last task was something Heather was terrified of doing, finding a job.

She visited her former high school to see her accounting teacher. She asked Mr. Marin about accounting in the current era, ten-plus years after her last accounting classes. He was nice enough to tell her that while accounting was mainly done by computer, it still required people knowledgeable in manual accounting practices.

There were the odd businesses out there that still did their books on paper, the old-fashioned way, but it would be difficult to find such a place. It would behoove Heather to update her skills with some computer-based accounting classes at the local community college in the neighboring town. He recommended she get an associate degree while she was there.

Heather's morale sank, but she decided to look up the courses at the college and talk with the professor Mr. Marin had identified as the instructor. The trip was partially fruitful. The professor had explained the two courses he thought Heather should take as a minimum. Neither was terribly expensive, and in her predicament, she was likely to qualify for some grant money to cover the fees.

Better still, the courses had day and evening as well as supervised online sessions. That would make it easier to attend while her children were either in school, daycare, or bed at her parents' house.

Unfortunately, the fall semester was almost over. She'd have to wait until the spring semester to start the first course, then take the second part in either a summer session or during the fall semester. Either way, it would be nearly a full year before she finished the sessions she needed.

Heather invested her free time searching for bookkeeping jobs. As it turned out, her mother found her a job. Macie Boyden had begun taking the three children to church as soon as they moved into the house. Before their stay at Grandma's, they had never been to church. Macie was an active member of the ladies group at church and well-known by the congregation. She enjoyed introducing her three grandchildren to her friends and to Reverend Bart.

Reverend Bart had heard about Heather's circumstances, so he was pleased to welcome them into the church community. Peter and Nicholas started church school to bring them up to speed on their catechism. The pastor also knew Heather was looking for a job and had been keeping his own eyes and ears open for any bookkeeping jobs that might be available.

MID-DECEMBER 2018

Timothy told Marla that the fire was far worse than he had imagined. A portion of the histology laboratory had been heavily damaged by flames and smoke before the sprinkler system knocked it down. The adjacent laboratory spaces were also damaged by smoke. All the clinical areas farther away were less smoke damaged, although every surface would need to be washed clean of the sooty film. The computers and biomedical analyzers, all finely engineered instruments, would need to be serviced before being used again.

Dr. Timothy Brighton and his core staff worked endless hours trying to get portions of the laboratory fit to reopen as swiftly as possible. Rather than lose customers to other laboratories, specimens were still accepted at the front office. Those that could not be analyzed in the Seattle facility were packaged and transported by a courier system to the closest private airport, where four hired planes carried the specimens to receivers at the landing airport. From there, the samples were analyzed at the San Francisco facility and reported out. It cost the company a fortune but was better than trying to regain lost clients.

Endless issues cropped up, including the need to replace many of the more sensitive biomedical analyzers when cleaning proved futile. All of their supplies, including unopened boxes of testing materials, had to be discarded.

In all, it took over twelve weeks for the entire laboratory to get up to running at fifty percent capacity.

Timothy managed to call Marla three times in those three weeks. She offered to fly out to help, either at his laboratory or his home. Timothy dissuaded her. He was working eighteen-hour days, seven days a week, trying to handle repairs, renovations, and new problems as well as the regular problems with day-to-day operations, with a dozen couriers, four planes, and fourteen pilots thrown into the mix.

He'd taken a small, furnished corporate apartment in Seattle, around the corner from the laboratory to make life easier. His Bainbridge Island condo waited for life to resume a more normal course. Marla was welcome to come, but she shouldn't expect to see him.

"I can't even promise to have dinner with you. I barely eat. I haven't been out since our day trip." Timothy had said, uncharacteristically harsh. "Frankly, Marla, I can't handle seeing you now." Tension, exhaustion, frustration, and anger simmered beneath the surface.

"It's okay. It was just a suggestion. I'll stay here. Call me when you have time," Marla said in a quavering voice. "Goodbye, Timothy," and she hung up.

"Marla. I'm sorry—" Timothy said before the dial tone assaulted his eardrum.

• • • •

REVEREND BART CALLED the Boyden household one morning to notify Heather about a job opening. Church member Gigi Price owned a local wholesale florist shop. By the end of the week, Heather had a job. It didn't pay terribly well, but it was far better than welfare, and she might still qualify for government assistance. The children still had health insurance through Billy's new employer, as he had promised Heather.

The stress of the new job, the instability, and abandonment had uncharacteristically kept Heather in an anorexic frame of mind. She found she wasn't hungry most of the time, and while her mother coaxed her to eat, she mainly appeased her mother's anxiety by eating fruits and yogurts. She missed every other Calorie Counters meeting because the money just wasn't available. Not that she was following the program much anyway. Her life was too complicated and erratic to pay attention to it. Plus, St. Elizabeth's was now far across town instead a few blocks away. Yet at each weigh-in she did make, Heather found she was dropping the pounds anyway.

She worried the kids would revert to all their old eating habits. Surprisingly, the children were influencing Grandma's cooking. They'd ask for fruits and raw vegetables, yogurts, and cheeses. They refused to eat the hot dogs, hamburgers, baloney sandwiches, beefaroni, and mac and cheese she prepared for them. Heather felt a welling of pride in her children for wishing to maintain the new food choices she had taught them.

In the end, Mr. and Mrs. Boyden's eating habits improved. Snoopy had to make do with his usual kibble as Grandma and Grandpa didn't take well to feeding the dog table scraps like Billy had, so eventually, even Snoopy lost a few pounds living at the Boyden's.

• • • •

AT THE BEGINNING OF December, Gemma knew the projected membership renewal numbers for NACET were worse. Overall, the membership was already down thirty-five percent. The board of directors teleconferenced to restructure the organization before the new fiscal year to stop the financial strain that was sure to come.

Gemma awaited the news in her office. She expected to lose another staff member. Downsize the list to three or four conferences. Each conference itself would have to be downsized for reduced participation. Hopefully, the hotel room blocks weren't so large that the organization wouldn't be responsible for unsold rooms.

When the call came, she walked into Mike's office, knowing the score. Or so she thought.

"Gemma, you know the situation. I don't have to tell you anything you don't already know," Mike said calmly, not meeting her eyes. "I'm afraid the board has decided to let the entire conference planning staff go."

"WHAT!!?" Gemma erupted. This was too much. Had she heard correctly?

"The board is hiring an outside firm to handle the conferences. They'll take over the files as they are, finish whatever planning is required, and then leave. No persons will be on payroll constantly for event planning." Mike tried explaining the reasoning and the logistics of the new system the board was implementing.

"You've got to be kidding me? An organization this size, with conferences the size you hold? You think a run-of-the-mill, overnight operation is going to be able to give you the same results?" Gemma stuttered, flabbergasted.

"It's certainly going to take some time to get used to. But there isn't much choice. The financial situation is too bleak. If things change, you know you'll be the first person we call back to refill the position." Mike offered a weak smile.

"When? How about Marilyn and Jeremy? If you're firing me, you better be the one telling them," Gemma spouted in anger.

"I'll tell them. This Friday will be the last day. I'm hoping all of you can be professional about this development, tie up as many of the loose strings as you can, put the files together cohesively, and leave them behind in such a way that the contractor can understand what has been done and what needs to be done yet," Mike said a little more firmly.

Gemma stared at him, her mouth gaping open in shock. "Sure." *Thanks for waiting until just before Christmas, asshole.* She strode out of his office, head held high until she turned the corner out of Mike's sightline. Then, head down, she tried to keep her tears from spilling until outside on the sidewalk.

Tempting as it was to commit sabotage, Gemma and her remaining staff tidied up the files as requested and left them in order for their replacements. The only items they took with them, with permission, were pictures of them working together at some of the NACET events. They remained in professional mode up until the office door swung shut for the last time.

However, their last official act was to pile into Jeremy's car. They went to the local pub, where they drank themselves silly for the next four hours. Taxis took them all home long after last call.

• • • •

TIMOTHY RETURNED ONLY half of Marla's text messages and emails. Considering how busy he was trying to get the lab running again, she should feel grateful for that. At night, Marla would stare at her phone or her computer screen, trying to think of something to say. More times than not, she couldn't think of anything that wasn't so mundane he'd ignore it as a waste of time.

Many times she considered hopping on a plane to Seattle and surprising him. But her cast would make it difficult. And she wasn't sure she could handle the rejection.

Marla stayed in Pittsburgh, going to work and going home. Sometimes she met with Gemma, Heather, and Chelsea or talked with them on the phone. The women hadn't met since before Thanksgiving. It was funny, but Marla got teary-eyed and a lump formed in her throat when she thought of them. Their friendship and love, yes, love, had become vital to her. Especially since Timothy's departure back to Seattle. After the last months, she couldn't fathom why she had been so reluctant to reunite with them. Yes, her weight had been up, but they had accepted her just as they did on the first day of camp.

LATE DECEMBER 2018

The lab renovations put a huge dent in Marla and Timothy's relationship. They spoke less than once a week for only a few minutes. Marla could hear the tension and exhaustion in his voice. A voice that had been so beautiful to her ears now sounded rough and crackly from over use.

Once again, she offered to fly out to see him for Christmas and was declined.

"It's just not necessary. I'll be at the lab or the airport or on the phone the entire holiday. We're short-staffed because a dozen techs quit after the fire. I might end up running one of the blood chemistry analyzers."

"Well, I can help out in the hematology lab. And we can be together."

A heavy sigh came over the phone. "Please, Marla, don't push. Let's just pretend we're each going to our parents' homes for Christmas."

"But I already sent your Christmas present."

"If you sent it to my Bainbridge house, I'll have to call my neighbors to collect it. I haven't been there except for a few short visits for clothing."

The sound of muffled talking came over the phone. Timothy must have cupped his hand over it to speak with someone.

"I've got to go, Marla." The call disconnected immediately.

Her heart aching, Marla hung up. She noticed he hadn't even mentioned a Christmas present for her.

• • • •

GEMMA GLANCED BACK before shutting the door of her condo for the last time. No, not her condominium any more.

Unemployment payments would not cover her mortgage. Rather than whittle down her savings, she abruptly decided to sell it. Except now, for the first time since her surgery, her chest felt heavy, and she could barely breathe. *Was it the right thing to do?*

She shook her head clear of fuzzy thoughts. It was Mr. and Mrs. Underwood's condominium now, as of eleven a.m. today, if all went as planned at the closing. Who knew what the future would hold? She might end up getting a position in DC, four hours and two hundred and forty-six miles away. Having this done would free her to start anywhere immediately.

Tears started to leak from her eyes, but she brushed them aside. She wanted to remain strong in the face of this final step, which would be the first step of her new life. She stood on the front stoop, taking one last survey of the view. To her surprise, Mrs. Hoskins came out of her own door, startling Gemma.

"Oh, Gemma dear, I was hoping I would catch you." Mrs. Hoskins hobbled over to Gemma's stoop.

"Hi, Mrs. Hoskins. It's so nice of you to say goodbye," Gemma said, taking the elderly woman's hands in her own.

"Well, dear. I wish you all the best. I hope you're able to find a new job soon," she said, her head twitching with Parkinson's.

"So do I."

"It's a pity to have this place turn over again. At least this time, it's not to another young woman who will end up seduced by Charlie whatever-his-name-is. Eight in a row is eight too many," tsked Mrs. Hoskins.

Gemma nearly fell over. Her mouth gaped open for a few seconds. She had only been half listening to Mrs. Hoskins's words. She was silent for a minute while the words sank into her skin, raising a fever first, then a rash.

"Mrs. Hoskins, did you say Charlie Hanover has dated seven other women in this complex before me?" Gemma asked carefully, trying to keep her emotions reined in until the answer.

"Oh, yes, he gets around this complex. He dated the last two ladies that lived in your unit. When the romance broke off, they both left. Karen Setton was broken-hearted, poor dear. Couldn't stand to live here, bumping into him. Before her, Mary Lou Kulas stuck it out a little while, then got a transfer in her job. They each sold and left. Over the last several years, he's dated women in areas B, F, and R. In my day, he'd have been called a regular Tom Cat or a Rake," She reported with a wily grin and a shake of her head. "But he was with you the longest, I think."

Lucky me.

"Thank you for telling me, Mrs. Hoskins. This makes me feel a whole lot better." Gemma smiled at her while seething inside at the audacity of the man to sleep his way into the beds scattered around the complex. Revenge shall be sweet, she thought, while ideas hatched in the back of her brain.

"Goodbye, Mrs. Hoskins. I'll miss you," Gemma said. "Take good care of yourself."

"You too, dear. Watch out for Tom Cats." She smiled. "They may be slick, but there's always a bad smell to them."

"Yes, ma'am. I believe you are right," Gemma whispered to herself as she got into her overloaded car to drive to the nearest copy center.

Before Gemma signed the papers to finalize the transaction in the attorney's office, the laundry and storage areas in all twenty buildings in the condo complex had at least four warning posters. She had worked them up on her computer and printed them at a copy center. Each warned the female residents to beware of the conniving charm of Charlie Hanover, the Tom Cat of the condominium complex. Gemma fervently hoped Charlie's days of dallying in the complex like it was his own personal sexual playground were over.

"How'd it go?" her cousin, Rose Anne asked, lounging out on the couch, bag of chips in one hand, TV remote in the other.

"Okay, at least it's over. I put the last of my bulky things in the storage unit," Gemma said from the comfort of the third-generation hand-me-down couch. "Thanks for letting me crash here for a few weeks. I need to make sure the money is free and clear before I spend it."

She held up a hand to silence her cousin. "Yes, I know, it should be at the closing. I want to make sure before I spend a dime. Buyer's remorse and all that," Gemma wearily offered as an excuse.

"There's no such thing as buyer's remorse in real estate," Rose Anne corrected. "Besides, you won't get the money for at least a couple weeks."

"Yeah, yeah. What if eight-five-year-old Mrs. Underwood dies tomorrow, and Mr. Underwood wants to back out of the deal? I'd feel like a schmuck not giving it back to him," Gemma badgered back.

"He can't. You can't. It's a done deal," Rose Anne stated firmly. "Want some chips?" Rose slid the bag of potato chips toward Gemma's end of the coffee table.

"No. I don't eat chips anymore."

Rose Anne stuck her potato chip-covered tongue out at Gemma. It was easy for Gemma to avoid these kinds of foods when she lived alone—she just didn't buy them. Or she hid them in the back of the kitchen cabinet so they never saw the light of day. She knew that if they were opened, she'd devour them completely.

It was going to be a little harder now at Rose Anne's apartment. Rose Anne ate whatever she pleased and never seemed to gain an ounce. They sat in silence for a few minutes, watching a TV commercial.

"Did you find any apartments you liked?" Rose Anne asked in a more conciliatory manner.

"I found one I liked. It was a studio. Big enough living space with a large storage area in the basement for my things. Unfortunately, they wanted to run a credit check, which is fine, except they also insist on having a tenant who's employed."

"Scumbags. What if you pay six months up front?"

"I don't want to do that in case I get a job offer somewhere else, like DC," Gemma explained. "Mobility is key for my profession. I can't tie myself to a lease." She sighed.

Rose Anne crumpled the chip bag into a ball. "So stay here as long as you need to."

"Thanks, I'll try not to." Gemma smiled. "I know it cramps your style."

"Nonsense. But don't complain if the volume gets a little loud." Rose Anne giggled.

"Incorrigible! You slut!" Gemma hissed, playfully throwing a pillow at her cousin's head.

"I try!" Rose Anne giggled outright and tossed it back.

• • • •

MARLA, GEMMA, HEATHER, and Chelsea huddled in the kitchen of Chelsea and Seth's apartment. It took some doing, but they all looked happy to spend the first hours of the new year together.

"Any luck with a new job?" Heather asked Gemma.

"Not a chance. I have to get something soon, or I'll wear out my welcome."

Marla raised an eyebrow. "Is your cousin unhappy sharing her place?"

"No. Rose Anne is fine with it, but I do want to move into my own space."

"Speaking of moving ... how are you and the kids doing at your parents' house?" Marla asked Heather.

"The kids think it's grand to have Grandma and Grandpa around all the time. It certainly makes my life easier. Between work and their school activities, it's hard to keep up. And the daycare savings are a Godsend."

Chelsea turned to Marla. "Any news on your leg? Shouldn't that cast be coming off soon?"

"Yes. Hopefully next week."

The TV sound grew louder in the living room as Seth watched the countdown to 2019. "Five, Four, Three, Two, One, Happy New Year!" the TV commentaries cried.

Marla held up her champagne glass. The other three did the same, the rims clinking together. "To the women of cabin four!"

JANUARY 2019

Gloria was looking at her with intense love and something else Chelsea couldn't name. Was it sorrow? She'd planned her wedding for July 8th. Momma couldn't understand why the two of them didn't marry earlier. As a result, she rarely visited her mother. But Gloria had asked for her help taking down curtains. They were seated in the kitchen, the curtain task completed.

"Chelsea, why are you waiting so long?" asked Gloria, deep frown lines crossing her forehead, impatience in her voice. She'd made tea for her and Chelsea. The salmon pink Formica tabletop was battered; it had been battered long ago when she and her husband, Thomas, bought it used as newlyweds.

"Momma, I want to wear this fabulous dress I bought from the salon. You know the one we saw, the one I picked out." Chelsea blew over her green tea, trying to cool it down.

Gloria's hands stretched out on the tabletop, palms up, beseeching. "So, what's the problem? You need money? I've got some money for you. I saved some from the insurance settlement when your father died. Let's move this along," Gloria urged.

Here we go, Chelsea thought. She didn't want to have to lay it all out for her mother, but it looked like a full explanation was going to be necessary. "Momma, it's not the money. I need to lose some weight to fit into the dress."

"Didn't you buy it in the right size, honey?" Gloria sat back in her chair looking exasperated. Her tea was going cold, untouched on the table. "Did they order the wrong size, or did you gain more weight?"

Geesh, gain weight? Hasn't she even noticed I've lost weight? Course not. Nobody beyond her camp friends had noticed yet. "The only one left was a size twelve. I couldn't find the right size anywhere. So I bought the size twelve, and I've been losing weight."

"So, buy a dress to fit you and move the wedding date up. You and Seth have been together since high school, for Christ's sake. Just do it, honey!" Gloria shouted, slapping her palms on the tabletop.

Stunned, Chelsea sat back and stared at her mother. Losing her patience was uncharacteristic, as was swearing. Her face was etched with deep agitation. She was more perturbed than Chelsea had ever seen her before.

"No, Momma. It's my wedding day, I want to look great in my wedding dress. I've been doing the Slimline System. I'm down sixty-one pounds already," Chelsea argued back, asserting her authority over the matter. *Why does it have to be like this? Why do I constantly have to explain to people why we're waiting until July? Is it any of their business what's holding it up?*

"I don't understand why you have to wait so long. Life doesn't last forever, Chelsea. We don't all get to live forever." This time, Gloria's fist pounded the table, rattling more than the teacups and spoons. Her eyes flashed with anger at her daughter.

Chelsea jumped back in her seat, mouth hung open, speechless for a few seconds. "What do you mean by that?" Chelsea cried. "Do you think Seth's going to get tired of waiting and leave me?"

"No, no, I'm just saying, a lot of things can happen in the six months while you're waiting to lose enough weight to get into a stupid dress," Gloria sputtered. Chelsea watched as her mother's anger ebbed. Tears began to slide from her eyes, spilling over the dark circles and mottled cheeks.

"It's not a stupid dress, it's beautiful. The most beautiful dress I've ever seen." Chelsea burst into tears also. "Why don't you want me to wear the dress I want?"

Gloria softened, her tears tumbling down her face unabashedly. "Baby, it has nothing to do with the dress. I only want you to get married sooner."

"Why, Momma? Why?" Chelsea sobbed, "Why can't I wait until July?"

Gloria reached across the table to grasp her daughter's hand. She sighed heavily, "Because I might not be here in July."

Chelsea didn't think she heard her mother correctly. "What? What are you talking about?" Chelsea asked, her sniffles easing so she could hear better.

Walking around the table to hug her daughter close, pressing Chelsea's head to her stomach, Gloria said, "Chelsea, I saw the doctor last month for some pain I've been having. I went through some tests, and they found some cancer." Fresh rivulets of tears poured down her cheeks now.

Chelsea's head rose up from resting on her mother's stomach. Her vision whirled, her mouth went bone dry. "Cancer? When? How? What are they going to do about it?" Chelsea watched her mother's face, searching desperately for more information, more answers.

"There's not much they can do about it. It started in my colon, and it's spread already. They see it in my bones, my lung, my liver, and a small spot on my spinal cord. It's too far gone now to do anything about it. Rather than give me treatments that will make me sick and may only extend my life a few extra weeks, I'm not doing anything. I have about four to five months left." Gloria said, her voice strong as though she had already resigned herself to the decision.

Chelsea blinked back her tears to clear her vision. "But Momma, what if you don't make it to my wedding?"

"That's why I'm asking you to reconsider the wedding date. Which is more important to you? Having your mother at your wedding or wearing a smaller-sized wedding dress?" asked Gloria with brutal honesty.

Gloria pulled her closer in a hug reminiscent of all those hugs long ago when Chelsea was little. At five or six, her head barely cleared her mother's waist, and she could hear her mother's heartbeat when Chelsea pressed her ear to her stomach. She tried with all her might to ingrain that sound now. *Oh, God, to be that child again.* To have her mother so young again. Back when her father was still alive. Back when everyone was healthy and happy.

Three days later, Chelsea and Seth rescheduled their wedding for Friday night, May 17th. It hadn't been easy. They lost the band and the venue but the Hungarian Society hall was available.

The invitations were ordered immediately, with "Save the date" notes going out by week's end. The bridesmaids and maid of honor were quickly assembled to plan the bridal shower, to be held in four weeks. Seth had long ago selected his best man and all his brothers as groomsmen.

• • • •

IN THE MIDDLE OF JANUARY, Heather started taking the night course in computer accounting programs, as her teacher had suggested. Again, because of her predicament, a full grant from the State of Pennsylvania paid for her tuition. Heather only needed to pay for school fees and her books.

The second good thing was that the Pennsylvania Department of Child Services could garnish Billy's wages for child support. Heather started getting regular, dependable child support checks through the state. They weren't enough to live on, but with her job, she was in a better situation. But not enough to make those ends meet.

Overall, it wasn't an easy time, as transitions never are in life. Heather often burned the candle on both ends, despite her mother's help babysitting and cooking.

The boys, particularly Peter, acted out at times in anger over the loss of their father. Billy never came to visit them; he neither called nor wrote. Not even a birthday card or gift for his eldest son, Peter, on his birthday, in January.

Afraid of how it might hurt him, Heather prepared a gift from "Daddy" for him. Peter unwrapped it but ignored the set of matchbox cars. He gave her a look as if to say he knew his father had nothing to do with the gift.

Perhaps someday Billy would want to reconnect with his three children if it wasn't too late for him or them. While Heather was happy he stayed out of their lives, she also knew Billy's absence was hurting the boys deeply, especially Peter.

She made a point to talk with Reverend Bart about the situation, not knowing what to tell the children when they asked for their father. Again, Rev. Bart came to their rescue. He found some free child psychology services. Weekly ongoing services were scheduled for both boys to help them deal with their father's abandonment. They also helped Heather assess each child's state of acceptance, their level of understanding and helped her tell them in a way they could understand that Daddy had gone away and she didn't know when he was coming back.

• • • •

FROM HER POSITION IN the company, Marla could keep track of the Seattle lab's functional status with the help of her assistant, Ashley. Upper management had already decided that until it was completely operational, Marla would not be re-inspecting the laboratory. She was made privy to the incident reports, police, fire, and insurance reports, investigation findings, and of course, the weekly updates from Medical Director Dr. Timothy Brighton. The fire marshal had determined a cell phone charging cord had started the fire in the flammable working environment and, fed by solvent vapors, had exploded in a conflagration. The histology staff was lucky to have gotten out alive.

Every time Marla read Timothy's name, a dull ache resounded in her gut, and tears flooded her eyes. There had been no direct communication between them since Marla's offer to fly to Seattle was rejected. She sent funny memes to his social media accounts. She texted him too. After texting every day for the first two weeks, her heart couldn't take the daily rejection, and she only texted every other day. After the first month, with not a single reply, she stopped entirely.

His last two calls had been voice messages. The first to apologize for his tone when she called about Christmas. The second, a week later, just to say hi, thinking of you but can't talk right now. Then nothing more than endless weeks of silence. Not a call, text, present, or card on Christmas. And no thank you for the present she sent. The disappointment of not seeing him open it settled in her chest. It was a book about the history of every U.S. national park. She knew he would like it.

She tried to remind herself he was dealing with a major disaster. Somehow it didn't help. If he really wanted to contact her, he knew how. Leaving a voice message on her work phone after hours was lame. She had a cell phone, and like him, she even had a home phone though it never rang except for spam calls. Maybe he was looking for a way out and decided this was his chance to ease out of the relationship? Whatever it was, Marla no longer expected to hear from him ever again.

It was questionable how she would handle the inspection once the laboratory was ready. Could she remain objective with Timothy so near? He'd been her only true love in so many ways.

A shiver went up her spine thinking of his exquisite lovemaking. Not that she had anyone to compare him with; she could tell he was incredibly sensitive to her body and needs. Her pleasure was his pleasure, he told her often enough.

It was a good thing they had been so discreet about their relationship. No one at corporate knew about it, and the same was true at the Seattle facility. They had been silent and secretive for the exact situation they were now experiencing. Fortuitous, Marla thought. There were no pitiful stares at work, no whispers. Moreover, this way, she didn't have to worry about anyone informing Timothy of her former self, *all* three hundred and seven former pounds of her.

• • • •

FAR TOO MANY WEEKS had passed without any luck finding a job or a place to live. Everywhere Gemma went, either a lease was required and/or a current job was a prerequisite. Every contact she had was located and tweaked for information. The jobs weren't out there. Worse yet, more of her colleagues at other companies were being let go, replaced by contract event planning companies. It looked bleak for her and for Marilyn and Jeremy, who were also struggling.

There were jobs in Washington, DC, but the cost of living there and the paltry salaries no bigger than her current, eh, former salary would not suffice. Besides, she liked living in Pittsburgh. It was a great city, and she had many friends there. She thought of Heather and Chelsea, and Marla. They had truly turned into sisters to her. After living without them for so long, she knew how bleak her world would be if she left. It would almost be like leaving camp all over again. No doubt, there'd be promises to stay in contact. But over time, they would fall to the wayside, just as it happened before.

Swirling her wine in a glass one night, contemplating the situation, Gemma had an epiphany. Who was this contract event planning company? She spent the next two hours searching the web for information. There were only two major companies out there doing special event planning consulting. Neither were hiring.

Gemma called Jeremy and Marilyn and asked them for lunch at Artiotis Café. There she told them her idea.

She handed out a one-page dossier on each of the two companies. "Main Event and Strategic Planners are the two major event planning companies. All my contacts and networks tell me they are gobbling business between New York and Washington DC. I did some digging about them online, and here's what I found out: they're small. Less than twenty employees each. I think we should do some thorough digging into them, figure out how they operate and then consider forming our own company, just the three of us," Gemma said. "Perhaps we can win over NACET to start."

Marilyn looked aghast at the suggestion until a sly smile crept across her face. Jeremy started fanning his face with the factsheets. "Gem, that's a super-hot idea! I love how you think."

Over the next two weeks, they dug up as much information as possible on the companies, their employees, client lists, and pricing.

Jeremy's brother Michael owned a business. To help dig for information, Jeremy got Michael's permission to impersonate him and called each company asking for a Request for Proposal for a fictitious event. He quizzed each company CEO as deeply as he dared to ferret out the companies' business plan, management scheme, and financial pricing structures. Last, he asked for five references from each company, which Gemma and Marilyn then contacted for more intelligence gathering. They meet at Rose Anne's kitchen table two weeks later to review the findings.

Jeremy started, "The email reports I sent out two days ago sum up the information I've been able to gather on their management, marketing, and pricing."

Marilyn added, "The references Gemma and I checked had some good and bad things to say about each of their performances.

Overall, they handled things well, but attention to detail was absent. They were sloppy. Registration and website problems were rampant with most of them. Hotel problems were always referred back to the hotel. They refused to intervene for attendees' issues."

Gemma took the leap of faith. "Well, I don't know about you, but I think there's plenty of room for a third event planning company."

"I think you're right." Marilyn nodded, smiling.

"Oh yeah. I'm in." Jeremy grinned.

"Any ideas for a name?" Gemma sat back in her chair. It was important for her to step back, not be the boss, just be a partner in this endeavor. If they wanted her to be CEO, they would have to ask.

"No." Marilyn dropped her chin in her hand and tried to brainstorm.

A few minutes elapsed before Jeremy threw out a suggestion. "How about Trilogy? Since it's the three of us."

Gemma nodded in approval. "I like it."

"I love it." Marilyn beamed.

"Well, then," Jeremy said, raising his coffee mug, "to Trilogy!"

"Trilogy," the ladies echoed in unison, thumping their coffee mugs together.

At the conclusion of their planning session, they had formed the Trilogy Event Planning and Management Corporation, LLC. Each of them agreed to invest five thousand dollars into their venture. They set up an office in Marilyn's garage and proceeded to incorporate their new business legally.

Their first line of business was to go after the NACET account. One afternoon, they showed up at the office asking to see Mike. They were friendly and professional and gave him their best offer. Mike was more than pleased to relay the information to the board of directors. At the board's next meeting, NACET switched to Trilogy for all their event-planning needs. With such a huge client under its belt, Trilogy was on its way. Next, they went after the five clients referenced by each company in their RFPs for the bogus event. By the end of the month, they had half of them as clients.

FEBRUARY 2019

Saturday, February 16th, Chelsea's maid of honor and bridesmaids held a bridal shower for her at the VFW hall. Heather's father had helped procure the space since he was a member. The fact that Seth and Chelsea had been living together for ten years skewed the party theme from the usual household items to more romantic items. Box after box held lingerie, sex toys, and other things that turned Chelsea into a blushing bride.

Gemma had fun running some sexually-orientated games that kept the sixty-five women entertained. She had even procured a penis cake with white cream frosting inside. Meanwhile, Heather and Marla remained helpful but silent.

When Chelsea's mother rolled her eyes at the cake and stared at her, Heather could only shrug. Heather thought it a bit much, but she didn't say anything. Diana and Gemma had put their heads together to plan and pay for the event, so who was she to object?

• • • •

HEATHER'S NEW JOB WAS going well, as was the online class through the college. There were days when the tension and frustration left her feeling weak and unable to focus. Every day she took care of the children, worked an eight-hour day, and then took the online course after the children went to bed. Only to be repeated the next day and every day thereafter. The weight of the responsibilities was heavy on her heart and her shoulders. The only time she had for herself was in the bathroom, where she frequently turned on the shower to keep the kids from hearing her sobs.

• • • •

THE SEATTLE LABORATORY was running at eighty percent. The histology laboratory relocated to a building on the same city block while the old space was completely rebuilt. Andrea said the procedures were still the same; it was only a different workspace. The fire marshal had personally inspected the laboratory and was satisfied, so Marla did not feel the need to venture out there, but she knew the day was coming closer.

When Beverly asked for the inspection, her assistant was out on maternity leave. There was no way she could get out of the situation. Marla made a plan. First, she'd call Timothy at his Bainbridge condo to say she was cool with the arrangement. That way, he wouldn't get the message at work. Or worse, answer the phone. He had nothing to worry about. He could excuse himself from the process, letting Andrea work with her on-site.

She'd stay at the Hyatt, work crazy fourteen-to-sixteen-hour days to get the job done in two days, then leave as quickly and silently as she had arrived. She would not participate in any fanfare, welcoming party, dinners ... nothing extra.

It took Marla the better part of two days to get up the nerve to call Timothy's Bainbridge condo. With the time difference, he was likely at work, which was exactly what she wanted. He wasn't the only chicken. Marla's palms became sweaty as she dialed the number. She repeated the phrases in her mind, pacing her bedroom as the phone rang on the other end. Then someone picked up.

"Hello?" a silky female voice asked.

Not expecting a human to answer, never mind a female, Marla was dumbstruck. Dizziness swayed her, forcing her to reach for the bed for support. Her lips moved, but nothing came out.

"Hello?" she said again. Then "Tim, it must be for you."

"Hello?" Timothy's voice sounded gruff in Marla's ear.

Marla came to her senses and hung up. All resolve and bravado crumbled with her into a heap on her bed. She sobbed uncontrollably for hours.

MARCH 2019

Gloria's revelation and the moving of the wedding date forced Chelsea to take her Slimline diet seriously. She'd called Rebecca immediately to let her know about her mother's illness and the change in date, warning her that all Chelsea's efforts now involved slimming down as quickly as possible.

Why haven't I been following the plan? I could be almost at goal by now? Chelsea chastised herself. However, she hadn't, and she wasn't anywhere close. She'd only lost seventeen of the twenty-five more pounds necessary to get into her size twelve dress.

Immediately, Chelsea started sticking to the diet plan. Seth was impressed with her tenacity. She even cut all alcohol from her diet, one of the biggest issues Rebecca insisted had stymied her weight loss.

Her efforts didn't last long.

When Gloria's health started to decline, so did Chelsea's tenacity. She visited the doctors with her mother, asking questions, seeking answers to some questions that had no answers but from God. The responses were delivered as gently as medical professionals knew how to give them: Gloria's cancer was far advanced. The only treatments they could provide would be palliative. They would only extend her life a few extra weeks at the expense of her health now. The treatments might even accelerate the "outcome."

Chelsea kept a stiff upper lip through a conversation while driving her mother home. She saw her mother settled at home, made a meal she knew would not be eaten, then left for the evening. Around the corner from her mother's house, she pulled over to the side of the road and crumpled into a wailing heap on the car seat. She was there so long a neighbor came out to see if she was all right. It took another half hour for Chelsea to contain her grief long enough to drive home.

By the time she got there, she was angry. Enraged with the situation she could not forestall. In her fury and pain, she reached out for the only thing in the house that would give her comfort. She binged her way through every single cupboard in the house, every refrigerator shelf, and through the freezer. If she guessed, over twenty thousand calories were consumed before she finished three hours later. By the time she stopped, her stomach ached, and she didn't feel any better about her mother. She certainly didn't feel any better about her weight. For as much as she tried every day after that, Chelsea could not stop herself from eating anything and everything she wanted as she tried to stifle the despair she felt watching her mother visibly deteriorate every day.

• • • •

WITHIN WEEKS, TRILOGY had expanded enough to warrant adding a fourth person. By unanimous vote, the three business partners chose to contact Tony. He was excited at the prospect of joining the team again under the new circumstances. The narrow realm of engineering technologists had cramped Tony's style. Knowing Trilogy would be taking on a myriad of different organizational contexts "sends shivers up my designing spine!"

Tony's first assignment was giving the company brand pizzazz, from tweaking the new logo to designing the company stationary and the tiny office when they outgrew Marilyn's garage. The partners hoped that this integrated and contemporary brand would give their company the extra boost needed to impress clients and, in turn, rocket past the other two planning companies competing for business.

Trilogy heard about a neighborhood library that was under renovation through Jeremy's partner, James. Sensing a great opportunity, they offered to sponsor the grand reopening celebration to highlight their talent to the Pittsburgh business community. Squirrel Hill was one of Pittsburgh's more affluent outlying residential neighborhoods, housing a large percentage of downtown corporate executives. Making an impression with them was going to be essential to Trilogy's future.

Gemma contacted the chairman of the library's board of directors. Simon Crofton, III was a far more pleasant man than Gemma imagined he would be, given his name, his title of chairman, and his position both in the community as a philanthropist and as owner and CEO of Croftlite Industries, Inc. Not only did he insist the library board jump at Trilogy's offer for event planning services, but he also would bankroll the entire event. This happened after he also paid for the library renovations in the first place. Simon gave Trilogy carte blanche to give his neighborhood's library a reopening grander than its initial opening back in the early 1920s.

While he gave them free rein, Gemma reported back to him several times a week on the plans and costs incurred to bring them to fruition. They spoke on the phone daily after their initial meeting with the library board. He was easy to talk with and even easier to get on the phone. Rarely did he not take her calls immediately, something Gemma found incredible. How could a man who ran a multi-billion-dollar business designing, manufacturing, and marketing outdoor recreational furniture and equipment be almost always available for her telephone reports?

His availability wasn't the only thing Gemma found interesting. The man was physically stunning. With immaculately cut, prematurely silvery white hair, a charismatic manner, and a hint of bridled energy, he towered over her at about six-two if Gemma guessed correctly. In his early forties, his shoulders were broad, his chest solid, his clothing expensive and immaculately tailored. And Gemma felt an undercurrent of one hundred percent alpha male testosterone though he hid it well. The pheromones the man gave off drew her to his side whenever they met in person.

He was very different from any man she found herself attracted to, and she didn't quite know what to do about him. First, he was technically a client, which put him off-limits until their contract was fulfilled. Second, he was so manly in a subdued manner. Gemma giggled to herself thinking about this. Simon Crofton III was not a metrosexual, which she now clearly saw was the category of men she had been dating. She would think Simon Crofton was one hundred percent two Y chromosomes if it were biologically possible. There was no doubt about it. The thought gave her goosebumps.

It also gave her pause. She had no history dealing with this kind of man. He was out of her ballpark in many disturbing ways.

Trilogy planned a three-day event beginning on Friday and lasting through the weekend. The media coverage alone was such a frenzy about the variety of shows, parties, and contests, as well as the local celebrities attending, that Trilogy became a common word on Pittsburgh corporate event planning lips nearly overnight.

APRIL 2019

Chelsea tried to involve her mother in the wedding planning as much as she wanted.

Together with Seth, they met the photographer to select the photography package. With the finality of her mother's life in mind, Chelsea ordered the complete package, with coverage from preparations before the wedding all the way through to the reception. On her cousin's suggestion, they also intended to place disposable cameras on the tables so the guests could take candid shots to pad their album.

It took several trips to the bridal salon to select Gloria's dress. During the first trip, sudden nausea forced Chelsea to take Gloria home when they had only just begun to look through the dress racks. The second time, Gloria was well enough to select a dress, from the clearance rack, of course. But again, she could not muster enough energy to try it on for size. Three was the charm, and the dress was ready for minor alterations, mainly hemming. The unspoken question hung heavy in the salon the entire visit: how well would it fit on her disintegrating frame when the wedding day arrived?

An evening trip to the reception site gave Chelsea, Seth, and Gloria the opportunity to taste-test some of the menu options for the reception. Gloria took only a few bites of each option, clearly forcing herself to participate for her daughter's sake. By the end of the two-hour dinner, Gloria was shockingly pale and gaunt. Seth had to carry her to the car. While Gloria asked them not to fuss, Chelsea was stunned at the transformation in her mother's appearance over the course of two hours. Initially, she was afraid it might have been a case of food poisoning, until her cousin Diane reminded her it takes at least four hours for the first of the food poisoning symptoms.

Her mother was very ill and, yes, dying. Chelsea had to admit it and had to face it. Later that night, she surrendered to the ugly truth in Seth's arms, staining his favorite dress shirt with her tears until her eyes swelled shut.

The sudden realization of life's finite nature affected Chelsea. She didn't wait for permission to call her mother anymore. She did it every day. A daily visit was required during which Chelsea cooked food her mother would not eat, cleaned the house, and helped her mother bathe and dress. Her brother, Toby, and her aunt and uncle were informed and visited or called daily as well.

Even Seth's mother, Peggy, helped by stopping by to assist when she was available. Chelsea was grateful for her support.

As the weeks progressed, it became clear that Gloria's health was declining faster than she had anticipated. By early April, her skin was turning a light yellowish hue, as were the whites of her eyes. Fatigue was as constant a state as the pain. Gloria was wheelchair-bound for safety's sake. The painkillers made her dizzy at times, leaving her prone to falls. Chelsea could still keep her comfortable and involved in the chair, although safely ensconced in a seated position.

At her mother's badgering, Chelsea tried on the size twelve dress. The seams were stretched taut even as she couldn't zip up the back all the way. There was no way Chelsea was going to fit into that dress in time.

"It's beautiful, Chelsea. It almost looks like my dress. A little fancier with the crystals on the bodice and hem. The shape is the same," Gloria said hoarsely. She wheezed and inhaled from the oxygen tubing that supplemented her breathing twenty-four hours a day.

"Really, Mom?" Chelsea asked, trying to remember the dress her mother wore in her parents' wedding picture on the fireplace mantel.

"It's in the back of my closet. Been there for forty-seven years." She wheezed again.

Chelsea looked at herself in the mirror, appraising the wedding dress she had chosen and the alterations the seamstress had yet to make. Would it even be possible to let out the seams enough to fit?

"You're going to be a beautiful bride," Gloria choked out. "I hope I'm here to see it."

• • • •

THE PARENT-TEACHER conference was in full swing by the time Heather and Peter arrived. Peter dragged her all over the classroom to see his desk, cubby hole, and artwork hanging on the wall. He also introduced her to several of his friends.

A light-blond-haired man approached. Peter said, "Mom, it's Mr. Morgan."

"Hello, you must be Mrs. Laulier." His light blue eyes crinkled as he smiled. "Welcome to our classroom. If you have a minute, I'd like to speak with you."

Heather sent Peter off to talk with some friends then followed Mr. Morgan to his desk. They both sat. He took a file folder from the stack on his desk and said, "I'm glad you came tonight. I wanted to see what's going on."

"Going on?" Heather brushed a stray lock of hair aside.

"Yes, Peter's a great kid and an asset to the class. For the most part, he's even-tempered, happy, laughing, and playful. A quick learner, and he grasps new concepts well."

"But ..." Heather said, knowing there was more and it wasn't good.

Mr. Morgan sighed, his lovely eyes meeting hers. "Frankly, there are days when he's agitated, angry, and sometimes, a bit mean. On those days, he can't focus, can't get his work done, and doesn't work well with classmates." He was quiet a moment. "Is there something going on at home that could explain the variations?"

Heather dropped her eyes to the floor, feeling the heat of a blush rise. "We ..." She stopped and looked up at Mr. Morgan. "His father has abandoned us. Peter didn't spend much quality time with him, but his absence clearly disturbs him. He goes to counseling, and it has helped considerably. But some days, he acts out his frustration and sorrow."

Mr. Morgan nodded. "That explains a lot. I'll try to help him deal with it while he's in the classroom. Thank you for telling me."

Heather nodded. "His work is okay?"

"Absolutely, he's one of the top students in class. I'll let you know if that changes." He glanced up and looked around the room. Peter was watching the class hamster in its cage across the room.

Heather noticed she and Peter were the only ones left in the classroom.

"I know this is highly unusual. But I'd love to have a cup of coffee with you sometime. Get to know you better."

Heather blinked rapidly. This man, so opposite of Billy, wanted to talk with her. Well-dressed, well-spoken, clear English, nicely groomed. And the most beautiful eyes Heather had ever seen on a man. "Sure. I'd like that."

• • • •

GEMMA BIT HER NAIL. The one Chelsea had manicured the day before. The library event started Friday with the ribbon-cutting ceremony, including the mayor of Pittsburgh, the governor of Pennsylvania, and the neighborhood and library dignitaries. A more formal reception for dignitaries and the press followed for picture taking and interview options.

On Saturday, the fun began when the party expanded to the community. For adults, there was a reception for book signings by local authors and book raffles in the adult area. It was the kids' library area celebration that became the talk of the town. Trilogy booked not only the usual clowns with balloons and face painters. They booked Clifford the Dog, Angelina Ballerina, Scooby-Doo, Blues Clues, Darth Vader, Eragon, Bilbo Baggins, and more hobbits to wander the children's section while books were read aloud by the volunteers. Afterward, there were pizza sticks, jelly sandwiches, popcorn, punch, cookies, and a huge cake shaped like a castle.

The adults had a Book Character Ball Saturday night during which a raffle for an Acura MDX SUV raised an additional twenty-one thousand dollars for the library book acquisitions fund.

Sunday afternoon, a teen's Lego castle contest would commence. Midafternoon, there would be a kids' costume ball. Each child was asked to come dressed as their favorite book character. The Wiggles were scheduled to entertain the massive crowd of pint-sized costumed characters with a forty-five-minute show. A poetry slam would occur simultaneously for adults in the quieter adult section.

The responsibilities for handling the dignitaries on Friday before and after the ceremony fell on Gemma's shoulders. Thankfully, she had some helpful assistance from Simon Crofton.

In planning the Saturday night ball, Simon asked for a Midsummer Night's Dream theme, complete with live indoor trees, shrubs, vines, flowers, grassy areas with benches for sitting, and even koi-filled artificial garden ponds. He donated thousands of dollars of company merchandise for the venue.

Tony had fallen in love with the idea and gone wild with the design of the convention center space. It took three days to assemble the scenery, dining tables, the band's stage, and the dancing area.

When word seeped out about the extent of the ball, it became the event of the decade for all of Pittsburgh. Two hundred couples vied for the limited number of tickets, each at five hundred dollars. Entire tables of eight were bought out by corporations at ten thousand each. Demand was so hot that tickets were scalped, some reportedly going for over a thousand dollars apiece.

It was nearly midnight at the ball when Simon found Gemma sitting on a park bench on an arbored bridge covered with fragrant bougainvillea vine. It crossed over a stream running down to the koi pond. Tiny white twinkling lights festooned the shrubs alongside the bridge and over the entire vista of make-believe. The only light so far back from the stage and dance floor.

"Here you are, hiding. How are you?" Simon asked, leaning down to rest his forearms on the handrail. His eyes gazed out at the rippling water that ran beneath the bridge.

Gemma smiled. "I'm fine. Weary. Is everything alright? Did you need me for something?" Gemma asked, turning sideways to look at him in his tux. He looked marvelous. Like a movie star of yesteryear. She'd spied on him all night, but tiny issues had kept her busy until this moment of quiet and calm.

"No, heavens, no. Everything is perfect, has been perfect all night, all weekend so far. I cannot believe how magnificent it is. Beyond my imagination. Tony's sensational."

"He sure is. It's enchanting. I think it lived up to everyone's expectations, don't you?" She rested against the rail. Her eyes focused on his handsome face.

Simon put his left hand over hers on the handrail. "It's incredible. Everyone is beside themselves with delight. You pulled off the most significant event this town has seen in the last decade. Well, minus a few Super Bowl championships, of course." He chuckled.

His hand was almost twice the size of hers. Warm and firm but not rough. He didn't work with his hands like a tradesman, but he didn't wear kid gloves either.

She regarded him further, trying to figure out which character he was portraying. His white hair was parted in the middle and slicked back with product. It belied his age of forty-two. His tux was vintage, more early teens or nineteen-twenties. His dark brown eyes were black in the dim lighting of their area of the hall. He was cleanly shaven along his strong jawline. Dimples, softening his face, one on either side of his mouth, were prominent when he smiled, as he was now.

"What are you thinking, Gemma?" he asked, cocking an eyebrow, his smile growing into a smirk.

"I was trying to figure out your character. For the ball, I mean," Gemma stammered, feeling a sudden heat rising out of her empire neckline, climbing up her neck to her cheeks.

"I'll give you a hint. He's written by one of America's bad boy authors," Simon teased, leaning back on the bridge rail, crossing his arms, then throwing them open to give Gemma a good look at the costume.

Look, she did. At his broad chest hinting at strength, his muscular arms, his trim waistline, firm thighs, and long legs. *Yum. I wonder if he has a date tonight?*

"Clearly not the *Old Man and the Sea*," Gemma sarcastically mumbled. "How about ... from a Steinbeck novel?"

"No, you are way off. Think more East Coast, Long Island, Redford ..."

"Oh, ah, it's, ah, damn, on the tip of my tongue!" Gemma snapped her fingers, trying to remember the name of the character. Fitzwilliam? No. Fitzgerald? Yes! No? That was the author.

"Let me help you figure it out," Simon said, wrapping his left arm around her waist, pulling her against his chest, and pressing his lips to hers.

Startled by his embrace, Gemma did not return the kiss. Simon broke off his kiss and leaned back to give her room. "No?" he breathed gruffly, starting to step back.

Gathering her senses, her wits, her lust, Gemma whispered, "Yes!" and pulled him back to resume the kiss, doing her best this time to let go rather than let shock paralyze her into losing this opportunity.

Their lips matched, fitted, and melded. Gemma parted her lips, letting her tongue slip out to taste his. His lips tasted delicious as she sensed he would. The attraction between them might have been slowly smoldering but it was bursting into flame. Or at least, she was bursting into lust.

Simon responded, opening his mouth to accept her tongue play, giving her a taste of his own.

Her insides quivered, screaming for more. Gemma's hand slid up to his neck, keeping him to her while her other hand, once around his waist, now slid down his trousers to his butt. She rubbed and caressed it, letting Simon's tongue penetrate her mouth, one hand on the back of her neck, the other wrapped around her waist, pulling her close to his broad chest.

Gemma broke away and murmured, "Gatsby."

"Yes, Elizabeth Bennett." Simon chuckled softly, before nibbling at her exposed collarbone.

"How did you know I was Elizabeth Bennett?" Gemma whispered, clinging to his tux lapel now for steadiness as her knees wobbled.

"There must be at least two dozen here tonight, along with two dozen Fitzwilliam Darcys, a dozen or so Jay Gatsbys, and a few Pucks." Simon smiled down at her. He lowered his head to kiss her again.

Suddenly, Gemma jumped back as if pinched.

"What?" Simon asked hastily, startled by her reaction. Then laughed when he saw Gemma pull her cell phone out of the pocket of her dress.

"Hello," Gemma said into the phone. "Okay, yes. That's fine. Leave them out on the table so people can take some when they leave. Thanks." She snapped it shut and tucked it back in her pocket.

Simon raised another eyebrow inquisitively.

"The catering staff is leaving the desserts on the table with small takeout boxes if anyone wants to bring some home. It was that or have them throw the leftovers out now before they leave."

"Think there's any more of those chocolate-covered strawberries and stemmed cherries?"

"Maybe."

"Let's check it out. I thought those were grand," he said, his arm sweeping behind her, his hand hovering over the small of her back to guide her along.

She was pleased he didn't go for her hand or wrap his arm around her shoulder. It would be inappropriate in the more public areas of the hall. Besides, she still didn't know the answer to her question about date or no date.

"I want to check on the band for a few minutes. Meet you at the dessert table, okay?" Gemma suggested, spotting the lead singer giving her a kind of wave that indicated he wanted to talk with her.

"Sure, but hurry back. I want to discuss some plans with you for the rest of the weekend." Simon's soft breath caressed her ear. All she could do was nod and float away toward the stage.

About three that morning, Gemma found out the answer to her question when Simon drove her home in his Lexus, leaving her with dinner plans for Sunday night and her panties damp from his goodnight kiss.

Sunday's poetry slam went well enough, though not as well attended as Gemma had hoped, which was serendipitous considering the amount of noise coming from the Wiggles concert in the community room.

By four p.m., Gemma was home, down for a quick power nap before getting ready for her dinner date with Simon.

They started at Café Zinho for dinner and then retired to the Martini Bar at the Sunny Boutique Hotel. Anticipation fluttered in Gemma's stomach at the thought of hotel beds upstairs, up that lobby elevator, easily within reach of her and this sexy hunk of man. Had he made a hopeful reservation?

Like earlier that day, Simon drove her home, walked her to Rose Anne's door, and after a sensational goodnight kiss, bid her adieu.

Twenty minutes after getting home, the phone rang.

"Hello?" she answered.

"Thanks for having dinner with me tonight. I know it could not have been easy after such a hard weekend."

"I enjoyed it, and I enjoy talking with you. Thank you for a delicious dinner. I think otherwise, I'd have ended up with Cheerios or toast."

"I know the feeling. My personal favorite is Wheaties. Don't think you've seen the last of me after tonight. I enjoy talking with you too. Good night, see you again soon."

Gemma hung up, snuggled down into her bed, and clicked off the light, inviting sweet dreams to invade her sleep so long as Simon was in them.

The phones rang off the hook in Trilogy's office the next day. Dozens of people called to rave about the events, the ball, the costumes, the media coverage. Before noon, a huge bouquet of three dozen pink roses arrived with a five-pound box of chocolates. The attached card, addressed simply "To Trilogy," said, "Bravo! Simon Crofton."

Within a week, the verbal feedback and resulting business from the library reopening allowed Trilogy to hire Mei part-time permanently, giving them the help they needed with the increasing workload.

Within that same month, Gemma's relationship with Simon fermented rapidly into a hot, rolling boil.

• • • •

IT HAD BEEN OVER SEVEN months since Billy had walked out on his family. Heather had been uncharacteristically quiet with her children in the last week.

"Is everything alright, Heather?" Macie slipped her arm around her daughter's waist and hugged her.

"Yeah. As right as it's ever going to be, for now." Heather hugged her mother, resting her chin on the shorter woman's shoulder. "I went to see a lawyer at the Legal Aid office ..." She sighed and drew back to look her mother in the eyes. "I filed for a divorce."

• • • •

THE FLIGHT WAS TOO short and repressive. Marla wished she were experiencing the return flight—that this was over instead of just beginning. Her phone call to Timothy's home made it clear why he never called again. He'd moved on to another woman. Marla gnashed her back molars whenever she thought of that sultry "hello?" echoing in her ear.

She chastised herself for thinking such a gorgeous man could possibly want to have any kind of lasting relationship with fat tub of lard, Marla. He'd probably sniffed her out as a virgin and taken his aim. What a little fool she had been to think it was anything more than a modern deflowering. He probably had a bet going with someone over the entire episode. Yet as she thought these horrible things, she knew deep in her core, Timothy was not likely to do them. Whatever it was that kept him from her now, it was not malicious.

She checked into her hotel and had the bellhop deliver her bag to her room while she took a cab to the laboratory. Knowing the layout, she found Andrea's office and knocked.

"Come in," Andrea called through the half-open door.

"Hi, Andrea. How are you holding up?" Marla asked, trying desperately to be nonchalant about her presence.

"Fine, I'm fine. I wasn't expecting you until tomorrow," Andrea said, gesturing toward an office chair.

"I just got in and decided to start as soon as possible if that's okay with you. I have a midafternoon flight on Thursday, so I don't have much time—family commitment." She shrugged to help along the little white lie tacked on the end.

"Let me call Dr. Brighton and Dr. Wimker to let them know you're here." Andrea reached for the phone.

"No! No, please don't bother them today. They're busy enough and I don't need them for this quick visit." Marla's voice sounded shaky to her own ears. *Please, Andrea, please agree with me.*

"Okay, I guess you can see them tomorrow," Andrea said a little warily, clearly unsure of Marla's adamant forestalling of the meeting.

"In fact, I can wander around on my own if that's okay with you. I don't expect to find any problems. You're a pro at this. It's only a formality for corporate," Marla explained, trying to keep her visit so far under the radar that Timothy wouldn't even know she was there.

"Okay, well, the staff knows you're coming, so ... have at it, I guess. You know where to find me if there are any issues," Andrea said again, returning to her desk chair.

"Thanks," Marla said, slipping out the door with briefcase in hand. She walked down the hall and around the corner, entered the ladies' room, and leaned against the wall to catch her breath. Her heart was speeding at the audacity of her plan. She hoped she could pull it off, get herself out of this site without setting eyes on Timothy Brighton.

Four hours later, stomach growling, Marla decided to call it a night. She'd been able to slog through the entire chemistry department, but it was finished. One department down, the hardest, and five more departments to go. Maybe she could get them all done tomorrow and change her reservation for the latest flight out.

LITTLE BIT OF WAIT

Marla was back at the inspection by six a.m. the next morning. At noon, she slipped down to the vending machines for a diet cola and a package of peanut butter crackers. She stepped outside onto the sidewalk for a breath of fresh air, then, hunger sated, dove back into the process.

By six p.m., she had only one more department to inspect. She decided it wouldn't be possible to make the late flight, but she would finish later this evening and catch an early morning flight back to Pittsburgh. She left the building, heading around the corner for a burger at a café. She took her time eating, savoring the burger with roasted peppers, portabella mushroom, and gorgonzola cheese.

It was the most decadent food she had eaten in months. Later, when she finished the inspection, she would find ice cream, even if she had to order the ridiculously expensive ice cream sundae on the room service menu.

When Marla returned to the building, she pulled the door handle, but it would not open. Her heart skipped a beat, and she tried another door. No go. Her heart sank as each door refused to open. Every outside door was locked. She pulled out her cell phone and called the main telephone number.

"Hello, Peabody Laboratories. How may I assist you?" A woman's voice answered.

"Hello, this is Marla Devine, the inspector from the corporate office in Pittsburgh. I stepped out for a bite to eat, and now the outside doors of the building are locked. Could someone let me in so I can finish the inspection tonight?" Marla asked as sweetly as she could.

"I don't know anything about an inspector from the corporate office being here. Let me check with my supervisor. Someone will be down," she said and hung up abruptly before Marla could suggest calling Andrea. Marla checked the time. It was 7:43 p.m.

Crap! You should have plowed on and finished, then eaten dinner. What if you can't get in tonight? Marla thought. She leaned against one of the doors to watch the street life while she waited. She checked her watch again, 7:47.

A soft knock on the door behind her startled Marla, and she turned.

The streetlights' yellow glare highlighted Timothy's gaunt, but beautiful features. The minimal lights behind silhouetted him, revealing his own weight loss. She stepped away from the door, unsure whether to enter or to bolt. Every nerve fiber in her body was telling every muscle in her body to leave.

It was the look in his eyes that nailed her to that spot on the sidewalk. His beautiful eyes were filled with more anguish than she had ever seen on anyone's face. The door slowly opened, and he stepped aside to give her room to pass. Marla paused on the sidewalk another moment, then silently brushed past him without stopping.

With her chin high and her head forward, she took the lobby escalator to the second floor, Timothy trailing behind her like a zombie in a trance.

"Marla," he called in a voice so dark and beaten she hardly recognized it.

Ignoring him, she rounded the hallway corner, ducking into the stairwell before Timothy could see her. She flew up the stairs, taking two at a time. Before she hit the third-floor landing, she heard another heavier set of feet running up the stairs.

"Marla, please," he pleaded, panting, continuing the climb.

"Dr. Brighton, we have nothing to say to each other." Marla panted, tired and nauseous from running on a full stomach.

"Marla, I'm sorry. Please stop." His voice cracked.

He must have stopped pursuing her; she didn't hear his steps anymore. *What if something's wrong? What if he's having a heart attack?* Suddenly, she was deeply worried about him. The stress he'd been under the last six months could have killed anyone.

"Dr. Brighton?" Marla asked gingerly, peering over the banister. Down two flights, she could see his figure leaning against the wall. His face was not visible.

"Marla ... I ... come ... down." His voice was weak and low.

Marla flew down the stairs until she was beside him. He was hunched over, hands on thighs, still trying to catch his breath. When she neared, he leaned back against the concrete wall. His face was flushed and sweaty from the chase.

Marla didn't know what to do. She wanted to take him in her arms and smother him with kisses. It was several months too late for that now.

"Are you alright? Is it your heart?" She asked hastily, reaching out to grasp his upper arm. Maybe he needed an ambulance or oxygen.

"You are my heart, Marla. Please don't run away from me again." He stared at her with wretched sorrow in his eyes.

She was speechless.

Timothy put both his hands on her shoulders and spoke into her eyes. "I can't live another day without you."

"Timothy, I—" Marla began. "I thought this was what you wanted. You've made few attempts to contact me in five months. What was I supposed to think?" she ended in a whisper.

"I've been an idiot. The longer it was, the harder it was for me to convince myself you wanted me to call you. I thought you would have moved on to someone else by now. I couldn't have tolerated knowing that for sure. That doesn't make any sense, I know. Love doesn't make any of us intelligent; it brings us down to the most common denominators, feelings of insecurity and unworthiness." He ran his fingers through his tousled hair. "I love you, Marla. I can't believe I'm getting another chance to say it. This time I'm taking it. I love you, Marla. Please come back to me."

He gripped her shoulders tighter, giving them a little shake. An odd combination of love and terror filled his eyes. Eyes brimming with love that clutched at her heart and gave it a galloping rhythm ... and terror that she wouldn't give him another chance.

She put her hands on his chest and pushed him back, not willing to concede so swiftly. He had some things to answer for yet.

"What about that woman?" Marla stammered.

"What woman?" Timothy cocked his head to one side, narrowing his eyes.

"The woman who answered the telephone at your condo."

He stared at her, brow furrowed, then instantly his eyes twinkled, and his face smoothed. "That was you? Of course it was you! That was my sister. She came to stay at the condo for a two-week vacation," Timothy said, trying to pull her fully into his arms.

Marla still resisted.

"What? You don't believe me?" Timothy's eyes narrowed again.

She eyed him with suspicion but said nothing. What could she say? He would deny it. Of course, he would.

Timothy huffed, dropped his hands from her shoulders, and pulled his cell phone out of his pants pocket. "Do you remember her voice?"

Marla nodded. She'd remember that voice to the day she died.

"Good. Do you remember what my only sister's name was?" Timothy quizzed her, flipping open the phone and holding it out to her.

"Amanda?"

"Good, here's my cell phone. Scroll through my contacts, select Amanda, and press send. See if that's the same voice." Timothy stood a little straighter, watching as she refused to take the phone.

Timothy's face darkened again as he cursed, "Damn it, Marla." He scrolled through the list and pressed send. Then he put it on speaker for her to hear.

"Hello?" a groggy voice answered.

"Hi Amanda, it's Timothy."

"What are you doing this time of night? Did you forget the time difference?" she asked, her voice a little less gravelly.

"Sorry, but this is important. Listen up. Remember that woman I told you about?"

"Yeah, Marilyn or Mary or something like that."

"Marla. Yeah, the one I'm crazy about." He winked at Marla.

"Yeah, I remember. What about her?" Amanda's voice was a little stronger and clearer as she had awoken a little more.

"She wants to say hello to you," Timothy said, winking again.

"Hello, Marla," Amanda's silky voice said, then she yawned.

"Hello, Amanda," Marla said, nodding. Yes, it was the same sultry voice she heard on the condo telephone.

"Thanks, Amanda, Sleep tight," Timothy said with a huge smile.

"That's it?" Amanda asked, a tone of disappointment noted in her voice. "You woke me to say 'hello'?"

"I'll explain tomorrow." Tim disconnected the call.

When Timothy tried to pull Marla into his arms there was no resistance this time. There was no resistance when he told her she was done inspecting the lab for the evening, no resistance when he told her he couldn't wait the long ferry ride across the Sound to go to his island condo, and definitely, no resistance when they made love for the next four hours in her hotel room.

Shortly after two a.m., Marla sat on the edge of the bathtub, working up the courage to tell Timothy her dirty secret. Since their first sexual encounter, she'd debated whether she needed to tell him. Did he need to know about her previous obesity? Would it be possible to keep it from him forever?

Somehow he hadn't noticed the stretch marks in her skin, those telltale lightning bolt-shaped signs of expansion. She was fortunate she had worked out with weights so hard it had not only formed the muscles beneath her skin but also tugged her skin into place enough that it didn't hang like flaps requiring surgical removal. It had been a lot of sweat, but she had trusted her personal trainer. There were few, if any, signs to give her dirty fat secret away. Maybe he suspected something but didn't say anything? Marla pondered, her eyebrows knitting into one long line across her forehead.

Her coworkers in Pittsburgh knew her fat secret. If any of them spoke to Timothy it could be mentioned. Did she want him to find out from someone else or from herself?

It came down to that. She knew the answer to that question. She asked herself how he would take it. Would he be reasonable, see what an achievement it was, congratulate her, and then ignore the fact? Or would he be totally grossed out by by her?

Marla thought she knew the answer to that question as well. She got up from the rim of the tub, snuggled into the thick hotel robe, and went to the bed, reaching for her purse as she passed by the desk. She pulled a cropped picture of an obese college graduate out of her purse and handed it to Timothy, who reclined naked in bed, a sheet thrown over his lower half. "I want you to meet someone."

Timothy took the photo and stared at it for a few seconds. "Your sister?" he asked, his eyebrows knitted.

"No, that's me. That's pretty much what I looked like until about eighteen months ago," she said, sitting on the edge of the bed, pulling her legs up to hug herself tightly.

Timothy stared at her, then glanced back at the photo, his brows pulled together tighter.

Marla held her breath, hoping she hadn't lost him again. "I've lived thirty-two years of my life being that fat or fatter. Eighteen months ago, I finally had enough. I turned my life around with the help of a dietician, a personal trainer, a behavioral psychologist, and a fitness center membership, as well as a yogi. I've lost a lot of weight. Weight I hope I never have to contend with again."

"I'm ... I'm amazed." Timothy's eyes swept over her body. "Did you do bariatric surgery?"

"No, I didn't want to mess with my body in that way. I knew what was causing my problem, it was a simple matter of more calories in than expended. I chose to take care of the root problem, not surgically alter my stomach. It's been a long journey of redemption. But one I will never have to take again," Marla said firmly. She watched his eyes, but they remained glued to the picture still held in his hand.

"I can't believe it," Timothy said with more than a little awe in his voice. "I guess that explains some of your eating habits." He tossed a smile at her but returned his eyes to the picture.

"Yes, it does," she said. "I have no intention of gaining weight again."

"Marla, I'm amazed. But knowing you the way I do, I can see how you're strong enough to do it." His voice still held a stunned tone. He didn't look at her.

They sat in silence a minute. Abruptly Timothy handed her the photo. She left the bed to stow it back in her purse.

She leaned against the bureau at the end of the bed. "I don't know if this changes the way you think of me," Marla said, tiptoeing on the eggshells she hoped would not crack to reveal rotten odors.

"It does!" Timothy exclaimed and got off the bed in all his splendid nakedness. "Are you kidding?"

The shells crumbled beneath her feet. She flushed scarlet and turned away to keep Timothy from seeing the tears burst from her eyes at his looming rejection.

"Now I know you are the most incredible woman I have ever met, Marla Devine." Timothy turned her to face him and slipped the robe off her shoulders.

Marla's tears continued to spill. She was weeping uncontrollably now, unable to say anything.

"What did you think? I was going to leave?" Timothy held her chin up to stare into her flooded eyes.

Marla nodded as best she could. "I was hoping not," she croaked out between sobbing gasps.

"Did you think so little of me?" His tone was filled with shock.

Marla could only shrug.

"Wait until you see my high school pictures. I'd say we're even."

"What?" Marla croaked out again, unable to believe what she heard.

"I was overweight as a teenager. When I started college, everyone else's freshman twenty was my sixty. It took me most of medical school to drop all the excess weight. Best diet I ever had. Too broke and no time to eat," Timothy said, gathering her into his arms. "How do *you* feel about that bit of news?" He shimmied his naked body against hers suggestively and dropped a kiss on her bare shoulder.

Marla started laughing. It wasn't funny, but it was very ironic to find out that gorgeous Timothy Brighton not only didn't care she'd been obese, but he had been too.

"You okay?" Timothy raised one eyebrow, his tone revealing his concerned of her hysterical laughter.

"Never been better in all my life!" Marla's peals of laughter continued.

MAY 2019

By May 1st, it was clear Gloria was not likely to make it to the wedding day. She was hospitalized the night before for an erratic heartbeat and evaluated the next morning. Her oncologist suggested a hospice placement, which Chelsea knew was the beginning of the final road to the end. Seth and Chelsea fought about the wedding. Seth suggested canceling it. Their mothers both said no. Not now. Maybe it would have to be canceled at the last minute. But it wasn't going to be canceled prematurely.

The staff at the hospice were incredible, as far as Chelsea and her brother could tell. They kept Gloria well cared for, physically, emotionally, and spiritually. On hearing about the imminent wedding, the staff were thoughtful about the circumstances. Two days into Gloria's stay, the bereavement counselor asked to speak with Chelsea and Seth.

"I know you two are planning to be married on the seventeenth. Your mother was quick to make sure everyone here knew about it as soon as she arrived," Mrs. Crumb said. "I know we have talked about the process here and the timeline we anticipated."

Chelsea, sensing where the woman was going, began to cry softly. "She's not going to make it to the wedding."

"No," said Mrs. Crumb. "She's not going to make it to the seventeenth. We've had situations similar to this before. Would you consider getting married here, in front of her with other immediate family, say tomorrow? Then you could do it all again on the seventeenth in front of your remaining family and friends, whose support you will need." Mrs. Crumb went on, "We've had quite a few weddings here." She smiled. "It's one of our happier moments."

Seth looked at Chelsea, who nodded in assent. "Sounds like a great idea. How can we set it up?"

"Tomorrow's Saturday, but I can arrange for the justice of the peace if that's okay with you. Can you get the license and bridal party together for tomorrow morning, say, eleven o'clock?"

"If we can't, it will just be the two of us. That's all we need," Seth said.

"Good, get to work!" Mrs. Crumb ordered with a smile.

A flurry of phone calls led to Chelsea and Seth getting the license after leaving the hospice. Chelsea called Diane, who contacted the bridal party. Seth's parents rounded up four "bouquets" of flowers from the local grocery store floral department and a rush order cake at the bakery department.

The big problem came with Chelsea's dress. The salon wouldn't have the alterations completed until the scheduled wedding day. It would not be available for her to wear tomorrow. Chelsea didn't have a wedding dress to wear unless she wanted to pick something else off the rack for the day.

Crying hysterically, she hunched over in a chair with her face buried in her hands. They were bitter tears that, once again, it all came down to that stupid dress and her weight. The Slimline System had been started and abandoned, and restarted after Gloria's revelation. The stress of the situation and the increasing depression and anxiety over her mother's rapid decline had reactivated Chelsea's eating habits preventing her from losing any more weight than she already had. It always came down to her weight.

Seth's mother tried to console her. "Maybe there's something else in the closet you could use for an hour or two? Why don't you look?"

Chelsea's mind echoed the phrase "in the closet."

"That's it." Chelsea leaped up, drying her eyes with the back of her hands. "My God, Peggy, you're a genius."

"What did I do?" Her eyes widened behind her plastic frames.

"My mother's wedding dress is in her closet. She was a size fourteen when she got married. Maybe it would fit me." Hope filled her lungs and face, making her breath come easier and halting her tears altogether.

"Let's give it a shot." Peggy drove them over to Gloria's silent house. Chelsea found the dress exactly where her mother said it was in the closet. Chelsea shucked her clothes while Peggy carefully pulled the old dress out of the white garment bag. In minutes, the dress was settling around Chelsea like a cloud of chiffon. It fit! Snugly, but it would be workable for one day. A tad long in the hem but with her high heels, it would not be noticeable.

"Oh, my!" Peggy said, stepping back to admire her soon-to-be daughter-in-law.

"Oh, yes!" Chelsea whispered. A feeling of intense calm and love swirled through her chest, washing the stress from her body.

On May 10th, Gloria Whitcom witnessed the marriage of her daughter Chelsea to Seth Symmonds in a bedside ceremony complete with bridesmaids and ushers, a piano player for the wedding march, fresh flower bouquets, a justice of the peace, and a cake. A photographer, donating his services for the happy couple, snapped over a hundred pictures of that half-hour event. Gloria's eyes lit up when she recognized her own wedding dress on her daughter. She wept with love and admiration for the special moment everyone had worked so hard to bring together for her.

As Chelsea and Seth left that night, Gloria stopped them, asking for a promise.

"Promise me you will never forget to love each other every single day for the rest of your lives."

"We will," They said in unison, squeezing each other's hands and giving each other smiles of deep, abiding love.

A coma descended that night, leaving Gloria unresponsive for her remaining days. Seth, Chelsea, and Toby were by her bedside when she took her last peaceful breaths on earth.

On Friday night, May 17th, Chelsea and Seth Symmonds repeated their vows by candlelight at St. Sebastian's Church, this time with a sense of unification and solidity they had not known existed. Knowing the great loss Chelsea had endured, family and friends were surprised she could put aside her sorrow seven days after her mother's death. Until they heard what transpired beforehand at the hospice center.

For those who did not know any better, Chelsea looked beautiful on her wedding day, beaming as brightly as if her mother had been there. She smiled, knowing her mother was with her every step on her journey that night.

As she got ready for her big day, she'd hung both dresses up on the shower curtain, side by side. She had to choose which one to wear. The wedding dress she had bought fit after all the weight Chelsea had lost in her grief. Her mother's size fourteen wedding dress was looser but still would look fine.

"Which one?" Diana asked as she watched Chelsea's eyes dart back and forth between them.

It took only a second for Chelsea to reach out for her mother's dress. "This one."

• • • •

SPRING ALWAYS CAME early along the Sound, the moist environment, the temperatures. Over the last month, Marla and Timothy had resumed their long-distance romance, with Marla flying in every Thursday night and leaving on the red-eye flight every Sunday. This second chance romance was more wonderful than the first. Wildflowers sprouted along the sides of the roadways and bike trails as they drove by on their way to Rialto Beach. Marla wanted to go back there again. It had been such a magical place for her: the tide pools, the buttes, the napping seal, her first kiss, and all it had led to.

Timothy was quieter than usual the last couple weeks. Marla thought perhaps something was going on at the laboratory he felt he couldn't discuss with her. Whatever it was, Marla hoped the trip to La Push and the beach would ease his mind for the day.

She was right, to a certain extent. Timothy was thrilled she wanted to go back there. Like before, they brought a picnic lunch, poked through the tide pools like little kids, and splashed in the water up to their ankles before strolling quietly, hand in hand, as the sun began to set. They sat on the picnic blanket, while the sun slipped beneath the horizon and shared the western sky's beautiful orange and pink glow.

"Marla?"

"Hmm," She replied, turning to look at him. He was on one knee.

"Marla, I love you. I want you with me all the time. Please, marry me?" Timothy asked softly, hopefully, as he took her left hand and slid an engagement ring on her ring finger.

Dumbstruck, speechless, and sightless from the flood of tears in her eyes, Marla fell into his arms and whispered "yes" into his ear before Timothy devoured her with kisses.

She pushed him away slightly. "Wait. I have stipulations."

Her serious tone of voice stopped Timothy's playfulness. "Anything for you, my love. What is it?"

"I want to keep my job but try to move my office to Seattle. My assistant can stay in Pittsburgh."

"Sure, why not. You'll have to fight for that with corporate." He eyed her neck as though he was going to pounce again.

Her palms held him back a moment longer. She had never told him of Sam and her aborted wedding. Now might not be the right time, but she knew she had to tell him. "And we must drive to the wedding together."

Timothy's face took on a quizzical look. "Whatever you say."

Marla's face brightened, and she pulled him back to resume their kisses, grateful he hadn't had a chance to ask her any questions about her request.

• • • •

THE SUPERMAN THEME music blared from Gemma's cell phone. She pulled it from her pocket without breaking stride. "Hello, Simon."

"Gemma. Bad time?"

Simon's sultry voice with the remnants of a Boston accent sent a shiver down her spine. "Never a bad time with you. Besides, I wouldn't answer if I was busy."

His chuckle was deep and real. If Gemma had to define it, she would call it heartfelt.

"I have the same policy." He paused a few seconds before adding, "Want to do lunch? I know it's short notice, but I'm just down the street. My meeting finished early, so I have a free hour."

"I'm power walking to Frick Park for a hotdog. Care to join me?" Maintaining her pace, she crossed the street to enter the park.

"Intriguing. Where shall we meet?"

"At the Reynold's Street entrance. There's a park bench beside the trail about two hundred feet from the arch."

"My favorite entrance. See you in two minutes." Simon disconnected.

Two minutes? Was he that close, or was he taking the chauffeured car to the park? Gemma decided to wait at the entrance. They could walk to her favorite park bench together.

A black town car pulled up to the gate, and Simon got out of the backseat. The car drove away, destination unknown.

Simon kissed her cheek before turning to admire the gatehouse.

"Why is it your favorite entrance?" Gemma asked as her small hand disappeared into Simon's larger one.

He pulled her closer to the gatehouse. Stopping in front of the door, he tipped his head toward the sign beside it.

Gemma read the sign and turned toward him, a smirk on her face. "You paid for the renovation?"

He shrugged. "It's a good cause." He tugged at her hand, and they began walking the trail that started at the gate. "Where's this hotdog stand?"

"At the corner of this trail and Forbes Avenue, about two hundred feet farther on." Gemma's heart lifted. It was a gorgeous late May day. The sun shone through sporadic clouds, the birds flitted about, and the spring flowers danced on the light, fragrant breeze. Trilogy's business was exploding, and she had this sexy man walking with her, holding her hand. She could see the quilted pattern of the stainless steel hotdog cart gleaming in the sunshine ahead. Life couldn't get much better today.

They placed their order, and Simon paid. His hotdog plain, and hers covered in chili and raw onions. Simon raised an eyebrow. "Raw onions?"

"Yup," Gemma said. "How come yours is plain? No toppings?"

He chuckled. "There's nothing to spill on my suit that way."

They walked along, rounding the bend where her favorite bench was. Gemma stopped in her tracks as they got a clear view of it.

Sitting on her favorite bench was Charlie. *Damn it, I should have remembered he liked to sit there and read scripts.* The last thing she wanted was for Charlie to see her, especially with Simon. Charlie hadn't seen her yet, his eyes on his cell phone. She had to think fast.

"Darn, someone's sitting on my bench. Why don't we go back to the gatehouse? There's a few Parisian-style tables under the trees there." Gemma turned around and headed back to the gate.

Simon glanced down the trail to the bench. "I could ask him to move over."

Gemma dared to turn back to him. "Nah, that's alright. Let's go. I don't have as much time for lunch as you apparently do." Deep in her gut, she trembled hoping Simon would acquiesce.

She sighed with relief when Simon turned to join her on the trek back the way they had come. Her only worry now was that Charlie would exit by way of Reynold's Street and see them there.

"I've been meaning to ask you if you'll be my date for an awards banquet next month."

She nodded. "If I'm free that night, sure. Text me the date and time when you get back to your office."

His hand reached out and held her upper arm, stopping their motion. "It could be a late night. Perhaps you could stay with me that night." His eyes softened, his face a weird mixture of apprehension and promise.

Gemma knew this moment would come. She'd been anxious about it, wanting to move their relationship into intimacy, and yet terrified. Terrified Simon would be revolted by the huge scar on her torso. He knew nothing about her asthma or the surgery that had brought it under control. He didn't know her body was scarred permanently. What would he think? And yet, the thrill of the intimacy left her feeling giddy like a schoolgirl. The more time they spent together, the more she yearned for it. But Simon had been the perfect gentleman since they first met. They had yet to add a sexual side to their relationship. It sounded like he was intent on taking it to the next level.

Gemma looked him right in the eyes. "I have something to tell you." Spotting the tables, she offered, "Let's sit and eat. I have a story to tell you."

Over the next fifteen minutes, Gemma told Simon everything. Everything except her relationship with Charlie.

He took her hand. "I don't care if you have a hundred scars. I'm captivated by you, and I think you are just as willing to explore this," his hand twirled in the air, "as much as I am."

The thundering of her heart in her chest added to the heat in her face. "I'm glad," she whispered. "I think it's time."

Simon's dazzling smile melted her insides. "So, yes to the event and afterward?"

"Yes," Gemma said with surety in her voice.

JUNE 2019

While Marla and Tim tried to visit each other every weekend, negotiations ensued between Marla and the corporate office. She told them only that she wanted to move to the Seattle area. She wanted to keep her job, work from Seattle, and fly into the corporate office when needed. As expected, they balked.

But Marla's boss, Beverly, won the day for them. There was no logical reason Marla couldn't telecommute from Seattle using modern technology. Marla had enough skill, experience, and savvy intuition that her boss did not want to see her leave and wasn't afraid to admit it. If that meant Marla emailed reports from Seattle rather than from down the hall, so be it. Beverly added that her assistant, Ashley, had returned to work after her maternity leave and would stay in Pittsburgh. After a month of haggling, the corporate powers that be relented.

Marla was assigned an office in the Seattle laboratory, two floors down from Dr. Timothy Brighton's office. Her immediate supervisor would remain Beverly, and her on-site supervisor would be Dr. Robert Wimker.

A month later, Marla and Timothy told the corporate office they were getting married. The legal team was consulted for fear of sexual harassment claims. They concluded there was no harassment as neither party had any supervisory status over the other, the relationship was consensual, and the company had no policy against married employees. In the end, they could say nothing except that any inspections necessary for the Seattle facility would have to be handled by Marla's assistant.

• • • •

SIMON STEERED THE CAR into the hotel's circular driveway. As he approached, the small band of valets began tussling to be the one to drive the car to the designated valet parking lot. When he stopped, the doorman opened the car door for Gemma while Simon handed over the keys to the closest valet. "Not a scratch or extra mileage, boys," he said with a tone of authority.

There were some things Simon wasn't willing to compromise on, Gemma thought with a smile. "I'm surprised you drove rather than use your town car."

Simon shrugged as he rounded the car. "That's for business use. This is my fun car. Which I rarely get to drive."

Gemma cocked her head. "Still, your Aston Martin must have cost a fortune."

They climbed the steps to the front entrance shimmering with gold and glass and crystal. "It did. It's well insured. If I hadn't given the key to the calmest guy, those valets would be fighting over the opportunity to drive her."

"Maybe they'll play rock, paper, scissors."

Simon chuckled, his hand slipping to her lower back to guide her to the Sheffield Ballroom.

They were greeted at the door and led through the crowded room. It was your typical banquet setup, round tables of eight with white linens. *How boring!* The table settings looked like real china, and the wine and water goblets sparkled like crystal. The centerpieces were an array of brightly colored flowers in all colors of the rainbow.

The head table on the stage was swagged with the same multicolored flowers in a garland. A podium and microphone were set up between the two tables on the stage.

Other attendees stopped them along the way to shake hands with Simon. Gemma had no idea who these people were so she just smiled sweetly and shook any hand proffered. Until the mayor of Pittsburgh approached them.

"Simon, good to see you."

"Thank you sir, it's a pleasure to see you again," Simon said before introducing Gemma.

The mayor directed his gaze at her. "Ah, yes. The owner of Trilogy. After your success at the library grand opening, I told my staff you are doing my re-election party." His smile looked genuine.

"I'm one of three owners. And we'd be thrilled to organize your victory party."

"Excellent." His eyes caught someone or something over her shoulder. "There's someone I need to speak with." He turned back to Simon. "Congratulations, Simon. We'll talk."

They continued their walk, heading for the stairs leading to the stage. "Congratulations?" Gemma threw Simon a long stare. "Are you getting an award or something?"

"Didn't I mention that?" He offered her his hand as they climbed the stairs. Their guide led them to seats nearest the podium. The place card beside it had Simon's name. The setting to his left held Gemma's.

"No, you didn't. Whose event is this? What did you win?"

As others seated at the head table began converging on the stage, Simon whispered in her ear, "This is the Pittsburgh LGBTQIA Business Alliance's event. I've been selected for the Distinguished Good Neighbor Award."

Gemma tried not to look too startled in front of several hundred people now settling themselves at tables in front of them. Suddenly, it all made sense: the flowers and garlands in colors of the rainbow, some rather flamboyantly dressed people, men standing beside other men, women paired with other women.

Simon motioned for her to sit, pulling out her chair. Gemma sat, no words forming in her brain. It was all scrambled. After taking a sip of her water, she calmed. She had no qualms about this community, the organization, or the lifestyle they had chosen to live. But it felt odd that Simon had never mentioned his involvement with this organization over the three months they had been together. She froze in her seat as a crippling thought crossed her mind.

She took another sip of water before confronting him. "Simon," she whispered in his ear. "Are you trying to tell me something? Are you, umm, a member of this community?"

Simon's mouth dropped open before he closed it and his eyes. "No, to both questions. I'm an active supporter and donor." His eyes opened and latched on to hers. "In memory of my brother. He was gay. My parents had a fit when he came out at seventeen. They made him feel ashamed, threatening to kick him out and disown him. He shot himself in the head a week later."

Gemma's mouth went dry, her breathing halted. "I'm so sorry," she whispered just before a server set a salad plate before her. The ache in her chest for Simon grew as the knowledge that his only sibling had been made to feel so worthless as a human being, he'd ended his own life. Her hand slipped under the table to rest on his thigh. His own rested on top of hers, giving it a squeeze before he withdrew it to eat.

The rest of the event was a blur. Food eaten, clapping at whatever everyone else was clapping at or for, all of it in a daze. She hadn't known he had a brother. Hadn't known of this side of him, beyond the library support. It warmed her heart to hear how he chose to honor his brother by his commitment to making the lives of other LGBTQIA persons a little easier.

When he received his award after dinner, Simon told the story of his brother. There probably wasn't a dry eye in the place when he ended. "Many of you have experienced hate for being who you truly are. If you remember nothing of tonight but this, I will be satisfied. You are valued. You are perfect. And you are loved by this community and many others for being the person God made you. Thank you."

Thunderous applause shook the ballroom as they gave him a standing ovation several minutes long. Simon merely sat, nodding his gratitude to the audience. As everything died down, he leaned over to Gemma. "Grab your purse. Let's get out of here now, or we'll be here half the night." He raised an eyebrow. "I think we have other plans for our evening together."

• • • •

THE WOMEN SAT AT THEIR usual table in Jitters Café two days later. The others were speechless after Gemma told them the story. Heather and Marla wiping their eyes, Chelsea chewing her fingernail. Their mugs of coffee getting tepid, forgotten.

"Stop that, Chel. It doesn't look good for a manicurist to have bitten nails," Gemma softly ordered. "I know. I was struck dumb when he told me. It's heartbreaking."

"How was the rest of your evening?" Heather asked.

"Ya'll know I don't like to wait for sex ... but I have to say it was worth the wait." Gemma thought for a moment. "It was quiet, slow, soft, generous." She paused as she could feel the heat of a blush rising on her face. "So peaceful. So unlike the wild monkey sex I usually have. I—" She paused again as she searched for words. "It felt like he was touching my soul."

Heather, Chelsea, and Marla could tell Gemma had fallen in love. For once, the four of them were silent.

JULY 2019

Six months after selling her condo, Gemma was still looking for her own home, a real house this time. She wanted it outside the center of the Squirrel Hill neighborhood but within easy walking distance to the most important amenities: pizza, Chinese, Mexican, Italian, post office, grocery store, and liquor store. Nothing had suited her. *There's no hurry. I can wait for the right place.*

Trilogy was fully booked for the rest of the year with corporate or city events. They had already expanded the staffing to eight and moved their office to bigger quarters. The three founders were beyond pleased with the outcome of their risk.

The houses Gemma was looking at were not too far from Simon's luxury home. Although she didn't know how long their relationship would last, she was seeing him on a routine basis multiple times each week. She liked it. There were no commitments between them, just a growing devotion. Neither of them was interested in making it a permanent situation. It was not even something they discussed. There was an understanding that they would continue as they had been with no strings attached. It was the type of relationship she had always wanted.

Gemma had just stepped into her old Chinese restaurant, Chow Fun, to pick up the order she and Simon had placed when she saw Charlie gathering his to-go bags at the register. She tried to back out of the door, but he spotted her when he turned to leave.

"Well, hello, Gemma!" Charlie said, trying to make it sound suave and sexy. He checked her out head to toe and back before beaming his best smile. There wasn't even a hint of remorse for Milwaukee anywhere on his face.

"Charlie." Gemma's tone was curt and surly. Her fingers curled into fists around her handbag strap of their own volition. God, how she wanted to punch him in the face! She tried to walk past him to the counter without stopping.

Charlie laid his takeout bag on the counter and turned back toward Gemma to talk rather than leave the restaurant. "I didn't realize you were still living in town. What a nice surprise. I thought you'd left."

"No, I've been here all along," Gemma said, clenching her back teeth to keep from spewing a tirade at him. She turned her attention to the clerk. "Simon's order, please." The clerk left to check on the order. Gemma remained facing the counter. Maybe Charlie would get the message she had no interest in talking with him.

"Simon? Already moved on, eh, Gemma?" He spied her hands. "No ring yet. I'll be damned." He smiled his charming smile again, the same smile that had greeted Gemma the first time she'd met him at the newspaper box. He leaned an elbow on the counter casually, his eyes appraising her looks.

"You sure are damned, Charlie." Gemma flung over her shoulder, paying for her order. Was he getting a kick out of making her uncomfortable, or was he ignoring her body language?

Charlie leaned half a foot closer to her. "It's good to see you, Gemma. I've missed you a lot." He gave her a sad puppy look with his eyes.

She wasn't falling for it. She wasn't even looking at him. "Get used to it." Gemma snagged up the food bags and marched for the door.

Charlie looked on, still leaning against the counter, his bags in hand. He followed her. "Can I call you?" Charlie flung the phrase at her receding back.

The feeling of rage and elation roiled inside Gemma's gut during her entire drive home. She glanced over her shoulder several times to make sure he wasn't following her, not that it was likely. Charlie didn't drive much.

Oh to have told the son-of-a-bitch off like I wanted to. It would have only gathered a crowd and the police in time. Once she got started, she didn't think she would be able to stop until she'd spit every ounce of venom with his name on it that still circulated in her body.

One of these days, I will have to get this out. Maybe kickboxing or plain old boxing. Put a picture of Charlie's face on a punching bag and go at it for a couple hours. She would probably feel like a new woman.

• • • •

"OMG, YOU GUYS WILL never guess who I ran into yesterday," Gemma said, dropping her handbag on the empty chair.

"Who?" Marla asked from Chelsea's computer screen. Since she was out in Washington, they were trying to Zoom with her for their weekly coffee meetings.

"You have to guess." Gemma returned from the barista's counter with her pre-ordered beverage.

"Charlie?" Heather asked, her voice unsure.

"Bingo!" Gemma said. "He wanted to see me again. But don't worry, I gave him the shove off."

Chelsea cut in. "How's Simon?"

"Wonderful. Tall, delicious, handsome, and sexy as hell. And he's too busy at work to become a nuisance. Just the way I like my men. Periodically seen and undemanding." Gemma sat back on the chair and sipped her latte. "We are consensually informal, and neither of us has any thoughts of going deeper into a relationship." She gave them a shy smile. "And the sex is still mind-blowing." She glanced at Chelsea. "How was your honeymoon, Chel?"

"Lovely, quiet, and peaceful. Exactly what we both needed." Chelsea turned to Heather. "How are you and the kids getting on?"

Heather smiled. "The kids are doing well in school. Michelle adores having my mother watch her during the day. And my boss gave me another raise last week."

"Bravo, Heather." Marla's voice echoed through the computer speaker as everyone else congratulated her.

"Hey ladies, I want to make extra sure you'll be coming to Washington for my wedding," Marla said, a nervous note in her voice.

They all said they were. All of them had airline tickets and were sharing an Airbnb rental for the weekend.

"I'm so honored to be your maid of honor," Heather gushed. "And my parents are more than ready at this point to handle the kids."

Chelsea added, "Don't you fret, Marla. We'll be there for you. Promise."

• • • •

TEARS SPRANG TO HEATHER'S eyes as the judge's gavel made the judgment final. She was a single woman again, with child support, health insurance for all three children, and a small monthly alimony. Billy did not contest the divorce, nor did he seek custody of his children. He did not seek visitation rights beyond one day a weekend, which he did not exercise before or after the divorce was finalized.

With the alimony and child support, Heather rented a small duplex apartment a few blocks away from her parents' house. The yard was fenced to keep the kids and Snoopy safe while playing outside on the swing set left by the previous owners.

When her computer class concluded, she used her newfound knowledge to upgrade the accounting system at her florist job from paper to computer. Her boss, Gigi, was so impressed with her abilities and initiative Heather received a nice bonus.

Once her financial future was finalized, Heather resumed attending weekly Calorie Counters meetings. By the time the divorce was final, she had reached her target weight of one hundred twenty-eight pounds. She wore the dress she'd bought for Marla's wedding. The look on Billy's face was priceless when he saw her walking down the courthouse hall with her attorney. She looked dynamite and she knew it. But seeing his jaw drop and tongue nearly hanging out of his mouth felt like the biggest victory that day.

Heather kept going to Calorie Counters, stuck with her new lifestyle's eating habits, and within six weeks, had maintained her goal weight to become a life member. While she knew her weight loss had more to do with nervous non-eating as much as sticking to the program, she was pleased to have met her weight range, no matter the circumstance. At her next program meeting, Pricilla approached her after the session.

"I'm so proud of you and all the hard work you've done here. Your story is inspirational. So many women are in the same place you were, struggling to do this. Do you think you could give a little talk about your experience with the Calorie Counters program and give tips and advice that may help them?"

"Me? Talk to the group? I don't think so," Heather declined, palms up to ward away the offer.

"Heather, you are what this meeting is all about. I know you have some words of wisdom to share that can help them," Pricilla reiterated with confidence despite Heather's shaking head. "Think about it. What things would you have liked someone to tell you earlier that would have made this process easier? Things you had to figure out for yourself?"

She thought about it for a week. Then she decided to tell Pricilla exactly what she would say, and let her decide if she still wanted Heather to speak.

When Pricilla heard her advice, she was even more excited to have Heather speak to the other members. The date was set for next month.

AUGUST 2019

On the 16th of August, Marla and Timothy were married on Rialto Beach. The guest list was small, only thirty, including Heather, Gemma, and Chelsea, a few relatives, and fewer coworkers. They picnicked in the sand for an intimate reception of salmon roasted on cedar over an open fire pit, roasted corn, grilled shrimp, fresh oysters, grilled steaks, roasted summer vegetables, and fruit kabobs. The cake was an Italian fruit cake.

After the sun went down and all the remaining guests had left, the four women had a fireside powwow. Timothy had gone to see his sister off back to his condo.

Heather said, "I have something to tell you guys." When she had their attention, she made her announcement. "I was asked to give a talk to my Calorie Counters group. I made life member a few weeks ago. Priscilla asked me to share my weight loss journey."

Chelsea, Marla and Gemma all congratulated her, and asked when her presentation was being held. Heather told them the date. "I know what I'm going to say. I hope you'll all wish me luck."

They assured her they were all behind her. Even Marla, who would be halfway around the world during the event.

Gemma stood up before the fire and her friends. "I think this is an auspicious moment to ask this question that we have all been avoiding since we first got together."

They all fell silent.

"Who started the fire in cabin four?" Gemma demanded in her most authoritative voice. "I didn't do it." She looked to her right at Marla.

"Wasn't me," Marla said and turned right to look at Chelsea.

"Nope. I didn't do it," Chelsea replied.

They all turned to look at Heather, whose cheeks were beet red.

"I ..." she stuttered, glancing away from them all. "I didn't do it either, but I know who did."

Three sets of eyes widened.

"It was Veronica from cabin eight. I heard voices outside our cabin that night and peeked out the window. She and another girl were outside. I wasn't sure what they were doing. Veronica was spraying something on the outside of the cabin. Then she lit a match and held it to the cabin wall. It ignited and spread in a flash." She paused. "It just exploded into flames. I couldn't believe they did that. I was stunned. Veronica saw me in the window. I finally got my wits about me and woke you guys up to get out."

"Why didn't you tell us?" Chelsea asked.

Heather shrugged. "I never said anything to anyone." She shook her head swiftly. "I was in total shock. Veronica approached me after the fire was out and threatened my life if I said a word. The way I figured it, we all got out alive, so why make a fuss." She sheepishly looked down at her feet. "I was afraid. I kept my mouth shut."

Marla took her hand. "It's a damn good thing you did get us out. That cabin didn't have any smoke detectors. We would have died if you hadn't woken us up. Thank you."

Marla and Chelsea joined hands with Gemma and Heather. "We owe you our lives, Heather," Gemma said. "Thank you."

"Me too, Heather. Thank you for saving all of us."

The clatter of the stones on the beach lulled everyone into silence to digest Heather's revelation. Timothy returned to claim his bride. As the campfire was extinguished, the three women left the newlyweds alone.

• • • •

MARLA AND TIMOTHY SPENT a sleepless night at a secluded oceanfront cabin. Sleep was indulged the next morning. Later that afternoon, they sat side by side in first class with their hands joined as they headed for a three-week honeymoon of boundless activity in New Zealand.

• • • •

ON THE NIGHT OF HER presentation, Heather wore Marla's dress again for the occasion. It fit her new slim figure beautifully, showing off every girly curve and adding height to her stature. When Pricilla introduced Heather, she mentioned everything about Heather's history with Calorie Counters: her five previous tries, her sporadic weigh-ins, and finally, her total weight loss and life membership status. The crowd greeted her with resounding applause as she took the tiny stage.

She stood uneasy on the platform, wringing her hands as she started to speak. Stuttering stops and starts had her blushing red from her blunders as she tried to ignore the wobbling of her knees and the sweat building under her armpits.

Then she began talking about her children, their ages, and personalities. Speaking of her children relaxed her. Her mouth wasn't so dry, and her knees stopped shaking. She spoke about their eating habits before she joined Calorie Counters. How she always ate their leftovers. Their food budget was so limiting it didn't make sense to waste any.

All the mothers in the room nodded unconsciously as Heather described the highly processed, boxed, canned and frozen foods she served for convenience's sake as well as because that's what TV advertising told her her children wanted to eat. Heather smiled then, knowing they understood her completely.

At last, she described that amazing day of carrots, celery sticks, and apple slices, the turning point when Calorie Counters' good nutritional advice hit her children's lives. How since that day, the children ate what she ate, what was fresh, unprocessed, even raw at times. How they didn't miss their chicken nuggets, corn dogs, or beefaroni. How even their grandparents were part of Calorie Counters' food revolution. Heather was chuckling at this point when she described Nicholas instructing Grandma how to make a proper salad.

She went on, "Sure, money's not plentiful. Fresh fruits and vegetables are expensive out of season. Frozen fruits and vegetables, bought as store brands, are more economical. Getting the kids to eat healthier has made them healthier. They haven't been as sick. Sure, Peter gets all the same germs from the kids at school and brings them home. They aren't as sick for as long. There was no need for a doctor's visit all winter, which has helped in the wallet, making it easier to afford the fruits and vegetables."

It wasn't until that moment that Heather scanned the entire room. She had a sharp intake of breath when she saw them. Chelsea and Gemma were beside the door smiling. And Gemma held up her laptop. Heather just knew in her heart, Marla was watching from New Zealand.

Tears stung her eyes, forcing her to blink them back. Smiling, her heart full of love for the support her friends gave unconditionally, she nodded a silent thank you to them and continued speaking.

She ended her talk by offering her fellow members a challenge. Stop making two separate meals: one for themselves and one for their family. Their families deserved the good food and health benefits of the good eating habits of the Calorie Counters revolution. Good habits that could save their lives from health consequences decades away. With that said, Heather smiled, gave a little bow as she thanked them for listening, and left the stage.

The audience broke out into thunderous applause, as did Pricilla and all the Calorie Counters staff. All agreed it was one of the most heartwarming and inspirational talks they had heard any member give.

Driving home that evening, rerunning the talk, the praise, and the positive comments afterward in her mind, Heather was overwhelmed by the members' gratitude. Priscilla had asked her to give that talk every year on the anniversary of her life membership. Heather said agreed.

The support from her cabin four friends deeply touched her heart. They were sisters now. Sisters by different parents, but sisters nonetheless. Gratitude filled her heart for each of them.

Her spirit rose buoyantly. She'd survived Billy's abandonment, the eviction, the divorce. Found a job, gone to college, got a raise at work. She'd provided her children with a steady income, good eating habits, a new roof over their heads, a fenced yard, and a mother who was happy, healthy, and adjusted to life's changes. A sense of empowerment filled Heather. She felt strong enough now to see her kids through no matter what life might throw their way.

• • • •

GEMMA SLAMMED HER HANDBAG down on the empty chair and slid onto the chair across from Simon. She cringed. She had been trying to retrain herself not to do that, but it was an old habit that wouldn't be tamed. She reached for the Cosmo glass in front of her, the exterior of the martini glass glistening with condensate. It was sweet of Simon to order her favorite drink so it would be ready the moment she arrived. "Did you order?"

Simon ignored her question. "How did it go this morning?"

"Total waste of my time." Gemma took another long sip from her drink, her eyes closing in appreciation of the cold, strong mix.

"How so?" Simon sipped his bourbon, his eyes never leaving her face.

She shook her head in disgust. "There's always something wrong. Windows that don't open, wet basements, ancient furnaces, no air conditioning. The list goes on."

"Those are things that you dicker with the seller about to get the price down."

"True, but I can't be bothered. I want move-in condition, not as-is." She sank back into the plush upholstered chair, her fingers turning the stem of her glass around and around.

Simon crossed his arms in front of his chest and leaned into the table before suggesting, "Buy it and flip it."

"Not this woman. I have far better things to do than chase contractors to get their jobs finished." She sighed. "Rose Anne will have to put up with me a little while longer."

The waiter approached the table, took their order, and left.

"Simon, why are you staring at me like I have three heads?" She cocked her own head. "Are you all right?"

He inhaled deeply and slowly. "Yes ... I'm fine. Never better." He exhaled and inhaled again. He sipped his drink, his eyes never leaving Gemma's. Setting the glass down, he clenched his hands together. "Why don't you move in with me?"

With a mouthful of Cosmo, Gemma started choking. Her hand flew to cover her mouth as she tried to prevent the alcohol from spewing out her nose in the posh restaurant. Her eyes blinking wildly at the burn of alcohol in her nasal passages, she choked out, "What?" She felt as though she had been kicked in the gut.

"Move in with me." He spoke a little softer and quieter, as though he didn't want anyone else in the crowded dining room to hear. They were already staring after Gemma's coughing fit.

Stuttering, Gemma could only reply, "But I—I can't."

"Why not?" Simon leaned across the table for two.

Gemma sputtered, fear rising into her chest. "I ... I have a business to help run."

Simon shook his head. "What does that have to do with it? I have a business to run too."

Stalling for time to think, Gemma fidgeted with her plate, her napkin, her flatware. Her mind was a swirling cloud of retorts and ideas. As she answered, her back straightened, her shoulders and neck tense. "I need my freedom."

"Do you?" he countered. "Do you really need that freedom? Haven't I been able to let you do whatever you need to do without question? Without complaint?"

She closed her eyes again, trying to harness the thoughts in her brain. The pros said it was the perfect solution to her living arrangement. She was at Simon's house more often than anywhere else. She even kept clothes and a full toiletries bag there.

But the cons could not be silenced. "Yes, you have. But I learned a long time ago to rely on myself. To not rely on a man. That tenet has saved me a lot of hardship and grief over the years." She stared him down. "Men take you for granted after a while, then discard you when someone else looks prettier, smarter, or sexier. And you're left in a boat without oars on whitewater rapids trying to navigate your life back to shore." She covered her eyes with her palm. "Look at Heather, for God's sake. Three children were evicted from their home because her husband rekindled his relationship with a former girlfriend."

"Do you think I'd do that to you?" His face darkened at her insinuation.

"You could." She shrugged. "That's why I'm not giving you the chance."

He reached for her hand, but she pulled it away. "We've been together for months. Haven't you felt like we're equally matched?"

She broke eye contact. "We do get along well. We like to talk about business and corporate taxes, the stock market, and our future expansion plans. We—"

His index finger pressed to her lips and stopped her in mid-sentence. "Gemma, I've found you to be the most enigmatic, obstinate, and enjoyable person to be around. We get each other. We understand how each other's minds think and what we dream of."

"Speak for yourself." Gemma shrugged, not meeting his eyes.

"And here you are, refusing to accept the love you deserve because your father left you over twenty-two years ago."

Tears welled under her eyelids, burning as she tried not to let Simon know how hard he'd hit home.

He snagged her hand this time and held on. "I get what Jerry Maguire meant in that movie when he told his girlfriend, 'You complete me.' I feel completely alive and whole with you, Gemma. I've never even known I wasn't before you arrived in my life."

Her free hand covered her mouth, trying desperately to rein in the emotions threatening to turn her into a pile of mush in this room full of staring strangers. Out of the corner of her eye, she noticed the maître d' stopping their waiter from delivering their entrées. "We can't have this conversation here."

"We already are." Simon bowed his head in an exasperated move.

"Not anymore." Gemma grabbed her handbag and bolted from the restaurant as the eyes of the other diners followed her.

• • • •

"YOU DID WHAT?" CHELSEA'S voice rose an octave in disbelief.

"I left." Gemma spread both her hands over her face. "I got scared. He said he loves me. I think."

"No doubt about it with that movie phrase," Heather replied.

"Did you sell your mother's house, Chel?" Gemma asked, wiping her tears away.

"We bought out my brother's share of Mom's house. Seth and I are all moved in." Chelsea squeezed her hand. "Now, back to you."

A ding on Chelsea's cell phone announced Marla was calling in.

"Hey, gals, what's up? I got your message and Zoomed as soon as I could," Marla said after her face appeared on Chelsea's screen.

Heather filled Marla in on the basics.

Marla laughed. "Ah, Gemma. You are one lucky woman."

Gemma shook her head. "I think I blew it. What should I do?"

Heather took one of Gemma's hands. "You acknowledge you are frightened. Don't you think we all were when we faced love? Marla and Timothy, Chelsea and Seth—"

"Heather and Christopher Morgan," Chelsea fake whispered none too softly.

Marla burst out with "What?" while Gemma demanded to know, "Who's Christopher?"

Heather's cheeks flamed bright red. "He's Peter's former school teacher. We, um, went out on a date after meeting at a parent-teacher conference."

"Tell us more." Gemma wanted to circumvent her issue with Simon, but none of them were letting her divert their attention.

Chelsea took Gemma's free hand in her own. "You march back over to his house and ring the doorbell with your suitcase in hand."

"What if he won't forgive me for making a scene at his favorite restaurant?"

"Don't worry about that. He'll forgive you with open arms," Marla said.

"And the fear?"

Chelsea squeezed her hand. "Focus on the good things, and you'll both be fine."

Heather interrupted. "We all have faced so much these past few years. The struggles with our weight, family issues, work dramas. We've all come out strong and whole. I'm sure we're more adept at life now than we ever were before we met each other at camp."

"Amen to that," Marla said, with the others echoing along.

• • • •

IT MIGHT HAVE BEEN the water in Pittsburgh, Pennsylvania. It might have been the confluence of two mighty rivers. Whatever it was, these four women resumed their relationship. Not knowing each other probably helped the girls in cabin four bond better. It sounds crazy. Other cabins had factions: two against two or three against one. Cabin four didn't. They were all in the same boat: all sisterless strangers. And they were ripe for girly companionship.

Their friendship was forged in the forests of hemlocks and oaks, amid clean, fresh, resinous scented air mixed with detritus, and in the stale-dust-smelling cabin that became their fortress. The fact they could get together so many years later, and re-establish that former connection was a miracle in their eyes.

Together they worked on their relationship with their weight. For Gemma, it began with the unexpected consequences of necessary surgery. For Marla, it was confronting an entire lifetime of poor eating habits, psychological fears, and emotional instability. A single purpose brought Chelsea to her weight loss adventure. After multiple failed attempts, Heather succeeded at Calorie Counters, not just for herself but for her family.

The actions they each chose had consequences in their lives, some expected and some completely unpredictable. Some welcome, some unwelcome. Each consequence was a growing experience for Gemma, Marla, Heather, and Chelsea. In the end, they each found that satisfaction and contentment in themselves had nothing to do with the weight of their flesh, and everything to do with the wait to find their own strength

COMING SOON

HAVILLAND'S HIGHLAND DESTINY
A Contemporary Highland Romance

• • • •

CHAPTER ONE

• • • •

"LET'S GO, HAVI, WE'RE going to be late!"

She primped one last time in the mirror beside her house's front door. "Okay, okay. I'm coming." She swiped at the curl dangling over her forehead, to no avail. Why was Jill, her co-worker, always rushing her.

It was only eight o'clock. They had plenty of time to get to the pub. She gave herself the once over. Brand-new tight-fitting jeans, a cross-over dark purple knit top with a plunging neckline she had pinned to held the girls in for the night and yet allowed a fine cleavage show. She usually stayed home every night. But she had been feeling lonely. *A little excitement might help get me out of this depression.*

Tonight, she and Jill were going to forget grad work and enjoy the band scheduled at Clancy's Pub near Hyannis. If they got there early enough they could eat free snacks before the band started. Not a very nutritious dinner but befitting their budget as grad students with limited stipends.

She grabbed her purse off the nearest chair, flicked off the light switch with the edge of her bag and shut the door. It slammed lightly behind her.

She almost retreated back inside. It was rare for her to be going out on a Friday night. Her life was defined by her graduate student status, her job with the institute and, well, it used to be defined by her grandmother. She didn't consider herself the sociable type.

Glancing down the porch stairs, she could see Jill was already down on the sidewalk. She slipped the deadbolt key into her pocket just as a crinkly voice from next door called out. "Havilland?"

It was Mrs. Faughn, the next-door busybody padding up the porch stairs. Havilland rolled her eyes before turning around with a smile pasted on her face.

Mrs. Faughn was dressed in her usual frumpy and faded robe, her pajama bottoms cut off above her ankles. As was the nightly mode, her hair was wrapped in tight pink curlers. Her feet encased in slippers that might have been pink and fuzzy when first bought, but now were a tan-pink color and matted. 'Havilland, dear. The mail man delivered this letter to me earlier this week. I've been trying to catch up with you." The woman's age-spotted hand held out an envelope.

"Mrs. Faughn, you could have just shoved it in my mailbox." She pointed to the black metal box on the exterior wall beside the front door. The mailman was frequently placing mail in the wrong mailboxes on the street.

Havilland grasped the envelope, noting with a small shudder the large bruise on her neighbor's hand. From previous inquiry, she knew the elderly woman was on blood thinners, which caused every little bump to bruise. Her frail hands were always covered with bruises in various stages of healing visible through her translucent skin. The bony, enlarged knuckles, a consequence of rheumatoid arthritis disappeared into her robe pocket. A dull ache thudded in her chest.

Those hands reminded her of her grandmother's hands. Havilland bent down to shove the envelope under her door.

The elderly woman shook her head. "Oh, no. Not this one. It's from Scotland."

"Scotland?" Havilland froze but it was too late, the envelope had already disappeared under the door. She jammed her key into the lock, opened the door and retrieved the business sized envelope. Sure enough, there were the stamps baring the profile of King Charles. The return address read, "Adair, Malcolm and Boyd, Esq., 4758 Queen Street, Edinburgh, EH16 5AF." On closer examination she noticed the postmark was nearly three weeks ago. Mrs. Faughn had it for three weeks?

"What is it?" Mrs. Faughn asked, peering over Haviland's arm.

"Havilland! Come on!" Jill's voice blasted up from the sidewalk.

"In a minute." She tore open the envelope being careful to not damage the stamp so she could add it to her collection. She opened the tri-folded paper. The impressive letterhead looked official. Havilland began to skim.

"Read it out loud, please." Mrs. Faughn whispered, a gleeful, excited expression lighting up her face. "I always wanted to go to Scotland."

Havilland shot her a frown before relenting. "Dear Ms. Tait, It is my pleasure to have found you, in a roundabout way. Please contact me at 584 458 2623 at your earliest convenience. Sincerely, Attorney Robert Boyd, Esquire."

"Oh my!" Mrs. Faughn exclaimed. "What could it be? Do you know anyone in Scotland?"

"No. It's a scam. It must be." Tucking the letter into the envelope tossed it on the floor inside the door. Slamming the door shut, she relocked it.

"Are you sure?" Mrs. Faughn asked, "It looked very official to me."

• • • •

Sign up for Diana's newsletter for more book release information at DianaRock.com

Don't miss out!

Visit the website below and you can sign up to receive emails whenever Diana Rock publishes a new book. There's no charge and no obligation.

https://books2read.com/r/B-A-YUKN-VWDFC

BOOKS2READ

Connecting independent readers to independent writers.

Also by Diana Rock

Colby County Series
Bid To Love
Courting Choices

Fulton River Falls
Melt My Heart
Proof of Love
Bloomin' In Love
First Christmas Ornament

MovieStuds
Hollywood Hotshot

Standalone
Little Bit of Wait

Watch for more at DianaRock.com.

About the Author

Diana lives in eastern Connecticut with her tall, dark and handsome hero. She works full time as a histotechnologist, writing in her spare time. Diana likes puttering about the yard, baking and cooking, hiking, fly-fishing, and Scottish Country Dancing. Follow her exploits on her website, in her blogs and newsletters.

Read more at DianaRock.com.

Printed in the USA
CPSIA information can be obtained
at www.ICGtesting.com
BVHW031625310823
668999BV00002B/15